SOULL

The vampire's hands shot forward, going for her neck. Apparently, he had decided if he could not suck her blood, strangulation was an acceptable alternative. Alexia jerked back, at the same time pressing her hair stick into the creature's white flesh. It slid in about half an inch. The vampire reacted with a desperate wriggle that, even without superhuman strength, unbalanced Alexia in her heeled velvet dancing shoes. She fell back. He stood, roaring in pain, with her hair stick half in and half out of his chest.

Miss Tarabotti scrabbled for her parasol, rolling about inelegantly among the tea things, hoping her new dress would miss the fallen foodstuffs. She found the parasol and came upright, swinging it in a wide arc. Purely by chance, the heavy tip struck the end of her wooden hair stick, driving it straight into the vampire's heart.

The creature stood stock-still, a look of intense surprise on his handsome face. Then he fell backward onto the much-abused plate of treacle tart, flopping in a limp-overcooked-asparagus kind of way. His alabaster face turned a yellowish gray, as though he was afflicted with the jaundice, and he went still. Alexia's books called this end of the vampire life cycle *dissanimation*. Alexia, who thought the action astoundingly similar to a soufflé going flat, decided at that moment to call it the Grand Collapse.

By Gail Carriger

The Parasol Protectorate

Soulless
Changeless
Blameless
Heartless
Timeless

SOULLESS

The Parasol Protectorate: Book the First

GAIL CARRIGER

www.orbitbooks.net

ORBIT

First published in the United States in 2009 by Orbit
First published in Great Britain in 2010 by Orbit
Reprinted 2011 (twice), 2012

A CIP catalogue record for this book
is available from the British Library.

ISBN 978-1-84149-972-7

Typeset in Times by Palimpsest Book Production Limited,
Falkirk, Stirlingshire
Printed and bound by CPI Group (UK) Ltd, Croydon, CR0 4YY

Papers used by Orbit are from well-managed forests
and other responsible sources.

MIX
Paper from
responsible sources
FSC
www.fsc.org   FSC® C104740

Orbit
An imprint of
Little, Brown Book Group
100 Victoria Embankment
London EC4Y 0DY

An Hachette UK Company
www.hachette.co.uk

www.orbitbooks.net

Acknowledgments

Tremendous thanks to the ladies of the WCWC and their multi-colored Pens of Doom: with criticism comes wisdom and, hopefully, tea. To Mum and Dad, who had the brilliant parental idea that good behavior be rewarded with trips to the bookshop. And to G and E: purveyors of fine feelings and patrons of the scribbling beast, however fiendish she may be.

CHAPTER ONE

In Which Parasols Prove Useful

Miss Alexia Tarabotti was not enjoying her evening. Private balls were never more than middling amusements for spinsters, and Miss Tarabotti was not the kind of spinster who could garner even that much pleasure from the event. To put the pudding in the puff: she had retreated to the library, her favorite sanctuary in any house, only to happen upon an unexpected vampire.

She glared at the vampire.

For his part, the vampire seemed to feel that their encounter had improved his ball experience immeasurably. For there she sat, without escort, in a low-necked ball gown.

In this particular case, what he did not know *could* hurt him. For Miss Alexia had been born without a soul, which, as any decent vampire of good blooding knew, made her a lady to avoid most assiduously.

Yet he moved toward her, darkly shimmering out of the library shadows with feeding fangs ready. However, the moment he touched Miss Tarabotti, he was suddenly no longer darkly doing anything at all. He was simply standing there, the faint sounds of a string quartet in the background as he foolishly fished about with his tongue for fangs unaccountably mislaid.

Miss Tarabotti was not in the least surprised; soullessness always neutralized supernatural abilities. She issued the vampire a very dour look. Certainly, most daylight folk wouldn't peg her as anything less than a standard English prig, but had this man not even bothered to *read* the vampire's official abnormality roster for London and its greater environs?

The vampire recovered his equanimity quickly enough. He reared away from Alexia, knocking over a nearby tea trolley. Physical contact broken, his fangs reappeared. Clearly not the sharpest of prongs, he then darted forward from the neck like a serpent, diving in for another chomp.

"I say!" said Alexia to the vampire. "We have not even been introduced!"

Miss Tarabotti had never actually had a vampire try to bite her. She knew one or two by reputation, of course, and was friendly with Lord Akeldama. *Who was* not *friendly with Lord Akeldama?* But no vampire had ever actually attempted to *feed* on her before!

So Alexia, who abhorred violence, was forced to grab the miscreant by his nostrils, a delicate and therefore painful area, and shove him away. He stumbled over the fallen tea trolley, lost his balance in a manner astonishingly graceless for a vampire, and fell to the floor. He landed right on top of a plate of treacle tart.

Miss Tarabotti was most distressed by this. She was particularly fond of treacle tart and had been looking forward to consuming that precise plateful. She picked up her parasol. It was terribly tasteless for her to be carrying a parasol at an evening ball, but Miss Tarabotti rarely went anywhere without it. It was of a style entirely of her own devising: a black frilly confection with purple satin pansies sewn about, brass hardware, and buckshot in its silver tip.

She whacked the vampire right on top of the head with it as he tried to extract himself from his newly intimate relations with the tea trolley. The buckshot gave the brass parasol just enough heft to make a deliciously satisfying *thunk*.

"Manners!" instructed Miss Tarabotti.

The vampire howled in pain and sat back down on the treacle tart.

Alexia followed up her advantage with a vicious prod between the vampire's legs. His howl went quite a bit higher in pitch, and he crumpled into a fetal position. While Miss Tarabotti was a proper English young lady, aside from not having a soul and being half Italian, she did spend quite a bit more time than most other young ladies riding and walking and was therefore unexpectedly strong.

Miss Tarabotti leaped forward—as much as one could leap in full triple-layered underskirts, draped bustle, and ruffled taffeta top-skirt—and bent over the vampire. He was clutching at his indelicate bits and writhing about. The pain would not last long given his supernatural healing ability, but it hurt most decidedly in the interim.

Alexia pulled a long wooden hair stick out of her elaborate coiffure. Blushing at her own temerity, she ripped open his shirt-front, which was cheap and overly starched, and poked at his chest, right over the heart. Miss Tarabotti sported a particularly large and sharp hair stick. With her free hand, she made certain to touch his chest, as only physical contact would nullify his supernatural abilities.

"Desist that horrible noise immediately," she instructed the creature.

The vampire quit his squealing and lay perfectly still. His beautiful blue eyes watered slightly as he stared fixedly at the wooden hair stick. Or, as Alexia liked to call it, hair *stake*.

"Explain yourself!" Miss Tarabotti demanded, increasing the pressure.

"A thousand apologies." The vampire looked confused. "Who are you?" Tentatively he reached for his fangs. Gone.

To make her position perfectly clear, Alexia stopped touching him (though she kept her sharp hair stick in place). His fangs grew back.

He gasped in amazement. "*What* are you? I thought you were

a lady, alone. It would be my right to feed, if you were left this carelethly unattended. Pleathe, I did not mean to prethume," he lisped around his fangs, real panic in his eyes.

Alexia, finding it hard not to laugh at the lisp, said, "There is no cause for you to be so overly dramatic. Your hive queen will have told you of my kind." She returned her hand to his chest once more. The vampire's fangs retracted.

He looked at her as though she had suddenly sprouted whiskers and hissed at him.

Miss Tarabotti was surprised. Supernatural creatures, be they vampires, werewolves, or ghosts, owed their existence to an overabundance of soul, an excess that refused to die. Most knew that others like Miss Tarabotti existed, born without any soul at all. The estimable Bureau of Unnatural Registry (BUR), a division of Her Majesty's Civil Service, called her ilk *preternatural*. Alexia thought the term nicely dignified. What vampires called her was far less complimentary. After all, preternaturals had once hunted *them,* and vampires had long memories. Natural, daylight persons were kept in the dark, so to speak, but any vampire worth his blood should know a preternatural's touch. This one's ignorance was untenable. Alexia said, as though to a very small child, "I am a *preternatural*."

The vampire looked embarrassed. "Of course you are," he agreed, obviously still not quite comprehending. "Again, my apologies, lovely one. I am overwhelmed to meet you. You are my first"—he stumbled over the word—"preternatural." He frowned. "Not supernatural, not natural, of course! How foolish of me not to see the dichotomy." His eyes narrowed into craftiness. He was now studiously ignoring the hair stick and looking tenderly up into Alexia's face.

Miss Tarabotti knew full well her own feminine appeal. The kindest compliment her face could ever hope to garner was "exotic," never "'lovely." Not that it had ever received either. Alexia figured that vampires, like all predators, were at their most charming when cornered.

The vampire's hands shot forward, going for her neck. Apparently, he had decided if he could not suck her blood, strangulation was an acceptable alternative. Alexia jerked back, at the same time pressing her hair stick into the creature's white flesh. It slid in about half an inch. The vampire reacted with a desperate wriggle that, even without superhuman strength, unbalanced Alexia in her heeled velvet dancing shoes. She fell back. He stood, roaring in pain, with her hair stick half in and half out of his chest.

Miss Tarabotti scrabbled for her parasol, rolling about inelegantly among the tea things, hoping her new dress would miss the fallen foodstuffs. She found the parasol and came upright, swinging it in a wide arc. Purely by chance, the heavy tip struck the end of her wooden hair stick, driving it straight into the vampire's heart.

The creature stood stock-still, a look of intense surprise on his handsome face. Then he fell backward onto the much-abused plate of treacle tart, flopping in a limp-overcooked-asparagus kind of way. His alabaster face turned a yellowish gray, as though he were afflicted with the jaundice, and he went still. Alexia's books called this end of the vampire life cycle *dissanimation*. Alexia, who thought the action astoundingly similar to a soufflé going flat, decided at that moment to call it the Grand Collapse.

She intended to waltz directly out of the library without anyone the wiser to her presence there. This would have resulted in the loss of her best hair stick and her well-deserved tea, as well as a good deal of drama. Unfortunately, a small group of young dandies came traipsing in at that precise moment. What young men of such dress were doing in a *library* was anyone's guess. Alexia felt the most likely explanation was that they had become lost while looking for the card room. Regardless, their presence forced her to pretend that she, too, had just discovered the dead vampire. With a resigned shrug, she screamed and collapsed into a faint.

She stayed resolutely fainted, despite the liberal application of smelling salts, which made her eyes water most tremendously, a cramp in the back of one knee, and the fact that her new ball gown was getting most awfully wrinkled. All its many layers of green trim, picked to the height of fashion in lightening shades to complement the cuirasse bodice, were being crushed into oblivion under her weight. The expected noises ensued: a good deal of yelling, much bustling about, and several loud clatters as one of the housemaids cleared away the fallen tea.

Then came the sound she had half anticipated, half dreaded. An authoritative voice cleared the library of both young dandies and all other interested parties who had flowed into the room upon discovery of the tableau. The voice instructed everyone to "get out!" while he "gained the particulars from the young lady" in tones that brooked no refusal.

Silence descended.

"Mark my words, I will use something much, much stronger than smelling salts," came a growl in Miss Tarabotti's left ear. The voice was low and tinged with a hint of Scotland. It would have caused Alexia to shiver and think primal monkey thoughts about moons and running far and fast, if she'd had a soul. Instead it caused her to sigh in exasperation and sit up.

"And a good evening to you, too, Lord Maccon. Lovely weather we are having for this time of year, is it not?" She patted at her hair, which was threatening to fall down without the hair stick in its proper place. Surreptitiously, she looked about for Lord Conall Maccon's second in command, Professor Lyall. Lord Maccon tended to maintain a much calmer temper when his Beta was present. But, then, as Alexia had come to comprehend, that appeared to be the main role of a Beta—especially one attached to Lord Maccon.

"Ah, Professor Lyall, how nice to see you again." She smiled in relief.

Professor Lyall, the Beta in question, was a slight, sandy-haired gentleman of indeterminate age and pleasant disposition, as agreeable, in fact, as his Alpha was sour. He grinned at her and doffed his hat, which was of first-class design and sensible material. His cravat was similarly subtle, for, while it was tied expertly, the knot was a humble one.

"Miss Tarabotti, how delicious to find ourselves in your company once more." His voice was soft and mild-mannered.

"Stop humoring her, Randolph," barked Lord Maccon. The fourth Earl of Woolsey was much larger than Professor Lyall and in possession of a near-permanent frown. Or at least he always seemed to be frowning when he was in the presence of Miss Alexia Tarabotti, ever since the hedgehog incident (which really, honestly, had not been her fault). He also had unreasonably pretty tawny eyes, mahogany-colored hair, and a particularly nice nose. The eyes were currently glaring at Alexia from a shockingly intimate distance.

"Why is it, Miss Tarabotti, every time I have to clean up a mess in a library, you just happen to be in the middle of it?" the earl demanded of her.

Alexia gave him a withering look and brushed down the front of her green taffeta gown, checking for bloodstains.

Lord Maccon appreciatively watched her do it. Miss Tarabotti might examine her face in the mirror each morning with a large degree of censure, but there was nothing at all wrong with her figure. He would have to have had far less soul and a good fewer urges not to notice that appetizing fact. Of course, she always went and spoiled the appeal by opening her mouth. In his humble experience, the world had yet to produce a more vexingly verbose female.

"Lovely but unnecessary," he said, indicating her efforts to brush away nonexistent blood drops.

Alexia reminded herself that Lord Maccon and his kind were only *just* civilized. One simply could not expect too much from them, especially under delicate circumstances such as these. Of course, that failed to explain Professor Lyall, who was always utterly urbane. She glanced with appreciation in the professor's direction.

Lord Maccon's frown intensified.

Miss Tarabotti considered that the lack of civilized behavior might be the sole provenance of Lord Maccon. Rumor had it, he had only lived in London a comparatively short while—and he had relocated from Scotland of all barbaric places.

The professor coughed delicately to get his Alpha's attention. The earl's yellow gaze focused on him with such intensity it should have actually burned. "Aye?"

Professor Lyall was crouched over the vampire, examining the hair stick with interest. He was poking about the wound, a spotless white lawn handkerchief wrapped around his hand.

"Very little mess, actually. Almost complete lack of blood spatter." He leaned forward and sniffed. "Definitely Westminster," he stated.

The Earl of Woolsey seemed to understand. He turned his piercing gaze onto the dead vampire. "He must have been very hungry."

Professor Lyall turned the body over. "What happened here?" He took out a small set of wooden tweezers from the pocket of his waistcoat and picked at the back of the vampire's trousers. He paused, rummaged about in his coat pockets, and produced a diminutive leather case. He clicked it open and removed a most bizarre pair of gogglelike things. They were gold in color with multiple lenses on one side, between which there appeared to be some kind of liquid. The contraption was also riddled with small knobs and dials. Professor Lyall propped the ridiculous things onto his nose and bent back over the vampire, twiddling at the dials expertly.

"Goodness gracious me," exclaimed Alexia, "what *are* you wearing? It looks like the unfortunate progeny of an illicit union between a pair of binoculars and some opera glasses. What on earth are they called, binocticals, spectoculars?"

The earl snorted his amusement and then tried to pretend he hadn't. "How about glassicals?" he suggested, apparently unable to resist a contribution. There was a twinkle in his eye as he said it that Alexia found rather unsettling.

Professor Lyall looked up from his examination and glared at the both of them. His right eye was hideously magnified. It was quite gruesome and made Alexia start involuntarily.

"These are my monocular cross-magnification lenses with spectra-modifier attachment, and they are invaluable. I will thank you not to mock them so openly." He turned once more to the task at hand.

"Oh." Miss Tarabotti was suitably impressed. "How do they work?" she inquired.

Professor Lyall looked back up at her, suddenly animated. "Well, you see, it is really quite interesting. By turning this little knob here, you can change the distance between the two panes of glass here, allowing the liquid to—"

The earl's groan interrupted him. "Don't get him started, Miss Tarabotti, or we will be here all night."

Looking slightly crestfallen, Professor Lyall turned back to the dead vampire. "Now, what *is* this substance all over his clothing?"

His boss, preferring the direct approach, resumed his frown and looked accusingly at Alexia. "What on God's green earth is that muck?"

Miss Tarabotti said, "Ah. Sadly, treacle tart. A tragic loss, I daresay." Her stomach chose that moment to growl in agreement. She would have colored gracefully with embarrassment had she not possessed the complexion of one of those "heathen Italians," as her mother said, who never colored, gracefully or otherwise. (Convincing her mother that Christianity had, to all intents and purposes, originated with the Italians, thus making them the exact opposite of heathen, was a waste of time and breath.) Alexia refused to apologize for the boisterousness of her stomach and favored Lord Maccon with a defiant glare. Her stomach was the reason she had sneaked away in the first place. Her mama had assured her there would be food at the ball. Yet all that appeared on offer when they arrived was a bowl of punch and some sadly wilted watercress. Never one to let her stomach get the better of her, Alexia had ordered tea from the butler and retreated to the library. Since she normally spent any ball lurking on the outskirts of the dance floor trying to look as though she did not want to be asked to waltz, tea was a welcome alternative. It was rude to order refreshments from someone else's staff, but when one was promised sandwiches and there was nothing but watercress, well, one must simply take matters into one's own hands!

Professor Lyall, kindhearted soul that he was, prattled on to no one in particular, pretending not to notice the rumbling of her stomach. Though of course he heard it. He had excellent hearing. *They* all did. He looked up from his examinations, his face all catawampus from the glassicals. "Starvation would explain why the vampire was desperate enough to try for Miss Tarabotti at a ball, rather than taking to the slums like the smart ones do when they get this bad."

Alexia grimaced. "No associated hive either."

Lord Maccon arched one black eyebrow, professing not to be impressed. "How could *you* possibly know *that*?"

Professor Lyall explained for both of them. "No need to be so direct with the young lady. A hive queen would never have let one of her brood get into such a famished condition. We must have a rove on our hands, one completely without ties to the local hive."

Alexia stood up, revealing to Lord Maccon that she had arranged her faint to rest comfortably against a fallen settee pillow. He grinned and then quickly hid it behind a frown when she looked at him suspiciously.

"I have a different theory." She gestured to the vampire's clothing. "Badly tied cravat and a cheap shirt? No hive worth its salt would let a larva like that out without dressing him properly for public appearance. I am surprised he was not stopped at the front entrance. The duchess's footman really ought to have spotted a cravat like *that* prior to the reception line and forcibly ejected the wearer. I suppose good staff is hard to come by with all the best ones becoming drones these days, but such a shirt!"

The Earl of Woolsey glared at her. "Cheap clothing is no excuse for killing a man."

"Mmm, that's what you say." Alexia evaluated Lord Maccon's perfectly tailored shirtfront and exquisitely tied cravat. His dark hair was a bit too long and shaggy to be de mode, and his face was not entirely clean-shaven, but he possessed enough hauteur to carry this lower-class roughness off without seeming scruffy. She was certain that his silver and black paisley cravat must be tied under sufferance. He probably preferred to wander about bare-chested at home. The idea made her shiver oddly. It must take a lot of effort to keep a man like him tidy. Not to mention well tailored. He was bigger than most. She had to give credit to his valet, who must be a particularly tolerant claviger.

Lord Maccon was normally quite patient. Like most of his kind, he had learned to be such in polite society. But Miss Tarabotti seemed to bring out the worst of his animal urges. "Stop trying to change the subject," he snapped, squirming under her calculated scrutiny. "Tell me what happened." He put on his BUR face and pulled out a small metal tube, stylus, and pot of clear liquid. He unrolled the tube with a small cranking device, clicked the top off the liquid, and dipped the stylus into it. It sizzled ominously.

Alexia bristled at his autocratic tone. "Do not give me instructions in that tone of voice, you . . ." she searched for a particularly insulting word, " . . . puppy! I am jolly well not one of your pack."

Lord Conall Maccon, Earl of Woolsey, was Alpha of the local werewolves, and as a result, he had access to a wide array of truly vicious methods of dealing with Miss Alexia Tarabotti. Instead of bridling at her insult (puppy, indeed!), he brought out his best offensive weapon, the result of decades of personal experience with more than one Alpha she-wolf. Scottish he may be by birth, but that only made him better equipped to deal with strong-willed females. "Stop playing verbal games with me, madam, or I shall go out into that ballroom, find your mother, and bring her here."

Alexia wrinkled her nose. "Well, I *like* that! That is hardly playing a fair game. How unnecessarily callous," she admonished. Her mother did not know that Alexia was preternatural. Mrs. Loontwill, as she was Loontwill since her remarriage, leaned a little too far toward the frivolous in any given equation. She was prone to wearing yellow and engaging in bouts of hysteria. Combining her mother with a dead vampire and her daughter's true identity was a recipe for disaster on all possible levels.

The fact that Alexia was preternatural had been explained to *her* at age six by a nice gentleman from the Civil Service with silver hair and a silver cane—a werewolf specialist. Along with the dark hair and prominent nose, preternatural was something Miss Tarabotti had to thank her dead Italian father for. What it really meant was that words like *I* and *me* were just excessively theoretical for Alexia. She certainly had an identity and a heart that felt emotions and all that; she simply had no soul. Miss Alexia, age six, had nodded politely at the nice silver-haired gentleman. Then she had made certain to read oodles of ancient Greek philosophy dealing with reason, logic, and ethics. If she had no soul, she also had no morals, so she reckoned she had best develop some kind of alternative. Her mama thought her a blue-stocking, which was soulless enough as far as Mrs. Loontwill was concerned, and was terribly upset by her eldest daughter's propensity for libraries. It would be too bothersome to have to face her mama in one just now.

Lord Maccon moved purposefully toward the door with the clear intention of acquiring Mrs. Loontwill.

Alexia caved with ill grace. "Oh, very well!" She settled herself with a rustle of green skirts onto a peach brocade chesterfield near the window.

The earl was both amused and annoyed to see that she had managed to pick up her fainting pillow and place it back on the couch without his registering any swooping movement.

"I came into the library for tea. I was promised food at this ball. In case you had not noticed, no food appears to be in residence."

Lord Maccon who required a considerable amount of fuel, mostly of the protein inclination, had noticed. "The Duke of Snodgrove is notoriously reticent about any additional expenditure at his wife's balls. Victuals were probably not on the list of acceptable offerings." He sighed. "The man owns half of Berkshire and cannot even provide a decent sandwich."

Miss Tarabotti made an empathetic movement with both hands. "My point precisely! So you will understand that I had to resort to ordering my own repast. Did you expect me to starve?"

The earl gave her generous curves a rude once-over, observed that Miss Tarabotti was nicely padded in exactly the right places, and refused to be suckered into becoming sympathetic. He maintained his frown. "I suspect that is precisely what the vampire was thinking when he found you *without a chaperone*. An unmarried female alone in a room in this enlightened day and age! Why, if the moon had been full, even I would have attacked you!"

Alexia gave him the once-over and reached for her brass parasol. "My dear sir, I should like to see you try."

Being Alpha made Lord Maccon a tad unprepared for such bold rebuttals, even with his Scottish past. He blinked at her in surprise for a split second and then resumed the verbal attack. "You do realize modern social mores exist for a reason?"

"I was hungry; allowances should be made," Alexia said, as if that settled the matter, unable to understand why he persisted in harping on about it.

Professor Lyall, unobserved by the other two, was busy fishing about in his waistcoat for something. Eventually, he produced a mildly beaten-up ham and pickle sandwich wrapped in a bit of brown paper. He presented it to Miss Tarabotti, ever the gallant.

Under normal circumstances, Alexia would have been put off by the disreputable state of the sandwich, but it was meant so kindly and offered with such diffidence, she could do nothing but accept. It was actually rather tasty.

"This is delicious!" she stated, surprised.

Professor Lyall grinned. "I keep them around for when his

lordship gets particularly testy. Such offerings keep the beast under control for the most part." He frowned and then added a caveat. "Excepting at full moon, of course. Would that a nice ham and pickle sandwich was all it took then."

Miss Tarabotti perked up, interested. "What do you *do* at full moon?"

Lord Maccon knew very well Miss Tarabotti was getting off the point intentionally. Driven beyond endurance, he resorted to use of her first name. "Alexia!" It was a long, polysyllabic, drawn-out growl.

She waved the sandwich at him. "Uh, do you want half of this, my lord?"

His frown became even darker, if such a thing could be conceived.

Professor Lyall pushed his glassicals up onto the brim of his top hat, where they looked like a strange second set of mechanical eyes, and stepped into the breach. "Miss Tarabotti, I do not believe you quite realize the delicacy of this situation. Unless we can establish strong grounds for self-defense by proving the vampire was behaving in a wholly irrational manner, you could be facing murder charges."

Alexia swallowed her bite of sandwich so quickly she partly choked and started to cough. "What?"

Lord Maccon turned his fierce frown on his second. "Now who is being too direct for the lady's sensibilities?"

Lord Maccon was relatively new to the London area. He had arrived a social unknown, challenged for Woolsey Castle Alpha, and won. He gave young ladies heart palpitations, even outside his wolf form, with a favorable combination of mystery, pre-eminence, and danger. Having acquired the BUR post, Woolsey Castle, and noble rank from the dispossessed former pack leader, he never lacked for a dinner invitation. His Beta, inherited with the pack, had a tense time of it: dancing on protocol and covering up Lord Maccon's various social gaffes. So far, bluntness had proved Professor Lyall's most consistent problem. Sometimes it even rubbed off on him. He had not meant to shock Miss Tarabotti, but she was now looking most subdued.

"I was simply sitting," Alexia explained, placing the sandwich aside, having lost her appetite. "He launched himself at me, totally unprovoked. His feeding fangs were out. I am certain if I had been a normal daylight woman, he would have bled me dry. I simply had to defend myself."

Professor Lyall nodded. A vampire in a state of extreme hunger had two socially acceptable options: to take sips from various willing drones belonging to him or his hive, or to pay for the privilege from blood-whores down dockside. This was the nineteenth century, after all, and one simply did not attack unannounced and uninvited! Even werewolves, who could not control themselves at full moon, made certain they had enough clavigers around to lock them away. He himself had three, and it took five to keep Lord Maccon under control.

"Do you think maybe he was forced into this state?" the professor wondered.

"You mean imprisoned until he was starving and no longer in possession of his faculties?" Lord Maccon considered the idea.

Professor Lyall flipped his glassicals back down off his hat and examined the dead man's wrists and neck myopically. "No signs of confinement or torture, but hard to tell with a vampire. Even in a low blood state, he would heal most superficial wounds in"—he grabbed Lord Maccon's metal roll and stylus, dipped the tip into the clear sizzling liquid, and did some quick calculations—"a little over one hour." The calculations remained etched into the metal.

"And then what? Did he escape or was he intentionally let go?"

Alexia interjected, "He seemed perfectly sane to me—aside from the attacking part, of course. He was able to carry on a decent conversation. He even tried to charm me. Must have been quite a young vampire. And"—she paused dramatically, lowered her voice, and said in sepulchral tones—"he had a fang-lisp."

Professor Lyall looked shocked and blinked largely at her through the asymmetrical lenses; among vampires, lisping was the height of vulgarity.

Miss Tarabotti continued. "It was as though he had never been trained in hive etiquette, no social class at all. He was almost a boor." It was a word she had never thought to apply to a vampire.

Lyall took the glassicals off and put them away in their little case with an air of finality. He looked gravely at his Alpha. "You know what this means, then, my lord?"

Lord Maccon was not frowning anymore. Instead he was looking grim. Alexia felt it suited him better, setting his mouth into a straight line and touching his tawny eyes with a determined glint. She wondered idly what he would look like if he smiled a real honest smile. Then she told herself quite firmly that it was probably best not to find out.

The object of her speculations said, "It means some hive queen is intentionally biting to metamorphosis outside of BUR regulations."

"Could it be just the once, do you think?" Professor Lyall removed a folded piece of white cloth from his waistcoat. He shook out the material, revealing it to be a large sheet of fine silk. Alexia was beginning to find the number of things he could stash in his waistcoat quite impressive.

Lord Maccon continued. "Or this could be the start of something more extensive. We'd better get back to BUR. The local hives will have to be interviewed. The queens are not going to be happy. Apart from everything else, this incident is awfully embarrassing for them."

Miss Tarabotti agreed. "Especially if they find out about the substandard shirt selection."

The two gentlemen wrapped the vampire's body in the silk sheet. Professor Lyall hoisted it easily over one shoulder. Even in their human form, werewolves were considerably stronger than daylight folk.

Lord Maccon rested his tawny gaze on Alexia. She was sitting primly on the chesterfield. One gloved hand rested on the ebony handle of a ridiculous-looking parasol. Her brown eyes were narrowed in consideration. He would give a hundred pounds to know what she was thinking just then. He was also certain she would tell him exactly what it was if he asked, but he refused to give her the satisfaction. Instead he issued a statement. "We'll try to keep your name out of it, Miss Tarabotti. My report will say it was simply a normal girl who got lucky and managed to escape an unwarranted attack. No need for anyone to know a preternatural was involved."

Now it was Alexia's turn to glare. "Why do you BUR types always *do* that?"

Both men paused to look at her in confusion.

"*Do* what, Miss Tarabotti?" asked the professor.

"Dismiss me as though I were a child. Do you realize I could be useful to you?"

Lord Maccon grunted. "You mean you could go around legally getting into trouble instead of just bothering us all the time?"

Alexia tried to keep from feeling hurt. "BUR employs women, and I hear you even have a preternatural on the payroll up north, for ghost control and exorcism purposes."

Lord Maccon's caramel-colored eyes instantly narrowed. "From whom, exactly, did you hear that?"

Miss Tarabotti raised her eyebrows. As if she would ever betray the source of information told to her in confidence!

The earl understood her look perfectly. "Very well, never you mind that question."

"I shall not," replied Alexia primly.

Professor Lyall, still holding the body slung over one shoulder, took pity on her. "We do have both at BUR," he admitted.

Lord Maccon elbowed him in the side, but he stepped out of range with a casual grace that bespoke much practice. "But what we do not have is any *female* preternaturals, and certainly not any gentlewomen. All women employed by BUR are good working-class stock."

"You are simply still bitter about the hedgehogs," muttered Miss Tarabotti, but she also bowed her head in acknowledgment. She'd had this conversation before, with Lord Maccon's superior at BUR, to be precise. A man her brain still referred to as that Nice Silver-Haired Gentleman. The very idea that a lady of breeding such as herself might want to *work* was simply too shocking. "My dearest girl," he had said, "what if your mother found out?"

"Isn't BUR supposed to be covert? I could be covert." Miss Tarabotti could not help trying again. Professor Lyall, at least, liked her a little bit. Perhaps he might put in a good word.

Lord Maccon actually laughed. "You are about as covert as a sledgehammer." Then he cursed himself silently, as she seemed suddenly forlorn. She hid it quickly, but she had definitely been saddened.

His Beta grabbed him by the arm with his free hand. "Really, sir, manners."

The earl cleared his throat and looked contrite. "No offense meant, Miss Tarabotti." The Scottish lilt was back in his voice.

Alexia nodded, not looking up. She plucked at one of the pansies on her parasol. "It's simply, gentlemen"—and when she raised her dark eyes they had a slight sheen in them—"I would so like something useful to do."

Lord Maccon waited until he and the professor were out in the hallway, having bid polite, on Professor Lyall's part at least, farewells to the young lady, to ask the question that really bothered him. "For goodness' sake, Randolph, why doesn't she just get married?" His voice was full of frustration.

Randolph Lyall looked at his Alpha in genuine confusion. The earl was usually a very perceptive man, for all his bluster and Scottish grumbling. "She is a bit old, sir."

"Balderdash," said Lord Maccon. "She cannot possibly have more than a quarter century or so."

"And she is very"—the professor looked for a gentlemanly way of putting it—"assertive."

"Pah." The nobleman waved one large paw dismissively. "Simply got a jot more backbone than most females this century. There must be plenty of discerning gentlemen who'd cop to her value."

Professor Lyall had a well-developed sense of self-preservation and the distinct feeling that if he said anything desultory about the young lady's appearance, he might actually get his head bitten off. He, and the rest of polite society, might believe Miss Tarabotti's skin a little too dark and her nose a little too prominent, but he did not think Lord Maccon felt the same. Lyall had been Beta to the fourth Earl of Woolsey since Conall Maccon first descended upon them all. With barely twenty years gone and the bloody memory still strong, no werewolf was yet ready to question why Conall had wanted the bother of the London territory, not even Professor Lyall. The earl was a confusing man, his taste in females equally mystifying. For all Professor Lyall knew, his Alpha might actually *like* Roman noses, tan skin, and an assertive disposition. So instead he said, "Perhaps it's the Italian last name, sir, that keeps her unwed."

"Mmm," agreed Lord Maccon, "probably so." He did not sound convinced.

The two werewolves exited the duke's town house into the black London night, one bearing the body of a dead vampire, the other, a puzzled expression.

CHAPTER TWO

An Unexpected Invitation

Miss Tarabotti generally kept her soulless state quite hush-hush, even from her own family. She was not undead, mind you; she was a living, breathing human but was simply . . . lacking. Neither her family nor the members of the social circles she frequented ever noticed she was missing anything. Miss Tarabotti seemed to them only a spinster, whose unfortunate condition was clearly the result of a combination of domineering personality, dark complexion, and overly strong facial features. Alexia thought it too much of a bother to go around explaining soullessness to the ill-informed masses. It was almost, though not quite, as embarrassing as having it known that her father was both Italian and dead.

The ill-informed masses included her own family among their ranks, a family that specialized in being both inconvenient and asinine.

"Would you look at this!" Felicity Loontwill waved a copy of the *Morning Post* at the assembled breakfast table. Her father, the Right Honorable Squire Loontwill, did not divert his concentrated attention from the consumption of an eight-minute egg and toast. But her sister, Evylin, glanced up inquiringly, and her mama said, "What is it, my dear?" pausing in midsip of her medicinal barley water.

Felicity pointed to a passage in the society section of the paper. "It says here that there was a particularly gruesome incident at the ball last night! Did you know there was *an incident*? I do not remember any incident!"

Alexia frowned at her own egg in annoyance. She had been under the impression Lord Maccon was going to keep everything respectfully quiet and out of the society papers. She refused to acknowledge the fact that the sheer number of people who had seen her with the dead vampire meant that any such endeavor was practically impossible. After all, the earl's purported specialty was accomplishing several impossible things before dawn.

Felicity elaborated, "Apparently someone died. No name has been released, but a genuine death, and I missed it entirely! A young lady discovered him in the library and fainted from the shock. Poor lamb, how horrific for her."

Evylin, the youngest, clucked her tongue sympathetically and reached for the pot of gooseberry jelly. "Does it say who the young lady is?"

Felicity rubbed her nose delicately and read on. "Unfortunately, no."

Alexia raised both eyebrows and sipped her tea in uncharacteristic silence. She winced at the flavor, looked with narrowed eyes at her cup, and then reached for the creamer.

Evylin spread jelly with great attention to applying a precisely even layer over the top of the toast. "How very tiresome! I should love to know all the relevant details. It is like something out of a gothic novel. Anything else interesting?"

"Well, the article continues on with a more extensive review of the ball. Goodness, the writer even criticizes the Duchess of Snodgrove for not providing refreshments."

"Well, really," said Evylin in heartfelt agreement, "even Almack's has those bland little sandwiches. It is not as if the duke could not see to the expense."

"Too true, my dear," agreed Mrs. Loontwill.

Felicity glanced at the byline of the article. "Written by

'anonymous.' No commentary on anyone's attire. Well, I call that a pretty poor showing. He does not even mention Evylin or me."

The Loontwill girls were quite popular in the papers, partly for their generally well-turned-out appearance and partly because of the remarkable number of beaux they had managed to garner between them. The entire family, with the exception of Alexia, enjoyed this popularity immensely and did not seem to mind if what was written was not always complimentary. So long as *something* was written.

Evylin looked annoyed. A small crease appeared between her perfectly arched brows. "I wore my new pea-green gown with the pink water lily trim simply so they'd write about it."

Alexia winced. She would prefer not to be reminded of that gown—*so many ruffles.*

The unfortunate by-product of Mrs. Loontwill's second marriage, both Felicity and Evylin were markedly different from their older half sister. No one upon meeting the three together would have thought Alexia related to the other two at all. Aside from an obvious lack of Italian blood and completely soul-ridden states, Felicity and Evylin were both quite beautiful: pale insipid blondes with wide blue eyes and small rosebud mouths. Sadly, like their dear mama, they were not much more substantive than "quite beautiful." Breakfast conversation was, therefore, not destined to be of the intellectual caliber that Alexia aspired to. Still, Alexia was pleased to hear the subject turn toward something more mundane than murder.

"Well, that's all it says about the ball." Felicity paused, switching her attention to the society announcements. "This is very interesting. That nice tearoom near Bond Street has decided to remain open until two AM to accommodate and cultivate supernatural clientele. Next thing you know, they will be serving up raw meat and flutes of blood on a regular basis. Do you think we should still frequent the venue, Mama?"

Mrs. Loontwill looked up once more from her barley and

lemon water. "I do not see how it can do too much harm, my dear."

Squire Loontwill added, swallowing a bite of toast, "Some of the better investors run with the nighttime crowd, my pearl. You could do worse when hunting down suitors for the girls."

"Really, Daddy," admonished Evylin, "you make Mama sound like a werewolf on the rampage."

Mrs. Loontwill gave her husband a suspicious glance. "You haven't been frequenting Claret's or Sangria these last few evenings, have you?" She sounded as though she suspected London of being suddenly overrun with werewolves, ghosts, and vampires, and her husband fraternizing with them all.

The squire hurriedly backed away from the conversation. "Of course not, my pearl, only Boodles. You know I prefer my own club to those of the supernatural set."

"Speaking of gentlemen's clubs," interrupted Felicity, still immersed in the paper, "a new one opened last week in Mayfair. It caters to intellectuals, philosophers, scientists, and their ilk—of all things. It calls itself the Hypocras Club. How absurd. Why would such a class of individual need a club? Isn't that what they have public museums for?" She frowned over the address. "Terribly fashionable location, though." She showed the printed page to her mother. "Isn't that next door to the Duke of Snodgrove's town house?"

Mrs. Loontwill nodded. "Quite right, my dear. Well, a parcel of scientists coming and going at all hours of the day and night will certainly lower the tenor of *that* neighborhood. I should think the duchess would be in a veritable fit over this occurrence. I had intended to send round a thank-you card for last night's festivities. Now I think I might pay her a call in person this afternoon. As a concerned friend, I really ought to check on her emotional state."

"How ghastly for her," said Alexia, driven beyond endurance into comment. "People actually thinking, with their brains, and right next door. Oh, the travesty of it all."

Evylin said, "I will come with you, Mama."

Mrs. Loontwill smiled at her youngest daughter and completely ignored her eldest.

Felicity read on. "The latest spring styles from Paris call for wide belts in contrasting colors. How regrettable. Of course, they will look lovely on you, Evylin, but on my figure . . ."

Unfortunately, despite invading scientists, the opportunity to gloat over a friend's misfortune, and imminent belts, Alexia's mama was still thinking about the dead man at the Snodgroves' ball. "You disappeared for quite a while at one point last night, Alexia. You would not be keeping anything important from us, would you, my dear?"

Alexia gave her a carefully bland look. "I did have a bit of a run-in with Lord Maccon." *Always throw them off the scent*, she thought.

That captured everyone's attention, even her stepfather's. Squire Loontwill rarely troubled himself to speak at length. With the Loontwill ladies, there was not much of a chance to get a word in, so he tended to let the breakfast conversation flow over him like water over tea leaves, paying only half a mind to the proceedings. But he was a man of reasonable sense and propriety, and Alexia's statement caused him to become suddenly alert. The Earl of Woolsey might be a werewolf, but he was in possession of considerable wealth and influence.

Mrs. Loontwill paled and noticeably mollified her tone. "You did not say anything disrespectful to the earl, now, did you, my dear?"

Alexia thought back over her encounter. "Not as such."

Mrs. Loontwill pushed away her glass of barley water and shakily poured herself a cup of tea. "Oh dear," she said softly.

Mrs. Loontwill had never quite managed to figure out her eldest daughter. She had thought that putting Alexia on the shelf would keep the exasperating girl out of trouble. Instead, she had inadvertently managed to give Alexia an ever-increasing degree of freedom. Thinking back on it, she really ought to have married Alexia off instead. Now they were all stuck with her outrageous behavior, which seemed to be progressively worsening as she got older.

Alexia added peevishly, "I did wake up this morning thinking of all the rude things I *could* have said but did not. I call that most aggravating."

Squire Loontwill emitted a long drawn-out sigh.

Alexia firmly put her hand on the table. "In fact, I think I shall go for a walk in the park this morning. My nerves are not quite what they should be after the encounter." She was not, as one might suppose, obliquely referring to the vampire attack. Miss Tarabotti was not one of life's milk-water misses—in fact, quite the opposite. Many a gentleman had likened his first meeting with her to downing a very strong cognac when one was expecting to imbibe fruit juice—that is to say, startling and apt to leave one with a distinct burning sensation. No, Alexia's nerves were frazzled because she was still boiling mad at the Earl of Woolsey. She had been mad when he left her in the library. She had spent a restless night fuming impotently and awoken with eyes gritty and noble feelings still on edge.

Evylin said, "But wait. What happened? Alexia, you must tell all! Why did *you* encounter Lord Maccon at the ball when we did not? He was not on the guest list. I would have known. I peeked over the footman's shoulder."

"Evy, you didn't," gasped Felicity, genuinely shocked.

Alexia ignored them and left the breakfast room to hunt down her favorite shawl. Mrs. Loontwill might have tried to stop her, but she knew such an attempt would be useless. Getting information out of Alexia when she did not want to share was akin to trying to squeeze blood from a ghost. Instead, Mrs. Loontwill reached for her husband's hand and squeezed it consolingly. "Do not worry, Herbert. I think Lord Maccon rather likes Alexia's rudeness. He's never publicly cut her for it, at least. We can be grateful for small mercies."

Squire Loontwill nodded. "I suppose a werewolf of his advanced age might find it refreshing?" he suggested hopefully.

His wife applauded such an optimistic attitude with an affectionate pat on the shoulder. She knew how very trying her second husband found her eldest daughter. Really, what *had* she been thinking, marrying an Italian? Well, she had been young and Alessandro Tarabotti so very handsome. But there was something else about Alexia, something . . . revoltingly independent, that Mrs. Loontwill could not blame entirely on her first husband. And, of course, she refused to take the blame herself. Whatever it was, Alexia had been born that way, full of logic and reason and sharp words. Not for the first time, Mrs. Loontwill lamented the fact that her eldest had not been a male child; it would have made life very much easier for them all.

Under ordinary circumstances, walks in Hyde Park were the kind of thing a single young lady of good breeding was not supposed to do without her mama and possibly an elderly female relation or two in attendance. Miss Tarabotti felt such rules did not entirely apply to her, as she was a spinster. Had been a spinster for as long as she could remember. In her more acerbic moments, she felt she had been born a spinster. Mrs. Loontwill had not even bothered with the expenditure of a come-out or a proper season for her eldest daughter. "Really, darling," Alexia's mother had said at the time in tones of the deepest condescension, "with that nose and that skin, there is simply no point in us going to the expense. I have got your sisters to think of." So Alexia, whose nose really wasn't that big and whose skin really wasn't that tan, had gone on the shelf at fifteen. Not that she had ever actually coveted the burden of a husband, but it would have been nice to know she could get one if she ever changed her mind. Alexia did enjoy dancing, so she would have liked to attend at least one ball as an available young lady rather than always ending up skulking in libraries. These days she attended balls as nothing more than her sisters' chaperone, and the libraries abounded. But spinsterhood did mean she could go for a walk in Hyde Park without her mama, and only the worst sticklers would object. Luckily, such sticklers, like the contributors to the *Morning Post,* did not know Miss Alexia Tarabotti's name.

However, with Lord Maccon's harsh remonstrations still ringing in her ears, Alexia did not feel she could go for a walk completely unchaperoned, even though it was midmorning and the antisupernatural sun shone quite brilliantly. So she took her trusty brass parasol, for the sake of the sun, and Miss Ivy Hisselpenny, for the sake of Lord Maccon's easily offended sensibilities.

Miss Ivy Hisselpenny was a dear friend of Miss Alexia Tarabotti's. They had known each other long enough to trespass on all the well-fortified territory of familiarity. So when Alexia sent round to see if Ivy wanted a walk, Ivy was very well aware of the fact that a walk was only the surface gloss to the proceedings.

Ivy Hisselpenny was the unfortunate victim of circumstances that dictated she be only-just-pretty, only-just-wealthy, and possessed of a terrible propensity for wearing extremely silly hats. This last being the facet of Ivy's character that Alexia found most difficult to bear. In general, however, she found Ivy a restful, congenial, and, most importantly, a willing partner in any excursion.

In Alexia, Ivy had found a lady of understanding and intelligence, sometimes overly blunt for her own delicate sensibilities, but loyal and kind under even the most trying of circumstances.

Ivy had learned to find Alexia's bluntness entertaining, and Alexia had learned one did not always have to look at one's friend's hats. Thus, each having discovered a means to overlook the most tiresome aspects of the other's personality early on in their relationship, the two girls developed a fixed friendship to the mutual benefit of both. Their Hyde Park conversation reflected their typical mode of communication.

"Ivy, my dear," said Miss Tarabotti as her friend bustled up, "how marvelous of you to find time to walk at such short notice! What a hideous bonnet. I do hope you did not pay too much for it."

"Alexia! How perfectly horrid of you to criticize my hat. Why should I not be able to walk this morning? You know I never have anything better to do on Thursdays. Thursdays are so tiresome, don't you find?" replied Miss Hisselpenny.

Miss Tarabotti said, "Really, I wish you would take me with you when you go shopping, Ivy. Much horror might be avoided. Why should Thursday be any different than any other weekday?"

And so on.

The day was quite a fine one, and the two ladies walked arm in arm, their full skirts swishing and the smaller, more manageable bustle, just come into fashion last season, making it comparatively easy to move around. Rumor had it that in France, certain ladies had dispensed with the bustle altogether, but that scandalous mod had yet to reach London. Ivy's and Alexia's parasols were raised against the sun, though, as Alexia was fond of saying, such an effort was wasted on her complexion. Why, oh why, did vampire-style paleness have to rule so thoroughly the fashionable world? They strolled along, presenting a fetching picture: Ivy in cream muslin with rose flowers, and Alexia in her favorite blue walking gown with velvet edging. Both outfits were trimmed with those many rows of lace, deep pleated flounces, and tucks to which only the most stylish aspired. If Miss Hisselpenny sported a slight overabundance of the above, it must be understood it was the result of too much effort rather than too little.

Partly due to the pleasant weather and partly due to the latest craze for elaborate walking dresses, Hyde Park was decidedly crowded. Many a gentleman tipped his hat in their general direction, annoying Alexia with constant interruptions and flattering Ivy with such marked attentions.

"Really," grumbled Miss Tarabotti, "what has possessed everyone this morning? One would think we were actually tempting marriage prospects."

"Alexia! You may see yourself as off the market," remonstrated her friend, smiling shyly at a respectable-looking gentleman on a handsome bay gelding, "but I refuse to accept such an injurious fate."

Miss Tarabotti sniffed.

"Speaking of which, how was the duchess's ball last night?" Ivy was always one for gossip. Her family being too nearly middle class to be invited to any but the largest of balls, she had to rely on Alexia for such detail as went unreported by the *Morning Post*. Sadly for Ivy, her dear friend was not the most reliable or loquacious source. "Was it perfectly dreadful? Who was there? What were they wearing?"

Alexia rolled her eyes. "Ivy, please, one question at a time."

"Well, was it a pleasant event?"

"Not a bit of it. Would you believe there were no comestibles on offer? Nothing but punch! I had to go to the library and order tea." Alexia spun her parasol in agitation.

Ivy was shocked. "You did not!"

Miss Tarabotti raised her black eyebrows. "I most certainly did. You wouldn't believe the fracas that resulted. As if that was not bad enough, then Lord Maccon insisted on showing up."

Miss Hisselpenny paused in her tracks to look closely into her friend's face. Alexia's expression showed nothing but annoyance, but there was something about the precise way she always spoke about the Earl of Woolsey that roused Ivy's suspicions.

Still she played the sympathy card. "Oh dear, was he utterly horrid?" Privately, Ivy felt Lord Maccon entirely respectable for a werewolf, but he was a little too, well, *much* for her particular taste. He was so very large and so very gruff that he rather terrified her, but he always behaved correctly in public, and there was a lot to be said for a man who sported such well-tailored jackets— even if he did change into a ferocious beast once a month.

Alexia actually snorted. "Pah. No more than normal. I think it must have something to do with being Alpha. He is simply too accustomed to having his orders followed all the time. It puts me completely out of humor." She paused. "A vampire attacked me last night."

Ivy pretended a faint.

Alexia kept her friend forcibly upright by stiffening her linked arm. "Stop being so squiffy," she said. "There is no one important around to catch you."

Ivy recovered herself and said vehemently, "Good heavens, Alexia. How *do* you get yourself into these situations?"

Alexia shrugged and commenced walking more briskly so that Ivy had to trot a few steps to keep up.

"What did you do?" She was not to be dissuaded.

"Hit him with my parasol, of course."

"You did not!"

"Right upside the head. I would do the same to anyone who attacked me, supernatural or not. He simply came right at me, no introduction, no nothing!" Miss Tarabotti was feeling a tad defensive on the subject.

"But, Alexia, really, it simply is not the done thing to hit a vampire, with a parasol or otherwise!"

Miss Tarabotti sighed but secretly agreed with her friend. There weren't very many vampires skulking around London society, never had been, but the few hives that were in residence included politicians, landholders, and some very important noblemen among their membership. To indiscriminately whack about with one's parasol among such luminaries was social suicide.

Miss Hisselpenny continued. "It's simply too outrageous. What's next? Charging indiscriminately about the House of Lords, throwing jam at the local supernatural set during nighttime session?"

Alexia giggled at the leaps made by Ivy's imagination.

"Oh no, now I am giving you ideas." Ivy pressed her forehead dramatically with one gloved hand. "What exactly happened?"

Alexia told her.

"You killed him?" This time Miss Hisselpenny looked like she might really faint.

"It was by accident!" insisted Miss Tarabotti, taking her friend's arm in a firmer grip.

"That was you in the *Morning Post*? The lady who found the dead man at the Duchess of Snodgrove's ball last night?" Ivy was all agog.

Alexia nodded.

"Well, Lord Maccon certainly covered things up adequately. There was no mention of your name or family." Ivy was relieved for her friend's sake.

"Or the fact that the dead man was a vampire, thank goodness. Can you imagine what my dear mother would say?" Alexia glanced heavenward.

"Or the detrimental effect on your marriage prospects, to be found unchaperoned in a library with a dead vampire!"

Alexia's expression told Ivy exactly what she felt about *that* comment.

Miss Hisselpenny moved on. "You do realize you owe Lord Maccon a tremendous debt of gratitude?"

Miss Tarabotti looked exactly as if she had swallowed a live eel. "I should think not, Ivy. It is his job to keep these things secret: Chief Minister in Charge of Supernatural–Natural Liaison for the Greater London Area, or whatever his BUR title is. I am certainly under no obligation to a man who was only doing his civic duty. Besides, knowing what I do of the Woolsey pack's social dynamics, I would guess that Professor Lyall, not Lord Maccon, dealt with the newspapermen."

Ivy privately felt her friend did not give the earl enough credit. Simply because Alexia was immune to his charm did not mean the rest of the world felt such indifference. He was Scottish, to be sure, but he had been Alpha for what, twenty years or so? Not long by supernatural standards, but good enough for the less discriminating of daylight society. There were rumors as to how he had defeated the last Woolsey Alpha. They said it had been far too rough for modern standards, though still legal under pack protocol. However, the preceding earl was generally known to have been a depraved individual wanting in all aspects of civility and decorum. For Lord Maccon to have appeared out of nowhere and eliminated him, however draconian his methods, had left London society part shocked, part thrilled. The truth of the matter was that most Alphas and hive queens in the modern age held power by the same civilized means as everyone else: money, social standing, and politics. Lord Maccon might be new to this, but twenty years in, he was now better at it than most. Ivy was young enough to be impressed and wise enough not to dwell on his northern origin.

"I really do think you are terribly hard on the earl, Alexia," said Ivy as the two ladies turned down a side path, away from the main promenade.

"It cannot be helped," Miss Tarabotti replied. "I have never liked the man."

"So you say," agreed Miss Hisselpenny.

They circumvented a coppice of birch trees and slowed to a stop at the edge of a wide grassy area. Recently, this particular meadow, open to the sky and off the beaten track, had come into use by a dirigible company. They flew Giffard-style steam-powered airships with de Lome propellers. It was the latest and greatest in leisurely travel. The upper crust, in particular, had taken to the skies with enthusiasm. Floating had almost eclipsed hunting as the preferred pastime of the aristocracy. The ships were a sight to behold, and Alexia was particularly fond of them. She hoped one day to ride in one. The views were reportedly breathtaking, and they were rumored to serve an excellent high tea on board.

The two ladies stood watching as one of the dirigibles came in for a landing. From a distance, the airship looked like nothing so much as a prodigiously long skinny balloon, with a basket suspended from it. Closer up, however, it became clear that the balloon was partly reinforced into semirigidity, and the basket was more like an overlarge barge. The barge part was painted with the Giffard company logo in bright black and white and suspended by a thousand wires from the balloon above. It maneuvered in toward the meadow and then, as the two ladies watched, cut and cranked down its propeller before sinking softly into a landing.

"What remarkable times we live in," commented Alexia, her eyes sparkling at the spectacular sight.

Ivy was not as impressed. "It is not natural, mankind taking to the skies."

Alexia tsked at her in annoyance. "Ivy, why do you have to be such an old fuddy-duddy? This is the age of miraculous invention and extraordinary science. The working of those contraptions is really quite fascinating. Why, the calculations for liftoff alone are—"

She was interrupted by a mellow feminine voice.

Ivy let her breath out in a huff of relief—anything to keep Alexia off all that loopy intellectual mumbo jumbo.

The two ladies turned away from the dirigible and all its wonders, Alexia reluctantly and Ivy with great alacrity. They found themselves facing an entirely different kind of spectacle.

The voice had come from atop a wholly fabulous phaeton that had drawn to a stop behind them without either woman noticing. The carriage was a high flyer: a dangerous open-topped contraption, rarely driven by a woman. Yet there, behind a team of perfectly matched blacks, sat a slightly chubby lady with blond hair and a friendly smile. Everything clashed about the arrangement; from the lady, who wore an afternoon tea gown of becoming dusty rose trimmed in burgundy rather than a carriage dress, to the high-spirited mounts, who seemed far better suited to draw some dandy of the Corinthian set. She had a pleasant expression and bobbing ringlets but kept iron-steady hands on the reins. Unfamiliar with the woman, the two young ladies would have turned back to their observations, presuming the interruption an embarrassing case of mistaken identity, except that the pretty young lady spoke to them again.

"Do I have the pleasure of addressing Miss Tarabotti?"

Ivy and Alexia looked at each other. It was such a remarkable thing to happen—in the middle of the park, by the airfield, *and* without any introduction—that Alexia answered in spite of herself. "Yes. How do you do?"

"Beautiful day for it, wouldn't you say?" The lady gestured with her whip at the dirigible, which had now completed its landing and was preparing to disgorge its passengers.

"Indeed," replied Alexia crisply, a bit put off by the woman's brash and familiar tone. "Have we met?" she inquired pointedly.

The lady laughed, a mellow tinkling sound. "I am Miss Mabel Dair, and now we have."

Alexia decided she must be dealing with *an original*.

"Pleased to make your acquaintance," she replied cautiously. "Miss Dair, might I introduce Miss Ivy Hisselpenny?"

Ivy bobbed a curtsy, at the same time tugging on Alexia's velvet-trimmed sleeve. "The *actress*," she hissed in Alexia's ear. "You know! Oh, I say, Alexia, you really must know."

Miss Tarabotti, who did not know, surmised that she ought to. "Oh," she said blankly, and then quietly to Ivy, "Should we be talking to an actress in the middle of Hyde Park?" She glanced covertly at the disembarking dirigible passengers. No one was paying them any notice.

Miss Hisselpenny hid a smile under one gloved hand. "This from the woman who last night accidentally"—she paused—"parasoled a man. I should think that talking to an actress in public would be the least of your worries."

Miss Dair's bright blue eyes followed this exchange. She laughed again. "That incident, my dears, would be the reason for this rather discourteous meeting."

Alexia and Ivy were surprised that she knew what they were whispering about.

"You must forgive my brazenness and this intrusion on your private confidences."

"Must we?" wondered Alexia under her breath.

Ivy elbowed her in the ribs.

Miss Dair explained herself at last. "You see, my mistress would like to visit with you, Miss Tarabotti."

"Your mistress?"

The actress nodded, blond ringlets bouncing. "Oh, I know they do not normally go in for the bolder artistic types. Actresses, I am under the impression, tend to become clavigers, since werewolves are far more intrigued by the performing arts."

Miss Tarabotti realized what was going on. "My goodness, you are a drone!"

Miss Dair smiled and nodded her acknowledgment. She had dimples as well as ringlets, most distressing.

Alexia was still very confused. Drones were vampire companions, servants, and caretakers who were paid with the possibility of eventually becoming immortal themselves. But vampires rarely chose drones from among those who occupied the limelight. They preferred a more behind-the-scenes approach to soul hunting: recruiting painters, poets, sculptors, and the like. The flashier side of creativity was universally acknowledged werewolf territory, who chose thespians, opera singers, and ballet dancers to become clavigers. Of course, both supernatural sets preferred the artistic element in a companion, for there was always a better chance of excess soul in a creative person and therefore a higher likelihood that he or she would survive metamorphosis. But for a vampire to choose an actress was rather unusual.

"But you are a woman!" objected Miss Hisselpenny, shocked. An even more well-known fact about drones or clavigers was that they tended to be male. Women were much less likely to survive being turned. No one knew why, though scientists suggested the female's weaker constitution.

The actress smiled. "Not all drones are after eternal life, you realize? Some of us just enjoy the patronage. I have no particular interest in becoming supernatural, but my mistress provides for me in many other ways. Speaking of which, are you free this evening, Miss Tarabotti?"

Alexia finally recovered from her surprise and frowned. She had no concrete plans, but she did not want to go into a vampire hive uninformed. So she said firmly, "Unfortunately, I am unavailable tonight." She made a quick decision to send her card round to Lord Akeldama, requesting he stop by for dinner. He might be able to fill her in on some of the local hive activities. Lord Akeldama liked perfumed handkerchiefs and pink neckties, but he also liked to *know things*.

"Tomorrow night, then?" The actress looked hopeful. This request must be particularly important to her mistress.

Alexia dipped her head in agreement. The long cascade feather on her felt hat tickled the back of her neck. "Where am I expected to go?"

Miss Dair leaned forward from her box seat, keeping a steady hand to her frisky horses, and handed Alexia a small sealed envelope. "I must ask you not to share the address with anyone. My apologies, Miss Hisselpenny. You understand the delicacy of the situation, I am sure."

Ivy held up her hands placatingly and blushed delicately. "No offense taken, Miss Dair. This entire affair is none of my concern." Even Ivy knew better than to ask questions of hive business.

"For whom do I inquire?" asked Miss Tarabotti, turning the envelope about in her hands but not opening it.

"Countess Nadasdy."

That was a name Alexia knew. Countess Nadasdy was purported to be one of the oldest living vampires, incredibly beautiful, impossibly cruel, and extremely polite. She was queen of the Westminster hive. Lord Maccon might have learned to play the social game with aplomb, but Countess Nadasdy was its master.

Miss Tarabotti looked long and hard at the bubbly blond actress. "You have hidden depths, Miss Dair." Alexia was not supposed to know many of the things that went on in Countess Nadasdy's circle, let alone her hive, but she read too much. Many of the books in the Loontwills' library were left over from her father's day. Alessandro Tarabotti had clearly felt a strong inclination toward literature concerning the supernatural, so Alexia had a tolerably clear concept of what occurred in a vampire hive.

Miss Dair certainly must be something more than blond curls, dimples, and a perfectly turned-out rose dress.

Miss Dair bobbed her ringlets at them. "Whatever the gossip columns may say, Countess Nadasdy is a good mistress." Her smile was slightly quirky. "If you like that sort of thing. It has been delightful to meet you ladies." She tightened the reins to her blacks and snapped them smartly. The phaeton jerked forward sharply on the uneven grass, but Miss Dair maintained a perfect seat. In mere moments, the high flyer was gone, rattling down the footpath and disappearing behind the small coppice of birch trees.

The two girls followed, the airship in all its technological glory having suddenly lost its appeal. Other more exciting events were afoot. They walked a little more slowly, conversing in a subdued manner. Alexia turned the small envelope around in her hands.

The jaunt through Hyde Park appeared to be doing the trick as far as Alexia's prickly feelings were concerned. All of her anger at Lord Maccon had dissipated to be replaced by apprehension.

Ivy looked pale. Well, paler than usual. Finally she pointed to the sealed envelope Alexia was fiddling with nervously. "You know what that is?"

Miss Tarabotti swallowed. "Of course I know." But she said it so quietly Ivy did not really hear her.

"You have been given the actual address of a hive, Alexia. They are either going to recruit you or drain you dry. No daylight humans but drones are allowed to have that kind of information."

Alexia looked uncomfortable. "I know!" She was wondering how a hive might react to a preternatural in their midst. Not very kindly, she suspected. She worried her lower lip. "I simply must speak with Lord Akeldama."

Miss Hisselpenny looked, if possible, even more worried. "Oh really, must you? He is so very outrageous."

Outrageous was a very good way of describing Lord Akeldama. Alexia was not afraid of outrageousness any more than she was afraid of vampires, which was good because Lord Akeldama was both.

He minced into the room, teetering about on three-inch heels with ruby and gold buckles. "My darling, *darling* Alexia." Lord Akeldama had adopted use of her given name within minutes of their first meeting. He had said that he just knew they would be friends, and there was no point in prevaricating. "*Darling!*" He also seemed to speak predominantly in italics. "How perfectly, deliciously, *delightful* of you to invite *me* to dinner. *Darling.*"

Miss Tarabotti smiled at him. It was impossible not to grin at Lord Akeldama; his attire was so consistently absurd. In addition to the heels, he wore yellow checked gaiters, gold satin breeches, an orange and lemon striped waistcoat, and an evening jacket of sunny pink brocade. His cravat was a frothy flowing waterfall of orange, yellow, and pink Chinese silk, barely contained by a magnificently huge ruby pin. His ethereal face was powdered quite unnecessarily, for he was already completely pale, a predilection of his kind. He sported round spots of pink blush on each cheek like a Punch and Judy puppet. He also affected a gold monocle, although, like all vampires, he had perfect vision.

With fluid poise, he settled himself on the settee opposite Alexia, a small neatly laid supper table between them.

Miss Tarabotti had decided to host him, much to her mother's chagrin, alone in her private drawing room. Alexia tried to explain that the vampire's supposed inability to enter private residences uninvited was a myth based upon their collective obsession with proper social etiquette, but her mother refused to believe her. After some minor hysterics, Mrs. Loontwill thought better of her objections to the arrangement. Realizing that the event would occur whether she willed it or no, Alexia being assertive—Italian blood—she hastily took the two younger girls and Squire Loontwill off to an evening card party at Lady Blingchester's. Mrs. Loontwill was very good at operating on the theory that what she did not know could not hurt her, particularly regarding Alexia and the supernatural.

So Alexia had the house to herself, and Lord Akeldama's entrance was appreciated by no one more important than Floote, the Loontwills' long-suffering butler. This caused Lord Akeldama distress, for he sat so dramatically and posed with such grace, that he clearly anticipated a much larger audience.

The vampire took out a scented handkerchief and bopped Miss Tarabotti playfully on the shoulder with it. "I hear, my little sugarplum, that you were a naughty, *naughty* girl at the duchess's ball last night."

Lord Akeldama might look and act like a supercilious buffoon of the highest order, but he had one of the sharpest minds in the whole of London. The *Morning Post* would pay half its weekly income for the kind of information he seemed to have access to at any time of night. Alexia privately suspected him of having drones among the servants in every major household, not to mention ghost spies tethered to key public institutions.

Miss Tarabotti refused to give her guest the satisfaction of asking how he knew of the previous evening's episode. Instead she smiled in what she hoped was an enigmatic manner and poured the champagne.

Lord Akeldama never drank anything but champagne. Well, that is to say, except when he was drinking blood. He was reputed to have once said that the best drink in existence was a blending of the two, a mix he referred to fondly as a Pink Slurp.

"You know why I invited you over, then?" Alexia asked instead, offering him a cheese swizzle.

Lord Akeldama waved a limp wrist about dismissively before taking the swizzle and nibbling its tip. "La, my dearest *girl*, you invited me because you could not *bear* to be without my company a single *moment* longer. And I shall be cut to the very quick of my extensive soul if your reason is *anything* else."

Miss Tarabotti waved a hand at the butler. Floote issued her a look of mild disapproval and vanished in search of the first course.

"That is, naturally, exactly why I invited you. Besides which I am certain you missed me just as much, as we have not seen each other in an age. I am convinced that your visit has absolutely nothing to do with an avid curiosity as to how I managed to kill a vampire yesterday evening," she said mildly.

Lord Akeldama held up a hand. "A moment please, my dear." Then he reached into a waistcoat pocket and produced a small spiky device. It looked like two tuning forks sunk into a faceted crystal. He flicked the first fork with his thumbnail, waited a moment, and then flicked the second. The two made a dissonant, low-pitched strumming sound, like the hum of two different kinds of bee arguing, that seemed to be amplified by the crystal. He placed the device carefully in the center of the table, where it continued to hum away discordantly. It was not entirely irritating but seemed like it might grow to be.

"One gets accustomed to it after a while," explained Lord Akeldama apologetically.

"What is it?" wondered Alexia.

"That little gem is a harmonic auditory resonance disruptor. One of my boys picked it up in gay Paris recently. Charming, isn't it?"

"Yes, but what does it do?" Alexia wanted to know.

"Not much in this room, but if anyone is trying to listen in from a distance with, say, an ear trumpet or other eavesdropping device, it creates a kind of screaming sound that results in the most tremendous headache. I tested it."

"Remarkable," said Alexia, impressed despite herself. "Are we likely to be saying things people might want to overhear?"

"Well, we were discussing how you managed to kill a vampire, were we not? And while I know *exactly* how you did it, *petal*, you may not want the rest of the world to know as well."

Alexia was affronted. "Oh really, and how did I do it?"

Lord Akeldama laughed, showing off a set of particularly white and particularly sharp fangs. "Oh, princess." In one of those lightning-fast movements that only the best athletes or a supernatural person could execute, he grabbed her free hand. His deadly fangs vanished. The ethereal beauty in his face became ever so slightly too effeminate, and his strength dissipated. "*This is how.*"

Alexia nodded. It had taken Lord Akeldama four meetings to deduce she was preternatural. Estranged from the hives as he was, he had never been officially informed of her existence. He considered this an embarrassing blight on his long career as a snoop. His only possible excuse for the blunder was the fact that, while preternatural men were rare, preternatural women were practically nonexistent. He simply had not expected to find one in the form of an overly assertive spinster, enmeshed in the thick of London society, companioned by two silly sisters and a sillier mama. As a result, he took any opportunity to remind himself of what she was, grabbing her hand or arm on the merest whim.

In this particular instance, he stroked her hand fondly. There was no attraction in the movement. "*Sweetling,*" he had once said, "you are at no more risk with me in *that* regard than you are in danger of me unexpectedly biting you—both being equal impossibilities. In the one case, I do not possess the necessary equipment upon contact, in the other case you do not." Her father's library had provided Alexia with any further explanation she might require. Alessandro Tarabotti had engaged in quite an adventurous life before marriage and collected books from all around the Empire, some of them with very fascinating pictures, indeed. He had an apparent passion for explanatory studies on primitive peoples, which resulted in the kind of documentation that might encourage even Evylin to enter a library—had she been made aware of their existence. Luckily, the entirety of Alexia's family felt that if it did not originate in the gossip section of the *Morning Post*, it was probably not worth reading. Alexia, as a result, knew considerably more on the ways of the flesh than any English spinster ought to know, and certainly enough not to mind Lord Akeldama's little gestures of affection.

"You have no idea how deliciously *restful* I find the miracle of your company," he had remarked the first time he touched her.

"It's like swimming in too-warm bathwater most of one's life and suddenly plunging into an icy mountain stream. Shocking but, I believe, good for the soul." He had shrugged delicately. "I enjoy feeling mortal again, if only for one moment and only in *your glorious* presence." Miss Tarabotti had granted him very unspinster-like permission to grasp her hand whenever he wished—so long as it was always done in complete privacy.

Alexia sipped her champagne. "That vampire in the library last night did not know what I was," she said. "He came charging right at me, went straight for my neck, and then lost his fangs. I thought most of your lot knew by now. BUR undoubtedly keeps close enough track of me. Lord Maccon certainly appeared last night more quickly than was to be expected. Even for him."

Lord Akeldama nodded. His hair glinted in the flickering flame from a nearby candle. The Loontwills had installed the latest in gas lighting, but Alexia preferred beeswax, unless she was reading. In the candlelight, Lord Akeldama's hair was as gold as the buckles on his shoes. One always expected vampires to be dark and slightly doomy. Lord Akeldama was the antithesis of all such expectations. He wore his blond hair long and queued back in a manner stylish hundreds of years ago. He looked up at her, and his face was suddenly old and serious, seeming not at all as ridiculous as his attire should make him. "They *do* mostly know of you, my pearl. All four of the official hives tell their larvae directly after metamorphosis that there is a soul-sucker living in London."

Miss Tarabotti winced. Usually Lord Akeldama was sensitive to her dislike of the term. He had been the first to use it in her presence, on the night he had finally realized what she was. For once in his long life, he had lost his perfectly donned charisma in shock at discovering a preternatural in the guise of a forthright spinster. Miss Tarabotti, understandably, had not taken to the notion of being called a soul-sucker. Lord Akeldama was careful never to use it again, except to make a point. Now he had a point to make.

Floote arrived with the soup, a creamy cucumber and watercress. Lord Akeldama received no nourishment from the consumption of food, but he appreciated the taste. Unlike some of the more repulsive members of his set, he did not engage in that tradition established by ancient Roman vampires. There was no need for Alexia to call for a purge bucket. He merely sampled each dish politely and then left the rest for the servants to partake of later. No sense in wasting good soup. And it was quite good. One could say a number of impolite things about the Loontwills, but no one had ever accused them of frugality. Even Alexia, spinster that she was, was given an allowance large enough to dress her to the height of fashion—although she did tend to stick to trends a little too precisely. The poor thing could not help it. Her choice of clothing simply lacked soul. Regardless, the Loontwills' extravagance extended to the keeping of a very fine cook.

Floote slid away softly to retrieve the next course.

Alexia removed her hand from her friend's grasp and, never one for dissembling, got straight to the point. "Lord Akeldama, please tell me, what is going on? Who was the vampire who attacked me last night? How could he not know who I was? He did not even know *what* I was, as if no one had told him preternaturals existed at all. I am well aware that BUR keeps us secret from the general public, but packs and hives are well informed as a rule."

Lord Akeldama reached forward and flicked the two tuning forks on the resonator again. "My *dearest* young friend. There, I believe, you have the *very* issue in hand. Unfortunately for you, since you eliminated the individual in question, every interested supernatural party is beginning to believe *you* are the one who knows the answers to those very questions. Speculation abounds, and vampires are a suspicious lot. Some already hold that the hives are being kept *purposefully* in ignorance by either you, or BUR, or *most likely* both." He smiled, all fangs, and sipped his champagne.

Alexia sat back and let out a whoosh of air. "Well, that explains her rather forceful invitation."

Lord Akeldama did not move from his relaxed position, but he seemed to be sitting up straighter. "Her? Her *who*? Whose invitation, my *dearest* petunia blossom?"

"Countess Nadasdy's."

Lord Akeldama actually did sit up straight at that. His waterfall of a cravat quivered in agitation. "Queen of the Westminster hive," he hissed, his fangs showing. "There *are* words to describe her, my *dear*, but *one* does *not* repeat them in polite company."

Floote came in with the fish course, a simple fillet of sole with thyme and lemon. He glanced with raised eyebrows at the humming auditory device and then at the agitated Lord Akeldama. Alexia shook her head slightly when he would have remained protectively in the room.

Miss Tarabotti studied Lord Akeldama's face closely. He was a rove—a hiveless vampire. Roves were rare among the bloodsucking set. It took a lot of political, psychological, and supernatural strength for a vampire to separate from his hive. And once autonomous units, roves tended to go a bit funny about the noggin and slide toward the eccentric end of societal acceptability. In deference to this status, Lord Akeldama kept all his papers in impeccable order and was fully registered with BUR. However, it did mean he was a mite prejudiced against the hives.

The vampire sampled the fish, but the delicious taste did not seem to improve his temper. He pushed the dish away peevishly and sat back, tapping one expensive shoe against the other.

"Don't you like the Westminster hive queen?" asked Alexia with wide dark eyes and a great show of assumed innocence.

Lord Akeldama seemed to remember himself. The foppishness reappeared in spades. His wrists went limp and wiggly. "La, *my dear daffodil*, the hive queen and I, we . . . have our differences. I am under the distressing impression she finds me a *tad*"—he paused as though searching for the right word—"flamboyant."

Miss Tarabotti looked at him, evaluating both his words and the meaning behind them. "And here I thought it was you who did not like Countess Nadasdy."

"Now, *sweetheart*, who has been telling you *little* stories like that?"

Alexia tucked into her fish, a clear indication that she declined to reveal her source. After she had finished, there was a moment of silence while Floote removed the plates and placed the main course before them: a delicious arrangement of braised pork chop, apple compote, and slow roasted baby potatoes. Once the butler had gone again, Miss Tarabotti decided to ask her guest the more important question she had invited him over to answer.

"What do you think she wants of me, my lord?"

Lord Akeldama's eyes narrowed. He ignored the chop and fiddled idly with his massive ruby cravat pin. "As I see it, there are two reasons. Either she knows exactly what happened last night at the ball and she wants to bribe you into silence, or she has no idea who that vampire was and what he was doing in her territory, and she thinks you do."

"In either case, it would behoove me to be better informed than I currently am," Miss Tarabotti said, eating a buttery little potato.

He nodded empathetically.

"Are you positive you do not know anything more?" she asked.

"My dearest *girl*, *who* do you think I am? Lord Maccon, perhaps?" He picked up his champagne glass and twirled it by the stem, gazing thoughtfully at the tiny bubbles. "Now there *is* an idea, my treasure. *Why not* go to the werewolves? They may know more of the *relevant* facts. Lord Maccon, of course, being BUR will know *most* of all."

Alexia tried to look nonchalant. "But as a minister of BUR's secrets, he is also the least likely to relay any cogent details," she countered.

Lord Akeldama laughed in a tinkling manner that indicated more artifice than real amusement. "Then there is nothing for it, *sweetest* of Alexias, but to use your plethora of feminine *wiles* upon him. Werewolves have been susceptible to the *gentler* sex for as long as I can remember, and that is a *very* long time, indeed." He wiggled his eyebrows, knowing he did not look a day over twenty-three, his original age at metamorphosis. He continued. "Favorable toward women, those *darling* beasties, even if they are a tad brutish." He shivered lasciviously. "Particularly Lord Maccon. So big and *rough*." He made a little growling noise.

Miss Tarabotti giggled. Nothing was funnier than watching a vampire try to emulate a werewolf.

"I advise you *most* strongly to visit him tomorrow *before* you see the Westminster queen." Lord Akeldama reached forward and grasped her wrist. His fangs vanished, and his eyes suddenly looked as old as he really was. He had never told Alexia quite how old. "*La*, darling," he always said, "a vampire, like a lady, *never* reveals his true age." But he had described to her in detail the dark days before the supernatural was revealed to daylight folk. Before the hives and packs made themselves known on the British Isle. Before that prestigious revolution in philosophy and science that their emergence triggered, known to some as the Renaissance but to vampires as the Age of Enlightenment. Supernatural folk called the time before the Dark Ages, for obvious reasons. For them it had been an age spent skulking through the night. Several bottles of champagne were usually required to get Lord Akeldama to talk of it at all. Still, it meant, by Alexia's calculations, that he was at least over four hundred years old.

She looked more closely at her friend. Was that fear?

His face was honestly serious, and he said, "My dove, *I* do not know what is transpiring here. *Me*, ignorant! Please take the gravest of care in this matter."

Miss Tarabotti now knew the real source of her friend's trepidation. Lord Akeldama had no idea what was going on. For years, he had held the trump card in every major London political situation. He was accustomed to having possession of all pertinent facts before anybody else. Yet at this moment, he was as mystified as she.

"*Promise me*," he said earnestly, "you will see what information you can extract from Lord Maccon on this matter *before* you go into that hive."

Alexia smiled. "To better your understanding?"

He shook his blond head. "No, sweetheart, to better *yours*."

CHAPTER THREE

Our Heroine Heeds Some Good Advice

"Bollocks," said Lord Maccon upon seeing who stood before him. "Miss Tarabotti. What did I do to merit a visit from you first thing in the morning? I have not even had my second cup of tea yet." He loomed at the entrance to his office.

Alexia ignored his unfortunate choice of greeting and swept past him into the room. The act of sweeping, and the fact that the doorway was quite narrow while Alexia's bosoms (even corseted) were not, brought her into intimate contact with the earl. Alexia was embarrassed to note she tingled a little bit, clearly a reaction to the repulsive state of the man's office.

There were papers everywhere, piled in corners and spread out over what might have been a desk—it was difficult to tell underneath all the muddle. There were also rolls of etched metal and stacks of tubes she suspected contained more of the same. Alexia wondered why he needed metal record-keeping; from the sheer quantity, she suspected it must be a cogent one. She counted at least six used cups and saucers and a platter covered in the remains of a large joint of raw meat. Miss Tarabotti had been in Lord Maccon's office once or twice before. It had always appeared a tad masculine for her taste but never so unsightly as this.

"Good gracious me!" she said, shaking off the tingles. Then

she asked the obvious question. "Where is Professor Lyall, then?"

Lord Maccon scrubbed his face with his hand, reached desperately for a nearby teapot, and drained it through the spout.

Miss Tarabotti looked away from the horrible sight. *Who was it that had said "only just civilized"?* She closed her eyes and considered, realizing it must have been she. She fluttered one hand to her throat. "Please, Lord Maccon, use one of the cups. My delicate sensibilities."

The earl actually snorted. "My dear Miss Tarabotti, if you possessed any such things, you certainly have never shown them to me." But he did put down the teapot.

Alexia looked more closely at Lord Maccon. He did not seem entirely well. Her heart moved with a funny little flipping motion in her chest. His mahogany-colored hair was standing up at the front, as though he had been running his hands through it repeatedly. Everything about his appearance seemed even more unkempt than usual. In the dim light, it also looked as though his canines were showing—a certain sign of distress. Alexia squinted to make certain. She wondered how close they were to full moon. The worry in her dark eyes, expressive even in their soullessness, softened her teapot-inspired disapproving expression.

"BUR business." Lord Maccon endeavored to explain away Professor's Lyall's absence and the state of his office in one curt phrase. He pinched the bridge of his nose between thumb and forefinger.

Alexia nodded. "I did not really expect to find you here, my lord, in the daytime. Shouldn't you be sleeping at this hour?"

The werewolf shook his head. "I can take the full sun for a few days running, especially when there's such a mystery as this. Alpha's not simply a meaningless title, you know? We can *do* things regular werewolves cannot. Besides which, Queen Victoria is curious." In addition to being BUR's supernatural liaison and Alpha of the Woolsey Castle pack, Lord Maccon was an agent of Queen Victoria's Shadow Parliament.

"Well, never mind that; you look positively ghastly," said Alexia baldly.

"Gee, thank you very much for your concern, Miss Tarabotti," replied the earl, straightening up and widening his eyes in an attempt to look more alert.

"What *have* you been doing to yourself?" asked his lady guest with all her customary bluntness.

"I have not slept since you were attacked," said Lord Maccon.

Alexia blushed slightly. "Concerned for my well-being? Why, Lord Maccon, now it is I who am touched."

"Hardly," he replied ungallantly. "Overseeing investigations, for the most part. Any concern you may note is over the idea that someone else may be attacked. You can obviously see to yourself."

Miss Tarabotti was torn between being crushed that he did not care one fig for her safety and pleased that he trusted in her competence.

She gathered up a small pile of metal slates from a side chair and sat down. Lifting one roll of thin metal, she held it open to examine with interest. She had to tilt it away from the shadows in order to make out the etched notations. "Rove vampire registration permits," she remarked. "You think the man who attacked me last night might have had a permit?"

Lord Maccon looked exasperated, marched over and snatched the stack of rolls away. They fell to the floor with a clatter and he cursed his sun-born clumsiness. But for all his sham annoyance at her presence, the earl was secretly pleased to have someone with whom to talk out his theories. Usually he used his Beta in that capacity, but with Lyall out of town, he'd been pacing about muttering to himself. "If he does have a permit, it is not in the London registry."

"Could he have come from outside the capital?" suggested Alexia.

Lord Maccon shrugged. "You know how territorial vampires are. Even without any hive ties, they tend to stay in the area of original blood metamorphosis. It is possible he traveled, but from where and why? What grave purpose would drive a vampire from his natural habitat? That is the information I've sent Lyall to hunt down."

Miss Tarabotti understood. BUR headquarters were stationed in central London, but they had offices all over England that kept tabs on the supernatural set in other parts of the country. During the Age of Enlightenment, when the supernatural became accepted instead of persecuted, what had been born out of a need to control turned into a means of understanding. BUR, a creature of that understanding, now employed werewolves and vampires, as well as mortals and even a ghost or two. Alexia also suspected there were a few sundowners still left among the ranks, though not used much anymore.

Lord Maccon continued. "He will travel by stagecoach during the day and in wolf form at night. He should be back before the full moon with a report from all six nearby cities. That is what I am hoping for, at any roads."

"Professor Lyall started in Canterbury?" Miss Tarabotti guessed.

Lord Maccon spun to stare at her intently. His eyes were more yellow than tawny gold, and particularly sharp in the dimly lit room. "I hate it when you do that," he growled.

"What, guess correctly?" Alexia's dark eyes crinkled in amusement.

"No, make me feel predictable."

Alexia smiled. "Canterbury is a port city and a center for travel. If our mystery vampire came from anywhere, it was most likely there. But you do not think he came from outside London, do you?"

Lord Maccon shook his head. "No, that does not feel right. He smelled local. All vampires get some indicative scent from their maker, particularly when they have been recently changed. Our little friend had the death odor of the Westminster hive about him."

Miss Tarabotti blinked, startled. Her father's books said nothing on this subject. *Werewolves could smell vampire bloodlines? Could vampires tell the difference between werewolf packs as well?*

"Have you spoken with the local queen?" she said.

The earl nodded. "I went straight to the hive house after leaving you that night. She completely denies any association with your attacker. If it was possible for Countess Nadasdy to be surprised, I would have said she looked shocked at my news. Of course, she would have to pretend such an appearance if she had metamorphosed a new vampire without proper paperwork. But usually the hive is proud to have made larvae. They host a ball, demand turnday presents, call in all the field drones, that kind of extravagance. BUR registry is customarily part of the ceremony. Local werewolves are even invited." His lip curled, showing several pointed teeth. "It is a sort of 'stick it in your face' to the packs. We have not gained any new members in over a decade." It was no secret how hard it was to make new supernaturals. Since it was impossible to tell beforehand how much soul a normal human had, it was a deadly gamble for humans to try and turn. Since many drones and clavigers made the attempt early on in life so their immortality might be blessed with youth, the deaths were all the more keenly felt. Of course BUR knew, and so did Miss Tarabotti, that low population numbers were part of what kept the supernatural set safe from public outcry. When they had first presented themselves to the modern world, daylight humans had overcome age-old terrors only upon realization of how few supernatural folk there really were in existence. Lord Maccon's pack numbered eleven in all, and the Westminster hive was slightly smaller—both were considered impressively large.

Miss Tarabotti cocked her head to one side. "Where does that leave you, my lord?"

"Suspecting that there is a rove queen making vampires illegally and outside of hive and BUR authority."

Alexia swallowed. "Inside Westminster territory?"

The earl nodded. "And of Countess Nadasdy's bloodline."

"The countess must be biting mad."

"You put it mildly, my dear Miss Tarabotti. As queen, of course, she insists your homicidal friend was from outside London. She has no understanding of how bloodlines smell. But Lyall identified the body as her get without doubt. He has generations of experience with the Westminster hive and the best nose of any of us. You know Lyall's been with the Woolsey Pack far longer than I?"

Alexia nodded. Everyone knew how recently Lord Maccon had risen to the earldom. She was given to wonder idly why Professor Lyall had not tried for Alpha himself. Then she assessed Lord Maccon's undoubtedly muscular form and imposing appearance and deduced the reason. Professor Lyall was no coward, but he was also no idiot.

The Alpha continued. "He could have been a direct metamorphic from one of Countess Nadasdy's bite-daughters. But then again, Lyall also noted that the countess has not managed to change over a female drone in his lifetime. She is understandably bitter over this fact."

Miss Tarabotti frowned. "So you have a genuine mystery on your plate. Only a female vampire, a queen, can metamorphose a new vampire. Yet here we find ourselves with a new vampire and no maker. Either Professor Lyall's nose or Countess Nadasdy's tongue is lying." Which explained more than anything else Lord Maccon's haggard appearance. Nothing was worse than werewolf and vampire at cross purposes, especially in this kind of investigation. "Let us hope Professor Lyall finds you some answers to these questions," she said with feeling.

Lord Maccon rang the bell for fresh tea. "Indeed. And, now, enough of my problems. Perhaps we might press on to what brought you to my doorstep at this ungodly hour."

Alexia, who was poking through another pile of rove paperwork she had scooped off the floor, waved one of the metal sheets at him. "*He* did."

Lord Maccon grabbed the metal she had gesticulated with out of her hand, looked at it, and huffed in annoyance. "Why do you persist in associating with that creature?"

Miss Tarabotti straightened her skirts, draping the pleated hem more carefully over her kid boots. She demurred. "I *like* Lord Akeldama."

The earl abruptly looked more livid than tired. "Do you, by George! What has he been luring you in with? Little pip-squeak, I shall wallop his scrawny hide to ribbons."

"I suspect he might enjoy that," murmured Alexia, thinking of what little she knew of her vampire friend's proclivities. The werewolf did not hear her. Or perhaps he simply chose not to use his supernatural auditory abilities. He paced about, looking vaguely magnificent. His teeth were now definitely showing.

Miss Tarabotti stood, marched over, and grabbed Lord Maccon's wrist. His teeth retracted instantly. The earl's yellow eyes went back to amber-brown. It was the color they must have been years ago before he yielded to the bite that made him supernatural. He also appeared slightly less shaggy, although no less large and angry. Remembering Lord Akeldama's comment on the subject of using feminine wiles, Alexia placed a second hand pleadingly above the first on his upper arm.

What she wanted to say was, *Do not be an idiot.* What she actually said was, "I needed Lord Akeldama's advice on supernatural matters. I did not want to disturb you for anything trivial." As if she would ever willingly go to Lord Maccon for help. She was only in his office now under duress. She widened her large brown eyes, tilted her head in a way she hoped might minimize her nose, and lowered her eyelashes beseechingly. Alexia had very long eyelashes. She also had very fierce eyebrows, but Lord Maccon seemed more interested in the former than repelled by the latter. He covered her small brown hand with his massive one.

Miss Tarabotti's hand became very warm, and she was finding that her knees reacted in a decidedly wobbly way to such close proximity to the earl. *Stop it!* she instructed them fiercely. What was she supposed to say next? Right: *Do not be an idiot.* And then: *I needed help with a vampire, so I went to a vampire for help. No, that was not right. What would Ivy say? Oh yes.* "I was so upset, you see? I encountered a drone in the park yesterday, and Countess Nadasdy has requested my presence, this very night."

That distracted Lord Maccon from his homicidal thoughts of Lord Akeldama. He refused to analyze why he was so opposed to the concept of Alexia liking the vampire. Lord Akeldama was a perfectly well-behaved rove, if slightly silly, always keeping himself and his drones in flawless order. Sometimes too flawless. Alexia *should* be entirely allowed to like such a man. His lip curled once more at the very idea. He shook himself and went on to the disturbing, in quite a different manner, idea of Miss Alexia Tarabotti and Countess Nadasdy in the same room together.

He hustled Alexia over to a small couch and sat them both, with a crackle, on top of the airship transit maps scattered across it.

"Start from the beginning," he instructed.

Miss Tarabotti commenced with Felicity reading aloud the newspaper, went on to the walk with Ivy and the meeting with Miss Dair, and ended with Lord Akeldama's perspective on the situation. "You know," she added when she felt the earl tense at the vampire's name, "he was the one who suggested I see you."

"What!"

"I must know as much as possible about this situation if I am to go into a hive alone. Most supernatural battles are over information. If Countess Nadasdy wants something from me, it is far better if I know what it is and whether I am capable of providing it."

Lord Maccon stood, slightly panicked, and said exactly the wrong thing. "I forbid you to go!" He had no idea what it was about this particular woman that made him lose all sense of verbal decorum. But there it was: the unfortunate words were out.

Miss Tarabotti stood as well, instantaneously angry, her chest heaving in agitation. "You have no right!"

He circled her wrists with an iron grip. "I am BUR's chief sundowner, I'll have you know. Preternaturals fall under my jurisdiction."

"But we are allowed the same degree of freedom as members of the supernatural set, are we not? Full societal integration, among other things. The countess has asked me to attend her for one evening, nothing more."

"Alexia!" Lord Maccon groaned his frustration.

Miss Tarabotti realized that the earl's use of her given name indicated a certain degree of irritation on his part.

The werewolf took a deep breath, trying to calm himself. It did not work, because he was too close to Alexia. Vampires smelled of stale blood and family lines. His fellow werewolves smelled of fur and wet nights. And humans? Even after all this time of trapping himself away at full moon, the hunt forbidden, humans smelled like food. But Alexia's scent was something else, something . . . not meat. She smelled warm and spicy sweet, like some old-fashioned Italian pastry his body could no longer process but whose taste he remembered and craved.

He leaned into her.

Miss Tarabotti characteristically swatted him. "Lord Maccon! You forget yourself!"

Which was, Lord Maccon thought, exactly the problem. He let go of her wrists and felt the werewolf return: that strength and heightened senses a partial death had given him all those decades ago. "The hive will not trust you, Miss Tarabotti. You must understand: They believe you to be their natural enemy. Do you keep abreast of the latest scientific discoveries?" He rummaged about on his desk and produced a small weekly news pamphlet. The lead article was titled THE COUNTERBALANCE THEOREM AS APPLIED TO HORTICULTURAL PURSUITS.

Alexia blinked at it, not comprehending. She turned the paper over: *published by Hypocras Press*. That did not help either. She knew of the counterbalance theorem, of course. In fact, she found the tenets, in principle, rather appealing.

She said, "Counterbalance is the scientific idea that any given force has an innate opposite. For example, every naturally occurring poison has a naturally occurring antidote—usually located in proximity. Much in the way that the juice of crushed nettle leaves applied to the skin relieves the nettle sting. What has this to do with me?"

"Well, vampires believe that preternaturals are their counterbalance. That it is your elemental purpose to neutralize them."

Now it was Miss Tarabotti's turn to snort. "Preposterous!"

"Vampires have long memories, my dear. Longer even than us werewolves, for we fight too often among ourselves and die centuries too young. When we supernaturals hid in the night and hunted humankind, it was *your* preternatural ancestors who hunted us. It was a violent kind of balance. The vampires will always hate you and ghosts always fear you. We werewolves are not so certain. For us, metamorphosis is part curse, one that sees us imprisoned each month for everyone's safety. Some of us see preternaturals as the cure for the full moon's curse. There are stories of werewolves who turned themselves to pets, hunting their own as payment for a preternatural's touch." He looked disgusted. "All this is better understood since the Age of Reason brought about the concept of a measured soul and the Church of England broke with Rome. But new science, such as this theorem, raises old memories in the vampires. They named preternaturals *soul-suckers* for good reason. You are the only one registered in this area. And you have just killed a vampire."

Miss Tarabotti looked grave. "I already accepted Countess Nadasdy's invitation. It would be churlish to refuse now."

"Why must you always be so difficult?" wondered Lord Maccon in utter exasperation.

Alexia grinned. "No soul?" she suggested.

"No sense!" corrected the earl.

"Nevertheless"—Miss Tarabotti stood—"someone has to

discover what is going on. If the hive knows anything about this dead vampire, I intend to find out what it is. Lord Akeldama said they wanted to know how much I knew because they either understood more or they understood less. It is to my advantage to figure out which is the case."

"Lord Akeldama again."

"His advice is sound, and he finds my company restful."

That surprised the werewolf. "Well, I suppose somebody must. How peculiar of him."

Miss Tarabotti, affronted, gathered up her brass parasol and made to leave.

Lord Maccon slowed her with a question. "Why *are* you so curious about this matter? Why do you insist on involving yourself?"

"Because someone is dead and it was by my own hand," she replied, looking gloomy. "Well, by my own parasol," she amended.

Lord Maccon sighed. He figured someday he might win an argument with this extraordinary woman, but clearly today was not that day.

"Did you bring your own carriage?" he asked, admitting defeat with the question.

"I shall hire a hackney, not to worry."

The Earl of Woolsey reached for his hat and coat in a very decisive manner. "I have the Woolsey coach and four here. At least let me drive you home."

Miss Tarabotti felt she had wrung enough concessions out of Lord Maccon for one morning. "If you insist, my lord," she acquiesced. "But I must ask you to drop me a little ways from the house. My mama, you see, is wholly unaware of my interest in this matter."

"Not to mention her shock at seeing you alight from my carriage without a chaperone. We would not want to compromise your reputation in any way, now, would we?" Lord Maccon actually sounded riled by the idea.

Miss Tarabotti thought she understood the reasoning behind his tone. She laughed. "My lord, you could not possibly think I have set my cap for *you*?"

"And why is that such a laughable idea?"

Alexia's eyes sparkled in merriment. "I am a spinster, long on the shelf, and you are a catch of the first water. The very notion!"

Lord Maccon marched out the door, dragging her behind him. "Don't ken why you should find it so devilish funny," he muttered under his breath. "Leastways you are nearer my age than most of those so-called incomparables the society matrons persist in hurling at me."

Miss Tarabotti let out another trill of mirth. "Oh, my lord, you are too droll. You are nearing what? Two hundred? As if my being eight or ten years older than the average marriage-market chit should matter under such circumstances. What delightful nonsense." She patted him approvingly on the arm.

Lord Maccon paused, annoyed at her belittling of herself and him. Then he realized what a ridiculous conversation they were having and how nearing dangerous it had become. Some of his hard-won London social acumen returned, and he held his tongue determinedly. But he was thinking that by "nearer his age" he had not meant nearer in years but in understanding. Then he wondered at his own recklessness in thinking any such thing. What was wrong with him today? He could not stand Alexia Tarabotti, even if her lovely brown eyes twinkled when she laughed, and she smelled good, and she had a particularly splendid figure.

He hustled his lady guest down the passageway, intent upon getting her into the carriage and out of his presence as quickly as possible.

Professor Randolph Lyall was a professor of nothing in particular and several subjects in broad detail. One of those generalities was a long running study on the typical human behavioral response when faced with werewolf transformation. His research on the subject had taught him it was best to change out of wolf shape away from polite company, preferably in a corner of a very dark alley where the only person likely to see him was equally likely to be crazy or drunk.

While the population of the greater London area, in specific, and the British Isle, in general, had learned well enough to accept werewolves on principle, to be faced with one engaging in the act of conversion was an entirely different matter. Professor Lyall considered himself rather good at the change—elegant and graceful despite the pain. Youngsters of the pack were prone to excessive writhing and spinal gyrations and sometimes a whimper or two. Professor Lyall simply melted smoothly from one form to the next. But the change was, at its root, *not natural*. Mind you, there was no glow, no mist, no magic about it. Skin, bone, and fur simply rearranged itself, but that was usually enough to give most daylight folk a large dose of the screaming heebie-jeebies. *Screaming* being the operative word.

Professor Lyall reached the Canterbury BUR offices just before dawn still in wolf shape. His animal form was nondescript but tidy, rather like his favorite waistcoat: his pelt the same sandy color as his hair but with a sheen of black about the face and neck. He was not very big, mostly because he was not a very big human, and the basic principles of conservation of mass still applied whether supernatural or not. Werewolves had to obey the laws of physics just like everyone else.

The change took only moments: his fur crawling away from his body and moving up to become hair, his bones breaking and reforming from quadruped to biped, and his eyes going from pale yellow to gentle hazel. He had carried a cloak in his mouth during his run, and he threw it on as soon as he was back to human form. He left the alleyway with no one the wiser to the arrival of a werewolf in Canterbury.

He rested against the BUR office's front doorjamb, dozing softly, until morning caused the first of the standard-issue clerks to make his appearance.

"Who are you, then?" the man wanted to know.

Professor Lyall eased himself away from the door and stepped aside so that the clerk could unlock it.

"Well?" The man barred the way when Lyall would have followed him inside.

Lyall bared his canines. It was not an easy trick in the morning sun, but he was an old enough werewolf to make it look easy. "Woolsey Castle pack Beta, BUR agent. Who is in charge of vampire registration in this office?"

The man, unperturbed by Lyall's demonstration of supernatural ability, replied without shilly-shallying. "George Greemes. He will be in around nine. Cloakroom is 'round that corner over there. Should I send the boot-boy to the butcher for you when he gets in?"

Professor Lyall moved off in the direction indicated. "Yes, do: three dozen sausages, if you would be so kind. No need to cook them."

Most BUR offices kept spare clothing in their cloakrooms, the architectural conceit of cloakrooms having spawned from generations of werewolf arrivals. He found some relatively decent garments, although not precisely to his exacting taste, and, of course, the waistcoat was significantly under par. He then gorged on several strings of sausage and settled in on a convenient ottoman for a much needed nap. He awoke just before nine, feeling much more human—or as human as was supernaturally possible.

George Greemes was an active BUR agent but not a supernatural one. He had a ghost partner who compensated for this disadvantage but who, for obvious reasons, did not work until after sunset. Greemes was therefore accustomed to quiet days full of paperwork and little excitement and was not pleased to find Professor Lyall waiting for him.

"Who did you say you were?" he asked as he came into his office to find Lyall already in residence. Greemes slapped his battered pork pie hat down over a pot full of what looked like the internal guts of several much-abused grandfather clocks.

"Professor Randolph Lyall, second in command of the Woolsey Castle pack and assistant administrator of supernatural relations in London central," said Lyall, looking down his nose at Greemes.

"Aren't you a mite scrawny to be Beta to someone as substantial as Lord Maccon?" The BUR agent ran a hand distractedly down his large sideburns, as if checking to ensure they were still affixed to his face.

Lyall sighed. His slender physique engendered this reaction all too often. Lord Maccon was so large and impressive that people expected his second to be of a similar stature and nature. Few understood how much it was to a pack's advantage having one who always stood in the limelight and one who never did. Lyall preferred not to illuminate the ignorant on this subject.

So he said, "Fortunately for me, I have not yet been called upon to physically fulfill my role. Few challenge Lord Maccon, and those who do, lose. However, I did attain Beta rank by fully following all aspects of pack protocol. I may not look like much for brawn, but I have other germane qualities."

Greemes sighed. "What do you need to know? We've no local pack, so you must be here on BUR business."

Lyall nodded. "Canterbury has one official hive, correct?" He did not wait for an answer. "Has the queen reported any new additions recently? Any blood-metamorphosis parties?"

"I should say not! The Canterbury hive is old and very dignified, not given to crass displays of any kind." He actually seemed a little offended.

"Has there been anything else out of the ordinary? Vampires turning up unexpectedly without metamorphosis reports or proper registration? Anything along those lines?" Professor Lyall kept his expression mild, but those hazel eyes of his were startlingly direct.

Greemes looked annoyed. "Our local hive is very well behaved, I will have you know; no aberrations in recorded history. Vampires tend to be fairly cautious in these parts. It is not comfortable to be supernatural in a port town—too fast-paced and changeable. Our local hive tends to produce *very* careful vampires. Not to mention the fact that all those sailors in and out means a ready supply of *willing* blood-whores down dockside. The hive is very little bother so far as BUR is concerned. It is an easy job I have here, thank heavens."

"What about new unregistered roves?" Lyall refused to let the subject drop.

Greemes stood and went to crouch over a wooden wine crate filled with documents. He rifled through them, pausing periodically to read an entry. "Had one in about five years ago. The hive queen forced him to register; no problems since."

Lyall nodded. Clapping his borrowed top hat to his head, he turned to leave. He had a stagecoach to catch for Brighton.

Greemes, sorting the parchment sheaves back into the crate, continued muttering. "Course, I have not heard from any of the registered roves in a while."

Professor Lyall stopped in the doorway. "What did you say?"

"They have been disappearing."

Lyall took his hat back off. "You made this fact clear in this year's census?"

Greemes shook his head. "I submitted a report on the matter to London last spring. Didn't you read it?"

Professor Lyall glared at the man. "Obviously not. Tell me, what does the local hive queen have to say on this particular topic?"

Greemes raised both eyebrows. "What does she care for roves in her feeding ground except that, when they are gone, things are easier for her household brood?"

The professor frowned. "How many have gone missing?"

Greemes looked up, his eyebrows arched. "Why, all of them."

Lyall gritted his teeth. Vampires were too tied to their territory to roam away from home for long. Greemes and Lyall both knew that missing roves most likely meant dead roves. It took all of his social acumen not to show his profound irritation. This might not interest the local hive, but it certainly was significant information, and BUR should have been told immediately. Most of their vampire problems involved roves. As most of their werewolf problems involved loners. Professor Lyall decided he had better push for Greemes's reassignment. The man's behavior smacked of drone thrall, those initial stages of over-fascination with the ancient mysteries of the supernatural. It did no one any good to have someone firmly in the vampire camp in charge of vampire relations.

Despite his anger, the Beta managed to nod a neutral good-bye to the repulsive man and headed out into the hallway, thinking hard.

A strange gentleman was waiting for him in the cloakroom. A man Professor Lyall had never met before but who smelled of fur and wet nights.

The stranger held a brown bowler hat in front of his chest with both hands, like a shield. When he saw Lyall, he nodded in a way that was less greeting and more an excuse to bare the side of his neck in obeisance.

Lyall spoke first.

Pack dominance games might seem complicated to an outsider, but very few wolves in England outranked Professor Lyall, and he knew all of them by face and smell. This man was not one of them; therefore, he, Professor Lyall, was in control.

"This office has no werewolves on staff," he said harshly.

"No, sir. I am not BUR, sir. There is no pack in this city as I am certain your eminence is well aware. We are under your lord's jurisdiction."

Lyall nodded, crossing his arms. "Yet, you are not one of the Woolsey Castle pups. I would know."

"No, sir. No pack, sir."

Lyall's lip curled. "Loner." Instinctively, his hackles raised. Loners were dangerous: community-oriented animals cut off from the very social structure that kept them sane and controlled. Alpha challenges invariably came from within the pack, following official lines, with Conall Maccon's unexpected ascension to power the most recent exception to that rule. But brawling, violence, feasting on human flesh, and other such illogical carnage—that was the loner's game. They were more common than vampire roves, and far more dangerous.

The loner clutched his hat tighter at Lyall's sneer, hunching down. If he had been in wolf shape, his tail would be tucked tight between his back legs.

"Yes, sir. I set a watch to this office waiting for the Woolsey Alpha to send someone to investigate. My claviger told me you had arrived. I thought I had best come myself and ascertain if you wanted an official report, sir. I am old enough to stand daylight for a little while."

"I am here on hive, not pack, business," Lyall admitted, impatient to get to the point.

The man looked genuinely surprised. "Sir?"

Lyall did not like being confused. He did not know what was going on, and he did not appreciate being put at a disadvantage, especially not in front of a loner. "Report!" he barked.

The man straightened, trying not to cower at the irate tone in the Beta's voice. Unlike George Greemes, he had no doubt of Professor Lyall's fighting capabilities. "They have stopped, sir."

"What has stopped?" Lyall's voice took on a soft deadly timbre.

The man swallowed, twisting his hat about further. Professor Lyall began to suspect the bowler might not survive this interview. "The disappearances, sir."

Lyall was exasperated. "I know that! I just found out from Greemes."

The man looked confused. "But he is on vampires."

"Yes, and . . . ?"

"It is werewolves who have gone missing, sir. You know, the Alpha had most of us loners stashed along the coast round these parts; keeps us well out of London's way. Also ensures we stay busy fighting pirates rather than each other."

"So?"

The man cringed back. "Thought you knew, sir. Thought the Alpha had started and then stopped it. It has been going several months now."

"You thought it might be Lord Maccon doing a culling, did you?"

"Packs never take to loners, sir. He is a new Alpha, needs to establish his authority."

Professor Lyall could not argue with that reasoning. "I have got to get moving," he said. "If these disappearances start up again, you will let us know immediately."

The man cleared his throat subserviently. "Cannot do that, sir. All apologies, sir."

Lyall gave him a hard look.

The man hooked a finger in his cravat to pull it down and expose his neck defensively. "Sorry, sir, but I am the only one left."

A cold shiver caused all the hairs on Professor Lyall's body to stick up on end.

Instead of going on to Brighton, he caught the next stagecoach back to London.

CHAPTER FOUR

Our Heroine Ignores Good Advice

Alexia was embarrassed to find that she was reduced to shamefully sneaking out of her own home. It simply would not do to tell her mama she was paying a late-night call on a vampire hive. Floote, though disapproving, proved an able ally in her transgression. Floote had been Alessandro Tarabotti's valet before Alexia was even a twinkle in that outrageous gentleman's eye. As such, he knew a lot more than just how to butler, and that included a thing or two on the organization of misdemeanors. He hustled his "young miss" out of the servants' entrance at the back of the house. He had her carefully shrouded in the scullery maid's old cloak and managed to stuff her into a hired cab maintaining a stiff but capable silence all the while.

The hackney rattled through the darkened streets. Miss Tarabotti, mindful of her hat and hair, nevertheless drew down the widow sash and stuck her head out into the night. The moon, three-quarters and gaining, had not yet risen above the building tops. Above, Alexia thought she could make out a lone dirigible, taking advantage of the darkness to parade stars and city lights before one last load of passengers. For once, she did not envy them their flight. The air was cool and probably unbearably chilly so high up; this was no surprise, as London was generally a city not celebrated for its balmy evenings. She shivered and closed the window.

The carriage finally stopped at a good-enough address in one of the more fashionable ends of town, although not an end Miss Tarabotti's particular collection of acquaintances tended to frequent. Anticipating a brief engagement, she paid the hackney to wait and hurried up the front steps, holding high the skirts of her best green and gray check visiting dress.

A young maid opened the door at her approach and curtsied. She was almost too pretty, with dark blond hair and enormous violet eyes, and neat as a new penny in a black dress and white apron.

"Miz Tarabotti?" she asked in a heavy French accent.

Alexia nodded, pulling at her dress to rid it of travel wrinkles.

"Zi comtesse, she iz expecting you. Right diz way." The maid led her down a long hallway. She seemed to sway as she moved with a dancer's grace and liquid movements. Alexia felt large, dark, and clumsy next to her.

The house was typical of its kind, though perhaps a touch more luxurious than most, and outfitted with every possible modern convenience. Miss Tarabotti could not help but compare it to the Duchess of Snodgrove's palatial residence. Here there was more real affluence and grandeur, the kind that did not need to display itself openly—it simply *was*. The carpets were thick and soft, in coordinating shades of deep red, probably imported directly from the Ottoman Empire three hundred years ago. There were beautiful works of art hanging on the walls. Some were very old; some were more contemporary canvases signed with names Alexia knew from newspaper gallery announcements. Luxuriant mahogany furniture showcased beautiful statues: Roman busts in creamy marble, lapis-encrusted Egyptian gods, and modern pieces in granite and onyx. Rounding a corner, Miss Tarabotti was treated to an entire hallway of polished machinery, displayed much as the statuary had been and with the same studied care. There was the first steam engine ever built, and, after it, a silver and gold monowheel; and, Alexia gasped, *was that a model of the Babbage engine?* Everything was perfectly clean and chosen with utter precision, each object occupying the space it had been given with immense dignity. It was more impressive than any museum Alexia had ever visited—and she was fond of museums. There were drones everywhere, all attractive and perfectly dressed, efficiently going about the business of running daylight interference and nighttime entertainment for the hive. They, too, were works of art, dressed in subdued elegance to match the tenor of the house, and collected with care.

Alexia did not have the soul to truly appreciate any of it. However, she understood style well enough to know that it surrounded her. It made her very nervous. She smoothed down her dress self-consciously, worried it might be considered too simple. Then she straightened her spine. A plain tan spinster like her could never compete with such grandeur; best take advantage of what assets she did have. She puffed up her chest slightly and took a calming breath.

The French maid opened a door to a large drawing room and curtsied her inside before gliding off, her feet silent on the red carpet, her hips swaying back and forth.

"Ah, Miss Tarabotti! Welcome to the Westminster hive."

The woman who came forward to greet Alexia was not at all what she had expected. The lady was short, plump, and comfortable-looking, her cheeks rosy and her cornflower-blue eyes sparkling. She looked like a country shepherdess stepped out of a Renaissance painting. Alexia glanced about for her flock. They were there, of a kind.

"Countess Nadasdy?" she asked tentatively.

"Yes, my dear! And this is Lord Ambrose. That is Dr. Caedes. That gentlemen there is His Grace the Duke of Hematol, and you know Miss Dair." She gestured as she spoke. Her movements were simultaneously too graceful and too contrived. They looked as though they had been well studied, as carefully articulated as a linguist speaking a foreign tongue.

Aside from Miss Dair, who smiled kindly from her place on the settee, no one seemed particularly pleased to see her. Miss

Dair was also the only drone present. Alexia was certain the other three were vampires. Though she knew none of them socially, she had read some of Dr. Caedes's research during her more adventurous academic pursuits.

"How do you do?" said Miss Tarabotti politely.

The party all made the requisite social murmurings.

Lord Ambrose was a large, exceedingly comely man, looking the way romantic schoolroom girls expect vampires to look— dark and broodingly arrogant with aquiline features and deep meaningful eyes. Dr. Caedes was also tall but skinny as a walking stick, with thinning hair stopped mid-retreat by metamorphosis. He had with him a doctor's bag, though Alexia knew from her readings that his Royal Society membership rested on his extensive engineering work, not a physician's license. The last hive member, the Duke of Hematol, was nondescript in a premeditated way that reminded Alexia of Professor Lyall. Consequently, she regarded him with great wariness and respect.

"If you do not mind, my dear, might I shake your hand?" The Westminster queen moved toward her with that abrupt and smooth supernatural suddenness.

Alexia was taken aback.

Up close, Countess Nadasdy looked less jolly, and it was clear her rosy cheeks were the product of artifice, not sunlight. Under layers of cream and powder, her skin was ashen white. Her eyes did not sparkle. They glittered as hard as the dark glass used by astronomers to examine the sun.

Miss Tarabotti backed away.

"We need to confirm your state," the hive queen explained, still coming at her.

She grabbed Alexia's wrist firmly. The countess's tiny hand was impossibly strong. The moment they touched, much of the hive queen's hardness vanished, and Miss Tarabotti was left wondering if once, long, long ago, Countess Nadasdy had actually *been* a shepherdess.

The vampire smiled at her. No fangs.

"I object most strenuously to this action, my queen. I want it known before the hive that I disagree with this approach to our situation." Lord Ambrose spoke curtly.

Alexia was not certain if he was angry at her preternatural state or at her physical effect on his queen.

Countess Nadasdy let go of her wrist. Her fangs reappeared. They were long and thin, almost biologically spiny, with what looked like barbed tips. Then, with a lightning-fast movement, she lashed out to the side with sharp clawlike fingernails. A long line of red appeared on Lord Ambrose's face. "You overstep your bond duties, child of my blood."

Lord Ambrose bowed his dark head, the shallow wound already closing and healing itself. "Forgive me, my queen; it is only your safety that concerns me."

"Which is why you are my *praetoriani*." In an abrupt change of mood, Countess Nadasdy reached to caress the very part of Lord Ambrose's face she had just sliced open.

"He speaks nothing but truth. You allow a soul-sucker to touch you, and once you are mortal, all it takes is one fatal injury." This time is was Dr. Caedes who spoke. His voice was slightly too high-pitched, with a fuzziness around the edges, a sound wasps make before they swarm.

To Alexia's surprise, the countess did not claw his face open. Instead she smiled, showing off the full length of her sharp barbed fangs. Alexia wondered if they had been filed into that extraordinary shape.

"And yet, this girl does nothing more threatening than stand before us. You are all too young to remember what real danger is inherent in her kind."

"We remember well enough," said the Duke of Hematol. His voice was calmer than the other two but more malicious in cadence—soft and hissing like steam escaping a boiling kettle.

The hive queen took Miss Tarabotti gently by the arm. She seemed to breathe in deeply, as though Alexia smelled of some scent she loathed but was trying desperately to identify. "We were never in any direct danger from the female preternaturals; it was only ever the males." She spoke to Alexia in a conspiratorial whisper. "Men, they do so enjoy the hunt, do they not?"

"It is not the ability to kill that worries me. Quite the opposite," said the duke softly.

"In which case it is you gentlemen who should avoid her and not I," replied the countess slyly.

Lord Ambrose laughed snidely at that remark.

Miss Tarabotti narrowed her eyes. "*You* asked me to come here. I do not wish to be an imposition, and I will not be made to feel unwelcome." She jerked her arm away, sharp enough to break the countess's grip, and turned to leave.

"Wait!" The hive queen's voice was sharp.

Miss Tarabotti continued moving toward the door. Fear made her throat tight. She comprehended what it must be like to be some trapped furry creature in a reptilian den. She stopped when she found her way barred. Lord Ambrose had moved with a vampire's characteristic swiftness to prevent her departure. He sneered at her, tall and distressingly gorgeous. Alexia found she much preferred Lord Maccon's brand of largeness: gruff and a little scruffy round the edges.

"Remove yourself from my path, sir!" hissed Miss Tarabotti, wishing she had brought her brass parasol. Why had she left it behind? What this man seemed most in need of was a good sharp prod to the nether regions.

Miss Dair stood and came over to her, all blond ringlets and troubled blue eyes. "Please, Miss Tarabotti. Do not leave just yet. It is only that their memories are longer than their tempers." She gave Lord Ambrose an evil look. Taking Alexia solicitously by the elbow, she led her firmly toward a chair.

Miss Tarabotti acquiesced, sitting with a rustle of green and gray taffeta and feeling even more at a disadvantage until the hive queen sat down across from her.

Miss Dair rang the bell rope. The pretty violet-eyed maid appeared in the doorway. "Tea, please, Angelique."

The French maid vanished and moments later reappeared pushing a fully laden tea trolley, complete with cucumber sandwiches, pickled gherkins, candied lemon peel, and Battenberg.

Countess Nadasdy served the tea. Miss Tarabotti took hers with milk, Miss Dair took hers with lemon, and the vampires took theirs with a dollop of blood, still warm and poured out of a crystal pitcher. Alexia tried not to think too hard about its origin. Then the scientific part of her wondered what would happen if that jug contained preternatural blood. Would it be toxic or just convert them to human state for a certain length of time?

Alexia and Miss Dair helped themselves to food, but no one else in the room bothered to partake. Unlike Lord Akeldama, they clearly did not appreciate the taste of food nor feel compelled by common courtesy to make a show of consuming it. Alexia felt awkward eating while her hostess touched nothing, but she was not the type ever to be put off good food, and the tea, like everything else in the hive house, was of the very highest quality. She refused to rush, sipping slowly from the exquisite blue and white bone china cup and even asking for a second helping.

Countess Nadasdy waited until Miss Tarabotti was halfway through a cucumber sandwich to reopen their conversation. They talked on safe and banal subjects: a new play down the West End, the latest art exhibit, the fact that full moon was just around the corner. Full moon was a regular holiday for working vampires, since werewolves *had* to absent themselves.

"I hear a new gentleman's club has opened near the Snodgrove town house," Miss Tarabotti offered, getting into the spirit of the small talk.

Countess Nadasdy laughed. "I understand the duchess is in high dudgeon. Apparently, it brings down the whole tenor of the neighborhood. She should count her blessings; if you ask me, it could be decidedly worse."

"It could be Boodles," giggled Miss Dair, clearly thinking how embarrassing the duchess would find country squires hanging about all day and night.

The duke added, "Or scandal of scandals, it could be Claret's."
He named the gentlemen's club that catered to werewolves.

The vampires all laughed uproariously at that. It was creepy in
its lack of decorum.

Miss Tarabotti decided in an instant that she did not like the
Duke of Hematol one jot.

"Speaking of the Duchess Snodgrove." The hive queen segued
in a slithery fashion onto the subject she had really summoned
Alexia in to discuss. "What was it that happened during her ball the
night before last, Miss Tarabotti?"

Alexia put her teacup down carefully into its saucer, then set
both onto the tea trolley with a faint clatter. "The papers described
it accurately enough."

"Except that you were not named in any of them," said Lord
Ambrose.

"And there was also no mention of the deceased young man
being supernatural," added Dr. Caedes.

"And no reference to the fact that you had executed the killing
blow." Countess Nadasdy sat back, a faint smile on her round
pleasant face. The smile did not sit well there, not with the four
fangs and the little dents they left in those full shepherdess lips.

Miss Tarabotti crossed her arms. "You seem well informed.
Why do you need me here?"

No one said anything.

"It was an accident," grumbled Alexia, relaxing her defensive
posture. She took a bite of Battenberg without really tasting it. It
was an insult to the little cake, for it was usually good and worth
appreciating: thick sponge with homemade marmalade and crys-
tallized almond paste on the outside. This sponge seemed dry
and the almond paste gritty.

"It was a very tidy stake to the heart," corrected Dr. Caedes.

Alexia went immediately on the defensive. "Too tidy: he barely
bled. Do not blindside me with accusations, venerable ones. *I* did
not drive him to starvation." No sane person would ever describe
Miss Tarabotti as a shrinking violet. When attacked, she fought

back with interest. It could have been the result of her preternatural state; then again, it could simply be a ridiculously stubborn disposition. She spoke decidedly, as though to a sulking child. "That vampire was suffering from serious hive neglect. He had not even been trained out of larvae stage well enough to recognize me for what I clearly am." If Alexia had been sitting close enough, she probably would have prodded the queen with a sharp finger to the sternum. *Scratch me*, Alexia thought. *I'd like to see her try!* She contented herself with frowning fiercely.

Countess Nadasdy looked taken aback, not having anticipated such a shift. "He was not one of mine!" she said defensively.

Miss Tarabotti stood, back straight, glad for once that she had an assertive figure: tall enough to tower over everyone but Lord Ambrose and Dr. Caedes. "Why do you play these games with me, venerable one? Lord Maccon said he could smell your bloodline in that dead boy. He *must* have been metamorphosed by you or one of your get. You've no right to pin *your* carelessness and inability to safeguard your own interests upon me, especially when I only acted in self-defense." She held up a hand to forestall interruption. "True, I have better defensive mechanisms than most daylight folk, but *I* am not the one being careless with hive blood."

Lord Ambrose hissed, his fangs fully extended, "You go too far, Soulless."

Miss Dair stood, one hand raised to her mouth in shock at such indelicate behavior. Her big blue eyes were wide and shifted between Alexia and Countess Nadasdy like those of a frightened rabbit.

Miss Tarabotti ignored Lord Ambrose, which was difficult, as her skin was prickling in reaction, and the prey part of her brain wanted desperately to run and hide behind the chaise longue. She forced down the instinct. It was preternaturals who hunted vampires, not the other way around. Technically, Lord Ambrose was *her* rightful prey. He should be trembling behind the sofa! She leaned on the tea trolley, bending toward the queen. She tried to loom like Lord Maccon loomed, but suspected her green and gray check visiting dress and ample bosom mitigated any threatening aspect.

Affecting indifference, Alexia spiked a second piece of Battenberg hard with a fork. Metal clanked loudly against serving plate. Miss Dair jumped.

"You are correct in one aspect, Miss Tarabotti. This is *our* problem," said the queen, "hive business. You should not be involved. BUR should not be involved, although they *will* continue to interfere. Not until *we* know more about the situation anyway. The werewolves should certainly keep their furry noses out of it!"

Miss Tarabotti pounced on the hive queen's indiscretion. "So there *has* been more than one of these mysterious vampire appearances?"

Countess Nadasdy sneered at her.

Alexia said, "The more BUR knows, the easier it will be to figure out why and how this is happening."

"This is hive business; it is not a matter for the Registry," the queen reiterated, saying nothing more.

"Not if unregistered roves are roaming London outside hive dominion. Then it is BUR business. Do you want to go back to the Dark Ages, when humans feared you and preternaturals hunted you? Vampires must at least *appear* to be under government control; that is part of BUR's mandate. You and I both know that. Everyone in this room must know that!" Miss Tarabotti spoke firmly.

"Roves! Do not talk to me about roves—nasty, ungoverned madmen, the lot of them." Countess Nadasdy bit her lip. It was a strangely endearing gesture from one of the oldest immortals in England.

At that sign of confusion, Alexia finally realized what was really going on. The hive queen was frightened. Like Lord Akeldama, she expected to fully comprehend what occurred in her territory. Hundreds of years of experience colored every new occurrence with predictability and ennui. Yet this was something new and thus outside her comprehension. Vampires did not like surprises.

"Tell me, please." Miss Tarabotti mollified her tone. It had worked with Lord Maccon. Perhaps the trick to dealing with the supernatural set was merely to play the social submissive. "How many have there been?"

"My queen, be cautious," the Duke of Hematol advised.

Countess Nadasdy sighed. She looked from one to the next of the three male vampires. Then she said, "Three in the past two weeks. We managed to catch two of them. They know nothing of vampire etiquette, are confused and disoriented, and usually die within a few days despite our best efforts. As you say, they are ignorant of the preternatural threat, of the proper respect due to a hive queen, and even the office of the potentate. They know little of BUR and its laws of registration. It's as though they sprung, fully formed, onto the streets of London—like Athena from the mind of Zeus."

"Athena was the goddess of war," said Alexia nervously.

"In all my centuries, nothing like this has ever occurred. There were vampire hives on this tiny island before there were human governments. The feudal system was based on hive and pack dynamics. The Roman Empire took its style of organization and efficiency from our kind. The hive structure is more than just a social institution. It is supernatural instinct. No vampire is born outside the hive, because only a queen can bring about metamorphosis. It has been our greatest strength, the control this engenders, but it has also been our greatest weakness." The countess looked down at her small hands.

Miss Tarabotti sat silent throughout this speech, watching the hive queen's face. Countess Nadasdy was definitely scared, but there was an edge of hunger to her fear. To make vampires without a queen! The hive wanted to know how it was occurring so they could master the technique themselves. Such a technology was more than any vampire could wish. It was one of the reasons they invested so heavily in the modern sciences. The gadgetry in the receiving room alone was meant for more than just to amaze and delight. The hive must boast several inventor drones. There were rumors Westminster held a controlling interest in the Giffard dirigible company. But their real hope was always for just such a scientific breakthrough—supernatural birth without blood bite. Miraculous, indeed.

"What will you do next?" Miss Tarabotti asked.

"I have already done it. I have involved a preternatural in hive business."

"The potentate will not be pleased." The Duke of Hematol seemed more resigned than annoyed. It was, in the end, his duty to support his queen and her decisions.

The potentate served as adviser to Queen Victoria, acting the vampire equivalent of a prime minister. Usually a well-known rove of extensive political acumen, the potentate was elected to the position by vote from all hives in the United Kingdom and served until someone better came along. It was the only way a rove could achieve any kind of serious social standing among the vampires of the ton. The current potentate had occupied the position since Queen Elizabeth I sat on the throne of England. Queen Victoria was reported to find his advice invaluable, and there were rumors that the success of the British Empire was due in large part to his skills. Of course, they said the same thing about the dewan, Her Majesty's werewolf adviser. He was a loner who had been around almost as long as the potentate, concerned himself mostly in military matters, and stayed out of pack squabbling. The two stood head and tail above other pack and hive outsiders as invaluable political liaisons to the daylight camp. But like all outsiders in good faith with the establishment, they tended to forget their revolutionary roots and side with the establishment. The potentate would bow to the hives in the end.

"The potentate is not a queen. This is hive business, not politics," countered Countess Nadasdy sharply.

"Nevertheless, he will have to be told," insisted the duke, running a fine-boned hand through his thinning hair.

"Why?" Lord Ambrose was clearly disinclined to tell anyone. He obviously objected to Alexia being consulted, and he certainly did not like the idea of involving a politician.

Miss Dair cleared her throat delicately, interrupting them. "Gentlemen, I am quite certain this is a subject best left for later." She gestured with her head at Miss Tarabotti, who had momentarily been forgotten.

Miss Tarabotti munched down her third piece of Battenberg and tried to look cunning.

Dr. Caedes swung around and gave her a very hard look. "*You*"—his tone was excessively accusatory—"are going to be trouble. Preternaturals always are. Just you keep a careful eye on those moon howlers you keep walking out with. Werewolves also have an agenda to keep to. You do realize that?"

"And you bloodsuckers, of course, are all sweetness and light with only my best interests at heart," Alexia shot back, brushing Battenberg crumbs casually off her lap.

"Look at the plucky young thing! She is trying to make a funny," said Lord Ambrose snidely.

Miss Tarabotti stood and nodded to the assembled company. The words being bandied about were getting dangerously rude. So rude, in fact, that unless she missed her guess, actions would soon be required. She would rather cut her visit short at words. This seemed an opportune moment to vacate the premises.

"Thank you for a delightful visit," she said, smiling in a way she hoped looked predatory. "It has been most"—she paused, deliberating, choosing her words carefully—"educational."

Miss Dair looked to the hive queen. At the countess's nod, she pulled a nearby bell rope that was discreetly hidden behind a heavy velvet drape. The beautiful blond maid appeared once more in the doorway. Miss Tarabotti followed her out, feeling a bit like she had just escaped the jaws of some unpleasant beast.

She was just starting down the front steps toward her cab when she was waylaid by a fierce grip on her upper arm. The lovely Angelique was far stronger than she appeared to be. It was not supernatural strength either; she was only a drone.

"Yes?" Miss Tarabotti tried to be polite.

"You are of ze BUR?" The maid's violet eyes were wide, earnest.

Alexia did not know quite what to say to that. She did not wish to lie, for she had no official sanction. A pox on Lord Maccon and his archaic principles! "I am not quite official, but—"

"You could take zem a message, yez?"

Miss Tarabotti nodded, leaning forward. Partly to appear interested, partly to ease the viselike grip the girl persisted in maintaining on her arm. *Tomorrow*, she thought, *I will be covered in bruises.*

"Tell me."

Angelique glanced around. "Ask zem. Ask zem, please, to look for ze missing ones. My master, he iz a rove. He vanishez last week. Poof." She snapped her fingers. "Like zat. Zey brought me to ze hive because I am pretty and do good work, but ze comtesse, she only just toleratez me. Without hiz protection, I do not know how long I will last."

Miss Tarabotti had no idea what the girl was on about. Lord Akeldama once said hive politics put the workings of the British government, whether daylight or shadow, to shame. She was beginning to understand the truth of his words. "Uh, I am not sure I quite follow."

"Please try."

Well, thought Alexia, *no harm in trying.* "Try to do what, exactly?"

"To find out where ze roves are gone. Az well az why ze new onez come." Clearly, Angelique liked listening at keyholes.

Miss Tarabotti blinked, trying to follow. "Vampires are going missing, as well as appearing out of thin air? You are certain they are not the same, with, say, lots of makeup and appalling shirts to make them look like new larvae?"

"No, miz." The maid gave Alexia's weak attempt at humor a reproachful look.

"No, I suppose they would not be so unfashionable, even as a hoax." Miss Tarabotti sighed and nodded. "Very well, I shall try." She was thinking that the world was getting even more confusing, and if the hive had no idea what was going on, and BUR even less, what could *she* possibly do to comprehend the situation?

Nevertheless, the maid seemed satisfied. Clearly, she did not share Alexia's reservations. She let go of Miss Tarabotti's arm and slipped back into the house, closing the massive door firmly behind her.

Alexia, frowning in puzzlement, marched down the stairs and into the waiting hackney. She did not notice that it was not the same hackney as the one she had originally arrived in, nor that it was driven by a different coachman.

She did, however, realize instantly that there was someone already residing inside the cab.

"Oh dear, I do beg your pardon! I thought this carriage was available," said Miss Tarabotti to the bulky individual slouched in the corner of the facing seat. "I told my driver to wait, and here you were in exactly the same spot, with the cab door open. I simply assumed. I do apologize. I . . ." She trailed off.

The man's face was in shadows, his features obscured by a wide coachman's hat. He did not seem to have anything to say. No greeting, no acceptance of her apologies. He did not even bother to move his gray-gloved hand to tip that horribly inappropriate hat to a strange lady blundering about in his rented transport.

"Well," said Miss Tarabotti, disgusted by his rudeness, "I shall just be off then."

She turned to leave, but the driver had climbed down off the box and now stood outside in the street, barring her exit. *His* features were not shadowed. A nearby gas lamp lit them silky gold and shiny. Alexia jerked backward in horror. *That face!* It was like a wax copy of something not quite human, smooth and pale with no blemish, no scar, and no hair to speak of. On the forehead four letters had been written in some sort of smudged black substance: VIXI. *And those eyes!* They were dark and curiously blank, so flat and expressionless it was as though nothing lived within the mind behind them. Here was a man who watched the world without blinking, yet somehow refrained from looking directly at anything.

Miss Tarabotti backed away from that smooth face in repugnance. The apparition reached forward and slammed the door to the cab, jerking the handle to lock it closed. Only then did his set expression change. He grinned a slow lazy grin that crept across his waxy face the way oil spreads over water. His mouth was full of straight white squares, not teeth. Alexia was certain that smile would haunt her dreams for years to come.

The wax man vanished from the door window, presumably to pull himself onto the driver's box, for, within the next moment, the carriage jerked and began to move. It rattled and creaked over the London street cobbles, heading toward a place Alexia was reasonably confident she had no desire to visit.

Miss Tarabotti grabbed the handle of the door, rattling it ineffectively. She braced one shoulder against it and pushed hard, putting her entire weight behind the shove. Nothing.

"Now, my dear," said the shadowed man, "no cause to carry on like that." His face remained obscured, although he was now leaning toward her. There was an odd smell in the air, like sweet turpentine. It was by no means a pleasant odor.

Miss Tarabotti sneezed.

"All we want to know is who you are and what you are doing visiting the Westminster hive. This will not hurt a bit." He lunged at her. He was holding a damp handkerchief in one hand—the apparent source of the unpleasant smell.

Alexia was not given to bouts of hysterics. However, she was also not one to stay quiet when circumstances warranted volume. She screamed, loud and long. It was one of those shrill, high shrieks, the kind only terrified women or very good actresses can produce. The scream exited the hackney cab as though no walls stood in the way and rent the quiet London night, cutting through the sound of horse hooves on stone. It rattled the leaded glass of the slumbering residences. It caused more than one stray cat to look about, suitably impressed.

At the same time, Miss Tarabotti braced herself back against the locked door. Without her parasol, her best defense was a good sharp-heeled kick. She was wearing her very favorite walking boots. They had lovely hourglass heels made of wood that gave her a little too much height for fashion but were pretty enough to make her feel almost elegant. They were also the pointiest pair of shoes she owned. Her mother had considered their purchase quite shockingly French. Alexia aimed one hard heel at the shadowed man's kneecap.

"No call for that!" he said, dodging the kick.

Miss Tarabotti was not certain if he was objecting to the kick or the scream, so she issued both again—with interest. He seemed to be having a difficult time negotiating Alexia's multiple layers of skirts and ruffles, which formed a particularly efficacious barrier in the tight confines of the hackney. Unfortunately, Alexia's own defensive movements were equally restricted. She leaned back stubbornly and kicked out again. Her skirts swished.

Despite Miss Tarabotti's best efforts, the shadowed man's handkerchief was coming inexorably toward her face. She twisted her head away, feeling dizzy. The sweet fumes were almost over-whelming. Her eyes began to water slightly.

Time seemed to slow. Alexia could not help wondering what she had done to offend the heavens so much they sent two attackers at her in the space of one short week.

Just when she felt there was no more hope and she was in imminent danger of succumbing to the fumes, there came an unexpected noise. One designed, Miss Tarabotti suspected, by this newfangled concept of evolution to chill the bones of mankind. It was a vast, roaring, snarling howl. It shivered the air and the blood and the flesh all up and down one's spine. It was the cry a predator made only once, when the prey was not yet dead, but the kill was assured. In this particular case, it was followed by a loud thump as something hit the front of the cab hard enough to rattle the two who struggled within.

The carriage, which had been picking up some speed, jerked to an abrupt halt. Alexia heard the screaming cry of a terrified horse. There came a snap as the animal broke free of its traces, and then the sound of galloping hooves as it took off alone through the London streets.

Another loud thump reverberated—flesh against wood. The cab shook again.

Miss Tarabotti's attacker became distracted. He left off forcing the handkerchief on her and instead pulled down the window sash and leaned out, craning his head around toward the driver's box. "What is going on out there?"

No answer was forthcoming.

Miss Tarabotti kicked the back of his knee.

He turned around, grabbed her boot, and jerked it forward.

She fell back against the door, hard enough to bruise her spine on the handle, her layers of dress and corset failing to shield her.

"You are beginning to annoy me," the shadowed man growled. He yanked her foot sharply upward. Alexia struggled valiantly to stand upright on only one leg and screamed again, this time more of a shriek of anger and frustration than distress.

As though in response, the door she leaned against opened.

With a small squeak of alarm, Miss Tarabotti fell backward out of the cab, legs and arms flailing. She landed with an "oof" on something solid but fleshy enough to comfortably break her fall.

She took a deep breath of the stale London air and then coughed. Well, at least it was not chloroform. She had not met the chemical in person before, it being only newly circulated among the most scientifically minded of the medical profession, but she had a good idea that must be what saturated the shadowed man's ominous handkerchief.

Her landing mattress squirmed and growled. "Good God, woman! Shift off."

Miss Tarabotti was no lightweight. She made no bones about enjoying food—on a fairly regular basis and generally of the toothsome variety. She kept her figure through regular exercise, not a tightly controlled diet. But Lord Maccon, for it was he who squirmed, was very strong and ought to have shifted her easily. Instead he seemed to be having some trouble removing her from atop of him. It took an inordinate amount of time for such a big man, even if such intimate contact with a preternatural canceled out his supernatural strength.

As a general rule, Lord Maccon appreciated a voluptuous woman. He liked a bit of meat on the female form, more to grab on to—and more to chew off. His voice, annoyed as always, belied the gentleness in his big hands as he took the excuse of removing Alexia's generous curves from his person to check for injuries.

"Are you unhurt, Miss Tarabotti?"

"You mean, aside from my dignity?" Alexia suspected Lord Maccon's handling was a tad more than was strictly called for under the circumstances, but she secretly enjoyed the sensation. After all, how often did a spinster of her shelf life get manhandled by an earl of Lord Maccon's peerage? She had better take advantage of the situation. She smiled at her own daring and wondered who could be said to be taking advantage of whom!

Eventually, the earl levered her into a sitting position. He then rolled out from under her and stood, jerking her unceremoniously to her feet.

"Lord Maccon," said Miss Tarabotti, "why is it that around you I always end up in some variety of indelicate and prone position?"

The earl arched a debonair eyebrow at her. "The first time we met, I believe it was I who took a particularly undignified tumble."

"As I have informed you previously"—Alexia brushed off her

dress—"I did not leave the hedgehog there intentionally. How was I to know you would sit on the poor creature?" She looked up from her ministrations and gasped in shock. "There is blood all over your face!"

Lord Maccon wiped his face hurriedly on his evening jacket sleeve, like a naughty child caught covered in marmalade, but did not explain. Instead he growled at her and pointed into the hackney. "See what you have gone and done? He got away!"

Alexia did not see, because there was nothing inside the cab to see any longer. The shadowed man had taken the opportunity her unfortunate tumble afforded to escape.

"*I* did not do anything. *You* opened the door. I simply fell out of it. A man was attacking me with a wet handkerchief. What else was I supposed to do?"

Lord Maccon could not say much in response to such an outlandish defense.

So he merely repeated, "A *wet* handkerchief?"

Miss Tarabotti crossed her arms and nodded mutinously. Then, in typical Alexia fashion, she opted to go on the attack. She had no idea what it was about Lord Maccon that always made her so inclined, but she went with the impulse, perhaps encouraged by her Italian blood. "Wait just a moment now! How did you find me here? Have you been following me?"

Lord Maccon had the good grace to look sheepish—if a werewolf can be said to look *sheepish*. "I do not trust vampire hives," he grumbled, as though that were an excuse. "I told you not to come. Didn't I tell you not to come? Well, look what happened."

"I would have you know I was perfectly safe in that hive. It was only when I left that things went all"—she waved a hand airily—"squiffy."

"Exactly!" said the earl. "You should go home and stay inside and never go out again."

He sounded so serious Alexia laughed. "You were waiting for me the entire time?" She looked curiously up at the moon. It was past three-quarters in size—an easy-change moon. She remembered the blood on his mouth and put two and two together. "It is a chilly night. I take it you were in wolf form?"

Lord Maccon crossed his arms and narrowed his eyes.

"How did you change so quickly and get dressed so fast? I heard your attack cry; you could not have been human at that point." Miss Tarabotti had a good idea how werewolves worked, though admittedly she had never seen the earl himself change shape. In fact, she had never seen anyone do it outside of the detailed sketches in some of her father's library books. Still, there the earl stood before her, top hat to tails, untidy hair and hungry yellow eyes, nothing out of place—apart from the odd bit of blood.

Lord Maccon grinned proudly, looking like a schoolboy who had just managed to translate his Latin perfectly. Instead of answering her question, he did the most appalling thing. He changed into wolf shape—but only his head—and growled at her. It was utterly bizarre: both the act itself (a weird melting of flesh and crunching of bones, most unpleasant in both appearance and sound) and the sight of a gentleman in perfect evening dress with an equally perfect wolf's head perched atop a gray silk cravat.

"That is quite revolting," said Miss Tarabotti, intrigued. She reached forward and touched his shoulder so that the earl was forced to return to fully human form. "Can all werewolves do that, or is it an Alpha thing?"

Lord Maccon was a bit insulted by the casualness with which she assumed control of his change. "Alpha," he admitted. "And age. Those of us who have been around the longest control the change best. It is called the Anubis Form, from the olden days." Brought to fully human state by Alexia's hand still resting on his shoulder, he seemed to register their surroundings with new eyes. The hackney's wild flight and sudden halt had placed them in a residential part of London, not quite so up-market as the hive neighborhood but not so bad as it could be.

"We should get you home," Lord Maccon asserted, looking around furtively. He removed her hand gently from his shoulder and curled it about his forearm, leading her at a brisk pace down the street. "Sangria is just a few blocks away. We should be able to hail a cab there at this time of night."

"And somehow you think it is a good idea for a werewolf and a preternatural to show up at the front door of the most notorious vampire club in London looking for a hackney?"

"Hush, you." Lord Maccon looked faintly offended, as though her statement were one of doubt in his ability to protect her.

"I take it you do not want to know what I found out from the vampire hive, then?" Miss Tarabotti asked.

He sighed loudly. "I take it you want to tell me?"

Alexia nodded, tugging down the sleeves of her over jacket. She shivered in the night air. She had dressed to go from carriage to house, not for an evening stroll.

"The countess seems an odd sort of queen," Miss Tarabotti began her story.

"You did not let her appearance mislead you, did you? She is very old, not very nice, and only interested in advancing her personal agenda." He removed his evening jacket and wrapped it around Alexia's shoulders.

"She is frightened. They have had three unexplainable new vampires appear inside Westminster territory in the past two weeks," said Miss Tarabotti, snuggling into the jacket. It was made from a high-end Bond Street silk blend, cut to perfection, but it smelled of open grassland. She liked that.

Lord Maccon said something very rude, and possibly true, about Countess Nadasdy's ancestry.

"I take it she did not inform BUR?" Alexia pretended artlessness.

Lord Maccon growled, low and threatening. "No, she most certainly did not!"

Miss Tarabotti nodded and looked at the earl with wide innocent eyes, imitating Ivy as best she could. It was harder than one would have thought. "The countess gave me tacit permission to involve the government at this time." Bat, bat, bat, went the eyelashes.

This statement, in conjunction with the lashes, seemed to make Lord Maccon even more annoyed. "As if it were her decision! We should have been informed at the onset."

Miss Tarabotti put a cautionary hand on his arm. "Her behavior was almost sad. She is quite frightened. Although she would never openly admit to being unable to cope with the situation. She did say the hive has managed to catch two of these mystery roves and that they died shortly thereafter."

Lord Maccon's expression said he would not put it past vampires to kill their own kind.

Alexia continued. "The mysterious newcomers seem entirely new. She said they arrive knowing nothing of customs, laws, or politics."

Lord Maccon walked along silently, processing this information for a few steps. He hated to admit it, but Miss Tarabotti had single-handedly ascertained more about what was transpiring than any of his agents. He was forced into feeling . . . What exactly was that sensation? Admiration? Surely not.

"Do you know what else these new ones do not know about?" asked Alexia nervously.

The earl suddenly had a very odd expression of confusion upon his face. He was eyeing her as though she had changed unexpectedly into something entirely non-Alexiaish.

"You seem to be far better informed than anyone else at the moment," responded the earl nervously with a sniff.

Miss Tarabotti touched her hair self-consciously under his appraising look, and then she answered her own question. "They do not know about me."

Lord Maccon nodded. "BUR, the packs, and the hives try to keep preternatural identity as secret as possible. If these vampires are being metamorphosed outside the hive, they would have no reason to know your kind even existed at all."

Miss Tarabotti was struck by something. She stopped in her tracks. "That man, he said they wanted to know *who* I was."

"What man?"

"The man with the handkerchief."

Lord Maccon groaned. "So they *were* after you specifically, blast it! I thought they might be after any drone or vampire, and you were just exiting the hive at the wrong time. You do realize they are going to try again?"

Alexia glanced up at him, pulling his jacket closer about her. "I guess I had best not give them another opportunity."

Lord Maccon was thinking exactly the same thing. He moved a little closer, curling her arm more firmly about his. He started them both moving once more toward Sangria, light, and company, and away from the empty, echoing side streets. "I'll have to set a watch on you."

Miss Tarabotti snorted. "And what happens at full moon?"

Lord Maccon winced. "BUR has daylight and vampire agents, as well as werewolves."

Alexia got on her proverbial high horse. "I will *not* have strangers dogging my every step, thank you. You, certainly, Professor Lyall if I must, but others . . ."

Lord Maccon grinned foolishly at that particular prioritization. His company had just merited a "certainly." What she said next, however, drove the smile right off his face.

"What if I arrange to be around Lord Akeldama during the full moon?"

The earl looked daggers. "I am certain he would be *extremely* helpful in a fight. He could ruthlessly flatter all your attackers into abject submission."

Miss Tarabotti grinned. "You know, your intense dislike of my dear vampire friend could almost sound like jealousy if the idea were not so patently absurd. Now, listen, my lord, if you simply let me—"

Lord Maccon let go of her arm, stopped, turned, and, to her complete surprise, kissed her full on the lips.

CHAPTER FIVE

Dinner with an American

The earl grabbed Miss Tarabotti's chin with one big hand and the small of her back with the other, pulling her toward him hard. He slanted his mouth over hers almost violently.

She jerked back. "What are you . . . ?"

"Only way to keep you quiet," he grumbled, taking her chin in a firmer grip and planting his mouth atop hers once more.

It was not the kind of kiss Alexia had ever experienced before. Not that she had been kissed all that frequently prior to this particular point in time. There were a few aberrations in her youth when some rogue or other thought a young and swarthy chaperone might be an easy mark. In such cases, the experience had been sloppy and, due to her ever-present and aptly applied parasol, brief. Lord Maccon's kiss was expertly administered. From his enthusiasm, Miss Tarabotti felt he might be trying to make up for her previous deficit in the arena of kissing. He was doing a bang-up job of it. Which was to be expected considering his years, possibly even centuries, of experience. Since she was holding his coat closed about her, Alexia's arms were effectively trapped by his sudden embrace, giving him full access without impediment. Not, Alexia thought, that she would be inclined to struggle.

The kiss itself was initially quite gentle: slow and soft. Alexia found it surprising given the violence of his embrace. She also found it faintly unsatisfying. She gave a little murmur of frustration and leaned in toward him. Then the kiss changed. It became harder, rougher, parting her lips with purpose. There was even, shockingly, tongue involved in the proceedings. Miss Tarabotti was not certain about *that*. It bordered on sloppy, but then again, the sheer heat of it . . . Her pragmatic preternatural self assessed the situation and realized that she could definitely learn to love the taste of him: like one of those expensive French soups, dark and rich. She arched her back. Her breath had gone all uneven, perhaps because her mouth was clogged with kisses. Alexia was just beginning to come to terms with the tongue concept and notice that she was now getting too warm to need the earl's jacket, when he left off kissing, pushed the coat roughly down, and started nibbling on her neck.

No need to think on that for any span of time. Miss Tarabotti knew instantly that she adored the sensation. She leaned into him even more, too lost in the gathering feelings to really register the fact that his left hand, which had been residing comfortably at the small of her back, had worked its way downward and, apparently unhindered by her bustle, was forming a newly intimate association with her posterior.

Lord Maccon moved her about, still nibbling, shoving the trailing ribbons of her perch hat aside so he could get at the back of her neck. He paused at one point to growl into her ear, sounding bewildered, "What *is* that spice you always smell like?"

Miss Tarabotti blinked. "Cinnamon and vanilla," she admitted. "I use it in my hair rinse." Not prone to flushing, even under the most trying of circumstances, her skin nevertheless felt strangely hot and full.

The earl did not reply. He simply went back to nibbling.

Alexia's head lolled, but she frowned for a second, certain there was something she was not supposed to be doing. Since engaging in a passionate embrace, with a peer of the realm, in the middle of the public street, did not occur to her as inappropriate just then, she immersed herself in the nibbles. They were becoming sharper and more insistent. Alexia found that she liked the idea of maybe a bite or two. As if in response to that thought, Lord Maccon sank his human—due to their shockingly informal embrace and the fact that she was a preternatural—teeth into the place where her neck and shoulder joined.

It sent tingling shocks through Alexia's entire body—a most delightful sensation, better than hot tea on a cold morning. She moaned and rubbed herself up against him, enjoying his big werewolf-sized body, pushing her neck against his mouth.

Someone cleared his throat delicately.

Lord Maccon bit down harder.

Miss Tarabotti lost complete control of her kneecaps, grateful for the wide hand firmly supporting her nether regions.

"Pardon me, my lord," said a polite voice.

Lord Maccon stopped biting Miss Tarabotti. He pulled away, putting about a finger's width of space between them. It felt like a yard. He shook his head, glanced at Alexia in shock, let go of her bottom, stared at his own hand as though accusing it of independent action, and then looked thoroughly ashamed of himself.

Unfortunately, Miss Tarabotti was too befuddled to truly appreciate the earl's uncharacteristic expression of chagrin.

He recovered himself soon enough and let loose a string of unsavory words Miss Tarabotti was certain no gentleman ought ever use around a lady, no matter how provoked. Then Lord Maccon turned to stand before her, shielding her decidedly mussed appearance from view.

Miss Tarabotti, knowing she should straighten her hat and probably the bodice of her dress and the fall of her bustle as well, could do nothing more than lean forward limply against Lord Maccon's back.

"Randolph, you could have chosen a better time," said the earl in exasperation.

Professor Lyall stood diffidently in front of his Alpha. "Possibly. But this is pack business, and it is important."

Alexia blinked stupidly at the Beta from around the earl's

upper arm. Her heart was doing crazy things, and she still could not locate her kneecaps. She took a deep breath and put some serious attention into tracking them down.

"Miss Tarabotti, good evening," acknowledged Professor Lyall, apparently unsurprised to find her the object of his lordship's amorous attentions.

"Didn't I recently send you on circuit?" Lord Maccon, back to his customary annoyed state, seemed to have turned all his considerable aggravation on to his Beta instead of Miss Tarabotti for once.

Alexia decided, then and there, that Lord Conall Maccon clearly had only two modes of operation: annoyed and aroused. She wondered which one she would prefer to deal with on a regular basis. Her body joined in that discussion without shame, and she actually managed to shock *herself* into continued silence.

Professor Lyall did not seem to require a response to his salutation from Miss Tarabotti. He answered Lord Maccon's question instead. "I uncovered a situation in Canterbury. It was unusual enough to drive me back here to London without bothering further on circuit."

"Well?" said Lord Maccon impatiently.

Alexia came back to her senses finally and straightened her hat. She pulled up on the neckline of her dress at the shoulder and fluffed out the fall of her bustle. Then she realized she had just engaged in a protracted act of lewdness, bordering on marital relations, in a public street, with Lord Maccon! She fervently hoped that very street would open up and swallow her whole. She became even hotter than she had been moments before, this time with abject humiliation. This was, it must be admitted, a far less pleasant sensation.

While Miss Tarabotti contemplated whether spontaneous human combustion might be due to acute embarrassment, Professor Lyall continued. "You had all the loners stationed along the coast 'round Canterbury, remember? Well, all but one has gone missing. Plus a number of rove vampires have also vanished."

Lord Maccon jerked in surprise.

Alexia realized that she was still plastered against his back. She stepped away and to one side quickly. Her knees were back in working order.

With a growl of possession, Lord Maccon snaked out one long arm and yanked her back against his side.

"Funny," said Miss Tarabotti, trying to ignore the growl and the arm.

"What is funny?" asked the earl, sounding stern. Despite his gruff tone, he used his free hand to adjust his coat more securely over her shoulders and neck.

Miss Tarabotti swatted at him and his solicitousness.

"Stop that," she hissed.

Professor Lyall's bright eyes followed the interaction. His expression did not change, but Alexia had an inkling he was secretly laughing at them both.

She said, "The drone maid said exactly the same thing about the *London* roves. A good number of them have been going missing for several weeks, apparently." She paused. "What about London lone werewolves? Are they still all accounted for?"

"There are none, aside from the dewan. Although he is sort of above the packs, rather than outside of them. Woolsey Castle has always kept strict loner regulations, and we enforce them to the letter," Professor Lyall said proudly.

"The dewan has even stronger feelings on the matter than I," added Lord Maccon. "Well, you know how conservative the Shadow Council tends to be."

Miss Tarabotti, who did not, as she had very little to do with Queen Victoria's government, nodded as though she knew exactly what they were talking about. "So we have got werewolves and vampires disappearing and new vampires appearing." She mulled over the quandary.

"And someone trying to make you disappear as well," added Lord Maccon.

Professor Lyall looked upset to hear that. "What?"

Alexia was touched by his concern.

"We will discuss it later," ordered Lord Maccon. "Right now I ought to get her back home, or we will have a whole new set of problems to cope with."

"Should I come along?" asked his second.

"In that state? You will only exacerbate the situation," mocked the earl.

Alexia noted for the first time—so embarrassed was she at her inadvertent assignation—that Professor Lyall was wrapped in a large coat and wore neither hat nor shoes. She looked with greater care; he did not have any trousers on either! Scandalized, she covered her mouth with one hand.

"You had better scamper off back to the den," instructed the earl.

Professor Lyall nodded and turned away, padding silently on bare feet round the corner of a nearby building. A moment later, a small lithe sandy-colored wolf, with intelligent yellow eyes and a cloak in its mouth, trotted back into the street. He nodded at Alexia once and then took off at a flat run down the cobbled road.

The rest of the night was comparatively uneventful. Outside Sangria, Miss Tarabotti and Lord Maccon ran into a handful of young bucks, dandies of the first order with pinked collars and high-shine shoes, who offered them use of a carriage. The dandies were so inoffensively foppish and so entirely inebriated that Lord Maccon felt comfortable enough taking them up on the offer. He saw Miss Tarabotti safely to her door, the servants' entrance, of course, and into the care of a worried Floote, the family none the wiser to her evening's peregrinations. Then Lord Maccon disappeared round the edge of a building.

Miss Tarabotti peeked out her window directly after she had dressed for bed. She was not certain what it said about her lifestyle that she found it immensely comforting to see an enormous wolf, his brown coat brindled gold and gray, pacing the back alley below her room.

"Lord Maccon did *what*?" Miss Ivy Hisselpenny set her gloves and beaded reticule down with a clatter onto the hall table of the Loontwills' entranceway.

Miss Tarabotti ushered her friend into the front parlor. "Keep your voice down, my dear. And please, for goodness' sake, remove that bonnet. It's positively scorching my eyeballs."

Ivy did as requested, staring at her friend all the while. She was so surprised by what she had just heard; she did not even have the capacity to take obligatory offense at Alexia's customary hat-related abuse.

Floote appeared with a heavy-laden tray and plucked the bonnet out of Miss Hisselpenny's grasp. He held the offensive article—a purple velvet affair covered with yellow flowers and a large stuffed guinea fowl—between thumb and forefinger and retreated out of the room. Miss Tarabotti closed the door firmly behind him . . . and the bonnet.

Mrs. Loontwill and the young lady-twills were out shopping, but they were due back at any moment. It had taken Ivy eons to gather momentum that morning, and now Alexia could only hope they remained uninterrupted for sufficient time to cover all the necessary gossip.

She poured raspberry cordial.

"Well!" insisted Miss Hisselpenny, sitting down in a wicker chair and fixing one curl of her dark hair absentmindedly.

Alexia passed her a glass of cordial and said flatly, "You heard correctly. I said that Lord Maccon kissed me last night."

Miss Hisselpenny did not touch the beverage, so prodigious was her shock. Instead she set her glass down on a small side table for safety's sake and leaned forward as much as her corset would allow. "Where?" She paused. "Why? How? I thought you disliked him most intensely." She frowned, her dark brows creasing. "I thought *he* disliked *you* most intensely."

Miss Tarabotti sipped her cordial, being poised and cagey. She did so like to torture Ivy. She relished the expression of avid curiosity on her friend's face. On the other hand, she was also itching to tell all.

Miss Hisselpenny peppered her further. "What exactly happened? Spare me no detail. How did it come to pass?"

"Well, it was a cold night, but there was still one last dirigible in the sky. Floote helped me sneak out the back and—"

Ivy groaned, "Alexia!"

"You said spare no detail."

Ivy gave her a dour look.

Miss Tarabotti smiled. "After I went to see the hive queen, someone tried to abduct me."

Ivy's jaw dropped. "What!"

Alexia passed her a plate of shortbread, drawing out the suspense. Miss Hisselpenny waved it away frantically. "Alexia, this is torment!"

Miss Tarabotti ceded to her friend's nervous constitution. "Two men tried to abduct me in a fake hackney cab as I left the hive house. It was actually somewhat frightening."

Ivy remained silent and enthralled while Alexia detailed the attempted abduction. Eventually she said, "Alexia, you should report this to the constabulary!"

Miss Tarabotti poured them more raspberry cordial from the cut-glass decanter. "Lord Maccon *is* the constabulary or, more properly, BUR's form thereof. He is keeping an eye on me in case they try again."

Miss Hisselpenny was even more intrigued by this bit of news. "Is he? Really? Where?"

Alexia led her to the window. They looked out onto the road. A man stood on the street corner leaning against a gas lantern post, his eyes firmly fixed on the Loontwills' front entranceway. He was vaguely disreputable-looking, wearing a long tan duster and the most ridiculous wide-brimmed John Bull hat. It looked like something favored by American gamblers.

"And you think my hats are bad!" Ivy giggled.

"I know," agreed Miss Tarabotti fervently. "But what can one do? Werewolves lack subtlety."

"That does not look like Lord Maccon," said Miss Hisselpenny, trying to make out the features under the hat. She had met the earl only a few times, but still . . . "Much too short."

"That is because it is not. Apparently, he departed this morning before I arose. That is his Beta, Professor Lyall, all in all a superior being so far as manners are concerned. According to him, Lord Maccon's gone home to rest." Miss Tarabotti's tone said she expected the earl to have told her that himself. "Well, we had a busy night."

Ivy twitched the heavy velvet curtains back to cover the front window once more and turned to her friend. "Yes, well, so it would seem with all that kissing! Which, I must point out, you have yet to address. You simply must tell me. What was it like?" Miss Hisselpenny found most of the books in Alexia's father's library shameful to read. She covered her ears and hummed whenever Miss Tarabotti even mentioned her papa, but she never hummed so loudly she could not hear what was said. But now that her friend possessed firsthand experience, she was simply too curious to be embarrassed.

"He simply, in a manner of speaking, grabbed me. I believe I was talking too much."

Ivy made the appropriate shocked noise of disagreement over such an outlandish idea.

"And the next thing I knew . . ." Alexia fluttered her hand in the air and trailed off.

"And do go on," encouraged Miss Hisselpenny, her eyes wide with avid curiosity.

"He used his tongue. It made me feel very warm and dizzy, and I do not know quite how to articulate it." Miss Tarabotti felt odd telling Ivy about the experience. Not because it was an indelicate topic but because she partially wished to keep the sensation to herself.

She had awoken that morning wondering if any of it had actually occurred. It was not until she noticed a large bite-shaped bruise on her lower neck that she accepted the previous night's events as reality and not some sort of torturous dream. She was forced to wear an ancient slate and navy striped walking dress as a result of the bite mark, one of the only garments in her wardrobe that boasted a high neckline. She decided it would be best not to tell Ivy about the bruise, particularly as she would then have to explain why it was impossible for Lord Maccon to ever give her a *real* werewolf bite.

Miss Hisselpenny blushed beet red but still wanted to know more. "Why would he do such a thing, do you think?"

"I am under the impression tongues are often involved in such exertions."

Ivy was not dissuaded. "You know what I mean. Why would he kiss you in the first place? And in a public thoroughfare!"

Miss Tarabotti had puzzled over that question all morning. It caused her to remain uncharacteristically silent during family breakfast. Statements from her sisters that just yesterday would have elicited cutting remarks had passed without a murmur. She had been so quiet her mother actually asked her, solicitously, if she was feeling quite the thing. She had acquiesced that she was a little out of sorts. It had given her an excuse not to go glove shopping that afternoon.

She looked at Ivy without quite seeing her. "I must conclude it was done entirely to keep me quiet. I cannot think of any other reason. As you said, we dislike each other most intensely, have done since he sat on that hedgehog and blamed me." But Miss Tarabotti's voice did not carry the same amount of conviction it once had on that subject.

Alexia was soon to discover that this did seem to be the case. That evening, at a large dinner party given by Lord Blingchester, Lord Maccon actively avoided talking to her. Miss Tarabotti was most put out. She had dressed with particular care. Given the earl's apparent partiality for her physique, she had chosen an evening dress of deep rose with a daringly low décolletage and the latest in small bustles. She had arranged her hair to fall over the side of her neck, covering the bite mark, which meant hours at the curling iron. Her mama had even commented that she looked very well for a spinster.

"Nothing we can do about the nose, of course, but otherwise quite creditable, my dear," she'd said, powdering her own tiny button specimen.

Felicity had even said the dress was a good color for Alexia's complexion, in a tone of voice that implied that *any* color found complementing Alexia's olive skin was truly a miracle of the first order.

It all went to no avail. For had Alexia looked like a vagabond, she was certain Lord Maccon would never have noticed. He greeted her with a shamefaced "Miss Tarabotti" and then seemed at a loss. He did not deliver her the cut direct, or imply anything that might affect her social standing; he simply seemed to have nothing to say to her. Nothing at all. For the entire evening. Alexia almost wished they were back at loggerheads.

She felt compelled to conclude that he was mortified to have kissed her in the first place and was hoping she would forget it ever happened. While knowing any well-bred lady would do simply that, Alexia had enjoyed the experience and did not feel like behaving properly over it. Still, she must conclude that all agreeable sensations were entirely one-sided, and now Lord Maccon felt nothing more than a palpable wish never to see her again. He would treat her with painful correctness in the meantime.

Well, Miss Tarabotti thought, what had she expected? She was nothing more than a soulless spinster, lacking both subtlety and grace. Lord Maccon was a peer of the realm, Alpha of his pack, owner of a considerable quantity of property, and, well, somewhat stunning. All her hopeful attention to appearance aside, and the fact that earlier in the evening the mirror had shown her looking, even to her critical eye, passably pretty, Alexia now felt utterly inadequate,

She must accept that Lord Maccon was providing her, to the best of his ability, with an out. He was being agonizingly polite about it. Throughout the Blingchesters' aperitifs, he arranged things so they were in each other's company, but when they were, he then had nothing to say to her. His behavior screamed acute embarrassment. He could barely stand to look in her direction.

Miss Tarabotti tolerated the ridiculous behavior for about half an hour and then went from confused and unhappy to extremely angry. It did not take much with Alexia. Italian temperament, her mother always said. She, unlike Lord Maccon, did not feel like being polite.

From that moment on, every time Lord Maccon entered a room, Miss Tarabotti arranged to leave it. When he moved purposefully across the receiving area toward her, Alexia sidled sideways and inserted herself seamlessly into a nearby conversation. It was usually something inane like the latest perfume from Paris, but it also involved various marriageable girls causing Lord Maccon to balk. When she sat, she did so between occupied chairs, and she was careful never to be alone or in any untenanted corner of a room.

When time came for supper, Lord Maccon's place card, originally near hers, had magically migrated to the other end of the table. There he spent an uncomfortable evening talking with a young Miss Wibbley on a string of utterly frivolous topics.

Miss Tarabotti, half a world away—eight whole place settings!—still managed to overhear the conversation. Her dinner partner, a scientist in some socially acceptable form, was ordinarily just the kind of personage Alexia hoped to be seated next to. In fact, her ability to converse comfortably with the intellectual set was openly acknowledged as the main reason a spinster of her shelf life continued to be invited to dinner parties. Unfortunately, she found herself uncharacteristically ill-equipped to assist the poor gentleman in his conversational inadequacies.

"Good evening. The name's MacDougall. You'd be Miss Tarabotti, correct?" was his opening gambit.

Oh dear, thought Alexia, *an American*. But she nodded politely.

The supper began with an array of petite oysters over ice with cool lemon cream. Miss Tarabotti, who thought raw oysters bore a remarkable resemblance to nasal excrement, pushed the offensive mollusks away and watched from under her eyelashes in horror as Lord Maccon consumed twelve of them.

"Is not that an Italy sort of a name?" asked the scientist timidly.

Miss Tarabotti, who always thought her Italian heritage far more embarrassing than her soulless state, considered this a weak topic—especially from an American. "My father," she admitted, "was of Italian extraction. Unfortunately, not an affliction that can be cured." She paused. "Though he did die."

Mr. MacDougall did not seem to know how to respond. He laughed nervously. "Didn't leave a ghost behind, did he?"

Alexia wrinkled her nose. "Not enough soul." *Not any soul at all*, she was thinking. Preternatural tendencies bred true. She was what she was because of her father's soullessness. The planet ought, by rights, to be overrun with her kind. But BUR, actually Lord Maccon—she winced—had said that there were simply too few of them to start with. In addition, preternaturals tended to live very short lives.

Another nervous laugh issued from her dinner companion. "Funny you should say, me boasting a bit of an academic interest in the state of the human soul."

Miss Tarabotti was only half listening. At the other end of the table, Miss Wibbley was saying something about her third cousin who had suddenly undertaken horticultural pursuits. Her family was evidently distrustful of this development. Lord Maccon, after glancing once or twice down the table at Alexia and her scientist, was now looking down at the vacuous girl with an expression of tolerant affection and sitting far too close.

"My particular study focus," continued Mr. MacDougall desperately, "would be the weighing and measuring of the human soul."

Miss Tarabotti looked miserably into her bouillabaisse. It was tasty as these things go. The Blingchesters kept a superb French chef. "How," asked Alexia, not really interested, "would one go about measuring souls?"

The scientist looked trapped; apparently this aspect of his work did not make for civilized dinner conversation.

Miss Tarabotti became more intrigued. She put down her spoon, a mark of how unsettled her feelings that she did not finish the stew, and looked inquiringly at Mr. MacDougall. He was a plumpish young man, adorned with a pair of dented spectacles and a hairline that looked like it anticipated imminent demise. The sudden full force of her interest seemed to unnerve him.

He babbled. "Haven't quite got around to ironing out the specifics, you might say. But I've drawn up plans."

The fish course arrived. Mr. MacDougall was saved from having to elaborate by pike breaded in a rosemary-and-black-pepper crust.

Miss Tarabotti took a small bite and watched Miss Wibbley bat her eyelashes at Lord Maccon. Alexia was familiar with the maneuver; it was the one Ivy had taught her. That made her angry. She pushed the fish away peevishly.

"So how would you approach such a study?" she asked.

"I had thought to use a large Fairbanks scale, customized with supports to hold a man-sized cot," Mr. MacDougall explained.

"Then what would you do, weigh someone, kill them, and then weigh them again?"

"Please, Miss Tarabotti! No need to be crude! I've not worked out the details yet." Mr. MacDougall looked faintly ill.

Alexia, taking pity on the poor sod, switched to theoretical avenues. "Why this particular interest?"

He quoted, "The affections of soul are enmattered formulable essences. That is precisely why the study of the soul must fall within the science of nature."

Miss Tarabotti was not impressed. "Aristotle," she said.

The scientist was delighted. "You read Greek?"

"I read Greek translations," Alexia replied curtly, not wishing to encourage his obvious interest.

"Well, if we could divine the soul's substance, we might measure for its quantity. Then we would know, before the death bite, whether a person might be able to become supernatural or not. Imagine the lives that could be saved."

Alexia wondered what she would weigh on such a scale. *Nothing? Probably, that would be a novel experience.* "Is that why you have come to England? Because of our integration of vampires and werewolves into regular society?"

The scientist shook his head. "Things are not so bad as all that across the pond these days, but, no, I'm here to present a paper. The Royal Society invited me to inaugurate the opening of their new gentlemen's club, Hypocras. Heard of it?"

Miss Tarabotti had, but she could not remember when, nor could she recall anything further about it. She simply nodded.

The fish course was taken away and the main dish set down before them: roasted beef short ribs with gravy and root vegetables.

At the far end of the table, Lord Maccon's dinner companion let out a tinkling laugh.

Miss Tarabotti asked Mr. MacDougall quite out of the blue, "Miss Wibbley is very attractive, wouldn't you say?" She tipped her rib from its upright presentation position and sawed away at the meat viciously.

The American, being an American, looked openly over at the girl in question. He blushed and said timorously into his food, "I prefer ladies with dark hair and a bit more personality."

Alexia was charmed despite herself. She decided she had wasted enough of the evening, not to mention the delicious meal, agonizing over Lord Maccon. She proceeded to give the hapless

Mr. MacDougall the full force of her attention for the remainder
of supper. A situation he seemed to regard with mixed terror and
delight.

Miss Tarabotti, never one to pass up an opportunity to display
her bluestocking tendencies, matched wits with the young scientist on a wide range of subjects. Leaving the weighing of souls for
another occasion, the salad course moved them on to recent inno-
vations in various engine designs. Over fruit and bonbons, they
broached the physiological correlation between mental and
behavioral phenomena and how this might affect vampire hive
dynamics. By coffee, which was served in the drawing room, Mr.
MacDougall had asked for and received permission to call upon
Miss Tarabotti the following day. Lord Maccon was looking as
black as thunderclouds, and Miss Wibbley seemed unable to
distract him further. Alexia did not notice the werewolf's disgrun-
tlement; new techniques in the capture of evanescent reflections
were just so riveting.

Miss Tarabotti departed the party still feeling rejected by the
earl but secure in the knowledge she could look forward to further
intellectual conversation the following day. She was also pleased
with herself, convinced that while she might be upset by Lord
Maccon's behavior, she had given no indication of this to him nor
to anyone else who mattered.

Lord Conall Maccon, Earl of Woolsey, paced his office like a
caged, well, wolf.

"I do not understand what she is playing at," he grumbled. He
was looking even scruffier than usual. This contrasted sharply
with the fact that he was still in evening dress, having just come
from the Blingchesters' dinner party. His cravat was terribly
mussed, as though someone had been pawing at it.

Professor Lyall, sitting at his own small desk in the far corner
of the room, looked up from behind a mound of metal scrolls. He
pushed a pile of wax rubbings to one side. He reflected sadly that
his Alpha really was a hopeless case so far as fashion was

concerned. He looked to be moving in that direction in the romantic arena as well.

Like most werewolves, they kept nighttime business hours. Essentially, the Blingchesters' dinner had been Lord Maccon's breakfast.

"I have had a report from the Westminster hive of yet another rove appearance," said Professor Lyall. "At least they *told* us this time. Funny that they should find out before we did; I did not think they concerned themselves so closely with rove activities."

His boss did not seem to hear this. "She completely ignored me, blasted female! Spent the entire evening flirting with a scientist. An *American* scientist, if you ken such an appalling thing!" The Alpha sounded particularly Scottish in his dudgeon.

Professor Lyall ceded to the fact that, for the moment, he was not likely to get any real work done. "Be fair, my lord. You undertook to ignore her first."

"Of course I ignored her! It is her responsibility to come to me at this juncture. I made my initial interest perfectly clear."

Silence.

"*I* kissed *her*," he explained, aggrieved.

"Mmm, yes, I had the dubious pleasure of witnessing that, ah-hem, overly public occurrence." Lyall sharpened his pen nib, using a small copper blade that ejected from the end of his glassicals.

"Well! Why hasn't she done anything about it?" the Alpha wanted to know.

"You mean like whack you upside the noggin with that deadly parasol of hers? I would be cautious in that area if I were you. I am reasonably certain she had it custom made and tipped with silver."

Lord Maccon looked petulant. "*I mean* like attempt to talk to me, or perhaps not talk at all but simply drag me off somewhere . . ." He trailed off. "Somewhere dark and soft and . . ." He shook himself like a wet dog. "But, no. Instead she utterly dismissed me, not a single word. I believe I liked it better when she was yelling at me." He paused and then nodded to himself. "I know I liked it better."

Professor Lyall sighed, put down his quill, turned his entire attention upon his boss, and attempted to explain. Ordinarily, Lord Maccon was not quite so thickheaded. "Alexia Tarabotti is not going to behave in accordance with pack dynamics. You are enacting the traditional courting ritual for Alpha females. It may be instinct for you, but this is the modern age; many things have changed."

"That woman," Lord Maccon spat, "is definitely Alpha and most certainly female."

"But not a werewolf." Professor Lyall's voice was aggravatingly calm.

Lord Maccon, who had been behaving entirely on instinct, looked suddenly crestfallen. "Have I handled this situation entirely wrong?"

Professor Lyall was reminded of his Alpha's origins. He might be a relatively old werewolf, but he had spent much of that time in a barely enlightened backwater city in the Scottish Highlands. All the London ton acknowledged Scotland as a barbaric place. The packs there cared very little for the social niceties of daytime folk. Highland werewolves had a reputation for doing atrocious and highly unwarranted *things,* like wearing smoking jackets to the dinner table. Lyall shivered at the delicious horror of the very idea.

"Yes. You have behaved, I would go so far as to say, badly. I suggest a well-crafted apology and an extended session of abject groveling," said the Beta. His expression remained mild, but the look in his eyes was flinty. His Alpha would find no sympathy there.

Lord Maccon stood up very straight. He would have towered over his second even if Lyall were not sitting down. "I am *not* a groveler!"

"It is possible to learn many new and interesting skills in one lifetime," advised Professor Lyall, unimpressed by the posturing.

Lord Maccon looked mutinous.

Professor Lyall shrugged. "Well, you had best give up now, then. I never quite understood your interest in the young lady to begin with. I am convinced the dewan would have much to say on the subject of unsanctioned intimacy between a werewolf and a preternatural regardless of your mistake with Miss Tarabotti." Of course, he was baiting his Alpha, perhaps unwisely.

Lord Maccon went red and sputtered. To tell the truth, he could not quite fathom his interest in her either. There was just something about Alexia Tarabotti that made her immensely appealing. Perhaps it was the turn of her neck or the secret smile she sometimes got when they argued that said she might be yelling at him for the pure fun of it. As far as Lord Maccon was concerned, nothing was worse than a timid woman. He was often prone to lamenting the loss of all those stalwart Highland lasses of his misspent youth. Alexia, he often felt, would adapt well to rough Scottish cold, and rock, and plaid. Was that the source of the fascination? Alexia in plaid? His mind carried that image one or two steps further, taking her out of the plaid and then on top of it.

He sat down with a sigh at his desk. Silence descended for about half an hour; nothing disturbed the night's stillness but the shuffling of papers, the tink of metal slates, and an occasional sip of tea.

Finally Lord Maccon looked up. "Grovel, you say?"

Lyall did not glance away from the latest vampire report he was perusing. "Grovel, my lord."

CHAPTER SIX

Driving with Scientists, Dabbling with Earls

Mr. MacDougall arrived promptly at eleven-thirty the next morning to whisk Miss Tarabotti away for a drive. His appearance caused quite a tizzy in the Loontwill household. Alexia was, naturally, expecting the gentleman. She sat awaiting his arrival calmly in the front parlor, wearing a forest green carriage dress with gold filigree buttons down the front, an elegant new broad-brimmed straw hat, and a cagey expression. The family surmised her imminent departure from the hat and gloves, but they had no idea who might be calling to take her out. Aside from Ivy Hisselpenny, Alexia did not entertain callers often, and everyone knew the Hisselpennys owned only one carriage, and it was not of sufficient quality to merit gold filigree buttons. The Loontwills were left to assume that Alexia was awaiting a *man*. There was little in the world at that moment that any of them could find more surprising. The possible reintroduction of the crinoline would have caused less shock. They had pestered her throughout the morning's activities to reveal the gentleman's name, but to no avail. So the Loontwills had finally settled into waiting with her, agog with curiosity. By the time the long-awaited knock came, they were quite frenzied with anticipation.

Mr. MacDougall smiled shyly at the four ladies who all seemed to have tried to open the front door at the same time. He issued a round of polite salutations to Mrs. Loontwill, Miss Evylin Loontwill, and Miss Felicity Loontwill. Miss Tarabotti introduced them with only minimal grace and an air of embarrassment before grabbing onto his proffered arm in a pointed manner and with an undisguised air of desperation. Without further ado, he helped her down the stairs and into his carriage, and settled on the box next to her. Alexia deployed her trusty brass parasol and tilted it in such a way she would not have to look any more at her family.

He drove a pair of elegant chestnuts: calm and quiet beasts, but well matched for pace and color, and goers even though they lacked a certain spirited fire in the eye. The carriage was equally unassuming, not a high flyer but a tidy little buggy well appointed with all modern conveniences. The chubby scientist handled all three like he owned them, and Alexia reassessed her opinion of him. Everything about the equipage was in tip-top condition, and he had clearly spared no expense, even though he was only visiting England for a short while. The carriage included a crank-operated water-boiling canteen for tea on-the-go, a long-distance monocular optical viewing device for the better appreciation of scenery, and even a small steam engine linked to a complex hydraulic system the purpose of which Alexia could not begin to fathom. Mr. MacDougall was a scientist, certainly, and an American, no doubt, but he also seemed to possess taste and the means by which to inventively display it properly. Miss Tarabotti was suitably impressed. As far as she was concerned, it was one thing to have wealth and quite another to know how to show it off appropriately.

Behind them, Alexia's family huddled in a delighted clucking mass. Thrilled upon seeing that it was, indeed, a *man* who had come to take the eldest daughter out, they were doubly delighted to find out that he was the respectable young scientist of the evening before. New heights of euphoria had been reached (especially by Squire Loontwill) once it was deduced that he seemed to possess more capital than was to be hoped for in any standard member of the intellectual set (even an American).

"He may actually be a very good catch," said Evylin to her sister as they stood on the stoop waving Alexia off. "A little portly for my tastes, but she cannot afford to be choosey. Not with her age and appearance." Evylin tossed one of her golden ringlets carelessly behind her shoulder.

"And we all thought her marriage prospects exhausted." Felicity shook her head at the wonders of the universe.

"They are suited," said their mother. "He is clearly bookish. I did not follow a single word of their conversation at dinner last night, not one jot of it. He must be bookish."

"You know what the best of this situation is?" added Felicity, catty to the last. Her father's murmur of "All that money" going either unheard or unacknowledged, she answered her own question. "If they do marry, he will take her all the way back to the Colonies with him."

"Yes, but we will have to put up with the fact that everyone important will know we have an *American* in the family," pointed out Evylin, her eyes narrowing.

"Needs must, my darlings, needs must," said their mother, ushering them back inside and closing the door firmly behind them. She wondered how little they could get away with spending on Alexia's future wedding and retreated to the study with her husband to consult on the matter.

Of course, Miss Tarabotti's relations were getting well ahead of themselves. Alexia's intentions toward Mr. MacDougall were of an entirely platonic nature. She simply wanted to get out of the house and talk with a person, any person, in possession of an actual working brain, for a change. Mr. MacDougall's intentions might have been less pure, but he was timid enough for Miss Tarabotti to easily ignore any verbal forays in the romantic direction. She did so initially by inquiring after his scientific pursuits.

"How did you get interested in soul measuring?" she asked pleasantly, delighted to be out of doors and disposed to be kind to the facilitator of her freedom.

It was an unexpectedly beautiful day, pleasantly warm with a light and friendly little breeze. Miss Tarabotti's parasol was actually being put to its intended use, for the top was down on Mr. MacDougall's buggy, and she certainly needed no more sun than was strictly necessary. The mere whiff of daylight and her tan deepened to mocha and her mama went into hysterics. With both hat and parasol firmly in place, her mama's nerves were assured complete safety—from that quarter at least.

Mr. MacDougall tsked to his horses, and they assumed a lazy walk. A vulpine-faced sandy-haired gentleman in a long trench coat left his station beneath the lamppost outside the Loontwills' front door and followed at a discreet distance.

Mr. MacDougall looked at his driving companion. She was not one to be considered fashionably pretty, but he liked the strong tilt to her jaw and determined glint in her dark eyes. He had a particular partiality for firm-willed ladies, especially when they came coupled with a jaw that was shapely, eyes that were large and dark, and a handsome figure to boot. He decided she seemed resilient enough for the real reason he wanted to measure souls, and it made for a nicely dramatic story anyway. "It's not bad to admit here, I suppose," he said to start, "but you should understand, in my country I'd not speak of it." Mr. MacDougall had a bit of flare for the dramatic well hidden behind the receding hairline and spectacles.

Miss Tarabotti placed a sympathetic hand on his arm. "My dear sir, I did not intend to be nosy! You are of a mind to think of my question as officious?"

The gentleman blushed and pushed at his spectacles nervously. "Oh no, of course not! No such thing. It's just that my brother was turned. Vampire you see. My older brother."

Alexia's response was characteristically British. "Felicitations on a successful metamorphosis. May he make his mark on history."

The American shook his head sadly. "Here, as your comment implies, it is generally thought a good thing. In this country, I mean to say."

"Immortality is immortality." Alexia did not mean to be unsympathetic, but there it was.

"Not when it comes at the price of the soul."

"Your family keeps the old faith?" Alexia was surprised. Mr. MacDougall, after all, was a scientist. Scientists were generally not given to overly religious backgrounds.

The scientist nodded. "Puritans to the very core. Not a progressive bone among them: so *supernatural* means 'undead' to them. John survived the bite, but they repudiated and disinherited him anyway. The family gave him three days' grace and then hunted him down like a rabid dog."

Miss Tarabotti shook her head in sorrow. The narrow-mindedness of it all! She knew her history. The puritans left Queen Elizabeth's England for the New World because the queen sanctioned the supernatural presence in the British Isle. The Colonies had been entirely backward ever since: religious fingers in all their dealings with vampires, werewolves, and ghosts. It made America into a deeply superstitious place. Fates only knew what they'd think of someone like her!

Curious that any man from a conservative family might opt to try for metamorphosis, she asked, "Why on earth did your brother turn in the first place?"

"It was against his will. I think the hive queen did it to prove a point. We MacDougalls have always voted against change—anti-progressive to the last breath and influential in government where it counts most."

Miss Tarabotti nodded. She had surmised his family's influence from the money he obviously possessed. She touched the fine leather of the buggy seat with one hand. Here was a scientist who needed no patronage. Strange place, that overseas land, where religion and wealth did the talking and history and age held so little sway.

Mr. MacDougall continued. "I think the hive thought that turning the eldest might make us MacDougalls all think differently."

"Did it?"

"None except me. I loved my older brother, you see? I saw him once after he'd changed. He was still the same person: stronger, paler, night-born, yes, but essentially the same. He probably still would have voted conservative, if they'd let him vote." He smiled slightly, and then his face fell back to round pudding blandness. "So I switched from banking to biology and have been studying the supernatural ever since."

Miss Tarabotti shook her head unhappily. Such a sad beginning. She contemplated the sunny day: the lovely green of Hyde Park, the bright hats and dresses of ladies walking arm in arm across the grass, the two plump dirigibles gliding sedately overhead. "BUR would never allow such behavior from any vampire—to bite without permission! Let alone for a hive queen to bite the unwilling with the intent to metamorphose! Such shocking behavior."

Mr. MacDougall sighed. "Yours is a very different world, my dear Miss Tarabotti. Very different. Mine is a land still at war with itself. The fact that the vampires sided with the Confederates still has not been forgiven."

Alexia did not wish to insult her new friend, so she refrained from criticizing his government. But what did the Americans expect if they refused to integrate the supernatural set into their society in any way? When they forced vampires and werewolves to hide and skulk about in a shoddy imitation of the European Dark Ages?

"Have you rejected your family's puritanical tenets?" Miss Tarabotti looked inquiringly at her companion. Out of the corner of her eye, she caught a flash of tan trench coat. It must be tough on Professor Lyall to be outside in all this sun, especially when full moon was soon due. She felt a moment's pity but was pleased to know that it was he who had relieved the night watch guard. It meant Lord Maccon was still thinking of her. Of course, he was thinking of her as a problem . . . but that was better than not thinking of her at all, was it not? Alexia touched her lips softly with one hand and then forcibly stopped all ruminations on the mental state of the Earl of Woolsey.

Mr. MacDougall answered her question. "You mean, have I abandoned the belief that supernatural folk have sold their souls to Satan?"

Miss Tarabotti nodded.

"Yes. But not necessarily because of my brother's misfortune. The idea was never scientific enough for me. My parents knew not what they risked, sending me to Oxford. You know, I studied for some time in this country? Several of the dons are vampires. I have come 'round to the Royal Society's way of thinking, that the soul must formulate a quantifiable entity. Some individuals have less of this soul-matter, and some have more. And those who have more can be changed into immortals, and those who have less cannot. Thus it is not lack of soul but overabundance that the puritans feared. And that very concept is heresy in my family."

Alexia agreed. She kept abreast of the Society's publications. They had yet to find out about preternaturals and the truly soulless. BUR was content to let daylight scientists blunder about without access to that particular knowledge. But Miss Tarabotti felt it was only a matter of time in this enlightened age before her kind were analyzed and dissected.

"You have been devising a way to measure the soul ever since?" She checked about casually for her supernatural shadow. Professor Lyall paced them several yards away, doffing his hat to ladies walking by: an everyday middle-class gentleman apparently unaware of their buggy nearby. But Alexia knew he was watching her the entire time. Professor Lyall knew his duty.

Mr. MacDougall nodded. "Wouldn't you like to know? Especially as a woman? I mean, ladies have a high risk of failing to survive metamorphosis."

Miss Tarabotti smiled. "I know exactly how much soul I have, thank you, sir. I need no scientist to tell me that."

Mr. MacDougall laughed, taking her confidence for jest.

A gaggle of dandified young men passed by. All were decked

to the height of fashion: three-buttoned swallowtails instead of frock coats, knotted silk cravats, and high collars. Alexia was certain she knew several of them from somewhere, but she did not recognize them well enough to name. These tipped their hats to her. One tallish specimen in blueberry satin breeches slowed to look with inexplicable interest at Mr. MacDougall before being whisked onward by his cohorts. Off to one side, Professor Lyall took note of their antics with interest.

Alexia glanced at her companion. "If you are successful in the measuring of souls, Mr. MacDougall, shouldn't you be worried such knowledge might be misused?"

"By scientists?"

"By scientists, by hives, by packs, by governments. Right now, what keeps the power of the supernatural set in check is their small numbers. If they knew ahead of time who to recruit, they could turn more females and increase their population drastically, and the very fabric of our social world would be rearranged."

"Yet the fact that they need us to procreate gives us normal folk some small advantage," he demurred.

It occurred to Miss Tarabotti that hives and packs had probably been working to uncover a way to measure the human soul for hundreds of years. This young man stood little chance of success where generations of advanced supernatural researchers had failed. But she held her tongue. Who was she to destroy a man's dreams?

She pretended interest in a group of swans floating across a pond to one side of the track. In truth, it was Professor Lyall who had caught her attention. Had he stumbled? It looked as though he had, falling against another gentleman and causing that man to drop some sort of metal device.

"So what topic will you address at the Hypocras inauguration?" Miss Tarabotti asked.

Mr. MacDougall coughed. "Well"—he looked embarrassed—"primarily what I have found the soul *not* to be. My initial research would seem to indicate that it is not an aura of any kind nor a pigmentation of the skin. There are several working theories: some think it may reside in part of the brain; others believe it to be a fluid element in the eyes or perhaps electrical in nature."

"What do you think?" Alexia was still feigning interest in the swans. Professor Lyall seemed to recover himself. It was hard to tell at this distance, but, under his John Bull hat, his angular face seemed oddly pale.

"From what I know of metamorphosis—and I have never been privileged enough to observe it in action, mind you—I believe the conversion to be the result of a blood-borne pathogen. The same kind of pathogen Dr. Snow has suggested resulted in the recent cholera outbreaks."

"You oppose the miasmatic hypothesis of disease transfer?"

The scientist inclined his head, delighted to converse with a woman so well educated in modern medical theory.

Miss Tarabotti said, "Dr. Snow suggests cholera transmission occurred through the ingestion of contaminated water. How exactly would you suggest supernatural transmission occurs?"

"That remains a mystery. As does the reason why some respond positively and others do not."

"A condition that we currently refer to as the presence or absence of excess soul?" suggested Alexia.

"Exactly." The scientist's eyes brightened with enthusiasm. "Identifying a pathogen will only show us *what* occurs to drive metamorphosis. It will not tell us *why* or *how*. My research until now has focused on hematology, but I am beginning to think I have been pursuing the wrong hypothetical angle."

"You need to deduce what is different between those who die and those who survive?" Alexia tapped the brass handle of her parasol with her fingertips.

"And what the survivor is like before and after metamorphosis." Mr. MacDougall drew the horses up so he could turn fully to face Alexia, animated in his enthusiasm. "If the soul has substance, if it is an organ or part of an organ that some possess and others do not—the heart, perhaps, or the lungs—"

Miss Tarabotti was equally enthusiastic; she finished the hypothesis for him. "Then it should be quantifiable!" Her dark eyes sparkled with the very idea of such a thing. Brilliant in concept, but it would require much further study. She understood now why he had not thought his research appropriate dinner conversation the evening before. "You are undertaking a number of cadaverous dissections?" she asked.

Mr. MacDougall nodded, having forgotten her ladylike sensibilities in his excitement. "But I am finding it most difficult to acquire dead werewolves and vampires for comparison. Particularly in the United States."

Miss Tarabotti shuddered. No need to ask why. Everyone knew the Americans burned to death any accused of being supernatural, leaving little behind for any scientist to study. "You think to procure specimens here and transport them back?"

The scientist nodded. "I hope that it will be considered in the best interest of science to pursue this kind of inquiry."

"Well," Alexia said, "your speech at Hypocras should pave the way if it at all approaches the conversation we are having. You have some of the newest and best ideas I have yet heard on the subject. You would have my vote of confidence, were I allowed to be a member of the club."

The young man grinned at her praise and began to think ever more fondly of Miss Tarabotti, who possessed enough intelligence to not only follow his thoughts, but perceive their worth as well. He tsked his horses into motion once more, guiding them off to one side of the path. "Did I mention how lovely you are looking today, Miss Tarabotti?" He pulled the carriage to a full stop.

Of course, Alexia could hardly point out the many flaws in his theories after such a compliment. So instead she steered their conversation on to more general topics. Mr. MacDougall cranked up the mechanical water boiler and brewed a pot of tea. Alexia used the carriage's monocular distance viewing device while he did so. She tilted the lenses about, commenting on the pleasures of a sunny day and the statuesque grace of distant dirigibles floating above the park. She also trained them briefly on Professor Lyall, who was leaning in the shade of a tree a little way away, only to find he had donned his glassicals and was watching her through them. She hurriedly put the optical magnification device down and turned amiably back to her host and tea.

While she sipped cautiously at the tin mug, surprised to find the offering a delicious Assam, he lit up the small hydraulic engine she had noticed at the back of the carriage. With much creaking and groaning, a massive parasol pulled itself upright and then unfolded to shade the open carriage. Alexia snapped her own small parasol shut, glaring at it with an entirely unwarranted sense of inadequacy. It was a good little parasol and hardly deserving of such a jaundiced look.

They passed a distinctly pleasant additional hour in each other's company, sipping tea and nibbling a box of rosewater and lemon Turkish delight that Mr. MacDougall had invested in for this occasion especially. In no time, it seemed, Mr. MacDougall was lowering the gigantic parasol and driving Miss Tarabotti back home.

The young gentleman helped her down from his carriage at the Loontwills' front steps feeling justifiably pleased with the success of their outing, but Alexia forestalled him when he tried to see her all the way to the door.

"Please do not mistake my refusal for rudeness," she explained delicately. "But you do not wish to encounter my relations just now. They are not up to your caliber of intellect, I am ashamed to say." She suspected her mother and sisters were out shopping, but she needed some excuse. The way his eyes looked right now, he might make a declaration, and then where would she be?

The scientist nodded gravely. "I completely understand, my dear Miss Tarabotti. My own relatives are similarly afflicted. May I call again?"

Alexia did not smile. It would not do to be coy when she had no intention of returning his advances. "You may, but not tomorrow, Mr. MacDougall. You will be preparing for your speech."

"The next day?" He was persistent. "That way I can tell you how the opening celebrations went."

Very forward, American men. Alexia sighed inwardly but nodded her acquiescence.

Mr. MacDougall assumed the driver's seat, tipped his hat, and urged his chestnut beauties into a sedate withdrawal.

Miss Tarabotti pretended she was remaining on the stoop to wave him off. Once he was out of sight, however, she nipped furtively back down the front steps and round the side of the house.

"You certainly kept a close watch," she accused the man lurking there.

"Good afternoon, Miss Tarabotti," he said in a polite if mild voice—milder than usual, even for Professor Lyall, almost weak sounding.

Alexia frowned in concern. She tried to get a good look at his face under the ostentatious hat. "How came you to be on duty today, sir? I would have thought Lord Maccon required your expertise elsewhere."

The professor looked pale and drawn, normal in a vampire but not in a werewolf. The lines on his face had deepened with strain, and his eyes were bloodshot. "Miss Tarabotti, it is getting on to full moon; his lordship has to be careful who he puts out to guard you come daylight. The young ones are not very stable at this time of the month."

Alexia sniffed. "I appreciate his concern for my well-being. But I had thought there were others in BUR who might not be so taxed by daylight service. When is the moon?"

"Tomorrow night."

Miss Tarabotti frowned. "Same time as Mr. MacDougall's speech at the Hypocras Club," she said softly to herself.

"What?" The professor looked too tired to be interested.

Alexia waved a hand in the air. "Oh, nothing of import. You

should go home, Professor, get some rest. You look absolutely awful. He should not work you so hard."

The Beta smiled. "It is part of my purpose."

"To exhaust yourself protecting me?"

"To safeguard his interests."

Miss Tarabotti gave him a horrified look. "I hardly think that an apt description."

Lyall, who'd seen the crested carriage parked just the other side of the Loontwill house, did not reply to that.

There was a pause.

"What did he do?" Alexia asked.

"Who?" replied Professor Lyall, although he knew perfectly well what she was asking about.

"The man you pretended to stumble into."

"Mmm." The werewolf was cagey. "It was more what he had."

Miss Tarabotti tilted her head and looked inquiring.

"I wish you a pleasant evening, Miss Tarabotti," said Professor Lyall.

Alexia gave him an exasperated look, then marched back up the front stairs and inside her house.

The family was clearly out, but Floote was waiting for her in the foyer with a most un-Floote-like expression of perturbation on his face. The door to the front parlor was open, a certain sign of visitors. Alexia was shocked. The Loontwills could not possibly have been expecting company, otherwise they would never have left the premises.

"Who is here, Floote?" she asked, fumbling with her hatpin.

The butler raised both eyebrows at her.

Alexia swallowed, suddenly nervous. She removed her hat and gloves and put them carefully on the hall table.

She took a moment to compose herself, checking her hair in the framed gilt hallway mirror. The dark mass was arranged a tad long for daytime, but she had a bite mark to cover up, and it was too hot for high necklines. She twitched several curls into place to better cover her bruise. Her own face looked back at her: firm chin, dark eyes, militant expression. Alexia touched her nose. *Mr. MacDougall thinks you are lovely*, she told her reflection.

Then she set her spine as straight as possible and marched into the front parlor.

Lord Conall Maccon whirled about from where he stood. He had been facing the closed velvet curtains of the front window, staring at them as though he might be able to see right through the heavy material. In the dim light of the room, his eyes looked accusatory.

Miss Tarabotti paused on the threshold. Without a word, she turned back around, reached out, and slammed the parlor door shut firmly behind her.

Floote gave the closed door a long, hard look.

Outside in the street, Professor Lyall set his bone-weary self toward the BUR offices—just a few more records to check before bed. With one free hand, he patted a new bulge in his many-pocketed waistcoat. Why, he wondered, was a man with a syringe wandering Hyde Park? He turned back once to look at the Loontwills' house. A sudden smile creased his angular face as he noted the Woolsey Castle carriage waiting nearby. Its crest shone in the late afternoon sun: a quartered shield, two parts a moon-backed castle, two parts a moonless starry night. He wondered if his lord and master would, in fact, grovel.

The Earl of Woolsey wore a suit of dark chocolate, a cravat of caramel silk, and an air of ill-disguised impatience. He had been holding his kid gloves in one hand and slapping them rhythmically into the other when Miss Tarabotti entered the front parlor. He stopped instantly, but she had noted the fidget.

"What bee has gotten into your britches?" Miss Tarabotti asked without any attempt at a formal greeting. Formality was wasted on Lord Maccon. She took up position, arms akimbo, standing on the round primrose rug before him.

The earl countered with a gruff "And where have you been all day?"

Miss Tarabotti was disposed to be elusive. "Out."

The earl would have none of it. "Out with whom?"

Alexia raised both eyebrows. He would find out from Professor Lyall eventually, so she said archly, "A nice young scientist."

"Not that butterball chap you were nattering away with at dinner last night?" Lord Maccon looked at her in horror.

Miss Tarabotti glared viciously down her nose at him. Inside she was secretly delighted. He had noticed! "It just so happens that Mr. MacDougall has some absolutely fascinating theories on a wide range of topics, and he is interested in *my* opinion. Which is more than I can say for certain other gentlemen of my acquaintance. It was a beautiful day and a lovely drive, *and* he makes for quite an enjoyable conversation partner. A position, I am certain, you are entirely unfamiliar with."

Lord Maccon looked suddenly very suspicious. His eyes narrowed, and their color lightened to the same caramel hue as his cravat. "What have you been telling him, Miss Tarabotti? Anything I should know?"

He was asking in his BUR tone of voice.

Miss Tarabotti looked around, expecting at any moment to see Professor Lyall emerge with a notepad or a metal plate and stylus. She sighed with resignation. Clearly, the earl had come to visit her only in his official capacity. Foolish of her to hope, she chided herself mentally. Then she wondered what exactly she was hoping for. An apology? From Lord Maccon! *Ha*. She sat down on a small wicker chair to one side of the sofa, careful to keep a proper distance between them. "What is interesting is more what *he* has been telling *me*," she said. "He thinks being supernatural is some kind of disease."

Lord Maccon, who was a werewolf and "cursed," had heard that description before. He crossed his arms and loomed at her.

"Oh, for goodness' sake," tsked Miss Tarabotti, "do sit down."

Lord Maccon sat.

Miss Tarabotti continued. "Mr. MacDougall . . . that *is* his name, you know? Mr. MacDougall. Anyhow, Mr. MacDougall believes that the supernatural state is brought about by a blood-borne pathogen that affects some humans but not others, because some possess a certain physical trait and others do not. Presumably under this theory, men are more likely to possess said trait, and that is why they survive metamorphoses more frequently than women."

Lord Maccon relaxed back, the tiny couch creaking under his weight. He snorted his contempt of the idea.

"There is, of course, one chief problem with his conjectures," Alexia went on, ignoring the snort.

"You."

"Mmmm." She nodded. There was no room in Mr. MacDougall's theory for those who had no soul at all and canceled out those who had too much. What *would* Mr. MacDougall make of a preternatural? Assume she was a kind of proximity antidote to the supernatural disease? "Still it is an elegant theory with what little knowledge he has to go on." She did not have to say that she respected the young man who had thought of it. Lord Maccon could see that in her face.

"So wish him joy of his delusions, and leave it be," the earl said grimly. His canines were beginning to show, and the color of his eyes had gone further toward the yellow end of brown.

Miss Tarabotti shrugged. "He shows interest. He is smart. He is wealthy and well connected, or so I understand." *He thinks I am lovely.* She did not say that out loud. "Who am I to complain at his attentions, or discourage them for that matter?"

Lord Maccon had cause to regret the words he had uttered to Professor Lyall the night Alexia killed the vampire. Apparently she *was* thinking of getting married. And she seemed to have found someone to marry her, despite being half Italian. "He will take you back to America, and you a preternatural. If he is as smart as you imply, he would figure that little fact out eventually."

Miss Tarabotti laughed. "Oh, I am not thinking of marrying him, my lord. Nothing so rash. But I enjoy his company; it relieves the monotony of the day, and it keeps the family off the offensive."

Lord Maccon felt a rush of palpable relief at this blithe assurance and was annoyed with himself for it. Why should he care so much? His canines retracted slightly. Then he realized she had specified *marry* and that in his experience, she was rather modern in her sensibilities for a spinster. "You are considering something else non-marriage with him, perhaps?" His voice was practically a growl.

"Oh, for pity's sake. Would it bother you if I were?"

Lord Maccon actually sputtered slightly at that.

Alexia suddenly realized what she was doing. She was sitting, having a polite conversation with Lord Conall Maccon, Earl of Woolsey—whom she did not like and with whom she was supposed to be extremely annoyed—about her romantic involvement (or lack thereof). It was just that his presence caused her to become overall addlepated.

She closed her eyes and took a deep breath. "Wait a moment. Why am I speaking with you at all? My lord, your behavior last night!" She stood and began to swish about the cluttered little room, her eyes sparking fiercely. She pointed an accusatory finger at him. "You are not simply a werewolf; you, my lord, are a rake. That is what you are! You took advantage the other night, Lord Maccon. Admit it! I have no idea why you felt it necessary to do"—she paused, embarrassed—"what you did, the evening of my near abduction. But you have clearly since thought better of it. Why, if you were not interested in me as anything more than a"—she stumbled, trying to find the right terminology—"momentary plaything, you might at least have just told me outright afterward." She crossed her arms and sneered at him. "Why didn't you? You think I was not strong enough to take it without causing a scene? I assure you, no one is better used to rejection than I, my lord. I think it very churlish of you not to inform me to my face that your breach in manners was an unfortunate impulse of the moment. I deserve *some* respect. We have known each other long enough for that at the very least." At that, her steam began to run out, and she felt a heat behind her eyes she refused to believe might be tears.

Now Lord Maccon was getting angry but for different reasons. "So you've figured it all out, have you? And why, pray tell, would I suddenly be thinking better of my . . . what did you call it? Unfortunate impulse of the moment?" He sounded particularly Scottish. Alexia would have been amused by the fact that the more angry the earl got, the more burr crept into his speech. But she was too angry to notice. All tears had retracted at that.

She stopped pacing and cast her hands heavenward. "I have no earthly idea. You started it. You ended it. You treated me like a distant and not-very-well-liked acquaintance all last evening. Then you turn up in my front parlor today. You tell *me* what you were thinking yesterday at dinner. As sure as I am standing here, I have no clue as to what you are about, Lord Maccon. That is the honest truth of it."

The earl opened his mouth and then closed it again. Truth be told, he did not know what he was doing there either, so he could not very well explain. Grovel, Lyall had said. He had no idea how to do such a thing. Alphas simply did not grovel; arrogance was part of the job description. Lord Maccon might only recently have won leadership of the Woolsey Castle pack, but he had always been an Alpha.

Miss Tarabotti could not help herself. It was rare that anyone left the Earl of Woolsey at a loss for words. She felt both triumphant and confused. She had tossed and turned most of the night over his disdainful treatment. She had even thought to call on Ivy to ask her opinion of his conduct. *Ivy* of all people! She must be desperate. Yet here before her sat the object of her perturbation, apparently at her verbal mercy.

So, of course, being Alexia Tarabotti, she cut straight to the heart of the matter. She looked down at the primrose rug, because, brave as she was, she could not quite face his yellow eyes. "I am not very"— she paused, thinking of the scandalous pictures in her father's books—"experienced. If I did something wrong, you know"—she waggled a hand in the air, even more embarrassed now but bound and determined to get it over with—"with the kissing, you must excuse my ignorance. I . . ."

Alexia trailed off, for Lord Maccon had stood up from the tiny couch, which creaked at the loss, and advanced purposefully toward her. He certainly was good at looming. Alexia was not used to feeling so small.

"That," the earl muttered gruffly, "was not the reason."

"Perhaps," Miss Tarabotti offered, hands up before her in a defensive position, "you thought better of it because you realized how ignoble it would be: the Earl of Woolsey and a twenty-six-year-old spinster?"

"Is *that* your real age?" he murmured, seemingly uninterested and still coming toward her. He moved in a hungry, stalking way, and under the brown of his expertly cut jacket, solid muscle shifted, all coiled energy directed at her.

Miss Tarabotti backed away and came up short against a large wingback armchair. "My father was an Italian; did you remember that all of a sudden?"

Lord Maccon moved closer, slowly, ready to pounce if she decided to bolt. His eyes were almost completely yellow now, with a ring of orange about the edge. Alexia had never noticed before how black and thick his eyelashes were.

He said, "And I hail from Scotland. Which origin is worse in the eyes of London society, do you think?"

Alexia touched her nose and considered the dark tenor of her skin. "I have . . . other . . . flaws. Perhaps time spent thinking over the matter made these more apparent?"

Lord Maccon reached forward and gently pulled her hand away from her face. Carefully he brought it down toward her other hand and then trapped both together in one big paw.

Miss Tarabotti blinked at him from a scarce few inches away.

She hardly dared breathe, not quite certain if he was *actually* going to eat her or not. She tried to look away, but it was nigh impossible. His eyes had turned back to tawny brown as soon as he touched her—his human eyes. But instead of being a relief, this color was more frightening because no threat masked the hunger there.

"Uh, my lord, I am not actually food. You do realize this, yes?"

Lord Maccon bent forward.

Alexia watched him until she went almost cross-eyed. This close, she could smell open fields and dark cold nights all about him.

Oh no, she thought, *it is happening again.*

Lord Maccon kissed the very tip of her nose. Nothing more.

Startled, she shied back, then opened her generous mouth, a bit like a fish. "Wha?"

He drew her back in toward him.

His voice was low and warm against her cheek. "Your age is not an issue. What does it matter to me how old or how much a spinster you may be? Do you have any idea how old I am, and how long a bachelor?" He kissed her temple. "And I love Italy. Beautiful countryside, fabulous food." He kissed her other temple. "And I find perfect beauty excessively boring, don't you?" He kissed her nose again.

Alexia could not help herself; she drew back and gave him the once-over. "Clearly."

He winced. "Touché."

Alexia was not one to let the matter drop. "Then why?"

Lord Maccon groveled. "Because I am a foolish old wolf who has been too long in the company of the pack and too little in the company of the rest of the world."

It was not an explanation, but Alexia decided she would have to settle for it. "That was an apology, was it?" she asked, just to make perfectly certain.

It seemed to have taken almost everything out of him. Instead of answering her in the affirmative, he stroked her face with his free hand, as though she were an animal that needed soothing. Alexia wondered what he thought of her as—a cat perhaps? Cats were not, in her experience, an animal with much soul. Prosaic, practical little creatures as a general rule. It would suit her very well to be thought catlike.

"Full moon," said Lord Maccon, as though this were some kind of clarification, "is just round the corner." A pause. "You understand?"

Miss Tarabotti had no idea what he was on about. "Uh . . ."

His voice dropped, low, almost ashamed. "Not much control."

Miss Tarabotti widened her dark brown eyes and batted her eyelashes to try and hide her perplexed expression. It was an Ivy maneuver.

Then he did kiss her properly and fully. Which was not exactly what she had intended by applying eyelash flapping, but she was not about to complain at the consequences. Ivy might be onto something.

As before, he started slowly, lulling her with soft drugging kisses. His mouth was unexpectedly cool. He ran a path of little fluttering nibbles over her lower lip and then applied the same treatment to her upper one. It was delightful but maddening. The tongue phenomenon occurred once again. This time, Alexia did not find it quite so startling. In fact, she thought she might even like it. But, like caviar, she suspected she'd have to try it more than once to be confident in her enjoyment. Lord Maccon seemed willing to oblige. He also appeared to be staying quite maddeningly calm and cool. Alexia was beginning to find the cluttered front parlor overly oppressive. This polarity annoyed her.

Lord Maccon stopped nibbling and went back to long soft kisses. Alexia, never one for patience, was now finding them entirely unsatisfying. A whole new source of annoyance. Clearly, she would have to take matters into her own hands—or tongue, as the case may be. Experimentally, she darted her tongue against his lips. That got a whole new agreeable reaction out of the man.

He deepened the kiss, almost roughly, angling his mouth over hers.

Lord Maccon shifted, drawing her closer. He let go of her hands and curved one of his up into her hair, tangling his fingers in the heavy curls. Alexia was certain, with a tiny modicum of offended sensibility, that he was probably mussing it up most dreadfully. He was using the maneuver to direct the angle of her head in harmony with his wishes. As his wishes appeared to prescribe further kissing, Alexia decided to let him have his way.

He began running his other hand up and down her back in long strokes. *Definitely a cat*, thought Alexia groggily. Her mind was becoming hazy. Those bizarre, sunshiny tingles that proximity to Lord Maccon seemed inevitably to produce were coursing through her body with alarming intensity.

The earl turned them both about where they stood. Alexia was not certain why, but she was inclined to cooperate so long as he did not stop kissing her. He did not. He arranged it so that he could sink slowly down onto the wingback armchair, taking her with him.

It was a most indelicate thing, but there Miss Alexia Tarabotti inexplicably found herself, bustle hiked up and all her layers of skirts askew, sitting in Lord Maccon's well-tailored lap.

He moved away from her lips, which was disappointing, but then began nibbling her neck, which was gratifying. He lifted one dark curl away from where the carefully arranged locks fell over one shoulder. He ran the strand between his fingertips and then pushed the silken mass aside.

Alexia tensed in anticipation, holding her breath.

Suddenly he stopped and jerked back. The wingback chair, already taxed by two occupants—neither of whom could be described as flimsy in physique—swayed alarmingly. "What the hell is that?" yelled Lord Maccon.

He had turned to anger so swiftly; Alexia could only stare at him, speechless.

She let out her pent-up breath in a *whoosh*. Her heart was beating a marathon somewhere in the region of her throat, her skin felt hot and stretched taut over her bones, and she was damp in places she was tolerably certain unmarried gentlewomen were not supposed to be damp in.

Lord Maccon was glaring at her coffee-colored skin, discolored between the neck and shoulder region by an ugly purple mark, the size and shape of a man's teeth.

Alexia blinked, and her brown eyes cleared of their dazed expression. A small crease of perturbation appeared between her brows.

"That is a bite mark, my lord," she said, pleased her voice was not shaking, though it was a little deeper than usual.

Lord Maccon was ever more enraged. "Who bit you?" he roared.

Alexia tilted her head to one side in utter amazement. "You did." She was then treated to the glorious spectacle of an Alpha werewolf looking downright hangdog.

"I did?"

She raised both eyebrows at him.

"I did."

She nodded, firmly, once.

Lord Maccon ran a distracted hand through his already messy hair. The dark brown strands stood up in small tufts. "Dog's bollocks," he said. "I am worse than a pup in his first season. I am sorry, Alexia. It is the moon and the lack of sleep."

Alexia nodded, wondering if she should point out that he had forgotten proper etiquette and used her first name. However, that seemed a little silly given their recent activities. "Yes, I see. Uh. What is?"

"This control."

She figured at some stage in the proceedings she might understand what was going on, but now did not seem to be that time. "What control?"

"Exactly!"

Miss Tarabotti narrowed her eyes and then said something very daring. "You could kiss the bruise and make it better." Well, perhaps not quite so daring for someone who was settled as intimately as she on Lord Maccon's lap. After all, she had read enough of her papa's books to know exactly what it was that pressed hard and flush against her nether regions.

Lord Maccon shook his head. "I do not think that is a very good idea."

"You do not?" Embarrassed by her own forwardness, Alexia squirmed against him, trying to extricate herself.

The earl swore and closed his eyes. There was a sheen of sweat on his brow.

Tentatively, Alexia squirmed again.

Lord Maccon groaned and leaned his head against her collarbone, clamping both hands about her hips to still the movement.

Alexia was scientifically intrigued. Had he gotten even larger down there? What was the maximum possible expansion ratio? she wondered. She grinned a tad maliciously. It had not occurred to her that she might have some sort of influence over the encounter. She decided then and there that, being a confirmed spinster and averse to allowing Mr. MacDougall his druthers, this might be her only chance to test some long-held and rather interesting theories.

"Lord Maccon," she whispered, squirming again despite his firm grip.

He snorted and said in a strangled voice, "I suspect you could get away with calling me by my given name at this juncture."

"Um?" said Alexia.

"Um, Conall," prompted Lord Maccon.

"Conall," she said, relinquishing the last hold on her scruples—once the egg was broken, might as well make an omelet with it. Then she got distracted by the feel of his back muscles under her hands. Hands that had run afoul of his coat and unceremoniously managed to strip it off him without her knowledge.

"Aye, Alexia?" He looked up at her. Was that fear in his caramel eyes?

"I am going to take advantage of you," she said, and without giving him a chance to reply, she began untying his cravat.

CHAPTER SEVEN

Revelations Over Chopped Liver

"Uh, probably not a good idea." Lord Maccon was panting a little.

"Hush, none of that, now," Miss Tarabotti admonished. "You started this."

"And it would be a devilish bad lot for all concerned were I to finish it," he said. "Or for you to finish it, for that matter." But he made no attempt to remove her from his lap. Instead, he seemed fascinated by the low neckline of her dress, which had sunk considerably during their exertions. One big hand was now tracing the lace frill tucked there, back and forth. Alexia wondered if he had a particular interest in ladies' fashions.

She dispensed with Lord Maccon's cravat, undid the buttons of his waistcoat and then those of his shirtwaist. "You are wearing entirely too much clothing," she complained.

Lord Maccon, who ordinarily could not agree more, was rather appreciative of it at the moment. Any additional time it took for her to undo buttons might give him back a modicum of restraint. He was sure his control was around somewhere, if he could simply find it. He tore his eyes away from the tops of those remarkable breasts of hers and tried to think unpleasant thoughts of particularly horrible things, like overcooked vegetables and cut-rate wine.

Alexia succeeded in her aim: peeling back Lord Maccon's clothing to expose his upper chest, shoulders, and neck. She had stopped kissing him for the moment. The earl considered that a godsend. He breathed a sigh of relief and looked up at her. Her expression seemed more one of avid curiosity than anything else.

Then Alexia bent forward and nibbled at his ear.

Lord Maccon writhed and let out an animal-in-pain sort of whimper. Alexia considered her experiment an unqualified success. Apparently what was good for the goose was, indeed, good for the gander.

She investigated further: moving along with little kisses down his throat and over his collarbone until she came to the same location on his neck that on hers was currently a decorative black and blue color. She bit him. Hard. Alexia never did anything by halves.

Lord Maccon almost reared right out of the armchair.

Alexia held on, teeth sinking into flesh. She did not want to draw blood, but she did intend to leave a mark and felt since he was a tough supernatural type, she had better do her worst. Any mark she left would not last long once they broke contact and he was out of her preternatural power. He tasted wonderful: of salt and meat—like gravy. She stopped biting and licked delicately at the red crescent-shaped brand she had left behind.

"Blast it all." Lord Maccon's breathing was very rapid. "We have got to stop."

Alexia nuzzled against him. "Why?"

"Because pretty bloody soon, I'm not going to be able to."

Alexia nodded. "I suppose that is sensible." She sighed. It felt like she had spent a lifetime being sensible.

The decision, it turned out, was taken away from them by some sort of commotion in the hallway.

"Well I never," said a lady's shocked voice.

Some quiet apologetic murmuring then ensued, the words of which were impossible to make out and probably emanated from Floote.

Then the woman issued forth once more, "In the front parlor?

Oh, here on BUR business, is he? I understand. Surely not . . ." The voice trailed off.

Someone knocked loudly on the parlor door.

Miss Tarabotti slid hurriedly off Lord Maccon's lap. Much to her surprise, her legs seemed to be working properly. She yanked her bustle back into position and hopped up and down hurriedly to shake her skirts back into place.

Lord Maccon, in the interest of time, simply buttoned the top of his shirtwaist and bottom of his waistcoat and jacket. But he seemed defeated in any effort to rapidly tie his cravat.

"Here, let me do that." Miss Tarabotti gestured him autocratic-ally over and tied it for him.

While she busied herself with an intricate knot, Lord Maccon tried, equally inexpertly, to fix her hair. His fingers brushed the bite mark on her lower neck.

"I am sorry about that," he said contritely.

"Do I detect an honest-to-goodness apology?" asked Alexia, but she smiled, still fiddling with his cravat. "I do not mind the bruise. What I mind is that I cannot produce the same." The bite mark she had given him only moments before had promptly vanished during the few seconds they separated while she straightened her dress. Then, she added, because Alexia never stayed silent when she ought, "These feelings you engender in me, my lord, are most indelicate. You should stop causing them immediately."

He gave her a quick look to assess the seriousness, and then, unable to determine if she was joking or not, remained silent.

Miss Tarabotti finished with the cravat. He had arranged her hair so that it at least covered all signs of his amorous attentions. She walked across the room to draw the curtains and look out the front window to see who might have arrived.

The knocking continued on the parlor door until finally it burst open.

Of all odd couples, Miss Ivy Hisselpenny and Professor Lyall entered the room.

Ivy was talking nonstop. She spotted Miss Tarabotti instantly and flitted over to her, looking like an excited hedgehog in a loud hat. "Alexia, my dear, did you know there was a BUR werewolf lurking in your hallway? When I came for tea, he was squaring off against your butler in a most threatening manner. I was terribly afraid there might be fisticuffs. Why would such a person be interested in visiting you? And why was Floote terribly set on keeping him away? And why . . . ?" She did not finish, having finally spotted Lord Maccon. Her large red and white striped shepherdess hat, with a curved yellow ostrich feather, quivered in agitation.

Lord Maccon was glaring at his second. "Randolph, you look awful. What are you doing here? I sent you home."

Professor Lyall took in his Alpha's disheveled appearance, wondering what atrocious thing had been done to his poor cravat. His eyes narrowed and shifted toward Miss Tarabotti's loose hair. However, Lyall had been Beta for three consecutive pack leaders, and he was nothing if not discreet. Instead of commenting or answering Lord Maccon's question, he simply walked over to the earl and whispered rapidly into his ear.

Miss Hisselpenny finally noticed her friend's tousled state. Solicitously, she urged Alexia to sit and took up residence next to her on the little settee. "Are you feeling quite well?" She removed her gloves and felt Alexia's forehead with the back of her hand. "You are very hot, my dear. Do you think you might be running a fever?"

Miss Tarabotti looked under her eyelashes at Lord Maccon. "That is one way of phrasing it."

Professor Lyall stopped whispering.

Lord Maccon's face flushed. He was newly upset about something. "They did *what*?" *Was he ever not upset?*

Whisper, whisper.

"Well, proud Mary's fat arse!" said the earl eloquently.

Miss Hisselpenny gasped.

Miss Tarabotti, who was getting very used to Lord Maccon's ribald mannerisms, snickered at her friend's shocked expression.

Issuing forth several additional creative statements of the gutter-born variety, the earl strode to the hat stand, shoved his brown topper unceremoniously on his head, and marched out of the room.

Professor Lyall shook his head and made a tut-tutting noise. "Fancy going out into public with a cravat like that."

The cravat in question, with head attached, reappeared in the doorway. "Watch her, Randolph. I will send Haverbink round to relieve you as soon as I get to the office. After he arrives, for all our sakes, go home and get some sleep. It is going to be a long night."

"Yes, sir," said Professor Lyall.

Lord Maccon disappeared once more, and they heard the Woolsey Castle carriage clattering off at a breakneck speed down the street.

Miss Tarabotti felt forsaken, bereft, and not entirely unworthy of the pitying glances Ivy was casting in her direction. What was it about kissing her that caused the Earl of Woolsey to feel it necessary to disappear with such rapidity?

Professor Lyall, looking uncomfortable, removed his hat and overcoat and hung them up on the stand just made vacant by vanished Lord Expletive. He then proceeded to check the room. What he was looking for, Alexia could not guess, but he did not seem to find it. The Loontwills kept to the height of what was required of a fashionable receiving parlor. It was greatly overfurnished, including an upright piano that none of the ladies of the house could play, and cluttered to capacity with small tables covered with embroidered drop cloths and crowded with assemblages of daguerreotypes, glass bottles with suspended model dirigibles, and other knickknacks. As he conducted his investigation, Professor Lyall avoided all contact with sunlight. In style since the supernatural set rose to prominence several centuries ago, the heavy velvet drapes over the front window nevertheless allowed some small amount of daylight to creep into the darkness. The Beta was fastidious in his avoidance of it.

Miss Tarabotti figured he must be very tired indeed to feel such ill effects. Older werewolves could go several days awake during the daytime. The professor must be pushing his time limit, or suffering some other ailment.

Miss Tarabotti and Miss Hisselpenny watched with polite curiosity as the urbane werewolf wandered about the room. He checked behind Felicity's insipid watercolors and underneath the infamous wingback armchair. Alexia blushed inwardly thinking about that chair and trying not to remember what had so recently occurred there. Had she really been so forward? Disgraceful.

When the silence became too unbearable, Miss Tarabotti said, "Do sit down, Professor. You look positively dead on your feet. You are making us dizzy wandering about the room like that."

Professor Lyall gave a humorless laugh but obeyed her order. He settled into a small Chippendale side chair, which he moved into the darkest recess of the room: a little nook near the piano.

"Should we order some tea?" Miss Hisselpenny asked, concern for both his peaked appearance and Alexia's obviously feverish condition outweighing all sense of propriety.

Miss Tarabotti was impressed by her friend's resource. "What an excellent notion."

Ivy went to the door to call for Floote, who magically appeared without needing to be summoned. "Miss Alexia is not feeling quite the thing and this gentleman here . . . " she faltered.

Alexia was appalled at her own lack of manners. "Ivy! You don't mean to say you have not been introduced? And here I thought you knew each other. You came in together."

Miss Hisselpenny turned to her friend. "We encountered one another on the front stoop, but we never formally made each other's acquaintance." She turned back to the butler. "I am sorry, Floote. What was I saying?"

"Tea, miss?" suggested the ever-resourceful Floote. "Will there be anything else, miss?"

Alexia asked from the couch, "Do we have any liver?"

"Liver, miss? I shall inquire of the cook."

"If we do, simply have her chop it small and serve it raw." Miss Tarabotti double-checked with a glance at Professor Lyall, who nodded gratefully.

Both Ivy and Floote looked aghast, but there seemed to be nothing they could do to gainsay Alexia's request. After all, in the absence of the Loontwills proper, this was Miss Tarabotti's house to rule over.

"And some jam and bread sandwiches," said Miss Tarabotti firmly. She felt a bit more composed, now that Lord Maccon had vacated the premises. Miss Tarabotti, once composed, was generally of a peckish proclivity.

"Very good, miss," said Floote, and glided off.

Alexia performed introductions. "Professor Lyall, this is Miss Ivy Hisselpenny, my dearest friend. Ivy, this is Professor Randolph Lyall, Lord Maccon's second in command and protocol adviser, so far as I can tell."

Lyall stood and bowed. Ivy curtsied from the doorway. Formalities over with, both returned to their seats.

"Professor, can you tell me what has occurred? Why did Lord Maccon depart in such haste?" Miss Tarabotti leaned forward and peered into the shadows. It was hard to read the professor's expression in the dim light, which gave him a decided advantage.

"Afraid not, Miss Tarabotti. BUR business." He shut her down shamelessly. "Not to worry, the earl should get it all sorted through in short order."

Alexia leaned back in the settee. Idly she picked up one of the many pink ribbon-embroidered cushions and began plucking at one of the tassels. "Then I wonder, sir, if I might ask you somewhat about pack protocol?"

Miss Hisselpenny's eyes went very wide, and she reached for her fan. When Alexia got that look in her eye, it meant her friend was about to say something shocking. Had Alexia been reading her father's books again? Ivy shuddered to even think such a thing. She always knew no good would come of those reprehensible manuscripts.

Professor Lyall, startled by this sudden switch in topic, looked uncomfortably at Miss Tarabotti.

"Oh, is it secret?" asked Alexia. One was never quite certain with the supernatural set. She knew there existed such concepts as pack protocol and pack etiquette, but sometimes these things were learned via cultural acumen and never taught or talked of openly. It was true that werewolves were more integrated into everyday society than vampires, but, still, one never knew unless one was actually a werewolf. Their traditions were, after all, much older than those of daylight folk.

Professor Lyall shrugged elegantly. "Not necessarily. I should caution, however, that pack rules are often quite blunt and not necessarily intended for a lady of Miss Hisselpenny's delicacy."

Alexia grinned at him. "As opposed to mine?" she asked, putting him on the spot.

The professor was not to be trifled with. "My dear Miss Tarabotti, you are nothing if not resilient."

Ivy, blushing furiously, spread open her fan and began fluttering it to cool her hot face. The fan was bright red Chinese silk with yellow lace at its edge, clearly selected to match the reprehensible shepherdess hat. Alexia rolled her eyes. Was Ivy's dubious taste now extending to *all* her accessories?

The fan seemed to give Miss Hisselpenny some courage. "Please," she insisted, "do not forbear needlessly on my account."

Miss Tarabotti smiled approvingly and patted her friend on the upper arm before turning expectantly back to face Professor Lyall in his darkened corner. "Shall I come to the point, Professor? Lord Maccon's manners have been highly bewildering of late. He has made several"—she paused delicately—"interesting incursions in my direction. These began, as you no doubt observed, in the public street the other evening."

"Oh, dear Alexia!" breathed Miss Hisselpenny, truly shaken. "You do not mean to tell me you were *observed*!"

Miss Tarabotti dismissed her friend's concern. "Only by

Professor Lyall here, so far as I am aware, and he is the soul of discretion."

Professor Lyall, though clearly pleased by her accolade, said, "Not to be rude, Miss Tarabotti, but your aspect of pack protocol is . . . ?"

Alexia sniffed. "I am getting there. You must understand, Professor Lyall, this is a smidgen embarrassing. You must permit me to broach the matter in a slightly roundabout manner."

"Far be it for me to require directness from *you*, Miss Tarabotti," replied the werewolf in a tone of voice Alexia felt might be bordering rudely on sarcasm.

"Yes, well, anyway," she continued huffily. "Only last night at a dinner event we both attended, Lord Maccon's behavior gave me to understand the previous evening's entanglement had been a . . . mistake."

Miss Hisselpenny gave a little gasp of astonishment. "Oh," she exclaimed, "how *could* he!"

"Ivy," said Miss Tarabotti a touch severely, "pray let me finish my story before you judge Lord Maccon too harshly. That is, after all, for me to do." Somehow Alexia could not endure the idea that her friend might be thinking ill of the earl.

Alexia continued. "This afternoon, I returned home to find him waiting for me in this very parlor. He seems to have changed his mind once again. I am becoming increasingly confused." Miss Tarabotti glared at the hapless Beta. "And I do not appreciate this kind of uncertainty!" She put down the ribbon pillow.

"Has he gone and botched things up again?" asked the professor.

Floote entered with the tea tray. At a loss for what proper etiquette required, the butler had placed the raw liver in a cut-glass ice-cream dish. Professor Lyall did not seem to care in what form it was presented. He ate it rapidly but delicately with a small copper ice-cream spoon.

Floote served the tea and then disappeared once more from the room.

Miss Tarabotti finally arrived at the point. "Why did he treat me with such hauteur last night and then with such solicitude today? Is there some obscure point of pack lore in play here?" She sipped her tea to hide her nervousness.

Lyall finished his chopped liver, set the empty ice-cream dish on the piano top, and looked at Miss Tarabotti. "Would you say that initially Lord Maccon made his interest clear?" he asked.

"Well," hedged Miss Tarabotti, "we have known each other for a few years now. Before the street incident, I would say his attitude has been one of apathy."

Professor Lyall chuckled. "*You* did not hear his comments after those encounters. However, I did mean more recently."

Alexia put down her teacup and started using her hands as she talked. It was one of the few Italian mannerisms that had somehow crept into her repertoire, despite the fact that she had barely known her father. "Well, yes," she said, spreading her fingers expansively, "but then again, not decisively. I realize I am a little old and plain for long-term romantic interest, especially from a gentleman of Lord Maccon's standing, but if he was offering claviger status, oughtn't I to be informed? And isn't it impossible for . . ." She glanced at Ivy, who did not know she was a preternatural. She did not even know that preternatural folk existed. "For someone as lacking in creativity as me to be a claviger? I do not know what to think. I cannot believe his overtures represent a courtship. So when he recently ignored me, I assumed the incident in the street had been a colossal mistake."

Professor Lyall sighed again. "Yes, that. How do I put this delicately? My estimable Alpha has been thinking of you instinctively, I am afraid, not logically. He has been perceiving you as he would an Alpha female werewolf."

Miss Hisselpenny frowned. "Is that complimentary?"

Seeing the empty ice-cream dish, Miss Tarabotti handed Professor Lyall a cup of tea.

Lyall sipped the beverage delicately, raising his eyebrows from behind the lip of the cup. "For an Alpha male? Yes. For the rest of us, I suspect, not quite so much. But there is a reason."

"Go on, please," urged Miss Tarabotti, intrigued.

Lyall continued. "When he would not admit his interest even to himself, his instincts took over."

Miss Tarabotti, who had a brief but scandalous vision of Lord Maccon's *instincts* urging him to do things such as throw her bodily over one shoulder and drag her off into the night, returned to reality with a start. "So?"

Miss Hisselpenny said to her friend, looking at Lyall for support, "It is an issue of *control*?"

"Very perceptive, Miss Hisselpenny." The professor looked with warm approval at Ivy, who blushed with pleasure.

Miss Tarabotti felt as though she was beginning to understand. "At the dinner party, he was waiting for *me* to make overtures?" She almost squeaked in shock. "But he was flirting! With a . . . a . . . Wibbley!"

Professor Lyall nodded. "Thereby trying to increase your interest—force you to stake a claim, indicate pursuit, or assert possession. Preferably all three."

Both Miss Tarabotti and Miss Hisselpenny were quite properly shocked into silence at the very idea. Though Alexia was less appalled than perturbed. After all, had she not *just* discovered, in this very room, the depth of her own interest in equalizing the male–female dynamic? She supposed if she could bite Lord Maccon on the neck and regret that she left no lasting mark, she might be able to claim him publicly.

"In pack protocol, we call it the Bitch's Dance," Professor Lyall explained. "You are, you will forgive my saying so, Miss Tarabotti, simply *too much* Alpha."

"I am not an Alpha," protested Miss Tarabotti, standing up and pacing about. Clearly, her father's library had failed her entirely on the niceties and mating habits of werewolves.

Lyall looked at her—hands on hips, full-figured, assertive. He smiled. "There are not many female werewolves, Miss Tarabotti.

The Bitch's Dance refers to liaisons among the pack: *the female's* choice."

Miss Hisselpenny maintained an appalled silence. The very idea was utterly alien to her upbringing.

Miss Tarabotti mulled it over. She found she liked the idea. She had always secretly admired the vampire queens their superior position in hive structure. She did not know werewolves had something similar. *Did Alpha females*, she wondered, *trump males outside the romantic arena as well?* "Why?" she asked.

Lyall explained. "It *has* to be up to the female, with so few of them and so many of us. There is no battling over a female allowed. Werewolves rarely live more than a century or two because of all the in-fighting. The laws are strict and enforced by the dewan himself. It is entirely the bitch's choice every step of the dance."

"So, Lord Maccon was waiting for me to go to him." Miss Tarabotti realized for the first time how strange it must be for the older supernatural folk to adjust to the changing social norms of Queen Victoria's daylight world. Lord Maccon always seemed to have such things well in hand. It had not even occurred to Alexia that he had made a mistake in his behavior toward her. "Then what of his conduct today?"

Miss Hisselpenny sucked in a gasp. "What did he do?" She shivered in delighted horror.

Miss Tarabotti promised to tell her the particulars later. Although this time, she suspected, she would not be able to reveal every detail. Things had progressed a little too far for someone of Ivy's delicate sensibilities. If merely looking at that wingback chair could make Alexia blush, it would certainly be too much for her dear friend.

Professor Lyall coughed. Miss Tarabotti believed he was doing so to hide amusement. "That may have been my fault. I spoke to him most severely, reminding him to treat you as a modern British lady, not a werewolf."

"Mmm," said Miss Tarabotti, still contemplating the wingback chair, "perhaps a little too modern?"

Professor Lyall's eyebrows went all the way up, and he leaned a little out of the shadows toward her.

"Alexia," said Miss Hisselpenny most severely, "you must force him to make his intentions clear. Persisting in this kind of behavior could cause quite the scandal."

Miss Tarabotti thought of her preternatural state and her father, who was reputed to have been quite the philanderer before his marriage. *You have no idea*, she almost said.

Miss Hisselpenny continued. "I mean to say, not that one could *bear* to think such a thing, but it must be said, it really must . . ." She looked most distressed. "What if he only intends to offer you *carte blanche*?" Her eyes were big and sympathetic. Ivy was intelligent enough to know, whether she liked to acknowledge it or not, what Alexia's prospects really were. Practically speaking, they could not include marriage to someone of Lord Maccon's standing, no matter how romantic her imagination.

Alexia knew Ivy did not intend to be cruel, but she was hurt nonetheless. She nodded glumly.

Professor Lyall, whose sensitivities were touched by Miss Tarabotti's suddenly sad eyes, said, "I cannot believe my lord's intentions are anything less than honorable."

Miss Tarabotti smiled, wobbly. "That is kind of you to say, Professor. Still, it seems as though I am faced with a dilemma. Respond as your pack protocol dictates"—she paused seeing Ivy's eyes widen—"risking my reputation with ruination and ostracism. Or deny everything and maintain as I have always done."

Miss Hisselpenny took Miss Tarabotti's hand and squeezed it sympathetically. Alexia squeezed back and then spoke as though trying to convince herself. She was, after all, soulless and practical. "Mine is not precisely a bad life. I have material wealth and good health. Perhaps I am not useful nor beloved by my family, but I have never suffered unduly. And I have my books." She paused, finding herself perilously close to self-pity.

Professor Lyall and Miss Hisselpenny exchanged glances. Something passed between them. Some silent pact of purpose to do . . . Ivy knew not what. But, whatever the future, Miss Hisselpenny was certainly glad to have Professor Lyall on her side.

Floote appeared in the doorway. "A Mr. Haverbink to see you, Miss Tarabotti."

Mr. Haverbink entered the room, shutting the door behind him.

Professor Lyall said, "Forgive me not standing, Haverbink. Too many days running."

"Not a worry, sir, not a bit of it." Mr. Haverbink was an extraordinarily large and thuglike man of working-class extraction. What origins his cultivated speech left in doubt, his physical appearance demonstrated. He was the type of good farming stock that, when the oxen collapsed from exhaustion, picked up the plow, strapped himself to it, and finished tilling the fields by hand.

Miss Tarabotti and Miss Hisselpenny had never before seen so many muscles on one individual. His neck was the size of a tree. Both ladies were suitably impressed.

Professor Lyall made introductions. "Ladies, Mr. Haverbink. Mr. Haverbink, this is Miss Hisselpenny, and this is Miss Tarabotti, your charge."

"Oh!" said Ivy. "You are from BUR?"

Mr. Haverbink nodded affably. "Aye, miss."

"But you are not . . . ?" Miss Tarabotti could not tell how she knew. Perhaps it was because he seemed so relaxed in the bright sunlight or because how grounded and earthy he seemed. He showed none of the dramatic flair one expects with excess soul.

"A werewolf? No, miss. Not interested in being a claviger either, so I shan't ever become one. Gone up against a couple in the boxing ring once or twice, so do not worry yourself on that account. Besides, the boss does not seem to think we will have trouble from that quarter, leastways not during the daytime."

Professor Lyall stood slowly. He looked bent and old, his mercurial face thin and drawn.

Mr. Haverbink turned to him solicitously. "Begging your pardon, sir, but his lordship gave me strict instructions to see you into the carriage and off to the castle. He has got the situation well in hand back at the office."

Professor Lyall, nearly to the point of utter exhaustion, made his way haltingly to the door.

The hugely muscled young man looked like he would prefer to simply pick the Beta up and carry him out to the street, relieving the werewolf of his obvious distress. But, showing that he did indeed have experience working with the supernatural set, he respected his superior's pride and did not even try to assist him with an arm.

Polite to the last, Professor Lyall collected his hat and coat, donned both, and bowed his farewell from the parlor doorway. Alexia and Ivy were afraid he might topple right over, but he righted himself and made it out the front door and into the Woolsey Castle carriage with only a few stumbles here and there.

Mr. Haverbink saw him safely on his way and then came back into the parlor. "I'll be just out the front by yon lamppost if you need me, miss," he said to Miss Tarabotti. "I'm on duty until sundown, and then there'll be three vampires in rotation all night long. His lordship is not taking any chances. Not after what just happened."

Though dying of curiosity, Ivy and Alexia knew better than to hound the young man with questions. If Professor Lyall would not tell them anything about what had taken the earl away so suddenly, this man would be equally unforthcoming.

Mr. Haverbink bowed deeply, muscles rippling all up and down his back, and lumbered from the room.

Miss Hisselpenny sighed and fluttered her fan. "Ah, for the countryside, what scenery there abides . . . " quoth she.

Miss Tarabotti giggled. "Ivy, what a positively wicked thing to say. Bravo."

CHAPTER EIGHT

Backyard Shenanigans

The Loontwills returned from their shopping expedition flushed with success. Except for Squire Loontwill, who was now less flush than he had been and wore an expression more often seen on men returning from battle—one that had been badly lost with many casualties. Floote appeared at his elbow with a large glass of cognac. The squire muttered something about Floote-liness being next to godliness and downed the liquor in one gulp.

No one was surprised to find Miss Tarabotti entertaining Miss Hisselpenny in the front parlor. The squire muttered a greeting only just long enough to satisfy politeness and then retreated to his office with a second glass of cognac and the mandate that he was not to be disturbed for any reason.

The ladies Loontwill greeted Miss Hisselpenny in a far more verbose manner and insisted on showing off all of their purchases.

Miss Tarabotti had the presence of mind to send Floote for more tea. It was clearly going to be a long afternoon.

Felicity pulled out a leather box and lifted the lid. "Look at these. Are they not utterly divine? Do you not wish you had some just like?" Lying in scrumptious grandeur on a bed of black velvet was a pair of lace elbow-length evening gloves in pale moss green with tiny mother-of-pearl buttons up the sides.

"Yes," agreed Alexia, because they were. "But you do not own an evening gown to match, do you?"

Felicity waggled her eyebrows excitedly. "Very perceptive, my dear sister, but I do now." She grinned in a most indecorous manner.

Miss Tarabotti thought she could understand her stepfather's deathly pallor. An evening gown to match such gloves would cost a small fortune, and whatever Felicity purchased, Evylin must have in equal value. Evylin proved this universal law by proudly displaying her own new evening gloves in silvery blue satin with rose-colored flowers embroidered about the edge.

Miss Hisselpenny was considerably impressed by such largesse. Her family's means did not extend into the realm of embroidered gloves and new evening gowns on a whim.

"The dresses are due next week," said Mrs. Loontwill proudly, as though her two daughters had accomplished something marvelous. "Just in time for Almack's, we hope." She looked down her nose at Ivy. "Will you be attending, Miss Hisselpenny?"

Alexia bridled at her mother, who was perfectly well aware that the Hisselpennys were not of a quality suitable to such an illustrious event. "And what new dress will you be wearing, Mama?" she asked sharply. "Something appropriate, or your customary style—a gown better suited to a lady half your age?"

"Alexia!" hissed Ivy, truly shocked.

Mrs. Loontwill turned flinty eyes on her eldest daughter. "Regardless of what I am wearing, it is clear *you* will not be there to see it." She stood. "Nor, I think, will you be permitted to attend the duchess's rout tomorrow evening." With that punishment, she swept from the room.

Felicity's eyes were dancing with merriment. "You are perfectly correct, of course. The gown she picked out is daringly low-cut, frilly, *and* pale pink."

"But really, Alexia, you should not say such things to your own mother," insisted Ivy.

"Who else should I say them to?" Alexia grumbled under her breath.

"Exactly, and why not?" Evylin wanted to know. "No one else will. Soon Mama's behavior will affect our chances." She gestured to Felicity and herself. "And *we* do not intend to end up old maids. No offense meant, my dear sister."

Alexia smiled. "None taken."

Floote appeared with fresh tea, and Miss Tarabotti gestured him over. "Floote, send my card round to Auntie Augustina, would you please? For tomorrow night."

Evylin and Felicity looked only mildly interested at this. They had no aunt named Augustina, but a meeting organized for a full-moon night with a personage of such a name must be a fortune-telling of some kind. Clearly, Alexia, unexpectedly and cruelly confined to the house by their mother's anger, must organize some kind of entertainment for herself.

Ivy was not so foolish as that. She gave Alexia a what-are-you-up-to? look.

Alexia only smiled enigmatically.

Floote nodded grimly and went off to do as he was bid.

Felicity changed the subject. "Have you heard? They are making jewelry out of this fantastic new lightweight metal—allum-ninny-um or something. It does not tarnish like silver. Of course, it is very dear at the moment, and Papa would not allow for the purchase of any." She pouted.

Miss Tarabotti perked up. Her scientific papers had been all agog over new ways of processing this metal, discovered twenty or so years ago. "Aluminum," she said. "I have read about it in several Royal Society publications. It has finally debuted in the London shops, has it? How splendid! You know, it is nonmagnetic, nonaetheric, and anticorrosive."

"It is what and what?" Felicity bit her bottom lip in confusion.

"Oh dear," said Evylin, "there she goes, no stopping her now. Oh, why did I have to have a bluestocking for a sister?"

Miss Hisselpenny stood. "Ladies," she said, "you really must excuse me. I should be getting on."

The Miss Loontwills nodded.

"Quite right. That is how we feel when she goes all scientific-ish as well," said Evylin with feeling.

"Only we have to live with her, so we cannot escape," added Felicity.

Ivy looked embarrassed. "No, really, it is simply that I must get home. My mother was expecting me a half hour ago."

Miss Tarabotti accompanied her friend to the door. Floote appeared with the offensive shepherdess hat, all white striped, red trim, and yellow ostrich glory. Alexia disgustedly tied it under Ivy's chin.

Looking out into the street, the two ladies observed Mr. Haverbink hovering across the way. Alexia gave him a tiny wave. He nodded to them politely.

Ivy flicked open her red parasol. "You never did intend to attend the duchess's rout tomorrow night at all, did you?"

Miss Tarabotti grinned. "You have caught me out."

"Alexia." Ivy's voice was deeply suspicious. "Who is Auntie Augustina?"

Miss Tarabotti laughed. "I believe you once referred to the individual in question as 'outrageous' and disapproved of our association."

Ivy closed her eyes in horror for a long moment. She had been thrown off by the gender switch, but that was simply the kind of code Alexia and her butler used around the Loontwills. "Twice in one week!" she said, shocked. "People will begin to talk. They will think you are turning into a drone." She looked thoughtfully at her friend. A practical, statuesque, stylish woman, not the type vampires usually went in for. But then, everyone knew: Lord Akeldama was no ordinary vampire. "You are not actually taking up as a drone, are you? That is a very big decision."

Not for the first time, Alexia wished she could tell Ivy about her true nature. It was not that she did not trust Miss Hisselpenny; it was simply that she did not trust Miss Hisselpenny's tongue not to run away with her at an inopportune moment.

In answer, she said only, "You have no idea how impossible that is, my dear. Do not worry. I will be perfectly fine."

Miss Hisselpenny did not look reassured. She pressed her friend's hand briefly and then walked off down the street, shaking her head softly. The long curling yellow ostrich feather swished back and forth like the tail of an angry cat—the motion of her disapproval.

Only Ivy, thought Alexia, *could emit censure in such a sunny and fluffy manner.*

Miss Tarabotti returned to the tender mercies of her half sisters and prepared herself for an evening of familial bliss.

Miss Tarabotti was awakened in the small hours of the night by the most phenomenal ruckus. It seemed to be emanating from just below her bedroom window. She crept out of bed, throwing a white muslin pelisse over her nightgown, and went to see what was occurring.

Her window, as it belonged to one of the less prestigious rooms of the house, looked out over the servants' kitchen entrance and into a back alley where tradesmen made their deliveries.

The moon, only one night away from being full, illuminated the struggling forms of several men below her with a silvery sheen. They were apparently engaged in a bout of fisticuffs. Alexia was fascinated. They seemed evenly matched and fought mostly in silence, which lent a decided aura of menace to the proceedings. The noise that had awakened her was apparently caused by a dustbin overturning; otherwise, only the sound of flesh hitting flesh and a few muffled grunts rent the air.

Alexia saw one man strike out hard. His punch landed full in the face of one of the others. It was a palpable hit that ought to have set the second man flat. Instead, the opponent whipped around and hit back, using the momentum of his own spin. The sound of fist on skin echoed through the alleyway, an unpleasantly wet thudding.

Only a supernatural could take a hit like that and remain unfazed. Miss Tarabotti remembered Professor Lyall saying there would be vampires guarding her tonight. Was she witnessing a vampire-on-vampire battle? Despite the danger, she was excited by this idea. Rarely was such a thing to be seen, for while werewolves often brawled, vampires generally preferred subtler methods of confrontation.

She leaned out her window, trying to get a better look. One of the men broke free and headed toward her, looking up. His blank eyes met hers, and Alexia knew that he was no vampire.

She bit back a scream of horror, no longer fascinated by the battle below. It was a visage she had seen before: the wax-faced man from her botched abduction. In the light of the moon, his skin had a dull metallic sheen like pewter, so smooth and lifeless she shuddered in abject revulsion. The letters still marked his forehead, sootlike, VIXI. He saw her, pale nightgown against the darkened interior of the slumbering house, and grinned. As before, it was like no grin she had ever seen, a slashed unnatural opening full of perfect square white teeth, splitting across his head as a tomato will split when it is dropped into boiling water.

He ran toward her. A smooth three stories of brick lay between them, yet somehow Alexia knew there was no safety in that.

One of the other men broke away from the fighting group and sprinted after her attacker. Alexia doubted he would arrive in time. The wax-faced man moved with utter efficiency and economy of motion, less a man running than a water snake slithering.

But his pursuer clearly was a vampire, and as Miss Tarabotti watched, she realized she had never before seen a vampire run at full speed. He was all liquid grace, his fine Hessian boots making only a buzzlike whispering on the cobblestones.

The wax-faced man reached the Loontwills' house and began to climb up the brick side. Unhindered, spiderlike, he oozed up the wall. That utterly expressionless face of his remained tilted up at Alexia. It was as though he were hypnotized by her face, fixated on her and only her. VIXI. She read the letters over and over and over again. VIXI.

I do not want to die, thought Alexia. *I have not yet yelled at Lord Maccon for his most recent crass behavior!* Thrown into a panic, she was just reaching to slam her shutters closed, knowing they were but flimsy protection from such a creature, when the vampire struck.

Her supernatural protector leaped up and forward, landing on the wax-faced man's back. He grabbed the creature's head and yanked it around, hard. Either the added weight or the yank caused the wax-faced man to let go of the brick wall. They both fell, landing with a horrendous bone-crunching crash in the alley below. Neither screamed nor spoke, even after such a fall. Their companions continued their equally silent battle behind them, without pausing to observe the tumble.

Miss Tarabotti was certain the wax-faced man must be dead. He had fallen nearly an entire story, and only supernatural folk could survive such an experience unscathed. As no werewolf or vampire would ever look the way the wax-faced man looked, he must, perforce, be some kind of normal human.

Her supposition was in error, for the wax-faced man rolled about on top of the vampire's fallen form and then sprang once more to his feet, turned, and single-mindedly headed back toward the house. And Alexia.

The vampire, hurt but not incapacitated, anticipated this move and had an iron grip with both hands on one of the wax-faced man's legs. Instead of trying to fight off the vampire, the man behaved in an entirely illogical manner. He simply kept jerking in Alexia's direction, like a child denied a treat and incapable of being distracted by anything else. He dragged the vampire behind him by slow degrees. Every time he surged toward her, Alexia flinched, even though she was high above him in her third-story room.

Impasse reigned. The fight in the alley beyond seemed evenly matched, and the wax-faced man could not get to Alexia so long as the vampire held on to his leg.

The sound of heavy-booted footsteps and a sharp, high-pitched whistle rent the night air. Running around the corner of the back street came two constables. Rows of protective silver and wooden straight pins decorated the front of their uniforms, gleaming in the moonlight. One of them held an Adam's cross pistol, cocked and loaded with a deadly sharp wooden stake. The other held a Colt Lupis revolver, the silver-bullet-slinger out of America—only the best from that most superstitious of countries. Upon seeing the nature of the participants, he put the Colt away and pulled out a large wooden policeman's baton stake instead.

One of the men fighting in the alley yelled something sharp and commanding in Latin. Then he and his companion ran off, presumably leaving only BUR agents behind. The wax-faced man stopped jerking toward Alexia's window. Instead, he turned on the hapless fallen vampire and lashed out at the supernatural man's face. There was a scrunch of breaking bone. Still, the vampire would not let go. The wax-faced man stepped inward, put all his weight on his trapped leg, and then shifted downward with his free foot, slamming the vampire's wrists with all his might. Alexia heard another ghastly wet crunching sound. With both wrists shattered, the vampire was forced to relax his grip. With one final, emotionless grin up at Alexia, the wax-faced man turned and raced away, battering through the two policemen as though they were not even there. The one with the cross pistol got off an excellent shot, but the wooden bullet did not even cause the wax man to stumble.

Alexia's vampire protector stood, shaky. His nose was broken, and his wrists hung limply, but when he looked up at Miss Tarabotti, his face was full of satisfaction. Alexia winced in sympathy at the blood spattered over his cheeks and chin. She knew he would heal quickly enough, especially if they could get him to fresh blood soon, but she could not help feeling empathy for his current pain, which must be acute.

A stranger, Alexia realized, a vampire, had just saved her from she knew not what unpleasantness. Saved *her*, a preternatural. She put her hands together and raised her fingertips to her lips, bowing forward in a silent prayer of thanks. The vampire nodded acknowledgment and then motioned her to step back inside the bedroom.

Miss Tarabotti nodded and retreated into the shadows of her sleeping chamber.

"What's going on here, then, me lad?" she heard one constable ask as she closed the shutters firmly behind her.

"Attempted burglary, I believe, sir," the vampire replied.

A sigh came from the constable. "Well, let me see your registration papers, please." To the other vampires, "And yours as well, please, gentlemen."

Miss Tarabotti had an understandably difficult time getting back to sleep after that, and when she finally managed it, her dreams were full of vampires with lifeless faces and shattered wrists who kept turning multiple Lord Maccons into wax statues tattooed with the word VIXI over and over again.

Miss Tarabotti's family was unexpectedly en masse and entirely in an uproar when she arose for breakfast the next morning. Usually this was the calmest time of day, with Squire Loontwill up first, Alexia second, and the remainder of the household a distant third. But, due to the excitement of the night, Miss Tarabotti was the last to awaken. She deduced she must be uncommonly late indeed, for when she went down the stairs, it was to find that her nearest and dearest were crowded in the hallway rather than the breakfast room.

Her mother came toward her, wringing her hands and looking more than usually dippy. "Fix your hair, Alexia, do, dear, do. Hurry! He has been waiting for nearly an hour. He is in the front parlor. Of course the front; nowhere else would do at all. He would not let us wake you. Lord knows why he wants to see *you*, but no one else will do. I hope it is not official business. You have not been *up* to anything, have you, Alexia?" Mrs. Loontwill left off wringing her hands to flutter them about her head like a herd of excited butterflies.

"He ate three cold roast chickens," said Felicity in a shocked voice. "Three, at breakfast time!" She spoke as though she was not certain which to be more offended by, the quantity or the hour.

"And he still does not look happy," added Evylin, big blue eyes even bigger and bluer than usual in awe.

"He arrived unfashionably early and did not even want to talk with Papa, and Papa was *willing* to visit with him." Felicity was impressed.

Alexia peeked in the hallway mirror and patted her hair into place. Today she had dealt with the bruises on her neck by donning a teal paisley shawl over her black and silver day dress. The shawl's pattern clashed with the geometric design trimming the fold of the dress, and it covered over the flattering square neckline of the bodice, but some things could not be helped.

Seeing nothing at all wrong with her hair, except that perhaps the simple knot was a bit old-fashioned, she turned to her mother. "Please calm yourself, Mama. *Who* exactly is waiting in the parlor?"

Mrs. Loontwill ignored the question, hustling her eldest daughter down the hall as though she were a blue frilly sheepdog and Alexia a reluctant black sheep.

Alexia opened the door to the parlor and, when her mother and sisters would have followed her inside, shut it firmly and unceremoniously in their faces.

The Earl of Woolsey was sitting in stony silence on the sofa farthest from the window, with the carcasses of three chickens on silver platters before him.

Before she could prevent herself, Miss Tarabotti grinned at him. He simply looked so bashful, with all those chickens, like poultry skeleton sentries, standing guard before him.

"Ah," said the earl, raising one hand as though to ward off her smile. "None of that, Miss Tarabotti. Business first."

Miss Tarabotti would have been crestfallen, except for the "first." She also remembered Professor Lyall's words. She was supposed to make the next move in this little dance of theirs. So, instead of taking offense, she lowered her eyelashes, filed her smile away for later, and took a seat near to him but not too near.

"Well, what brings you to call on me this morning, then, my lord? You certainly have thrown the Loontwill household into a tizzy." She tilted her head to one side and strove for cool politeness.

"Um, aye, apologies for that." He looked abashedly at the chicken carcasses. "Your family, they are a bit, well"—he paused, hunting for the right word and then appearing to have come up with a new one of his own—"fibberty-jibbitus, are they not?"

Alexia's dark eyes twinkled at him. "You noticed? Imagine having to live with them all the time."

"I'd as soon not, thank you. Though it certainly speaks highly of your strength of character," he said, smiling unexpectedly. The expression suffused his normally cross face.

Miss Tarabotti's breath caught. Until that moment, she had not actually thought of the earl as pretty. But when he smiled. Oh dear, it was most inconvenient to deal with. Particularly before breakfast. She wondered what exactly was entailed in her making a *first move*.

She removed her paisley shawl.

Lord Maccon, who had been about to speak, paused, arrested midthought by the low neckline of the dress. The stark silver and black coloration of the material brought out the creamy undertones of her Mediterranean skin. "That dress will make your complexion come over all tan," Mrs. Loontwill had criticized when she ordered it. But Lord Maccon liked that. It was delightfully exotic: the contrast of that stylish dress and the foreign tones of her complexion.

"It is unseasonably warm this morning, wouldn't you say?" said Miss Tarabotti, putting her wrap to one side in a way that caused her torso to dip forward slightly.

Lord Maccon cleared his throat and managed to track down what he had been about to say. "Yesterday afternoon, while you and I were . . . otherwise engaged, someonc broke into BUR headquarters."

Miss Tarabotti's mouth fell open. "This cannot possibly be good. Was anyone grievously injured? Have you caught the culprits? Was anything of value stolen?"

Lord Maccon sighed. Trust Miss Tarabotti to get straight to the meat of the issue. He answered her questions in order. "Not seriously. No. And mostly rove vampire and loner wolf files. Some of the more detailed research documentation also vanished, and . . ." He looked upset, pursing his lips.

Miss Tarabotti was worried more by his expression than by his words. She had never seen the earl with a look of such worry on his face. "And?" she prompted, sitting forward anxiously.

"Your files."

"Ah." She leaned back.

"Lyall returned to the office to check on something or other, even though I had ordered him home to bed, only to find all those on duty insensate."

"Good gracious, how?"

"Well, there was not a mark on them, but they were quite solidly asleep. He checked the office and found it ransacked and those certain records stolen. That was when he came to alert me here. I verified his information, although, by the time I arrived, everyone was awake once more."

"Chloroform?" suggested Alexia.

The earl nodded. "That does seem to be the case. He said a lingering scent was on the air. It would have taken quite a considerable amount of it too. Few have access to such a quantity of the chemical. I have all available agents tracking major scientific and medical institutions for any recent orders for large shipments of chloroform, but my resources are always taxed at full moon."

Alexia looked thoughtful. "There are a number of such organizations around London these days, are there not?"

Lord Maccon shifted toward her, his eyes soft caramel and affectionate. "You can see that there is further concern for your safety? Before, we could assume that they did not know exactly *what* you were, they thought you just an interfering daylighter. Now they know you are a preternatural, and they know it means you can neutralize the supernatural. They will want to dissect you and understand this."

Lord Maccon hoped to impress upon Miss Tarabotti the full range of the danger. She could be very stubborn over these kinds of things. Tonight, being full moon, neither he nor his pack could keep watch over her. He trusted his other BUR agents, even the vampires, but they were not pack, and a werewolf could not help whom he trusted most. That would always be pack. But no werewolf could guard on full moon—all the human parts of them vanished in the space of one night. In fact, he himself should not even be outside right now. He should be home safe and asleep, with his claviger handlers keeping an eye on everything. Especially, he realized, he should not be around Alexia Tarabotti, whom, like it or not, his carnal urges had taken an overly proprietary interest in. There was a reason werewolf couples were locked in the same cell together on full moon. Everyone else had to take solitary vigil in bestial form, vicious and relentless, but passion was passion and could be channeled into more pleasurable and slightly less violent pursuits, so long as the female was equally cursed and so able to survive the experience. *How*, he wondered, *would it be to weather the moon in human form, held there by the touch of a preternatural lover?* What an experience that would be. His baser instincts urged such musings on, driven by the damnable neckline of Miss Tarabotti's dress.

Lord Maccon picked up the paisley shawl and shoved it at Alexia's chest area. "Put that back on," he ordered gruffly.

Miss Tarabotti, instead of taking offense, smiled serenely, lifted the garment from his grasp, and placed it carefully behind her and out of his reach.

She turned back and, greatly daring, took one of his large rough hands in both of hers.

"You are worried for my safety, which is sweet, but your guards were most efficacious last night. I have no doubt they will be equally competent this evening."

He nodded. He did not withdraw his hand from her tentative touch but turned it to curl about hers. "They reported the incident to me just before dawn."

Alexia shivered. "Do you know who he is?"

"He who?" asked the earl, sounding like a donkey. Absentmindedly, he ran his thumb over her wrist in a reassuring caress.

"The wax-faced man," said Miss Tarabotti, eyes glazed with memory and fear.

"No. Not human, not supernatural, not preternatural," he said. "A medical experiment gone astray, perhaps? He *is* filled with blood."

She was startled. "How would you know such a thing?"

He explained. "The fight, at the carriage? When they tried to abduct you. I bit him; do you not recall?"

She nodded, remembering the way the earl had only changed his head into wolf form and how he had wiped the blood from his face onto his sleeve.

One shapely male lip curled in disgust. "That meat was not fresh."

Alexia shuddered. *No, not fresh.* She did not like to think of the wax man and his compatriots having *her* personal information. She knew Lord Maccon would do his best to see her protected. And, of course, last night had proved that these mysterious enemies knew where to find her, so nothing had fundamentally changed with the theft of the BUR papers. But now that the wax-faced man and the shadowed man with his chloroform handkerchief knew she was soulless, Miss Tarabotti felt somehow terribly exposed.

"I know this will not please you," she said, "but I have decided to call on Lord Akeldama this evening while my family is out. Do not worry. I will make certain your guards can follow me. I am convinced Lord Akeldama's residence is extremely secure."

The Alpha grunted. "If you must."

"He knows things," she tried to reassure him.

Lord Maccon could not argue with that. "He generally knows too many things, if you ask me."

Miss Tarabotti tried to make her position clear. "He is not interested in me, as anything, well . . . *significant.*"

"Why would he be?" wondered Lord Maccon. "You are a preternatural, soulless."

Alexia winced but strode doggedly onward. "However, you are?"

A pause.

Lord Maccon looked most put upon. His caressing thumb movement stopped, but he did not withdraw his hand from hers.

Alexia wondered if she should force the issue. He was acting as though he had not given the matter much thought. Perhaps he had not: Professor Lyall said the Alpha was acting entirely on instinct. And this *was* full moon, a notoriously bad time for werewolves and their instincts. *Was it appropriate to inquire as to his feelings on the matter of her good self at this particular time of the month?* Then again, wasn't this the time when she was most likely to get an honest answer?

"I am what?" The earl was not making this easy for her.

Alexia swallowed her pride, sat up very straight, and said, "Interested in me?"

Lord Maccon was quiet for a few long minutes. He examined his emotions. While admitting that at that moment—her small hands in his, the smell of vanilla and cinnamon in the air, the neckline of that damnable dress—his mind possessed all the clarity of pea soup full of ham-hock-sized chunks of need, there was something else lurking in said soup. Whatever it was, it made him angry, for it would desperately complicate everything in his well-ordered life, and now was not the time to tackle it.

"I have spent a good deal of time and energy during the course of our association trying not to like you," he admitted finally. It was not an answer to her question.

"And yet *I* find not liking *you* comparatively easy, especially when you say things such as that!" Miss Tarabotti replied, trying desperately to extract her hand from his odious caress.

The action backfired. Lord Maccon tugged and lifted her forward as if she weighed no more than thistledown.

Miss Tarabotti found herself sitting flush against him on the small couch. The day was suddenly as warm as she had previously implied. She was scorched from shoulder to thigh by intimate contact with his lordship's prodigious muscles. *What is it*, she wondered, *about werewolves and muscles?*

"Oh my," said Alexia.

"I am finding," said the earl, turning toward her and caressing her face with one hand, "it very difficult to imagine not not disliking you on a regular and intimate basis for a very long time to come."

Miss Tarabotti smiled. The smell of open fields was all about her, that breezy scent only the earl produced.

He did not kiss her, simply touched her face, as though he were waiting for something.

"You have not apologized for your behavior," Miss Tarabotti said, leaning into his hand with her cheek. Best not to let him get the upper hand, so to speak, in this conversation by getting her all flustered. She wondered if she dared turn her face to kiss his fingertips.

"Mmm? Apologize? For which of my many transgressions?" Lord Maccon was fascinated by the smoothness of the skin of her neck, just below her ear. He liked the old-fashioned way she had put up her hair, all caught up at the back like a governess— better access.

"You ignored me at that dinner party," Alexia persisted. It still rankled, and Miss Tarabotti was not about to let him slide without some pretense at contrition.

Lord Maccon nodded, tracing her arched black brows with a fingertip. "Yet you spent the evening engaging in a far more interesting conversation than I and went driving the next morning with a young scientist."

He sounded so forlorn, Alexia almost laughed. Still no apology, but this was as close as an Alpha got, she supposed. She looked him dead-on. "*He* finds me interesting."

Lord Maccon looked livid at that revelation. "Of that I am perfectly well aware," he snarled.

Miss Tarabotti sighed. She had not meant to make him angry, fun as that could be. "What am I supposed to say at this juncture? What would you, or your pack protocol, like me to say?" she asked finally.

That you want me, his baser urges thought. *That there is a future, not too far away in space or time, involving you and me and a particularly large bed.* He tried to grapple with such salacious visions and extract himself from their influence. *Blasted full moon*, he thought, almost trembling with the effort.

He managed to control himself enough so that he did not actually attack her. But with the dampening down of his needs, he was forced to deal with his emotions. There it was, like a stone in the pit of his stomach. The one feeling he did not want to acknowledge. Further than just need, or want, or any of those less-civilized instincts he could so easily blame on his werewolf nature.

Lyall had known. Lyall had not mentioned it, but he had known. *How many Alphas*, Lord Maccon wondered, *had Professor Lyall watched fall in love?*

Lord Maccon turned a very wolflike gaze on the one woman who could keep him from ever becoming a wolf again. He wondered how much of his love was tied into that—the very uniqueness of it. Preternatural and supernatural—was such a pairing even possible?

Mine, said his look.

Alexia did not understand that glance. And she did not understand the silence that came with it.

She cleared her throat, suddenly nervous. "Bitch's Dance. Is it . . . my move?" she asked, naming pack protocol to give herself some credence. She did not know what was required, but she wanted him to know she had come to understand some part of his behavior.

Lord Maccon, still bowled over by the revelation he had just come to, looked at her as though he had never really seen her before. He stopped caressing her face and tiredly scrubbed at his own with both hands, like a little child. "My Beta has been talking, I see." He looked at her through his hands. "Well, Professor Lyall has assured me that I have committed a grave transgression in my handling of this situation. That Alpha you may be, but werewolf you are not. Though I will add that, appropriate or not, I have enjoyed our interactions immensely." He looked over at the wing chair.

"Even the hedgehog?" Miss Tarabotti was not certain what was happening. *Had he just admitted intentions? Were they purely physical? If so, should she pursue a liaison?* No word of marriage had yet crossed his lips. Werewolves, being supernatural and mostly dead, could not have children. Or so her father's books purported. They rarely married as a result, professional experts in bedsport or clavigers being the preferred approach. Alexia contemplated her own future. She was not likely to get another opportunity such as this, and there were ways to be discreet. Or so she had read. Although, no doubt, given the earl's possessive nature, all would be revealed eventually. *Reputation be damned*, she thought. *It is not as though I have any significant prospects to ruin. I would simply be following in my father's philandering footsteps. Perhaps Lord Maccon would stash me away in a little cottage in the countryside somewhere with my library and a nice big bed.* She would miss Ivy and Lord Akeldama and, yes, she must admit, her silly family and sillier London society. Alexia puzzled. *Would it be worth it?*

Lord Maccon chose that moment to tilt her head back and kiss her. No gentle approach this time, but straight to that long, hot branding of lips, and teeth, and tongue.

Plastering herself against him, annoyed, as always seemed to be the case when he accosted her, with the amount of clothing between her hands and his torso. *Only one possible answer to that: yes, it would be worth it.*

Miss Tarabotti smiled against his lordship's insistent mouth. *Bitch's Dance.* She drew back and looked up into his tawny eyes. She liked the predator hunger she saw there. It spiced the delicious salty taste of his skin, that sense of risk. "Very well, Lord Maccon. If we are going to play this particular hand, would you be interested in becoming my . . ." Miss Tarabotti scrabbled for the right word. *What does one properly call a male lover?* She shrugged and grinned. "Mistress?"

"*What* did you say?" roared Lord Maccon, outraged.

"Uh. The wrong thing?" suggested Alexia, mystified by this sudden switch in moods. She had no more time to correct her gaffe, for Lord Maccon's yell had reached out into the hallway, and Mrs. Loontwill, whose curiosity was chomping at the proverbial bit, burst into the room.

Only to find her eldest daughter entwined on the couch with Lord Maccon, Earl of Woolsey, behind a table decorated with the carcasses of three dead chickens.

CHAPTER NINE

A Problem of Werewolf Proportions

Mrs. Loontwill did what any well-prepared mother would do upon finding her unmarried daughter in the arms of a gentleman werewolf: she had very decorous, and extremely loud, hysterics.

As a result of this considerable noise, the entirety of the Loontwill household came rushing from whatever room they had formerly been occupying and into the front parlor. Naturally, they assumed someone had died or that Miss Hisselpenny had arrived in a bonnet of unmatched ugliness. Instead, they found something far less likely—Alexia and the Earl of Woolsey romantically enmeshed.

Miss Tarabotti would have moved off the couch and seated herself an appropriate distance from Lord Maccon, but he coiled one arm about her waist and would not let her shift.

She glared at him in extreme annoyance from under dark brows. "What are you doing, you horrible man? We are already in enough trouble. Mama will see us married; you see if she does not," she hissed under her breath.

Lord Maccon said only, "Hush up now. Let me handle this." Then he nuzzled her neck.

Which naturally made Miss Tarabotti even more put out and uncomfortable.

Felicity and Evylin paused in the doorway, eyes wide, and then commenced hysterical giggling. Floote appeared at their heels and hovered in a worried but mostly invisible manner next to the hat stand.

Mrs. Loontwill continued to scream, more in surprise than in outrage. The earl and *Alexia*? What would this do to their social standing?

Miss Tarabotti fidgeted under the warmth of Lord Maccon's arm. Surreptitiously, she tried to pry his fingers off where they gripped her waist, just above her hipbone. His arm rested across the top of her bustle—shocking. He merely winked at her subtle struggles in apparent amusement. Winked!

I mean, thought Alexia, *really!*

Squire Loontwill bumbled into the front parlor with a handful of household accounts he had been in the middle of reckoning. Upon observing Alexia and the earl, he dropped the accounts and sucked his teeth sharply. He then bent to retrieve the paperwork, taking his time so as to consider his options. He ought, of course, to call the earl out. But there were intricate layers to this situation, for the earl and he could not engage in a duel, being as one was supernatural and the other not. As the challenger, Squire Loontwill would have to find a werewolf to fight the earl as his champion. No werewolf of his limited acquaintance would take on the Woolsey Castle Alpha. As far as he knew, no werewolf in London would take on such a Herculean task, not even the dewan. On the other hand, he could always *ask* the gentleman to do the right thing by his stepdaughter. But who would willingly take on Alexia for life? That was more of a curse than even werewolf change. No, Lord Maccon would probably have to be forced. The real question was whether the earl could be persuaded in a non-violent manner to marry Alexia or if the best the squire could hope for was for her to become simply one of Woolsey's clavigers.

Mrs. Loontwill, naturally, complicated the issue.

"Oh, Herbert," she said pleadingly to her silent husband, "you must *make* him marry her! Call for the parson immediately! Look at them . . . they are . . . " she sputtered, "canoodling!"

"Now, now, Leticia, be reasonable. Being a claviger is not so bad in this day and age." Squire Loontwill was thinking of the expense of Alexia's continued upkeep. This situation might turn out to be profitable for all concerned, except Alexia's reputation.

Mrs. Loontwill did not agree. "My daughter is *not* claviger material."

Alexia muttered under her breath, "You have no idea how true a statement that is."

Lord Maccon rolled his eyes heavenward.

Her mother ignored her. "She is *wife* material!" Mrs. Loontwill clearly had visions of drastically improved social status.

Miss Tarabotti stood up from the couch to better confront her relations. This forced the earl to release her, which upset him far more than her mother's hysterics or her stepfather's cowardice.

"I will *not* marry under duress, Mama. Nor will I force the earl into such bondage. Lord Maccon has not tendered me an offer, and I will not have him commit unwillingly. Don't you dare press the issue!"

Mrs. Loontwill was no longer hysterical. There was instead a steel-edged gleam in her pale blue eyes. A gleam that made Lord Maccon wonder which side Alexia had gotten her flinty personality from. Until that moment, he had blamed the deceased Italian father. Now he was not so certain.

Mrs. Loontwill said, voice high-pitched and abrasive, "You brazen hussy! Such sentiments should have prevented you from allowing him such liberties in the *first* place."

Alexia was belligerent. "Nothing of significance has occurred. My honor is still intact."

Mrs. Loontwill stepped forward and slapped her eldest daughter smartly across the face. The cracking sound echoed like a pistol shot through the room. "You are in no position to argue this point, young lady!"

Felicity and Evylin gasped in unison and stopped giggling.

Floote made an involuntary movement from his statuelike state near the door.

Lord Maccon, faster than anyone's eye could catch, suddenly appeared next to Mrs. Loontwill, a steel grip about her wrist. "I would not do that again, if I were you, madam," he said. His voice was soft and low and his expression bland. But there was a kind of anger in the air that was all predator: cold, impartial, and deadly. The anger that wanted to bite and had the teeth to back it up. This was a side of Lord Maccon that no one had seen before— not even Miss Tarabotti.

Squire Loontwill had the distinct impression that, regardless of his decision, Alexia was now no longer his responsibility. He also had the impression that his wife was actually in danger of her life. The earl looked both angry and hungry, and canines were inching down over his bottom lip.

Miss Tarabotti touched her hot cheek thoughtfully, wondering if she would have a handprint. She glared at the earl. "Let my mother go immediately, Lord Maccon."

The earl looked at her, not really seeing her. His eyes were entirely yellow, not simply the colored part either but the whites as well, just like a wolf. Miss Tarabotti thought werewolves could not change during daylight, but perhaps this close to full moon anything was possible. Or perhaps it was another one of those Alpha abilities.

She stepped forward and forcibly placed herself between Lord Maccon and her mother. He wanted an Alpha female, did he? Well, she would give him Alpha in spades.

"Mama, I will not marry the earl against his will. Should you or Squire Loontwill attempt to coerce me, I will simply not submit to the ceremony. You will be left looking like fools among family and friends, and me silent at the altar."

Lord Maccon looked down at her. "Why? What is wrong with me?"

This shocked Mrs. Loontwill into speaking again. "You mean you *are* willing to marry Alexia?"

Lord Maccon looked at her like she had gone insane. "Of course I am."

"Let us be perfectly clear here," said Squire Loontwill. "You are willing to marry our Alexia, even though she is . . . well . . . " he floundered.

Felicity came to his rescue. "Old."

Evylin added, "And plain."

"And tan," said Felicity.

The squire continued. "And so extraordinarily assertive."

Miss Tarabotti was nodding agreement. "My point exactly! He cannot possibly *want* to marry me. I will not have him forced into such an arrangement merely because he is a gentleman and feels he ought. It is simply that it is near to full moon, and things have gotten out of hand. Or"— she frowned—"should I say too much *in* hand?"

Lord Maccon glanced about at Alexia's family. No wonder she devalued herself, growing up in this kind of environment.

He looked at Felicity. "What would I possibly want with a silly chit just out of the schoolroom?" At Evylin. "Perhaps our ideas on beauty do not ally with one another. I find your sister's appearance quite pleasing." He carefully did not mention her figure, or her smell, or the silkiness of her hair, or any of the other things he found so alluring. "After all, it is *I* who would have to live with her."

The more Lord Maccon considered it, the more he grew to like the idea. Certainly his imagination was full of pictures of what he and Alexia might do together once he got her home in a properly wedded state, but now those lusty images were mixing with others: waking up next to her, seeing her across the dining table, discussing science and politics, having her advice on points of pack controversy and BUR difficulties. No doubt she would be useful in verbal frays and social machinations, as long as she was on his side. But that, too, would be part of the pleasure of marrying such a woman. One never knew where one stood with Alexia. A union full of surprise and excitement was more than most could hope for. Lord Maccon had never been one to seek out the quiet life.

He said to the squire, "Miss Tarabotti's personality is a large measure of her appeal. Can you see me with some frippery young thing whom I could push around at any opportunity and cow into accepting all my decisions?"

Lord Maccon was not explaining himself for Alexia's family's benefit but for hers. Although, he certainly did not want the Loontwills to think they were forcing him into anything! He was Alpha enough for that. This whole marriage thing was *his* idea, curse it. No matter that it had only just occurred to him.

Squire Loontwill said nothing in response to that. Because he had, in fact, assumed the earl would want just such a wife. What man would not?

Lord Maccon and the squire were clearly birds of entirely different feathers. "Not with my work and position. I need someone strong, who will back me up, at least most of the time, and who possesses the necessary gumption to stand up to me when she thinks I am wrong."

"Which," interrupted Alexia, "she does at this very moment. You are not convincing anyone, Lord Maccon. Least of all me."

She held up her hand when he would have protested. "We have been caught in a compromising position, and you are trying to do the best by me." She stubbornly refused to believe his interest and intentions were genuine. Before her family had interrupted them, and during all previous encounters, no mention of marriage had ever passed his lips. Nor, she thought sadly, had the word *love*. "I *do* appreciate your integrity, but I will not have you coerced. Nor will I be manipulated into a loveless union based entirely on salacious urges." She looked into his yellow eyes. "Please understand my position."

As though her family were not watching, he touched the side of her face, stroking the cheek her mother had hit. "I understand that you have been taught for far too long that you are unworthy."

Miss Tarabotti felt inexplicably like crying. She turned her face away from his caress.

He let his arm drop. Clearly, the damage done could not be

mended with a few words from him in the space of one disastrous morning.

"Mama," she said, gesturing expansively, "I will not have you manipulating this situation. No one need know what has occurred in this room. So long as you all hold your collective tongues for once." She glared at her sisters. "My reputation will remain intact, and Lord Maccon will remain a free man. And now I have a headache; please excuse me."

With that, she gathered what was left of her dignity and swept from the room. She retreated upstairs to the sanctity of her own boudoir to indulge in a most uncharacteristic but blessedly short-lived bout of tears. The only one who caught her at it was Floote, who placed a sympathetic tea tray on her bedside table, including some of Cook's extra-special apricot puffs, and issued orders with the household staff that she was not to be disturbed.

Lord Maccon was left in the bosom of her family.

"I believe, for the moment, we ought to do as she says," he said to them.

Mrs. Loontwill looked stubborn and militant.

Lord Maccon glared at her. "Do not interfere, Mrs. Loontwill. Knowing Alexia, your approbation is likely to turn her more surely against me than anything else possibly could."

Mrs. Loontwill looked like she would like to take offense, but given this was the Earl of Woolsey, she resisted the inclination.

Then Lord Maccon turned to Squire Loontwill. "Understand, my good sir, that my intentions are honorable. It is the lady who resists, but she must be allowed to make up her own mind. I, too, will not have her coerced. Both of you, stay out of this." He paused in the doorway, donning his hat and coat and baring his teeth at the Loontwill girls. "And, you two, keep quiet. Your sister's reputation is at stake, and never doubt that it drastically impacts your own. I am not one to be trifled with in this matter. I bid you good day." With that, he left the room.

"Well, I never," said Mrs. Loontwill, sitting down heavily on the couch. "I am not sure I want that man for a son-in-law."

"He is very powerful, my dear, no doubt, and a man of considerable means," said Squire Loontwill, attempting to establish a silver lining of some kind.

"But so rude!" persisted his wife. "And all that, after eating three of our best chickens!" She gestured limply at the carcasses in question, a blatant reminder that, whatever it was that had just occurred, she had clearly emerged the loser. The chickens were beginning to attract flies. She pulled the bell rope for Floote to come and clear them away, peeved with the butler for not disposing of them sooner.

"Well, I shall tell you one thing. Alexia is definitely not attending the duchess's rout tonight. Even if I had not already forbidden her, today's behavior would have sealed it. Full-moon celebration or not, she can stay at home and think long and hard on her many transgressions!"

Mr. Loontwill patted his wife's hand sympathetically. "Of course, my dear."

There was no "of course" about it. Miss Tarabotti, knowing her family's propensity for the dramatic, followed suit by keeping to her room most of the day and refusing to leave it even to see them depart that evening. Appreciating the tragedy of it all, her two sisters made sympathetic cluck-clucking noises outside her closed door and promised to bring back all the latest gossip. She would have been more reassured if they had promised not to engage in any gossip of their own. Mrs. Loontwill refused to speak to her, an occurrence that did not tax Alexia in the slightest. Eventually the house fell silent. She breathed a prodigious sigh of relief. Sometimes her family could really be very trying.

She stuck her head out of her bedroom door and called, "Floote?"

The butler appeared on cue. "Miss?"

"Hail a cab, please, Floote. I am going out."

"Are you certain that is wise, miss?"

"To be wise, one might never leave one's room at all," quoted Miss Tarabotti.

Floote gave her a skeptical look but went downstairs as bidden to flag down a hackney.

Miss Tarabotti summoned her maid and went about changing into one of her more serviceable evening gowns. It was an ivory taffeta affair with small puffed sleeves, a modest scooped neckline, and trimmed out with raspberry pin-tucked ribbon and pale gold lace edging. True, it *was* two seasons old and probably should have been made over before now, but it was comfortable and wore well. Alexia thought of the dress as an old friend, and knowing she looked passably well in it, tended to don it in times of stress. Lord Akeldama expected grandeur, but Miss Tarabotti simply hadn't the emotional energy for her russet silk fancy, not tonight. She curled her hair over her still-marked shoulder, coiling part of it up with her two favorite hair pins, one of silver and one of wood. She braided the rest loosely with ivory ribbon. It contrasted becomingly with her dark tresses.

By the time she was ready, it was dark outside her window. All of London nested safely in those few hours after sunset, before the moon climbed into the sky. It was a moment supernatural folk called twinight: just enough time to get werewolves under lock and key before the moon herself appeared and drove them to become mad unstoppable monsters.

Floote gave Miss Tarabotti one more long warning glance as he handed her up the steps of the cab. He did not approve of her going out on such a night. He was certain she would get into mischief. Of course, Floote tended to be under the impression that the young miss was up to no good *whenever* she was out of his sight. But on full moon in particular, no possible benefit could come of it.

Miss Tarabotti frowned, knowing exactly what the butler was thinking, despite his face remaining perfectly impassive. Then she smiled slightly. She must admit, he was probably correct in his opinion.

"Be careful, miss," Floote instructed severely but without much hope. He had, after all, been butler to her father before her, and just look what happened to Alessandro. Prone to willful and problematic lives, the Tarabottis.

"Oh, Floote, do stop mothering. It is most unbecoming in a man of your age and profession. I will only be gone a few hours, and I will be perfectly safe. Look." She pointed behind Floote to the side of the house, where two figures appeared out of the night shadows like bats. They moved with supernatural grace coming to stand several feet from Alexia's hackney, obviously prepared to follow it.

Floote did not look reassured. He snorted in a most unbutler-like manner and shut the carriage door firmly.

Being vampires, Miss Tarabotti's BUR guards needed no cab of their own. Of course, they probably would have preferred one. It was not quite apropos to the supernatural mystique, jogging after a public transport. But they experienced no physical taxation of any kind from the exertion. So that is precisely what Miss Tarabotti forced them to do, instructing her driver to walk on, before they had a chance to find a conveyance of their own.

Miss Tarabotti's little cab wended its way slowly through the throngs of moon-party traffic, ending up in front of one of the most dashing abodes in London, the town residence of Lord Akeldama.

The foppish vampire was waiting for her at the door when she alighted from the cab. "Alexia, *sugarplumiest* of the plums, what a *lovely* way to spend the full moon, in your ambrosial company! Who could possibly wish for *anything* else in life?"

Miss Tarabotti smiled at the excessive gallantry, knowing full well Lord Akeldama would far rather be at the opera, or the theater, or the duchess's rout, or even down the West End in the blood-whores' den gorging himself until he could not see straight. Vampires liked to misbehave on full moon.

She paid the cab and made her way up the front steps. "Lord Akeldama, how lovely to see you again so soon. I am delighted you could accommodate my visit at such short notice. I have much to talk with you about."

Lord Akeldama looked pleased. Just about the only thing that could keep him home at full moon was information. In fact, he had been motivated to change his plans at Miss Tarabotti's request in light of the fact that she would only contact him if she needed to know something. And if she needed to know something, she must perforce know something else significant already. The vampire rubbed his elegant white hands together in delight. Information: reason for living. Well, that and fashion.

Lord Akeldama was dressed to the pink for the evening. His coat was of exquisite plum-colored velvet paired with a satin waistcoat of sea-foam green and mauve plaid. His britches were of a perfectly coordinated lavender, and his formal cravat a treble bow of white lawn secured with a massive amethyst and gold pin. His Hessian boots were polished to a mirror shine, and his top hat was plum velvet to match the coat. Miss Tarabotti was not certain if this elaborate outfit was because he intended to go out after their assignation, if he actually considered her that important, or if he just always dressed like a sideshow performer on full moon. Regardless, she felt shabby and severe by comparison in her outmoded gown and practical shoes. She was glad they were not going out on the town together. How the ton would laugh at such a mismatched pair!

Lord Akeldama guided her solicitously up the last few steps. He paused on the stoop and looked back over his plum-colored shoulder at the spot where her cab had been and now was not anymore. "Your shadows will have to stay outside my domain, little *creampuff*. You *know* vampire territory laws, don't you, my *dove*? Not even *your* safety, or *their* jobs at BUR, can countermand such regulations. They are more than law; they are instinct."

Miss Tarabotti looked at him, wide-eyed. "If you deem it necessary, my lord, of course they must stay off the premises."

"Well, my *ravishing* one, even if you do not comprehend to

what I am referring, *they* certainly do." His eyes slitted as he glared out into the street.

Miss Tarabotti could not see what drew his attention, but she knew that did not mean they were not there: two vampire guards, standing supernaturally still in the night, watching them. She looked closely at her friend's face.

For a moment, Miss Tarabotti thought Lord Akeldama's eyes actually glowed, a sheen of warding, a spark of possession. She wondered if that look was the vampire equivalent of a dog peeing to mark his territory. *Stay out*, said Lord Akeldama's expression. *Mine*. What, then, did werewolves do? Lord Maccon had implied they were not as territorial as vampires, but still. The packs tended to stick to certain geographic regions; there was no doubt of that. Miss Tarabotti mentally shrugged. They actually were wolves, at least part of the time, and scent did seem to be particularly important to werewolves. They probably did pee. The thought of Lord Maccon cocking a leg to mark Woolsey Castle parklands was so absurd that Miss Tarabotti actually had to stop herself from chortling aloud. She filed the image away as an excellent and insulting question to ask the earl at an utterly inappropriate future moment.

A shadow across the street, empty darkness contrasting the light cast by flickering gas, materialized into the figure of two men. They doffed their hats at Lord Akeldama, who merely sniffed. Then they faded out of view once more.

Lord Akeldama grabbed Miss Tarabotti's hand, affectionately tucking it over his arm, and steered her into his fabulous house.

"Come along, my *dearest* girl." The sheen in his eyes vanished, as if it had never been, and he was back to his usual debonair self.

He shook his head as his butler closed the front door behind them. "Little better than drones, youngsters of the hive. They cannot even be bothered to think for themselves! First, obey the queen; second, obey BUR, spending their strongest years simply jumping from one set of orders to the next like trumped-up soldiers. Still, it is an uncomplicated life for the primitive of intellect." His tone was rancorous, but Miss Tarabotti thought she could detect an undercurrent of regret. He had a faraway look in his eyes, as if he were visiting some long-forgotten and far simpler time.

"Is that why you became a rove—too many orders?" Miss Tarabotti asked.

"What was that, my diminutive *gherkin*?" Lord Akeldama shook himself and blinked as though waking up from a long sleep. "Orders? No, the split was due to circumstances far *more* labyrinthine than that. It all started when gold buckles came back into vogue, progressed to heights of bitterness over spats versus gaiters, and wended down a slippery slope from there. I believe the defining moment was when certain persons, who shall remain nameless, objected to my fuchsia silk striped waistcoat. I loved that waistcoat. I put my foot down, right then and there; I do not mind telling you!" To punctuate his deeply offended feelings, he stamped one silver-and-pearl-decorated high heel firmly. "*No one* tells me what I can and cannot wear!" He snapped up a lace fan from where it lay on a hall table and fanned himself vigorously with it for emphasis.

It was clear he was skidding the conversation off track, but Miss Tarabotti did not mind. She responded to his distress with a noncommittal murmur of sympathy.

"Pardon me, my *fluffy cockatoo*," he said, pretending to rein in an excessively emotional state. "*Please* ignore my ramblings as those of a madman. It is just so uncomfortable to have two not of *my* bloodline in proximity to my home, you understand? It is a little like having those *disagreeable* shivers constantly running up and down one's spine. Something does not feel right with the *universe* when one's territory is invaded. I *can* bear it, but I do not *like* it. It makes me quite edgy and off kilter."

Lord Akeldama put the fan down. A personable young man appeared at his elbow with a solicitous cooling cloth draped artistically on a silver tray. Lord Akeldama dabbed at his brow delicately. "Oh, *thank* you, Biffy. *So* thoughtful." Biffy winked and skipped off again. He displayed impressive musculature for all his grace. Acrobat? wondered Alexia. Lord Akeldama watched the young man walk away appreciatively. "I should not have favorites, of course . . ." He sighed and turned to Miss Tarabotti. "But, now, on to more important topics! Such as your *scrumptious* self. To what do I owe the singular *pleasure* of your company this evening?"

Miss Tarabotti refrained from any direct answer. Instead, she looked about the interior of his house. She had never been inside before, and she was overwhelmed. Everything was to the height of style, if one were thinking in terms of style round about a hundred years ago. Lord Akeldama possessed real, substantial wealth and was not afraid to display it openly. Nothing in his home was substandard, or faux, or imitation, and all of it was well beyond the pale. The carpets were not Persian but were instead vibrant flower-ridden images of shepherds seducing shepherdesses under intense blue skies. Were those puffy white clouds? Yes, they were. The arched ceiling of the entrance hall was actually frescoed like the Sistine Chapel, only Lord Akeldama's ceiling depicted cheeky-looking cherubs up to nefarious activities. Alexia blushed. All kinds of nefarious activities. She turned her eyes hurriedly back down. Small Corinthian columns stood proudly all around, supporting marble statues of naked male gods that Miss Tarabotti had no doubt were authentically ancient Greek in origin.

The vampire led her through to his drawing room. It contained none of the style clutter but instead harkened back to a time before the French Revolution. The furniture was all white or gilded gold, upholstered in cream and gold striped brocade and riddled with fringe and tassels. Heavy layers of gold velvet curtains shielded the windows, and the plush rug on the floor sported yet another proximate shepherding event. Lord Akeldama's had only two nods to modern life. The first was evident in the room being well lit, with multiple gas lamps no less, elaborate candelabras appearing to be only for decorative purposes. The second facet of modernity took the form of a gilded pipe with multiple joints, mounted on the mantel. Alexia figured it must be some modern artwork. *Such an expense!* thought Miss Tarabotti.

She took a seat in a thronelike armchair and removed her hat and gloves. Lord Akeldama sat across from her. He produced the strange crystal tuning fork device, flicking it into dissonant resonance and placing it on a side table.

Alexia wondered that he thought such caution necessary inside his own home. Then she figured no one would be more worried about eavesdropping than a lifelong eavesdropper.

"Well," he demanded, "what do you think of my humble abode?"

For all its gilt pomposity and grandeur, the room had a feeling of regular use. There were multiple hats and gloves strewn about, here-and-there notes on slips of paper, and the odd abandoned snuffbox. A fat calico cat lounged in possession of an overstuffed hassock and one or two dead tassels near the fire. A grand piano stood prominently in one corner, well dusted, with sheets of music lying atop it. It clearly underwent more regular use than the one in the Loontwills' front parlor.

"It is unexpectedly welcoming," Miss Tarabotti replied.

Lord Akeldama laughed. "So speaks one who has visited the Westminster hive."

"It is also very, uh, Rococo," she said, attempting not to intimate she found it at all old-fashioned.

Lord Akeldama clapped his hands delightedly. "Isn't it just? I am afraid I never quite left that particular era. It was *such* a glorious time to be alive, when men *finally* and *truly* got to wear sparkly things, and there was lace and velvet everywhere."

A gentle hubbub arose outside the drawing room door, then subsided, and then broke into raucous laughter.

Lord Akeldama smiled affectionately. His fangs showed clearly in the bright light. "There are my little drone-y-poos!" He shook his head. "Ah, to be young again."

They were left untroubled by whatever it was that was occurring in the hallway. Apparently a closed door meant a well-respected "stay out" in Lord Akeldama's household. However, Alexia soon discovered that her vampire friend's domicile seemed to exist in a constant state of tumult-in-the-hallway.

Miss Tarabotti imagined this must be what it was like inside a gentlemen's club. She knew that there were no women among Lord Akeldama's drones. Even if his taste had extended in that direction, Lord Akeldama could hardly hope to present a female to Countess Nadasdy for metamorphosis. No queen would willingly turn a woman of a rove household; the chance of making a renegade queen, however slim, would never be risked. The countess probably only bit Lord Akeldama's male drones under sufferance—for the good of increasing the population. Unless, of course, Lord Akeldama was allied to a different hive. Miss Tarabotti did not ask. She suspected such a question might be impertinent.

Lord Akeldama sat back and twiddled his amethyst cravat pin with thumb and forefinger, pinky raised high into the air. "Well, my *captivating* crumpet, *tell* me about your visit to the hive!"

Alexia told him, as briefly as possible, about the experience and her evaluation of the characters involved.

Lord Akeldama seemed to agree with her general assessments. "Lord Ambrose you can disregard; he is her pet favorite but hasn't the brains of a *peahen*, I am afraid, for all his pulchritude. *Such* a waste!" He tut-tutted and shook his blond head sadly. "Now, the Duke of Hematol, he is a tricky character and in an outright sense of a one-on-one match, the most perilous of the Westminster inner circle."

Alexia ruminated on that nondescript vampire who had reminded her so strongly of Professor Lyall. She nodded. "He certainly gave that impression."

Lord Akeldama laughed. "Poor old Bertie, he works so hard *not* to!"

Miss Tarabotti raised her eyebrows. "Which is exactly why he does."

"But you are, my *daffodil*, and I do not mean to cause offense, a tad *insignificant* for his attentions. The duke contents himself mainly with attempting to rule the world and other suchlike *nonsense*. When one is guiding the patterns of the social *universe*, a single spinster preternatural is unlikely to cause one undue distress."

Miss Tarabotti fully understood where he was coming from and was not in the least offended.

Lord Akeldama continued. "But, my *treasure*, under your *particular* circumstances, I suggest Dr. Caedes is the one to be most wary of. More mobile than the countess, and he is . . . How do I put this?" He stopped spinning his amethyst pin and began tapping it with one finger. "He is interested in *minutia*. You know he takes an interest in modern inventions?"

"That was his collection on display in the hallway of the hive house?"

Lord Akeldama nodded. "He dabbles himself, as well as investing and collecting like-minded drones. He is also not altogether *compos mentis* in the daylight sense of the term."

"As opposed to?" Alexia was confused. Sanity was sanity, was it not?

"Ah"—Lord Akeldama paused—"we vampires tend to have an unfettered approach to the concept of mental health." He twiddlcd his fingers in the air. "One's moral clarity goes a *little* fuzzy after the first two centuries or so."

Miss Tarabotti said, "I see," although she did not.

There came a timid knock on the drawing room door.

Lord Akeldama stilled the vibrating sound disrupter device. "Come!" he then sang out.

It opened to reveal a gaggle of grinning young men, captained by the one Lord Akeldama had referred to earlier as Biffy. All of them were handsome, charming, and in high spirits. They bustled into the room.

"My lord, we are going out to enjoy the full moon," said Biffy, top hat in hand.

Lord Akeldama nodded. "The usual instructions, my dear boys."

Biffy and the other young bloods nodded, their smiles slipping ever so slightly. They were all dressed to the nines—dandified gentry of the kind welcome at any gathering and noticed at none. Alexia reasoned no man of Lord Akeldama's household would ever be less than perfectly fashionable, entirely presentable, and patently invisible as a result. A few favored his more outrageous mode of costuming, but most were toned-down, less eccentric versions of their lord. A few looked faintly familiar, but Alexia could not, for the life of her, pinpoint where or when she had seen them before. They were simply so very *good* at being exactly what was expected.

Biffy looked hesitantly at Miss Tarabotti before asking Lord Akeldama, "Anything in particular desired for this evening, my lord?"

Lord Akeldama waggled a wrist limply in the air. "There is a *sizable* game in motion, my *darlings*. I depend upon you all to play it with your usual consummate skill."

The young men released a spontaneous cheer, sounding like they had already got into Lord Akeldama's champagne, and trundled out.

Biffy paused in the doorway, looking less jolly and more apprehensive. "You will be all right without us, my lord? I could stay if you wished." There was something in his eyes that suggested he would very much like to do just that, and not only out of concern for his master's welfare.

Lord Akeldama stood and minced over to the doorway. He pecked the young man on the cheek, which was for show, and then stroked it gently with the back of his hand, which was not. "I must know the players." He used no excessive emphasis when he spoke: no italic intonation, no endearments—just the flat sure voice of authority. He sounded old and tired.

Biffy looked down at the toe tips of his shiny boots. "Yes, my lord."

Alexia felt a little discomfited, as though she were witnessing an intimate moment in the bedchamber. Her face heated with embarrassment, and she looked away, feigning sudden interest in the piano.

Biffy placed his top hat on his head, nodded once, and left the room.

Lord Akeldama closed the door behind him softly and returned to sit next to Miss Tarabotti.

Greatly daring, she put a hand on his arm. His fangs retracted. The human in him, buried by time, surfaced at her touch. *Soulsucker*, the vampires called her, yet Alexia always felt it was only in these moments that she actually got close to seeing the true nature of Lord Akeldama's soul.

"They will be fine," Miss Tarabotti said, trying to sound reassuring.

"I suspect that state would tend to depend on *what* my boys find out, and whether anyone *thinks* they have found out anything of import." He sounded very paternal.

"So far, no drones have gone missing," said Alexia, thinking about the French maid taking refuge at the Westminster hive, her rove master gone.

"Is that the *official* word? Or information from the source itself?" asked Lord Akeldama, patting the top of her hand with one of his appreciatively.

Alexia knew he was asking about BUR records. Since she did not know, she explained. "Lord Maccon and I are currently *not* on speaking terms."

"Good *gracious* me, why ever not? It is so much more fun when you are." Lord Akeldama had seen Miss Tarabotti and the earl through many an argument, but neither had ever resorted to silence before. That would defeat the purpose of their association.

"My mother wants him to marry me. And he agreed!" said Miss Tarabotti, as though that explained everything.

Lord Akeldama clapped a hand over his mouth in startlement,

looking once more like his old frivolous self. He stared down into Alexia's upturned face to determine the veracity of her words. Upon realization that she was in earnest, he threw his head back and let out a quite unvampirelike bark of laughter.

"Showing his hand at last, is he?" He chuckled further, extracting a large perfumed mauve handkerchief from one waist-coat pocket to dab at his streaming eyes. "Lordy, what *will* the dewan have to say about such a union? Preternatural and super-natural! That has not happened in my lifetime. And Lord Maccon *already* so powerful. The hives will be outraged. And the poten-tate! Ha."

"Now, hold just a moment," insisted Alexia. "I refused him."

"You did *what*?" Now Lord Akeldama really was startled. "After leading him on for so many years! That is *just* plain cruel, my *rosebud*. How *could* you? He is only a werewolf, and they can be *terribly* emotional creatures, you understand? *Quite* sensitive about these things. You could do permanent damage!"

Miss Tarabotti frowned at this unexpected diatribe. Wasn't her friend supposed to be on her side? It did not occur to her how confoundingly odd it was for a vampire to be lauding a werewolf.

The vampire in question continued his admonition. "What is *wrong* with him? A little crude, I grant you, but a *robust* young beastie? *And*, rumor has it, he is endowed most generously with copious other . . . attributes."

Miss Tarabotti let go of his hand and crossed her arms. "I would not have him coerced into matrimony, simply because we were caught in flagrante delicto."

"You were caught . . . *what*? This simply gets better and better! I *demand* all the particulars!" Lord Akeldama looked like he antici-pated a deliciously vicarious experience.

Outside in the hallway came another of those hubbubs that frequented the Akeldama household. For the moment, both were so involved in Alexia's gossip, neither remembered the house was supposed to be empty of such activity.

The door to the drawing room burst open.

"Here!" said the man at the entrance. A man who was not well dressed and clearly did not belong in Lord Akeldama's splendid house.

Lord Akeldama and Alexia both stood. Alexia grabbed her brass parasol, gripping it firmly in both hands. Lord Akeldama reached for the gold pipe art piece from the mantel. He pressed hard at a hidden button in the midpoint, and a curved, hooklike blade sprang out each end of the pipe and clicked into place. One was sharpened ironwood, the other solid silver. Not art, as it turned out.

"Where are my on-premises drones?" wondered Lord Akeldama.

"Never mind that," said Alexia. "Where are my vampire guards?"

The man in the doorway had no answer for either of them. He did not even appear to hear. He did not approach but merely stood, blocking their sole avenue of escape.

"He has got a female with him," he shouted back to someone in the hallway.

"Well, bring them both," came the sharp reply. Then some kind of complex Latin phrases were issued. The terms used were outside of Miss Tarabotti's limited education and spoken in such a strange old-fashioned accent as to make them particularly difficult to decode.

Lord Akeldama tensed. He clearly understood what was said, or at least what it implied. "*No.* That is impossible!" he whispered.

Miss Tarabotti felt that if he had not been vampire-white already, he would have blanched. His supernatural reflexes seemed stalled by some horrific realization.

The stranger in the doorway vanished to be replaced by an all-too-familiar figure: a man with a stagnant, wax-like face.

CHAPTER TEN

For the Good of the Commonwealth

Miss Tarabotti's nemesis held a brown glass bottle up high in one hand.

She was momentarily hypnotized by the repulsive fact that he seemed to have no fingernails.

Closing the door firmly behind him, the wax-faced man advanced toward Miss Tarabotti and Lord Akeldama, unstopping the bottle and spilling its contents about the room as he went. He did so with infinite care, as a conscientious flower girl scatters petals before an advancing bride.

Invisible fumes rose up from the drops of liquid, and an odd smell permeated the air. Alexia knew that odor well by now: sugary turpentine.

Miss Tarabotti held her breath, plugging her nose with one hand and raising her parasol into guard position with the other. She heard a dull thud as Lord Akeldama collapsed to the floor, his golden pipe weapon rolled away, unused. Clearly, all his plethora of information did not include the latest medical pamphlets on the application, use, and smell of chloroform. Either that, or vampires were more quickly affected by the drug than preternaturals.

Alexia felt light-headed, not certain how long she could hold her breath. She fought the sensation as much as possible and then broke toward the drawing room door and fresh air.

The wax-faced man, apparently unaffected by the fumes, shifted to prevent her egress. Miss Tarabotti remembered from the night before how fast he could move. Supernatural? Perhaps not if the chloroform had no effect. But assuredly faster than she was. Miss Tarabotti cursed herself briefly for not bringing her conversation with Lord Akeldama more rapidly around to the topic of this man. She *had* meant to ask. It was just, now . . . too late.

She swung her deleterious parasol. Brass haft and silver tip made satisfying contact with the man's skull, yet neither seemed to have any effect.

She hit him again just below the shoulder. He brushed her weapon aside with the flick of one arm.

Alexia could not help but gasp in astonishment. She had hit him *very* hard. But no sound of breaking bone came when buck-shot-filled ferrule met arm.

The wax-faced man grinned his horrible not-teeth grin.

Too late, Miss Tarabotti realized that she had breathed inward in her surprise. She cursed herself roundly for a fool. But self-recriminations were to no benefit. The sweet chemical smell of the chloroform invaded her mouth, permeated her nose and throat, and then her lungs. *Blast it*, thought Alexia, borrowing one of Lord Maccon's favorite curses.

She hit the wax-faced man one last time, mostly out of orneri-ness. She knew it would result in nothing. Her lips began to tingle and her head spun. She swayed dangerously and reached forward with her nonparasol hand, groping for the wax man, preternatural her last resort. Her hand came to rest against his horrible smooth temple, just below the *V* on VIXI. His skin felt cold and hard. Nothing at all happened to him at the contact. No change back to normal human, no return to life, no soul-sucking. Definitely not supernatural. *Here*, Miss Tarabotti realized, *was the real monster*.

"But," Alexia whispered, "I am the soulless one . . ." And with that, she dropped her parasol and pitched forward into darkness.

* * *

Lord Maccon arrived home in the nick of time. His carriage clattered up the long cobbled drive to Woolsey Castle just as the sun set behind the high trees planted along the western edge of its extensive grounds.

Woolsey Castle stood a respectable distance from town—far enough away for the pack to run and close enough for them to take advantage of all the amusements London afforded. Woolsey Castle was also not the impenetrable fortress its name implied but instead a sort of trumped-up family manor house with multiple stories and excessively excitable buttresses. Its most important feature, so far as the werewolves were concerned, was a very large and secure dungeon, designed to accommodate multiple guests. The original owner and designer was reputed to have had some rather indecent proclivities, outside of his fondness for flying buttresses. Whatever the cause, the dungeons were extensive. Also key, in the pack's opinion, was the large number of private bedchambers above dungeon level. Woolsey Castle had to house a goodly number of residents: werewolves, clavigers, and servants.

Lord Maccon jumped out of his carriage, already feeling those heady tingles and carnivorous urges only the full moon whipped into rampancy. He could smell the blood of prey on the evening air, and the urge to hunt, and maim, and kill, was approaching with the moon.

His clavigers were waiting for him in a large tense group at the door to the castle.

"You are cutting it a bit close for comfort, my lord," remonstrated Rumpet, head butler, taking the Alpha's cloak.

Lord Maccon grunted, shedding his hat and gloves onto a long hallway stand designed expressly for that purpose.

He squinted into the assembled masses, searching for Tunstell. Tunstell was his personal valet and default captain of the household clavigers. Spotting the gangly redhead, Lord Maccon barked, "Tunstell, you dreadful young blunt, report."

Tunstell bounced up and flourished a bow. His customary

smile dimpled his freckled face. "All the pack's accounted for and locked down, sir. Your cell is clean and waiting. Best we get you down there right quick, I'm thinking."

"There you go with the thinking thing. What have I told you?"

Tunstell only grinned wider.

Lord Maccon held his wrists outward. "Precautionary measures, Tunstell."

Tunstell's chipper smile diminished. "Are you certain that is necessary, sir?"

The earl felt his bones beginning to self-fracture. "Drat it, Tunstell, are you questioning orders?" The small part of his logical brain still functioning was saddened by this lapse. He had great affection for the boy, but every time he thought Tunstell might be ready for the bite, he behaved like a fathead. He seemed to have plenty of soul, but did he have enough *sense* to become supernatural? Pack protocol was not to be taken lightly. If the redhead survived the change but continued with this cavalier attitude toward regulations, would *anyone* be secure?

Rumpet came to his rescue. Rumpet was no claviger. He had no intention of bidding for metamorphosis, but he did enjoy executing his job efficiently. He had been butler to the pack for a long time and was easily double the age of any of the clavigers present in that hallway. Usually he exhibited more aptitude than all of them combined.

Actors, thought Lord Maccon in exasperation. It was one of the downsides of fleecing that particular profession. Men of the stage were not always men of sagacity.

The butler proffered a copper tray with a set of iron manacles atop it. "Mr. Tunstell, if you would be so kind," he said.

The redheaded claviger already carried his own set of handcuffs, as all clavigers did. He sighed resignedly, plucking them off the tray and snapping them firmly around his master's wrists.

Lord Maccon sighed in relief. "Quickly," he insisted, already slurring his words as the change re-formed his jawbone away from any capacity for human speech. The pain was intensifying as well, the horrible bone-wrenching agony to which, in all his long life, Lord Maccon had never yet become accustomed.

The proto-pack of clavigers surrounded him and hustled him down the winding stone staircase and into the castle dungeon. Some, the earl noticed in relief, were sensibly armored and armed. All wore sharp silver cravat pins. A few carried silver knives sheathed at their waists. These stayed to the outskirts of the crowd, carefully distanced from him, until such a time when he might make it necessary for them to use those knives.

The Woolsey Castle dungeon was full of snarling, slathering occupants. The youngest pups of Lord Maccon's pack could not resist change for several nights leading up to the full moon, let alone the moon itself. These had been in residence for days. The rest went with the sun as soon as it set on the actual night. Only Lord Maccon was strong enough to still be outside of confinement so late in the evening.

Professor Lyall was sitting suavely on a small three-legged footstool in one corner of his cell, wearing only his ridiculous glassicals and reading the evening paper. He was struggling to slow the change. Most of the pack simply let themselves be taken, but Lyall always resisted as long as he could, testing his will against the inevitability of the moon. Through the heavy iron bars of his Beta's cell, Lord Maccon could see that Lyall's spine was curled forward inhumanly far, and he boasted considerably more hair than was acceptable for any more social occasion than reading the evening paper in the privacy of one's own . . . prison.

The professor gave his Alpha a long look from yellow eyes over the tops of his spectacles.

Lord Maccon, holding his manacled hands stiffly in front of him, ignored his Beta in a very pronounced manner. He suspected Lyall would have said something embarrassing about Alexia if his Beta's jaw were not already changed well beyond human speech.

The earl continued down the passageway. His pack settled down as he passed. As each wolf caught sight and scent of the Alpha, he instinctively quieted. Several flattened down their forelegs in a kind of bow, and one or two rolled over, presenting their stomachs. Even in the thrall of full moon, they acknowledged his dominance. None wished to even hint at a challenge. He would brook no disobedience, on this of all nights, and they knew it.

The earl stepped inside his own waiting cell. It was the largest but also the most secure, empty except for chains and bolts. Nothing was safe when he changed. No footstool or periodical was in residence, just stone and iron and emptiness. He sighed heavily.

His clavigers slammed and triple bolted the iron door behind him. They stationed themselves outside it but across the passageway, so as to be entirely out of reach. In this, at least, they followed his orders impeccably.

The moon rose above the horizon. Several youngsters of the pack began to howl.

Lord Maccon felt his bones completely breaking and reforming, his skin stretching and shrinking, his tendons realigning, his hair shifting downward and becoming fur. His sense of smell sharpened. He caught a faint whiff of some familiar scent riding an air current down from the castle above.

Those few older members of the pack still partly human completed their final changes with him. The air was rent with growls and whines as the dregs of daylight disappeared. Bodies always resisted the cursed change, making the pain ever more excruciating. With flesh held together only by the threads of what remained of their souls, all sensibility converted to frenzy. The noise they made was the rampaging death-lust cry of the damned.

Any who heard those particular howls felt nothing but fear: vampire, ghost, human, or animal, it mattered not. Nor would it, in the end, for any werewolf freed of his fetters would kill indiscriminately. On full-moon night, the blood moon, it was not a matter of choice or necessity. It simply was.

However, when Lord Maccon raised his muzzle up to howl, his was not a mindless cry of wrath. The low tones of the Alpha's voice were immeasurably mournful. For he had finally recognized the smell wafting down into the dungeon. Too late to say anything in human tongue. Too late to warn his clavigers.

Conall Maccon, Earl of Woolsey, crashed up against the bars of his cell, the last vestiges of his human side crying out: not to kill, not to be free, but to protect.

Too late.

For that little whiff bore the scent of sweet turpentine, and it was getting stronger.

The sign above the door to the Hypocras Club read PROTEGO RES PUBLICA, engraved into white Italian marble. Miss Alexia Tarabotti, gagged, trussed, bound, and carried by two men—one holding her shoulders, the other her feet—read the words upside down. She had a screaming headache, and it took her a moment to translate the phrase through the nauseating aftereffects of chloroform exposure.

Finally she deduced its meaning: *to protect the commonwealth.*

Huh, she thought. *I do not buy it. I definitely do not feel protected.*

There also appeared to be the emblem of some kind bracketing either side of the words. A symbol or some sort of excitable invertebrate? Was it a brass octopus?

Miss Tarabotti was strangely unsurprised to be brought to the Hypocras Club. She remembered Felicity reading out the *Post's* proclamation detailing the "inception of an innovative social establishment catering to gentlemen of a scientific inclination." Of course, she realized now that it made perfect sense. After all, it was at the duchess's ball, right next door to the new club, that she had killed that first mysterious vampire who started it all. This made for a rather tidy full circle. And, with all that chloroform, there would have to be scientists involved.

Had Lord Maccon discovered this as well? she wondered. *Did he suspect just the club, or was the Royal Society itself implicated?* Alexia doubted even the earl's suspicious nature would stretch as far as that.

Her captors carried her into a small boxlike room with a concertina-style grating for a door. She could turn her head just enough to see the violet-clad form of Lord Akeldama being treated with equal disrespect: slung over someone's shoulder like a side of beef and crammed into the tiny room with her.

Well, Miss Tarabotti reasoned, *at least we are still together.*

The wax-faced man, unfortunately still with them, was not engaged directly in Tarabotti/Akeldama transport. He closed the grated door and then cranked some sort of pulley device inset into one wall of the chamber. The most peculiar thing resulted. The whole of the tiny room began to move listlessly downward, carrying everyone inside with it. It was like falling slowly, and Alexia's stomach, combining this with the added bonus of chloroform exposure, was not particularly thrilled by the experience.

She choked down a convulsive gag.

"This one does not like our ascension room," snickered the man who held her feet, jiggling her rudely.

One of the other men grunted his agreement.

Through the grating, a flabbergasted Alexia watched as the first floor of the club vanished, and the ground itself appeared, then the foundations of the building, then a new ceiling, and, finally, the furniture and floor of underground chambers. It was really quite a remarkable experience.

The tiny room jolted to a stop. Miss Tarabotti's stomach joined up with them shortly thereafter. The human transport flunkies slid back the grating, carried her and Lord Akeldama out, and laid them side by side on a plush Oriental carpet in the middle of a respectably sized receiving room. One of them took the precautionary measure of sitting on Lord Akeldama's legs, although he was still asleep. They did not seem to feel Alexia warranted the same level of consideration.

A man, sitting in a comfortable brown leather armchair with silver studs and smoking a large ivory pipe, stood up at their arrival and walked over to look down at the two prisoners.

"Excellent work, gentlemen!" He bit down on his pipe and rubbed his hands together enthusiastically. "Akeldama, according to the BUR records, is one of the oldest vampires in London. Next to one of their queens, his blood should be the most potent we have yet analyzed. We are in the middle of a transverse-sanguinity procedure at the moment, so put him into storage for now. And what is this?" He turned to look down at Alexia.

There was something familiar about the set of his face, although at that particular angle it was almost completely in shadow. That shadow was also familiar. The man from the carriage! Miss Tarabotti had almost forgotten about him in the horror of her recent encounters with the wax-faced monster.

He clearly had not forgotten about her. "Well, what do you know? This one simply keeps turning up, does she not?" He puffed thoughtfully on his pipe. "First visiting the Westminster hive, now found in the august presence of specimen Akeldama. How does she fit into the picture?"

"We do not know yet, sir. We will have to consult the records. She is no vamp: has neither the teeth nor queen-level protection. Though she did have two vampire guards tailing her."

"Ah, so, and . . . ?"

"We eliminated them, of course. Could be BUR agents; difficult to tell these days. What do you want done in the meantime?"

Puff, puff, puff. "Put her into storage as well. If we cannot find anything out about how she fits into our investigations, we will have to force it out of her. Terribly gauche thing to do to a lady, of course, but she is clearly fraternizing with the enemy, and sometimes sacrifices must be made."

Miss Tarabotti was confused by the players in this little game. These men did not seem to know who or, more precisely, *what* she was. Yet, clearly they were the ones who wanted her. They had sent the wax-faced man to her house in the middle of the night only recently. Unless there existed two wax-faced men in London, both of them after her. Alexia shuddered at the very idea. They must have gotten her home address from her BUR records. Yet, now they did not seem to know who she was. It was as though they were thinking of her as two separate persons. The one who kept interfering with their plans, and the Miss Alexia Tarabotti, preternatural, of BUR's records.

Then Alexia recalled that BUR did not keep sketches on file, for safety reasons. Her record contained only words, notes, and brief descriptive details, and most of that in code. These men had not made the connection to the fact that she *was* Alexia Tarabotti, because they did not know what Alexia Tarabotti looked like. Excepting only the wax-faced man, who would have seen her face in her bedroom window. She wondered why he had not revealed her secret.

Her question remained unanswered. The thugs lifted her up, in response to the shadowed man's order, and carried her after Lord Akeldama out of the plush reception room.

"And, now, where is my precious baby?" she heard the shadowed man ask as they departed. "Ah, there he is! And how did he behave on this outing? Good? Of course he did, my darling." Then his words degenerated into Latin.

Miss Tarabotti was carried through a long narrow corridor, painted white and lined with institutional-looking doors. It was lit with white ceramic oil lamps atop short marble pedestals dispersed between the doors. It all looked very ritualistic, like some sort of ancient place of worship. Oddly, the door handles were made to look like octopuses and so, upon closer inspection, were the lamps.

Miss Tarabotti was maneuvered down a long flight of stairs and into another corridor with more doors and lamps, exactly the same as the first.

"Where shall we put them?" asked one of the men. "Space is scarce, since we have *vamped* up operations, so to speak."

The other three snickered at the terrible pun.

"Just put them in the cell at the end. It does not matter much if they are left together; the doctors will be taking Akeldama off soon enough for processing. The gray coats have been waiting to get their hands on him a good long while now."

One of the others licked his fatty lips. "We ought to be getting quite large bonuses for this little collection venture."

Murmurs of agreement met that statement.

They reached the last door in the corridor and slid aside the body section of its brass octopus handle, revealing a large keyhole. Opening the door, they unceremoniously deposited Miss Tarabotti and the supine form of Lord Akeldama inside the room. Alexia landed hard on her side and attempted not to cry out in pain. They slammed the door shut, and Alexia heard them chatting as they walked away.

"Bodes well for a success in the experiments, eh?"

"Hardly."

"What do we care so long as the pay is good?"

"Too true."

"You know what I think? I think . . ."

And then their voices became faint and faded to silence.

Miss Tarabotti lay wide-eyed, staring about at the chamber in which she now found herself. Her pupils took a while to adjust to the blackness, for there were no oil lamps here and no other source of illumination. The cell did not have bars, just a seamless door with no inside handle, and felt more like a closet than a prison. Nevertheless, she knew instinctively that it *was* a prison. It had no windows, no furniture, no rug, and no other decoration of any kind—just herself and Lord Akeldama.

Someone cleared his throat.

With difficulty, her limbs being tightly bound and her physical dexterity further impeded by her dratted corset and bustle, Miss Tarabotti wiggled from lying on her back to lying on her side, facing Lord Akeldama.

The vampire's eyes were open, and he was staring at her

intently. It was as though he were trying to speak to her with simply the power of a glare.

Alexia did not speak glare-ish.

Lord Akeldama began undulating toward her. He managed to writhe his way across the floor, like some sort of purple snake, the velvet of his beautiful coat slippery enough to aid his progress. Eventually he reached her. Then he flipped about and twiddled his bound hands until Miss Tarabotti understood what he was after.

Alexia flipped back over, inched down, and pressed the back of her head to his hand. The vampire was able to undo the gag tied over her mouth with his fingertips. Her wrists and legs, unfortunately, wcrc manacled with steel bonds, as were his. Such cuffs were beyond even a vampire's ability to break.

With great difficulty, they managed to reverse positions so that Miss Tarabotti could untie Lord Akeldama's gag. Then they were at least able to talk.

"Well," said Lord Akeldama, "this is a *pretty* kettle of fish. I think those miscreants have just *ruined* one of my best evening jackets. How *very* vexing. It is a *particular* favorite of mine. I am sorry to have dragged *you* into this, my dear, almost as much as having dragged the evening jacket into it."

"Oh, don't be so nonsensical. My head is still spinning from that blasted chloroform, and there is no need for you to be tiresomc on top of it," remonstrated Miss Tarabotti. "This situation could not possibly be misconstrued as your fault."

"But they were after me." In the dark, Lord Akeldama actually looked guilty. But that could have been a trick of the shadows.

"They would have been after me as well, if they only knew my name," insisted Miss Tarabotti, "so let us hear nothing more about it."

The vampire nodded. "Well," he said, "my *buttercup*, I suggest we *keep* that name of yours quiet as long as possible."

Alexia grinned. "You should not find that a particularly difficult endeavor. You never do use my real name anyway."

Lord Akeldama chuckled. "Too true."

Miss Tarabotti frowned. "We may not need to bother with subterfuge. The wax-faced man knows. He saw me in the carriage outside the Westminster hive, *and* he saw me at my window one night when they came to abduct a known preternatural. He will put two and two together and realize I am the same person."

"Cannot be done, *dewdrop*," said Lord Akeldama confidently.

Alexia shifted, trying to relieve the pain in her manacled wrists. "How could you possibly know that?" she asked, wondering at his confident tone.

"The wax-faced man, as you call it, cannot tell anyone *anything*. He has no voice, little tulip, *none* at all," replied Lord Akeldama.

Alexia narrowed her eyes at him. "You know what he is? Do tell! He is not supernatural; I can tell you that much."

"*It*, not *him*, my lightning bug. And, yes, I know what *it* is." Lord Akeldama wore a coy expression, one that usually accompanied his fiddling with his cravat pin. As his arms were cuffed behind his back, and his pin had been judiciously removed, he could do nothing to add to the expression but purse his lips.

"Well?" Miss Tarabotti was itching with curiosity.

"*Homunculus simulacrum*," said Lord Akeldama.

Miss Tarabotti looked back at him blankly.

He sighed. "A *lusus naturae*?"

Alexia decided he was playing with her and gave him a nasty look.

He explained further. "A synthetic creature formed by science, an alchemical artificial man . . ."

Miss Tarabotti wracked her brain and finally came up with a word from some long-ago religious text in her father's library. "An automaton?"

"Exactly! They have existed before."

Miss Tarabotti's generous mouth fell open. She had thought

them mere creatures of legend, like unicorns: freaks of a purely mythical nature. The scientific side of her intellect was intrigued. "But, what is it made of? How does it work? It seems so very much alive!"

Lord Akeldama took exception to her word choice once again. "It is moving, animated, and active, yes. But, my dear bluebell, *alive* it most certainly is *not*."

"Yes, but how?"

"Who knows what *dastardly* science went into its creation—a metal skeleton perhaps, a small aetheromagnetic or steam engine of some kind. Perhaps it has clockwork parts. I am no engineer to know the truth of it."

"But why should anyone wish to build such a creature?"

"*You* are asking *me* to explain the actions of a scientist? I hardly know how to put it, petunia petal. Your friend there would appear to be the perfect servant: unflagging and loyal to the last. Of course, one would suppose all orders must be *very* precise." He would have continued, but Miss Tarabotti interrupted him.

"Yes, yes, but what about killing them?" Alexia went straight for the heart of the matter. Really, she quite adored Lord Akeldama, but he did tend to blather on.

Lord Akeldama looked at her reprovingly. "Now, do not be *too* hasty, my darling. All in good time."

"That is easy for you to say," grumbled Miss Tarabotti. "You are a vampire; all you have is time."

"Apparently not. I need hardly remind you, sweetheart, that those men are coming back for *me*. Shortly. Or so they implied."

"You were awake the entire time." Miss Tarabotti was somehow unsurprised.

"I awoke in the carriage on the way here. I feigned sleep, as there seemed nothing advantageous in alerting them to my consciousness. Pretending afforded me an opportunity to over-hear interesting information. Unfortunately, I heard *nothing* of any consequence. Those"—he paused as though searching for the right way to describe the men who had abducted them—

"*degenerates* are mere minions. They know only what they have been told to do, not why they were told to do it. Just as bad as the automaton. They were not interested in discussing this business, *whatever* it is, among themselves. But, marigold—"

Miss Tarabotti interrupted him again. "Please, Lord Akeldama, I do not mean to be rude, but the *homunculus simulacrum*?"

"Quite right, my dear. If I am to be taken off presently, you should have as much information as I can relay. In my limited experience, automatons cannot be killed. Because how does one *kill* something that is not *alive*? The *homunculus simulacrum* can be disanimated, though."

Miss Tarabotti, who had developed rather unladylike homicidal tendencies toward the repulsive wax-faced thing, asked eagerly, "How?"

"Well," said Lord Akeldama, "activation and control is usually in the form of a word or phrase. If one can find a way to undo that phrase, one can, in effect, turn the *homunculus simulacrum* off, like a mechanical doll."

"A word like VIXI?" suggested Alexia.

"Very like. You have seen it?"

"Written across its forehead, in some kind of black powder," Miss Tarabotti confirmed.

"Magnetized iron dust, I would hazard a guess, aligned to the domain of the automaton's internal engine, possibly through an aetheric connection. You must find a way to undo it."

"Undo what?" she asked.

"The VIXI."

"Ah." Miss Tarabotti pretended to understand. "That simple, is it?"

In the darkness of their lonely cell, Lord Akeldama grinned at her. "Now you are playing *me* for a lark, my sweet. I am sorry I do not know any more. I have never had to deal with a *homunculus simulacrum* personally. Alchemic sciences have never been my forté."

Alexia wondered what *was* his forté but asked, "What else do you think they are doing at this club? Aside from building an automaton."

The vampire shrugged as much as his handcuffs would allow. "Whatever they do must, perforce, involve experimentation on vampires, possibly a *forcing* of metamorphosis. I am beginning to suspect that rove you killed—when was it, a week or so ago?— was not *actually* made supernatural at all but was manufactured as a counterfeit of some kind."

"They have been abducting loner werewolves too. Professor Lyall found out about it," Alexia told him.

"Really? *I* did not know that." Lord Akeldama sounded more disappointed in his own abilities than surprised at the news. "Stands to reason, I suppose; might as well work with both sides of the supernatural living. I assure you, even *these* scientists cannot figure out a way to cut open or replicate a ghost. The real question is, *what* are they doing with all of us in the end?"

Miss Tarabotti shuddered, remembering that Countess Nadasdy had said the new vampires rarely lived beyond a few days. "It cannot be pleasant, whatever it is."

"No," Lord Akeldama agreed quietly. "No, it cannot." He was silent for a long moment, and then he said soberly, "My dear child, may I ask you something, in all seriousness?"

Alexia raised her eyebrows. "I do not know. Can you? I did not think you actually possessed the capacity for seriousness, my lord."

"Ah, yes, it is an assumption I have taken great care to cultivate." The vampire cleared his throat. "But, let me give it my best attempt this once. It seems unlikely that I will survive this little misadventure of ours. But if I do, I should like to ask a favor of you."

Miss Tarabotti did not know what to say at that. She was struck by how bleak her life suddenly looked without Lord Akeldama to color it. She was also amazed by his calm acceptance of his impending demise. She supposed that after so many centuries, death was no longer a fearsome thing.

He continued. "It has been a very, very long time since I have experienced the sun. Do you think you might wake me early one evening, with contact, so that I could see it set?"

Miss Tarabotti was touched by such a request. It would be a very dangerous endeavor for him, for he would have to trust her implicitly not to let go. If they broke contact for even a moment, he would immolate instantly.

"Are you certain?"

He breathed out acknowledgment as though it were a benediction. "Absolutely positive."

Just then, the door to the cell banged open. One of the flunkies came in and unceremoniously lifted Lord Akeldama over one bulky shoulder.

"Promise?" said the vampire, hanging limply upside down.

Miss Tarabotti said, "I promise," hoping she would have the chance to live up to her vow.

With that, Lord Akeldama was carried from the room. The door was closed and bolted behind him. Miss Tarabotti, with nothing but her own thoughts for company, was left alone in the dark. She was particularly annoyed with herself; she had meant to ask about the brass octopuses appearing everywhere.

CHAPTER ELEVEN

Among the Machines

Miss Tarabotti could think of nothing to do but wiggle her hands and feet to keep up blood circulation within the tight confines of the manacles. She lay there for what seemed like an age, simply wiggling. She was beginning to infer she had been forgotten, for no one came to check up on her, nor, indeed, showed any interest at all in her physical condition. She was quite uncomfortable, for corsets, bustles, and all other accoutrements of a lady's appropriate dress were not conducive to lying, bound, on a hard floor. She shifted, sighed, and stared up at the ceiling, trying to think about anything but Lord Maccon, her current predicament, or Lord Akeldama's safety. Which meant she could do nothing but reflect on the complex plight of her mama's most recent embroidery project. This, in itself, was a worse torture than any her captors could devise.

Eventually, she was saved from her own masochistic meditations by the sound of two voices in the corridor outside her cell. Both seemed vaguely familiar. The conversation, when they were in close enough proximity for Alexia to overhear the particulars, bore a distinct semblance to a guided museum tour.

"Of course, you must acknowledge that in order to eliminate the supernatural threat, we must first understand it. Professor Sneezewort's most worthwhile research has shown ... Ah, in *this* cell, we have another rove vampire: splendid example of *Homo sanguis*, although rather young for exsanguination. Unfortunately, his origin and original hive association are unknown. This is the sad result of having to rely so heavily on rove specimens. But, you understand, here in England, members of a hive tend to be too much in the public eye and too well guarded. We are having a very difficult time convincing this one to speak. He was transported over from France, you see, and has not been quite right in the head since. There appear to be some serious physical and mental repercussions when one removes a vampire from his immediate localized area: tremulations, disorientation, dementia, and the like. We have not determined the exact mathematical nature of the distance, whether bodies of water are key factors, and so forth, but it promises to be a fascinating branch of research. One of our younger, more enthusiastic, investigators is producing some interesting work utilizing this particular specimen as his main study source. He has been trying to convince us to mount a collecting trip across the Channel into the farther reaches of Eastern Europe. I believe he wants Russian specimens, but we are concerned with remaining inconspicuous at the moment. I am certain you understand. And, of course, there is the cost to consider."

A second male voice answered in a flattish accent, "This is quite fascinating. I had heard of the territorial aspect of vampire psychology. I did not know of the physiological repercussions. I would be quite interested to read the research once it is published. What little gem do you hold in the last cell?"

"Ah, well, it did house Akeldama, one of the oldest vampires in London. His capture this evening was quite the coup. But he is already on the exsanguination table, so we have our mystery guest in residence for the moment."

"A mystery?" The second voice sounded intrigued.

Miss Tarabotti was still unable to determine why this voice seemed so very familiar.

"Indeed," answered the first, "a spinsterly young lady of

moderate breeding who has persisted in turning up during the course of our investigations. After one too many appearances, we brought her in."

The second voice said, shocked, "You have imprisoned a *lady*?"

"Unfortunately, she has made it increasingly necessary. It is the end result of her own meddling. Quite a puzzle she is too." The first man was sounding equal parts annoyed and enthralled. He continued. "Would you be interested in meeting her? You might be able to provide some insight. You are, after all, approaching the supernatural problem from an entirely unique perspective, and we would value your input."

The second man sounded genuinely pleased. "I would be delighted to offer my assistance. How kind of you to ask."

Miss Tarabotti frowned in ever increasing frustration at her terribly inconvenient inability to place the man's voice. There was something about his accent. What was it? Fortunately (or more accurately unfortunately), she did not have to live in confusion much longer.

The door to her closet of a prison swung open.

Miss Tarabotti blinked and inadvertently coiled away from the seemingly blinding light of the hallway.

Someone gasped.

"Why, Miss Tarabotti!"

Miss Tarabotti, eyes watering, squinted at the two backlit figures. Eventually, her eyes adjusted to the unsteady light of the oil lamps. She squirmed about, trying to assume a more elegant position on the floor. She was only mildly successful, remaining ungracefully prone and manacled. She did manage a better angle, which enabled her to see her visitors with greater clarity.

One proved to be the shadowed man, and for the first time in their unsavory acquaintance, his face was not actually in complete shadow. It was he who was playing the part of tour guide. Seeing his countenance at last was an unsatisfactory experience. Alexia had hoped for something particularly horrific and evil. But it was nothing singular, comprised of large graying muttonchops, excessive jowls, and watery blue eyes. She had expected at least some kind of dramatic scar. But there stood her great and sinister nemesis, and he was disappointingly ordinary.

The other man was plumpish, bespectacled, and in possession of a hairline midretreat. His was a countenance Alexia was quite familiar with.

"Good evening, Mr. MacDougall," she said. Even when one was horizontally prone, there was no call for rudeness. "How nice to see you again."

The young scientist, with a cry of profound surprise, came instantly over to kneel solicitously next to her. He helped her gently into a sitting position, apologizing profusely for having to manhandle her person.

Miss Tarabotti did not mind in the least; for, once upright, she felt considerably more dignified. She was also pleased to know Mr. MacDougall had no intentional hand in her abduction. That would have grieved her sorely, for she liked the young man and did not wish to think ill of him. She had no doubt his surprise and concern were genuine. She might, she thought, even be able to turn his presence to her advantage.

Miss Tarabotti then realized the state of her hair and was mortified. Her captors had, of course, removed her hair ribbon and her two deadly hair pins—the one of wood and the other of silver. Without them, heavy dark curls fell down her back in wild abandon. Pathetically, she raised a shoulder and bent to the side, trying to push it away from her face, not realizing, of course, how fetchingly exotic she looked with loose hair in combination with her strong features, wide mouth, and tan skin.

Very Italian, thought Mr. MacDougall when he could spare a moment in his concern for her well-being. He was genuinely worried. He also felt guilty, for if Miss Tarabotti was caught up in this mess, it must be of his doing. Had he not encouraged her interest in the supernatural during their drive together? And her, a lady of good breeding! What could he have been thinking to talk so unguardedly of scientific pursuits? A woman of Miss Tarabotti's caliber would not be content to let matters lie, if she was really intrigued. It *must* be his fault that she had been imprisoned.

"You know the young lady?" asked the shadowed man, pulling out his pipe and a small velvet tobacco pouch. There was an octopus embroidered on the outside of the pouch, golden thread on chocolate brown velvet.

Mr. MacDougall looked up from where he knelt. "I certainly do. This is Miss Alexia Tarabotti," he said angrily before Miss Tarabotti could stop him.

Oh dear, Alexia thought philosophically, *the cat is well and truly out of the bag now.*

Mr. MacDougall continued speaking, a flush staining his pasty, pudgy cheeks and a small sheen of sweat lining his brow. "To treat a young lady of such standing as shabbily as this!" he sputtered. "It is a grave blow, not only to the honor of the club, but also to that of the scientific profession as a whole. We should remove her restraints this moment! Shame on you."

How did that saying go? Alexia wondered. Ah, yes, "Brash as an American." Well, they had won their independence somehow, and it was not with politeness.

The man with the muttonchops filled his pipe bowl and nipped back into the hallway briefly to light it with one of the oil lamps. "Why does that name sound familiar?" He turned back and puffed for a moment, blowing fragrant vanilla-scented smoke into the cell. "Of course—the BUR records! Are you telling me this is *the* Alexia Tarabotti?" He took the pipe out of his mouth and pointed the long ivory stem at Alexia for emphasis.

"The only one I've met in your country so far," answered Mr. MacDougall, sounding unbelievably rude—even for an American.

"Of course." The shadowed man finally put two and two together. "This explains everything: her involvement with BUR, her visiting the hive, and her association with Lord Akeldama!"

He looked to Miss Tarabotti severely. "You have led us a merry dance, young lady." Then he looked back at Mr. MacDougall. "Do you know *what* she is?"

"Aside from manacled? Which she should not be. Mr. Siemons, give me the keys this minute!"

Miss Tarabotti was suitably impressed by Mr. MacDougall's insistence. She had not thought he would be such a champion or possess such backbone.

"Ah, yes, of course," Mr. Siemons said. At last the shadow man had a name. He leaned backward out the doorway and yelled up the hallway. Then he came inside the cell and bent down toward Miss Tarabotti. He grabbed her face quite roughly and turned her toward the light in the hall. He continued to puff on his pipe, blowing smoke into her eyes.

Alexia coughed pointedly.

Mr. MacDougall was further shocked. "Really, Mr. Siemons, such crass treatment!"

"Amazing," said Siemons. "She seems perfectly normal. One would never be able to tell simply by looking, would one?"

Mr. MacDougall finally got over his gentlemanly instincts enough to allow the scientific part of his mental faculties to participate in the conversation. In a voice colored with both hesitation and dread, he asked, "Why shouldn't she be?"

Mr. Siemons stopped blowing smoke in Miss Tarabotti's face and blew it instead at the American scientist. "This young lady is a *preternatural*: a *Homo exanimus*. We have been looking for her since we first deduced her existence here in London. Which, I might add, was only shortly after finding out that preternaturals existed at all. Of course, if you follow the counterbalance theorem, her kind seems perfectly logical. I am surprised we never before thought to look. And, of course, we knew the supernatural set had ancient legends pertaining to certain dangerous creatures that were born to hunt *them*. The werewolves have their curse-breakers, the vampires their soul-suckers, and the ghosts their exorcists. But we did not know they were all the same organism and that that organism was a scientific fact, not a myth. They are startlingly uncommon, as it turns out. Miss Tarabotti here is a rare beast, indeed."

Mr. MacDougall looked shocked. "A *what*?"

Mr. Siemons did not share his shock; in fact, he looked particularly delighted all of a sudden—a lightning change of mood that did not strike Miss Tarabotti as entirely sane.

"A preternatural!" He grinned, waving his pipe about haphazardly. "Fantastic! There are so many things we need to know about her."

Alexia said, "*You* stole the paperwork from BUR."

Mr. Siemons shook his head. "No, my dear, we liberated and then secured important documents in order to prevent dangerous societal elements from fraudulently identifying themselves as normal. Our initiative in this matter will enhance our ability to assess threat and confirm identity of those enabling the supernatural conspiracy."

"She is one of them?" Mr. MacDougall said, still stuck on Miss Tarabotti's preternatural state. He jerked away from her and thus stopped supporting Alexia in her seated position. Luckily, she managed not to fall backward.

He seemed almost repelled by her. Alexia began to wonder about the story of his brother becoming a vampire. *How much of that had been truth?*

Mr. Siemons slapped Mr. MacDougall's back delightedly. "No, no, no, my good man. Quite the opposite! She is the antidote to the supernatural. If you can think of an entire living organism as an antidote. Now that we have her, the opportunities for study are endless! Simply think of what we could accomplish. Such possibilities." He was positively gregarious. His watery blue eyes shone with an excess of scientific enthusiasm.

Alexia shuddered at the idea of what such a study might entail.

Mr. MacDougall looked thoughtful and then stood and pulled his companion out into the hallway. They engaged in a whispered conversation.

During their brief absence, Miss Tarabotti tried frantically to slip free of her handcuffs. She had a sinking suspicion that she would not like anything they wanted to do to her in this ghastly place. But she could not even manage to stand upright.

She heard Mr. Siemons say, "It is an excellent suggestion and could not hurt. If she is as intelligent as you purport, she may yet perceive the merits of our work. It would certainly be novel to engage with a willing participant."

The most miraculous change in Miss Tarabotti's circumstances then proceeded to occur. She found herself gently lifted by a pair of subdued lackeys. She was carried upstairs into the lavish precincts of the foyer, with its plush Oriental carpets and luxuriant furnishings. Her restraints were unlocked and removed, and she was given a small private dressing room in which to wash and compose herself. Her ivory taffeta dress was a little worse for the experience; one of the puffed sleeves and some of the gold lace had ripped, and it was stained beyond redemption in several places. Alexia was annoyed. True, it was out of fashion, but she had liked the gown. She sighed and did her best to smooth out the wrinkles while looking with interest around the dressing room.

There was no means of escape, but there was a bit of ribbon for her to tie back her unruly hair and a looking glass in which she could check up on the generally disreputable state of her appearance. The mirror was ornate, framed but carved gilded wood, more suited to Lord Akeldama's house than a modern setting. The frame seemed to be made up of a long chain of octopuses, arms linked. Alexia was beginning to find the whole octopus prevalence slightly sinister.

She broke the looking glass as quietly as possible, tapping with the back of the ivory hairbrush she had been given. She wrapped a sharp shard of glass carefully in a handkerchief and tucked it down the front of her bodice, between dress and corset, for safekeeping.

Feeling slightly more the thing, she exited the changing room and was escorted downstairs back into the receiving area, with its brown leather armchair. There she found a hot cup of tea and an interesting proposition awaiting her.

Mr. MacDougall made introductions.

"Miss Tarabotti, this is Mr. Siemons. Mr. Siemons, Miss Alexia Tarabotti."

"Enchanted," said the pipe-smoking gentleman, bending over Alexia's hand as though he had not just abducted her, imprisoned her for several hours, and probably done unspeakable things to one of her dearest friends.

Miss Tarabotti decided to play whatever hand was dealt her, at least until she learned the rules of the game. It was typical of her character that she simply assumed she would, eventually, gain control over the situation. Only one man had ever consistently bested her in life's ongoing vocal scuffle, and Lord Maccon used underhanded nonverbal tactics. Thinking of Lord Maccon made Alexia cast a covert glance about the room, wondering if they had brought her parasol when they nabbed her.

"Let me come straight to the point, Alexia," said her jailer. Alexia had no doubt that, while her immediate bonds had been removed, she was still very far from free.

He sat in the leather chair and gestured for her to sit opposite him on a red chaise longue.

She did so. "Please do, Mr. Siemons. Directness is a very admirable quality in kidnappers"—she paused in thought—"and scientists." She was nothing if not fair, and she had read her share of scientific articles that prevaricated and waffled most dreadfully. A strong thesis was very important.

Mr. Siemons proceeded on.

Miss Tarabotti sipped her tea and noted that the silver studs on the leather armchair were also very small octopuses. Really, why the obsession with invertebrates?

Mr. MacDougall hurried about worriedly while Mr. Siemons spoke, fetching this and that to make Alexia more comfortable. Would she like a cushion? Some sugar? Another spot of tea? Was she warm enough? Had the restraints harmed her wrists in any way?

Finally Mr. Siemons rounded on the young man and glared him into silent stillness.

"We should like very much to study you," he explained to Alexia. "And we should like to do so with your cooperation. It would be much easier and more civilized for all concerned if you were a willing participant in the proceedings." He sat back, a strange look of eagerness on his jowly face.

Alexia was confused. "You must understand," she said at length, "that I have several questions. Although, as you intend my participation whether willing or not, you can naturally refrain from answering them."

The man laughed. "I am a scientist, Miss Tarabotti. I appreciate a curious mind."

Miss Tarabotti raised her eyebrows. "Why do you wish to study me? What information do you hope to acquire? And what would these studies entail, exactly?"

He smiled. "Good questions, all of them, but none very enlightened in essence. Obviously, we wish to study you because you are a preternatural. And while both you and BUR might know much of what that means, we know very little and are quite eager to comprehend the whole. We hope, most importantly, to understand the sum components of your ability to cancel out the supernatural. To distill that ability and harness it, what a weapon you might make!" He rubbed his hands together gleefully. "Also, it would be a true joy simply to watch you in action."

"And the studies themselves?" Miss Tarabotti was beginning to feel most apprehensive, though she prided herself on the fact that it was not visible in her general demeanor.

"I understand you have heard some of Mr. MacDougall's theories?"

Miss Tarabotti thought back to that morning drive. It seemed to have occurred an age ago, to a different person, in a different time. However, she did remember much of the conversation, for it had been most diverting. "I recall some," she replied cautiously, "to the best of my recollection and limited feminine capacities, of course." Alexia hated to do it, but it was always advantageous to undermine one's enemy's confidence in one's intelligence.

Mr. MacDougall gave her a shocked glance.

As subtly as possible, Alexia winked at him.

He looked as though he might faint but sat back in his chair, clearly of a mind to let her deal with the situation in whatever way she saw fit.

Miss Tarabotti had the transitory idea that he might be suitable husband material after all. And then realized that a lifelong alliance with a man of such weak character would certainly turn her into a veritable tyrant.

She said, pretending timidity and lack of understanding, "He believes that the supernatural may either be blood-borne, a type of disease, or present as a special organ that those who can become supernatural possess and the rest of us do not."

Siemons smiled in a superior manner at this explanation. Alexia was seized with a quite unladylike desire to slap the smug expression right off his fat face. With those jowls, her hand would probably make a very satisfying smack. She took a hurried gulp of tea instead.

"That is near enough to the truth," he said. "We at the Hypocras Club find his theories intriguing but instead favor the idea that metamorphosis occurs as a result of energy transmission: a type of electricity. Although, a small minority holds out for aethero-magnetic fields. Have you heard of electricity, Miss Tarabotti?"

Of course I have, you nincompoop, was what Alexia wanted to say. Instead she said, "I believe I have read something on the subject. Why do you think this might be the answer?"

"Because supernatural beings react to light: werewolves to the moon and vampires to the sun. Light, we are beginning to theorize, is but another form of electricity; thus, we believe the two may be connected."

Mr. MacDougall leaned forward and joined in the conversation, as it had become one safely within his purview. "Some have suggested that the two theories are not mutually exclusive. After my lecture this evening, there was discussion of possible electricity within blood transfer, or organs whose purpose is to process this light-borne energy. In other words, that the two hypotheses could be combined."

Miss Tarabotti was interested despite herself. "And it is the capacity to process this electrical energy that you believe correlates to the soul?"

The two scientists nodded.

"How do I fit into this?"

The two men looked at each other.

Finally, Mr. Siemons said, "That is what we hope to find out. Do you somehow dampen this energy? We know that certain materials do not conduct electricity. Are preternaturals the living equivalent of a grounding agent?"

Great, Alexia thought, *I have gone from soul-sucker to electrical ground. The epithets just get sweeter and sweeter.* "And how, exactly, do you plan to figure this out?"

She did not expect them to say they wanted to cut her open. Though she had a pretty good idea that Mr. Siemons, at least, rather relished such an eventuality.

"Perhaps it would be best if we showed you some of our experimental equipment so you can get an idea of how we conduct research," suggested Mr. Siemons.

Mr. MacDougall blanched at that. "Are you certain that is such a good plan, sir? She is a lady of gentle breeding, after all. It might be a bit much."

Mr. Siemons gave Miss Tarabotti an assessing look. "Oh, I think she is of a strong enough constitution. Besides, it might . . . encourage . . . her willing participation."

Mr. MacDougall looked whiter at that. "Oh dear," he muttered under his breath, his forehead creased in a frown. He shoved his spectacles up his nose nervously.

"Come, come, my dear sir," said Mr. Siemons jovially. "Nothing is so bad as all that! We have a preternatural to study. Science will rejoice—our mission's conclusion is finally in sight."

Miss Tarabotti looked at him with narrowed eyes. "And what *exactly* is your mission, Mr. Siemons?"

"Why, to protect the commonwealth, of course," he replied.

Miss Tarabotti asked the obvious question. "From whom?"

"From the supernatural threat, what else? We Englishmen have allowed vampires and werewolves to roam openly among us since King Henry's mandate without a clear understanding of what they really *are*. They are predators. For thousands of years, they fed upon us and attacked us. What they have given us in military knowledge has allowed us to build an empire, true, but at what cost?" He became impassioned, his tone the high-voiced raving of a fanatic. "They permeate our government and our defenses, but they are not motivated to protect the best interest of the fully human species. They are only concerned with advancing their own agenda! We believe that agenda to be world domination at the very least. Our goal is mobilization of research in order to secure the homeland from supernatural attack and covert infiltration. This is an exceedingly complex and delicate mission, requiring the focused effort from our entire association. Our main scientific objective is to provide a framework of understanding that shall eventually lead to a unified national effort toward wide-scale extermination!"

Supernatural genocide, Alexia thought, feeling her face blanch. "Good Lord, you are not papal Templars, are you?" She looked about for religious paraphernalia. Was *that* the meaning of the octopuses?

Both men laughed.

"Those fanatics," said the pipe man. "Certainly not. Although some of their tactics have proved moderately useful in our collection expeditions. And, of course, we have recently realized that Templars have in the past employed preternaturals as covert agents. We had thought those rumors mere religious embellishment, the power of faith to cancel the devil's abilities. Now we see there were scientific underpinnings. Some of their information, should we manage to get possession of it, will pave the way toward better understanding of your physiology, if nothing else. But, to answer your question, no, we of the Hypocras Club are of a purely scientific bent."

"Though advocating a political agenda," accused Miss Tarabotti, forgetting her ploy to lull them into a false sense of her stupidity in her amazement at such flagrant disregard for the tenets of scientific objectivity.

"Say instead, Miss Tarabotti, that we have nobility of purpose," said Mr. Siemons. But his smile was not unlike that of a religious fanatic. "We are preserving the freedom of those who matter."

Alexia was confused. "Then why are you creating more of them? Why the experiments?"

Mr. Siemons said, "Know thy enemy, Miss Tarabotti. To eliminate the supernatural, we must first understand the supernatural. Of course, now that we have you, further supernatural vivisections may be unnecessary. We can turn all our attention to deducing the nature and reproducibility of the preternatural instead."

The two men escorted her proudly through the seemingly endless labyrinthine white laboratories of that nightmarish club. Each contained complex machinery of some kind. Most appeared to be steam-powered. There were great pumping bellows with enormous gears and coils to facilitate up-and-down motion. There were shiny engines, smaller than hatboxes, with overly organic curves that were, in their way, more terrifying than the larger contraptions. They all, regardless of size, boasted a brass octopus, riveted somewhere about their casings. The contrast of engine and invertebrate was oddly sinister.

The steam produced by the mechanicals discolored the walls and ceilings of the laboratories, causing the white wallpaper to buckle and pimple outward in yellowed boils. Oil from the gears leaked across the floors in dark viscous rivulets. There were other stains there, too, rust-colored ones that Alexia did not care to think about.

Mr. Siemons proudly detailed the function of each machine, as though relating the accomplishments of his favorite children.

Though Miss Tarabotti heard wheezing gasps and clunks in nearby rooms, she was never shown any machine in action.

She also heard the screams.

At first the keening was so high in pitch she thought it might be sourced in one of the machines. She was not certain *when* she realized it came from a human throat, but the absolute knowledge of its origin hit her so hard she stumbled under the weight of it. No machine could make such a noise as that high, agonized moaning squeal, like an animal being butchered. Alexia leaned heavily against one wall of the hallway, her skin clammy, swallowing down the sour bile her writhing stomach produced in sympathy. She thought she had never before heard so pure a sound of pain.

The machines she had been seeing took on new and horrific meanings as she realized what they might do to a physical body.

Mr. MacDougall was concerned by her sudden pallor. "Miss Tarabotti, you are unwell?"

Alexia looked at him with wide dark eyes. "This place is all madness. Do you realize that?"

Mr. Siemons's jowls swam into her field of view. "I take it you will not cooperate willingly with our research?"

Another high keening scream rent the air. Inside that cry, Alexia could hear Lord Akeldama's voice.

Mr. Siemons cocked his head at the sound and licked his lips, as though savoring a pleasant taste.

Miss Tarabotti shuddered. There was something almost lustful in his gaze. Only then did she finally come to a realization of the truth.

"What does it matter, if *that* is to be my fate either way?" Miss Tarabotti asked.

"Well, it would be easier all round if you were a willing participant."

And why, Alexia wondered, *should I make this easier for you?* She grimaced and said, "What do you want me to do?"

Mr. Siemons smiled like he had just won some competition. "We need to observe and verify the extent of your preternatural abilities. There is no point in us undertaking extensive experimentation if we cannot determine if your purported soul-sucking curse-canceling powers are, in fact, genuine."

Miss Tarabotti shrugged. "So, bring me a vampire. All it takes is one touch."

"Really? Remarkable. Skin to skin, or does it work through clothing?"

"Through clothing most of the time. After all, I wear gloves like any respectable person. But I have not explored the particulars."

Mr. Siemons shook his head as though to clear it. "We will explore further, later. I was thinking of a little more definitive testing. After all, it is full moon night. As it happens, we have just received a substantial delivery of new werewolf specimens in full change. I should like to see if you can counteract such a substantial change."

Mr. MacDougall looked alarmed. "That could be dangerous, if her abilities are false or overexaggerated."

Mr. Siemons grinned wider. "That would be part of the test, would it not?" He turned to Miss Tarabotti. "How long does it usually take for you to neutralize the supernatural?"

Alexia lied instantly and without hesitation. "Oh, generally not much more than an hour."

The scientist, with no prior knowledge of the rapidity of her abilities, was forced to believe her. He looked at the goons, two of whom had been shadowing them throughout the tour. "Bring her."

Mr. MacDougall protested, but to no avail.

Once more prisoner instead of guest, Miss Tarabotti was

dragged unceremoniously back toward the confinement area on the other side of the club grounds.

They took her to the other hallway, the one in which she and Lord Akeldama had not been ensconced. Previously silent, it now resounded with snarling cries and howls. Periodically, some door or another would vibrate violently as though a large body had hurled itself against it.

"Ah," said Mr. Siemons, "I see they have awoken."

"Chloroform works better initially on werewolves than on vampires but does not seem to last as long," reported a young man in a gray jacket who appeared seemingly out of thin air, clutching a leather notepad. He wore a pair of those monocular cross-whatsit lens things, the glassicals, which somehow looked less ridiculous on him than they had on Professor Lyall.

"And which room is *he* in?"

The man pointed with his notebook at one of the doors. One of the few that was not vibrating but stood ominously still and quiet. "Number five."

Mr. Siemons nodded. "He should be the strongest and thus the hardest to change back. Toss her in with him. I will check back in an hour." With that, he left them.

Mr. MacDougall protested vociferously. He even struggled against the two goons, attempting to stop the inevitable. Miss Tarabotti's valuation of his moral fiber rose substantially. But it was all to no avail. The two lackeys were of the overly muscled variety. They tossed the pudgy scientist aside with barely any effort whatsoever.

"But she'll never survive. Not with one in full change! Not if she takes so long to counteract them!" Mr. MacDougall continued to protest.

Even knowing the full extent and rapidity of her skills, Alexia, too, was worried. She had never changed an angry werewolf before, let alone one fully moon-mad. She was pretty certain he could manage to get in at least one bite before her abilities would take full effect. Even then, if she managed to survive that, what kind of man would she be trapped with? Werewolves tended to be physically strong even without their supernatural traits. Such a man could do her considerable harm, preternatural or no.

Miss Tarabotti had very little time to cogitate the possible shortness of her future before she was thrust into the portentously quiet chamber. So quiet, in fact, she could hear the door being locked and bolted behind her.

CHAPTER TWELVE

Nothing but Werewolf

The werewolf charged.

Miss Tarabotti, whose eyes were not yet accustomed to the darkness of the cell, perceived the monster as nothing more than a bulky blur of darkness heading at supernatural speed in her direction. She dove awkwardly to one side, only just fast enough. Her corset stays creaked in a most alarming manner as she tried desperately to twist out of the way. She stumbled upon landing, nearly falling to her knees.

The wolf hit the closed door hard, behind where she had just stood, and slid to the floor in an ungainly heap of long legs and sweeping tail.

Alexia backed away, hands up before her chest in an instinctive, and entirely useless, defensive position. She was not ashamed to admit she was deathly frightened. The werewolf was huge, and she was becoming convinced that what preternaturals *could* do would not be fast enough to cancel out what *he* might be able to do first.

The wolf resumed an upright position, shaking himself like a wet dog. He had a long glossy pelt, silky in texture and of some changeable color difficult to determine in the shadowy room. He crouched down to charge again, powerful muscles quivering, saliva leaking out one side of his mouth in silver rivulets.

He leaped forward in another burst of speed and then twisted before he struck, yanking himself back mid jump.

He could have killed her easily that time. There was no doubt in Alexia's head that his fangs were coming straight for her jugular. Her initial dodge had been pure luck. She was nowhere near fit enough to go up against a regular wolf, let alone a supernatural one. True, she was an inveterate walker and had a decent seat for the hunt, but no one would ever make the mistake of calling Miss Tarabotti a sportswoman.

In an apparent state of confusion, the great beast circled to one side of the cell, then the other, weaving about Alexia and sniffing the air. He gave an odd, frustrated little whine and backed slowly away from her, swaying his bushy head back and forth in profound mental distress. The yellow of his eyes glowed faintly in the dark room. Alexia thought that their expression was one of worry more than hunger.

Miss Tarabotti watched in amazement as for several minutes the werewolf continued his internal struggle, pacing back and forth. Her respite did not last long, however. It soon became clear that despite whatever held him back, the urge to attack was overpowering. The wolf's mouth opened in a snarl of bloodlust, and he coiled his muscles to spring at her once more.

This time, Alexia was pretty darn certain she would not escape unscathed. She had never before seen so many sharp teeth in one place.

The werewolf attacked.

Miss Tarabotti could make out his form more clearly now, her eyes having adjusted fully to the gloom. Yet all she could really process mentally was a great shaggy mass of killing frenzy plunging toward her throat. She wanted desperately to run, but there was nowhere for her to go.

Keeping her wits about her, Alexia stepped toward the charging monster and a little to one side. In the same movement, she tilted sideways as much as her corset would allow and crashed against the beast's ribs, knocking him out of his leap. He was a big wolf, but Alexia Tarabotti was no lightweight either, and she managed to broadside him just enough to throw him off kilter. They fell to the ground together in a coil of skirts and bustle wires and fur and fangs.

Alexia twined her arms, her legs—as much as her underpinnings would allow—and anything else she could manage about the wolf's huge furry body and held on as tightly as humanly possible.

With a profound sense of relief, she felt his fur disappear and his bones re-form under her fingers. The sound of muscle, sinew, and cartilage breaking was truly gruesome, like a cow being butchered, but the feel of it was even worse. The sensation of fur disappearing at her touch, crawling away from any point of contact with her body, and the bones, liquidlike, changing their very nature under his flesh, was one that would haunt her for months. But, eventually, she held only warm human skin and solid lean muscles.

Miss Tarabotti took a long, deep, shaky breath and from the smell alone had no doubt at all whom it was she held. For the scent was all open grassy fields and night air. Involuntarily, her hands moved against his skin in relief. Then, of course, she realized something else.

"Why, Lord Maccon, you are stark naked!" Alexia said. She was appalled beyond all reason by this last in the long string of indignities she had had to suffer in the space of one torturous evening.

The Earl of Woolsey was indeed completely nude. He did not seem particularly perturbed by this fact, but Miss Tarabotti felt the sudden need to close her eyes tight and think about asparagus or something equally mundane. Coiled about him as she was, her chin wedged over one of his massive shoulders, she was being forced to look down directly at a nicely round, but embarrassing bare, moon. And not the kind that caused werewolves to change either. Although it did seem to be changing aspects of her own anatomy that she would rather not think about. It was all a very heady—or bottomy?—experience.

But, Alexia reasoned, *at least he is no longer trying to kill me.*

"Well, Miss Tarabotti," admitted the earl, "nakedness happens, I am ashamed to say, particularly to us werewolves. To compound the offense, I must ask you most cordially *not* to let go." Lord Maccon was panting, and his voice sounded funny, all low and gruff and hesitant.

With her chest pressed hard against his, Alexia could feel the rapid beat of his overtaxed heart. A strange series of questions ran through her head. *Was his exertion the result of the attack or the change? What happened if he changed into wolf form in full evening dress? Would the clothes rip? That was sure to be inconveniently expensive! How come it was socially acceptable for werewolves in the wolf state to run around completely starkers, but not anyone else?*

Instead she asked, "Are you cold?"

Lord Maccon laughed. "Practical as always, Miss Tarabotti. It is a little chilly in here, but I am well enough for the moment."

Alexia looked at his long, powerful, but bare, legs dubiously. "I suppose I could loan you my underskirt."

The earl snorted. "I hardly think that would look very dignified."

Miss Tarabotti reared back so she could look him in the face for the first time. "I meant to drape over you like a blanket, not to wear, you ridiculous man!" She was blushing heatedly, but with her dark skin, she knew it was not noticeable. "Besides, remaining exposed is hardly a dignified condition either."

"Aye, I see. Thank you for the thought, but . . ." Lord Maccon trailed off, becoming distracted by something far more interesting. "Uh, where exactly are we?"

"We are guests of the Hypocras Club. That new scientific establishment that opened recently right next door to the Snodgroves' town residence." She did not even pause to let him interject but hurried agitatedly on. Partly because she wanted to relay everything she could before she forgot something vital and partly because their intimate proximity was making her nervous. "It is the scientists here who are behind the supernatural disappearances," she said, "as I am certain you are now well aware. You yourself have become one of those very vanishing acts. They have quite the arrangement here. We are currently in underground facilities reached only by something called an ascension chamber. And there are rooms upon rooms of exotic steam and electric current machinery on the other side of the foyer. They have got Lord Akeldama hooked up to something called an exsanguination machine, and I heard the most horrible screams. I think it was him. Conall"—this was said most earnestly—"I believe that they may be torturing him to death."

Miss Tarabotti's big dark eyes welled with tears.

Lord Maccon had never before seen her cry. It did the most remarkable thing to his own emotions. He became irrationally angry that anything might make *his* stalwart Alexia sad. He wanted to kill someone, and this time it was not at all tied into being a werewolf. It couldn't be, as, held tightly in her arms, he was as human as possible.

Alexia paused to take a breath, and Lord Maccon said, in an attempt to distract her from her unhappiness and himself from homicidal thoughts, "Aye, this is all very informative, but why are *you* here?"

"Oh, they put me in with you to check the authenticity of my abilities as a preternatural," she answered, as though this fact were perfectly obvious. "They have your BUR files on me, the ones that were stolen, and they wanted to see if the reports were true."

Lord Maccon looked ashamed. "Sorry about that. I still do not know how they got through my security. But what I meant was, how did you get here, to the club?"

She tried to find the least embarrassing place to rest her hands. Finally she decided the middle of his back was safest. She was seized with a most irrational desire to rub her fingertips up and down the indentation of his spine. She resisted and said,

"Technically, I believe they were after Lord Akeldama, something about his being very old. Apparently this is an important factor in their experimentation. I was having dinner with him. I told you I was going to, remember? They chloroformed his entire residence and brought me along because I was with him. They only realized who I was when Mr. MacDougall came into my cell and saw me. He used my name, and the other man, he is called Siemons, remembered it from your paperwork. Oh! And you should know, they have an automaton." She tensed at the memory of that awful waxy thing.

Lord Maccon rubbed his big hands over her back in an absentminded soothing motion. Miss Tarabotti took it as an excuse to loosen her own grasp a mite. The temptation to begin her own rubbing was almost overwhelming.

He interpreted her relaxed hold the wrong way. "No, do not let go," he said, shifting his grip to pull her, if possible, even more intimately against his naked body. Then he answered her statement. "We had surmised that it was an automaton. Though I have never before encountered one filled with blood. It must be some newfangled construction. It may even be on a clockwork frame. I tell you, science can do amazing things these days." He shook his head. His hair brushed against Alexia's cheek. There was an edge of admiration mingled with the disgust in his voice.

"You knew it was an automaton, and you did not tell me?" Miss Tarabotti was most disgruntled, partly because she had not been informed and partly because Lord Maccon's hair was so very silky. So was his skin, for that matter. Alexia wished she had gloves on, for she had given up and was now running her fingers in circles against his back.

"I hardly see how your knowing might have improved matters. I am certain you would have continued to engage in your customary reckless behavior," said Lord Maccon rudely, not at all perturbed by her caress. In fact, though they were arguing, he had taken to nuzzling her neck between phrases.

"Ah-ha, I like that," replied Alexia. "I might remind you that *you*, too, have now been captured. Was that not a consequence of *your* reckless behavior?"

Lord Maccon looked worried. "Quite the opposite, actually. It was the consequence of too predictable nonreckless behavior patterns. They knew exactly where to find me and at what time I would return home on full-moon night. They used chloroform on the whole pack. Blast them! This Hypocras Club must hold a controlling interest in a chloroform company, given the sheer amount of the chemical that they seem to have access to." He cocked his head, listening. "From the number of howls, it sounds like they brought the entire pack in. I do hope the clavigers escaped."

"The scientists do not seem interested in drones or clavigers," said Miss Tarabotti reassuringly, "only fully supernatural and preternatural types. They seem to believe they must protect the commonwealth against some mysterious threat posed by yourself and others of your set. In order to do this, they are trying to *understand* the supernatural, to which end they have been conducting all sorts of horrendous experiments."

Lord Maccon stopped nuzzling, lifted his head, and growled, "They are *Templars*?"

"Nothing so church-bound as that," Miss Tarabotti said. "Purely scientific investigators, simply warped, so far as I can tell. And obsessed with octopuses." She looked sad, knowing the answer before she asked the next question. "Do you think the Royal Society is involved?"

Lord Maccon shrugged.

Alexia could feel the movement all up and down her body, even through her layers of clothing.

"I rather believe they must be," he said. "Though I suspect we would find that difficult to prove. There must have been others as well; the quality of the machinery and supplies alone would seem to indicate some considerable monetary investment on the part of several unknown benefactors. It is not entirely a surprise to us, you realize? After all, normal humans are right to suspect a supernatural agenda. We are basically immortal; our goals are likely to be a little different from those of ordinary people, sometimes even at odds. When all is said and done, daylight folk are still food."

Alexia stopped petting him and narrowed her eyes in mock suspicion. "Am I allied with the wrong side in this little war?"

In reality, she did not have much doubt. After all, she had never heard cries of pain and torture coming from the BUR offices. Even Countess Nadasdy and her hive seemed more civilized than Mr. Siemons and his machines.

"That depends." Lord Maccon lay passive in her arms. On full-moon night in human form, he was dependent upon her ability and her whim for his sanity. It did not sit well with an Alpha. All the choices were hers, including this one. "Have you decided which you prefer?"

"They did ask for my cooperation," she informed him coyly. Miss Tarabotti was enjoying having the upper hand over Lord Maccon.

The earl looked worried. "And?"

Alexia had never even contemplated Mr. Siemons's offer as a real possibility. Yet Lord Maccon was looking at her as though she had actually had a choice. How could she explain to the earl that, quite apart from anything else—including their constant arguments—*he* had her complete loyalty? She could not—not without having to admit, to herself or him, why that might be the case.

"Let us simply say," she said at last, "that I prefer your methods."

Lord Maccon went perfectly still. A gleam entered his beautiful tawny eyes. "Is that so? Which ones?"

Miss Tarabotti pinched him for such blatant innuendo. It did not matter where she pinched, as the earl was a bare canvas of pinchability.

"Ow!" said the Alpha, looking pained. "What was that for?"

"May I remind you we are in grave danger? I have managed to acquire for us, at most, an hour of grace time."

"How on earth did you finagle that?" he asked, rubbing the place she had just pinched.

Alexia smiled. "Luckily, your files on me did not report everything. I simply told Mr. Siemons my preternatural powers took an hour to activate."

"And they threw you into this cell with me anyway?" Lord Maccon was not pleased in the least by this bit of information.

"Did I not just say that I preferred your methods? Now you know why." Alexia twitched uncomfortably. She was getting a cramp in one of her shoulders. Lord Maccon's torso was rather too large to have one's arms wrapped around for an extended period of time, especially when one was lying on a hard wooden floor. Not that she was about to complain, mind you.

Her evident discomfort made the earl ask, in all seriousness, "I did not hurt you, did I?"

Miss Tarabotti cocked her head to one side and raised an eyebrow at him.

"I mean, when I attacked you just now, in wolf form? We werewolves do not remember much that happens during the full moon, you see. It is all embarrassingly instinctual," he admitted.

Miss Tarabotti patted him reassuringly. "I think you realized, almost despite yourself, that it was me you nearly killed."

"I smelled you," he admitted gruffly. "It sparked off a whole different set of instincts. I *do* remember being very confused, but not much else."

"What kind of different instincts?" Miss Tarabotti asked archly. She knew she was treading dangerous ground, but for some reason she could not resist encouraging him. She wanted to hear him say it. She wondered at what time she had become such a hardened flirt. *Well*, she reasoned, *one must get something from one's mother's side of the family.*

"Mmm. The reproductive variety." The earl began to nibble her neck with wholly concentrated interest.

Miss Tarabotti's innards turned toward a feel of mashed

potatoes. Fighting her own urge to nibble back, she pinched him again, harder this time.

"Ow! Stop that!" He left off nibbling and glared at her. It was a funny thing to see such an expression of wounded dignity on the face of such an enormous and highly dangerous man—even if he was naked.

Alexia said practically, "We have no time for such monkey-shines. We must determine a way out of this predicament. We have to rescue Lord Akeldama, and we absolutely must close this wretched club down. Your amorous intentions are not currently part of the agenda."

"Is there a way they might become so, in the not-too-distant future?" Lord Maccon asked meekly, shifting against her in a manner that ensured she realized the nibbling had affected his outsides just as much as her insides. Alexia was partly shocked, partly intrigued by the idea that as he was naked, she might actually get to *see* what he looked like. She had seen sketches of the nude male, of course, for purely technical purposes. She was given to wonder if werewolves were anatomically bigger in certain areas. Of course, she was touching Lord Maccon, so such supernatural traits ought rightly to be canceled out, but in the interest of scientific curiosity, she shifted her lower body away from him a handbreadth and peeked downward. She was thwarted by the material of her own skirt wadded between them.

Taking her movement as withdrawal rather than curiosity, the earl pulled her back against him possessively. He slid one leg between her two, trying to shift multiple skirts and petticoats out of his way.

Miss Tarabotti sighed in long-suffering style.

He returned to nibbling and then nipping and kissing softly up and down the entire column of her throat. This was causing most distractingly invigorating frissons of sensation up and down her sides, over her ribs, and toward her nether regions. It was almost uncomfortable, as though her skin itched from underneath. Also, due to his unclothed state, Alexia was learning ever more about the veracity of some of those sketches. Still, her father's books had not entirely done the situation justice.

Lord Maccon slid one hand up into her hair.

So much for tying it back, thought Alexia as he loosed it from her hard-won ribbon.

The earl tugged at the black tresses, pulling her head back so as to more fully expose her neck to his lips and teeth.

Miss Tarabotti decided that there was something excruciatingly erotic about being fully dressed with a large naked man pressed against her from breast to foot.

Since she had not been able to see for herself exactly what the earl's frontal area looked like, Alexia decided to try the next best thing and began to work her hand around to touch. She was not entirely sure this was the kind of action a young lady undertook in such situations, but then again, most young ladies did not get themselves into them to start with. *In for a penny, in for a pound*, she decided. Miss Tarabotti always was one to seize the moment. So she seized.

Lord Maccon, and the certain portion of his anatomy now firmly in her grasp, jerked violently.

Miss Tarabotti let go. "Oops," she said. "Should I not have?" She trailed off, humiliated.

He hastened to reassure her. "Oh no, you most certainly should. It was simply unexpected." He pressed up against her receptively.

Embarrassed but more curious than anything else, purely scientifically, mind you, Alexia continued her explorations, a little more tenderly this time. His skin in that area was very soft, and there was hair nested at the base. He produced the most delicious noises under her tentative touch. She became increasingly intrigued but was also getting more and more concerned with the logistics of any further proceedings.

"Um, Lord Maccon?" she said finally in a cautious whisper.

The earl laughed. "No choice at this point, Alexia; you simply must call me Conall."

She swallowed. He could feel the movement under his lips.

"Conall, aren't we getting a tad carried away given the circumstances?"

The earl pulled her head back so he could look her directly in the eyes. "What are you blathering on about now, you impossible female?" His tawny eyes were glazed with passion, and he was breathing hard. Alexia was shocked to discover her own breathing was far from relaxed.

She scrunched up her forehead, trying to find the right words. "Well, should we not be abed for this kind of sport? Plus, they are scheduled to return at any moment."

"They? Who?" He was clearly falling behind the conversation.

"The scientists."

Lord Maccon gave a strangled laugh. "Aye, yes. And we wouldn't want them to learn too much about interspecies relations, now, would we?" He reached down with a free hand and pulled hers away from its questing.

Miss Tarabotti was faintly disappointed. Until he raised it to his lips and kissed it. "I do not mean to rush into these things, Alexia. You are inexplicably tempting."

She nodded, bumping his head slightly. "The feeling is mutual, my lord. Not to mention unexpected."

He seemed to take that as encouragement and rolled so that she was beneath him, and he loomed above her. He was now lying between her legs, component parts flush against hers.

Alexia squeaked at the sudden shift in positions. She was not certain whether she should be grateful or upset that women's fashion demanded so many copious layers of fabric, as this was now all that prevented more intimate contact and, she was pretty certain, sexual congress.

"Lord Maccon . . . " she said in her best, most severe, spinster voice.

"Conall," he interrupted. He leaned back, and his hands began journeying over her chest.

"Conall! Now is *not* the time!"

He ignored her and asked, "How do I undo this blasted dress?"

Alexia's ivory taffeta gown was held together by a row of tiny mother-of-pearl buttons up the length of its back. Although she did not answer him, the earl eventually discovered this fact and began undoing them with a rapidity that bespoke consummate skill in the art of undoing ladies' clothing. Miss Tarabotti would have been disgruntled, except that she figured it was best if one of them knew what they were on about in the matter of fornication. And she could hardly expect a gentleman of over two hundred years or so to have remained celibate.

In no time at all, he had dexterously undone enough of the buttons to pull down the neckline of her dress and expose the tops of her breasts where they rose above her corset. He bent and began kissing them, only to stop, rear back very suddenly, and say in a voice harsh with suppressed need, "What in tarnation is that?"

Alexia lifted herself onto her elbows and looked down, trying to see what it was that had stopped the annoying but unfortunately delightful ravishment of her personage. However, given the nature of her copious endowments in the bosom department, she could not make out what it was about her corset that had so taken his attention.

Lord Maccon picked up the shard of mirror wrapped in a handkerchief and showed it to her.

"Oh, I forgot about that. I pinched it from the dressing room when the scientists left me alone for a moment. Thought it might come in handy."

Lord Maccon gave her a long, thoughtful, only mildly amorous look. "Very resourceful, my dear. It is at times like this when I really wish you could be on the BUR roster."

She looked up into his face, embarrassed more by the compliment and the endearment than she had been by their previous physical proceedings. "So, what is the plan?"

"*We* are not going to develop a plan," he growled, placing the mirror carefully down on the floor next to them, out of view of the doorway.

Alexia grinned at such foolish protectiveness. "Do not be ridiculous. You can hardly hope to accomplish anything more this night without my help. It is full moon, remember?"

Lord Maccon, who had, outrageously, forgotten the moon, had a momentary shock of terror that, in his absentmindedness, he might lose proximity with her. Alexia's preternatural abilities were the only thing currently keeping him sane. He quickly canvassed to make certain they were in firm physical contact. His body reminded him that, yes, *firm* was the operative word.

He tried to keep his head focused on their future nonamorous actions. "Well, in that case, you are to remain tangential as much as possible. None of those fire-eating antics you are so fond of. In order to get us out of here, I may have to use violence. In which case, you will need to hold on to me tightly and stay well out of the way. Do you ken?"

Alexia was going to get defensive and angry and explain quite severely that she was practical enough to avoid fisticuffs, especially when she had no brass parasol to protect herself with, but instead she said, "Did you just ask if I *kenned*?" She could not help grinning.

Lord Maccon looked ashamed of the verbal slip and muttered something about Scotland under his breath.

"You did! I was just kenned!" Miss Tarabotti's grin widened. She could not restrain herself; she did so like it when the earl's Highland lilt came out. It was currently her second favorite thing he did with his tongue. She leaned up on her elbows and kissed him softly on the cheek. Almost despite himself, Lord Maccon moved his own mouth toward her lips and turned it into a far deeper kiss.

When Alexia finally dropped back, they were both panting again.

"This has got to stop," she insisted. "We are in danger,

remember? You know, ruination and tragedy? Calamity just beyond that door." She pointed behind him. "Any moment now, evil scientists may come charging in."

"All the more reason to grasp the opportunity," he insisted, leaning in and pressing his lower body against her.

Miss Tarabotti pressed against his torso defensively with both hands, trying to stop him from kissing her again. She cursed fate that had set life up so that when she finally did get to touch Lord Maccon's bare chest, there was no time to appreciate it.

He nibbled her earlobe. "Just think of this as a sort of wedding-night prelude."

Alexia was not certain which part of that particular statement gave the most offense—the fact that he assumed there would be a wedding night or the fact that he assumed it would take place on the hard floor of a barren room.

"Really, Lord Maccon!" she said, pushing harder.

"Oh dear, back to that, are we?"

"Where do you keep getting this idea that we should marry?"

Lord Maccon rolled his tawny eyes and gestured expressively to his naked flesh. "I assure you, Miss Tarabotti, I do not do these kinds of things with a woman of your caliber without contemplating marriage in the very near future. I may be a werewolf and Scottish, but despite what you may have read about both, we are not cads!"

"I do not want to force you into anything," Alexia insisted.

Keeping hold of her with one hand, the Alpha rolled off her prone body and sat back. Although he kept in contact to keep himself from changing, most of him was now separated from Alexia.

Miss Tarabotti's eyes, having entirely adjusted to the dim interior of the room, received a full-frontal view. Those sketches in her papa's books had been far more restrained than she realized.

"Really, we must discuss this silly notion of yours," he said with a sigh.

"What?" she croaked, goggling at him.

"That you will not marry me."

"Must we discuss it here and now?" she said, not realizing what she was saying. "And why is it silly?"

"Well, at least we have some privacy." He shrugged. The movement shifted all the muscles of his chest and stomach.

"Uh . . . uh . . . " stuttered Miss Tarabotti, "couldn't it wait until I am home and you are, uh, clothed?"

Lord Maccon realized he had the advantage over Alexia; he was not about to sacrifice it. "Why, you think your family will allow us some privacy? My pack certainly will not. They have been eager to meet you ever since I came home covered in your scent. Not to mention Lyall and his gossiping."

"Professor Lyall gossips?" Alexia tore her eyes away from his body to look up into his face.

"Like an old churchyard biddy."

"And what exactly has he told them?"

"That the pack is getting an Alpha female. I am not giving up, you realize?" He said it with deadly calm.

"But I thought it was my move? Isn't that the way this works?" Miss Tarabotti was confused.

Lord Maccon's grin was all wolf. "Up to a certain point. Let us simply say you have made your preferences known."

"I thought you found me utterly impossible."

He grinned cheerfully. "Most assuredly."

Alexia's stomach flipped over, and she was seized with the sudden impulse to tackle him and rub up against him. Lord Maccon naked was one thing; naked and smiling that gently crooked smile of his—devastating.

"I thought I was too bossy," she said.

"And I shall provide you with an entire pack to boss around. They could use the discipline. I have been getting lax in my old age."

Miss Tarabotti highly doubted that. "I thought you found my family impossible."

"I shall not be marrying them," he began, inching back in toward her, sensing a weakness in her resolve.

Miss Tarabotti was not certain his return was a good thing. True, that most disturbing view was blurring as he moved toward her, but he had that look on his face that said the kissing would start up again presently. She wondered exactly how she had managed to get herself into such an untenable position.

"But I am tall, and brown, and have a large nose, and large everything else." She gestured ineffectually at her hips and chest.

"Mmm," said the earl, agreeing with her entirely, "you most certainly do." He found it interesting she did not mention those things that had worried him from the start: his age (advanced) and her state (preternatural). But he was not about to assist in her protestations by giving her more ammunition in objecting to his suit. They could talk about his own concerns later—preferably after they were married; that is, he grimaced mentally, if they managed to survive their current predicament and make it to the altar.

Finally, Alexia came round and about to the thing that really troubled her. She looked down at her free hand as though finding its palm fascinating. "You do not love me."

"Ah," said the Alpha, looking pleased at this, "says who? You never asked me. Should it not be *my* opinion you take into account?"

"Well," sputtered Miss Tarabotti, at a loss for words. "Well, I never."

"So?" He raised an eyebrow.

Alexia bit her lip, white teeth gnawing at the full swollen flesh. Finally, she lifted trembling lashes and cast a very worried glance up at him, now too close to her once more.

Naturally, because fortune is a fickle beast, it was precisely at that moment that the door to their cell opened.

Standing in the doorway was a backlit figure, clapping slowly but with evident approval.

CHAPTER THIRTEEN

The Last Room

In a lightning-fast movement, which bespoke his dexterity as a human before he had become a werewolf, Lord Maccon shifted around Miss Tarabotti so that his back was to the intruder and he was shielding her with his body. In the same motion, Alexia saw he had managed to grab the shard of mirror off the floor next to them. He held it between them, protected from Mr. Siemons's view.

"Well, Miss Tarabotti," said the scientist, "you certainly do excellent work. I never thought to see a werewolf Alpha in human form on full-moon night."

Alexia moved to sit, lifting the bodice of her dress over her shoulders as subtly as possible. The back had entirely come undone. She glared at Lord Maccon, who looked back at her in an utterly unapologetic way.

"Mr. Siemons," she said flatly.

As the scientist moved into the room, she saw that behind him stood at least six other men of varying sizes, mostly on the larger end of the spectrum. He was clearly taking no chances should her preternatural abilities be simply a superstitious hoax. But, having found no werewolf in residence, he stared at Lord Maccon's back with a decidedly clinical expression.

"Does his brain return to human reason as well as his body to human form, or is he still essentially a wolf inside?" the scientist asked.

Alexia saw the earl's intent in the narrowing of his eyes and the way he shifted his grip on the shard. With his back to the door, Lord Maccon had not seen Mr. Siemons's large retinue. Miss Tarabotti shook her head almost imperceptibly at him. Taking the hint, he subsided slightly.

Mr. Siemons came closer. Bending over their prone forms, he made to grab the earl's head so he could tilt it up and look into his face. With a spark of malicious humor, Lord Maccon growled loudly and snapped at him as though he were still a wolf. Mr. Siemons hurriedly backed away.

He looked at Alexia. "Really," he said, "quite remarkable. We are going to have to study your abilities extensively, and there are several tests . . ." He trailed off. "Are you certain I cannot persuade you to our cause—that of justice and security? Now that you have experienced the true terror of a werewolf attack, you must admit to how incontrovertibly hazardous these creatures are! They are nothing more than a plague on the human race. Our research will lead to empire-wide prevention and protection against this threat. With your capabilities, we could determine new neutralization tactics. Don't you see how valuable you could be to us? We would simply want to do a few physical assessments now and again."

Alexia was not quite sure what to say. She was both repulsed and frightened by the eminently reasonable way in which the man spoke. For there she sat, flush against a werewolf, a man whom this kidnapper, this torturer, thought of as an abomination. Yet a man whom, she realized with no surprise whatsoever, she loved.

"Thank you for the kind offer—" she began.

The scientist interrupted her. "Your cooperation would be invaluable, but it is not necessary, Miss Tarabotti. Understand, we will do what we must."

"Then I would act in accordance with my conscience, not

yours," she said firmly. "Your perception of me must logically be as warped as your perception of him." She dipped her chin at Lord Maccon. He was glaring at her intently, as though trying to get her to stay silent. But Miss Tarabotti's tongue had always gotten the better of her—hinged in the middle as it undoubtedly was. "I would as soon not be a willing participant in your fiendish experiments."

Mr. Siemons smiled a tight little psychopathic smile. Then he turned away and yelled something in Latin.

A brief silence descended.

There was a rustle among the scientists and thugs gathered in the doorway, and the automaton pushed them aside to enter the cell.

Lord Maccon could see the revulsion on Miss Tarabotti's face, but he still did not turn around to find out what had caused it. He remained resolutely facing away from the scientist and those who stood behind him, keeping his naked back to the events. He had grown tenser and tenser as Alexia and Mr. Siemons exchanged barbs.

Miss Tarabotti could feel his vibrating aggravation at every point of contact between their bodies. She could see it in the hard muscles under his bare skin. He practically quivered, like a dog straining at its lead.

Alexia knew he was going to break a moment before he did.

In one smooth movement, Lord Maccon turned and lashed out with the mirror shard. Mr. Siemons, seeing a certain apprehension enter Alexia's face, stepped out of range.

At the same time, the automaton came forward and to one side, lunging for Miss Tarabotti.

Caught midswing and hampered by having to stay in physical contact with her, Lord Maccon could not switch to strike against the automaton quickly enough.

Alexia was not so restricted. As soon as the evil thing closed in on her, she screamed and lashed out, certain she would die if that repulsive imitation of a man touched her.

Notwithstanding her aversion, the automaton grabbed Miss Tarabotti under the armpits with its cold fingernail-less hands and picked her up bodily. The monster was amazingly strong. Alexia kicked out, and though she made definitive contact with the heel of her boot, it did not seem to affect the creature. It threw her, still kicking and screeching like a banshee, over one waxy shoulder.

Lord Maccon whirled back toward her, but the combination of his lunge and the automaton's attack had broken contact between them. Alexia, draped facedown, caught his panicked expression through the tangle of her hair and then the flash of something sharp. With his last conscious thought, Lord Maccon had thrown the shard of mirror into the automaton's lower back, just under where she hung suspended.

"He is changing back!" yelled Mr. Siemons, retreating rapidly from the room. The automaton, carrying the squirming Miss Tarabotti, followed.

"Neutralize him! Quickly!" Mr. Siemons ordered the men waiting in the doorway. They rushed into the chamber.

Miss Tarabotti felt a little sorry, realizing they had no idea how fast the change would occur. She had claimed it would take her an hour to change a werewolf back into human form. They must have thought it took equally long to change back. She hoped this gave Lord Maccon some kind of advantage. It would be a mixed blessing in any event, his animal instincts now taking over completely, placing everyone, even her, at risk.

As they moved rapidly down the corridor, Miss Tarabotti heard a portentous snarl, a sad wet crunching sound, and then terrified screams. Those cries being so much more impressively blood-curdling than her own, she stopped her bansheelike screeching and turned her attention to trying to get the automaton to drop her. She kicked and writhed with animalistic vigor. Unfortunately, the construct's grip was like iron about her waist. Since she had no idea exactly what the monstrosity was made of, she figured its grip could actually *be* iron.

Whatever the skeletal superstructure of the *homunculus*

simulacrum, it was coated in a layer of fleshy substance. Miss Tarabotti eventually stopped struggling, a waste of energy, and stared morosely down at the shard of mirror sticking out of its back. A small amount of dark viscous liquid was leaking from where it stuck. In fascinated horror, she realized Lord Maccon was right. The being was filled with blood—old, black, dirty blood. *Was everything,* she wondered, *about blood with these scientists?* And then: *Why had Lord Maccon been so intent on wounding the automaton?* It came to her. *He needs a trail to follow. This will never do,* she thought. *It's not bleeding enough to leave drops behind.*

Trying not to think about it too closely, she reached for the piece of mirror embedded in the automaton's oozing flesh. She slashed the soft underside of her arm against an exposed corner of the sharp shard. Her own blood, a healthy bright red, welled fast and clean and dripped in perfect droplets onto the carpeted floor. She wondered if even her blood smelled of cinnamon and vanilla to Lord Maccon.

No one noticed. The automaton, following its master, carried her back through the receiving room of the club and toward the machinery chambers. They passed by those rooms Miss Tarabotti had visited on her tour of the Hypocras facilities and on toward parts she had not been allowed to see. This was the area from which she had heard those terrible screams.

They reached the last room at the very end of the corridor. Alexia managed to twist about enough to read a small slip of paper tacked to the side of the door. It said, in neat black calligraphy, framed on either side by an etched octopus, EXSANGUINATION CHAMBER.

Miss Tarabotti could see nothing of the interior from where she hung, until Mr. Siemons issued instructions in that undecipherable Latin of his, and the automaton put her down. Alexia bounced away from the creature like a not-very-agile gazelle. Undeterred, the automaton grabbed both her arms and wrenched her back to itself, holding her immobilized.

She stiffened in revulsion. No matter that it had just carried her the length of the club, her skin still shivered away in horror whenever the monster touched her.

Swallowing down bile, she took a deep breath and tried to calm herself. Reaching some kind of equilibrium, she shook her hair out of her face and looked about.

The room contained six iron platforms of equal size and shape, bolted to the floor and paired off into three groups of two. Each platform, the size of a large man, was equipped with a plethora of restraints made of various materials. Two young scientists in gray frock coats and glassicals bustled about. They clutched leather-bound notepads and were jotting observations in them using sticks of graphite wrapped in sheepskin. An older man, about Mr. Siemons's age, was also in attendance. He wore a tweed suit, of all horrible things, and a cravat tied with such carelessness it was almost as much a sin as his actions. He also wore glassicals, but of a larger, more elaborate kind than Alexia had seen before. All three gentlemen paused to look at them when they entered the room, their eyes distorted to hugeness by the optical glass. Then they were back to moving between the lifeless figures of two men lying on one pair of platforms. One figure was tied down with sisal rope, and the other . . .

Alexia cried out in horror and distress. The other wore an extravagant plum-colored velvet evening coat stained with blood and a satin waistcoat of sea-foam green and mauve plaid torn in several places. He, too, was tied down with rope, but he had also been crucified through both hands and feet with wooden stakes. The stakes were bolted into the platform on which he lay, and Alexia could not tell if he lay still because of the pain they caused him or because he could no longer move at all.

Miss Tarabotti wrenched toward her friend convulsively, but the automaton held her fast. Finding reason only at the very last, Alexia figured this was probably a good thing. If she touched Lord Akeldama when he was in such a weakened state, her preternatural abilities might bring about his immediate demise. Only his supernatural strength was keeping him alive—that is, if he *was* still alive.

"You," she sputtered at Mr. Siemons, searching for a word horrible enough to describe these so-called scientists, "you *philistines*! What have you done to him?"

Not only had Lord Akeldama been strapped and nailed down, but they had hooked him into one of their infernal machines. One sleeve of his beautiful coat had been cut away, as had the silk shirt underneath, and a long metal tube emerged from under the skin of his upper arm. The tube ran into a mechanical steam-driven contraption of some kind, from which came another tube, which hooked into the other man. This second man was clearly not supernatural; his skin was tan and his cheeks rosy. But he, too, lay as still as death.

"How far along are we, Cecil?" Mr. Siemons asked one of the gray-clad scientists, completely ignoring Miss Tarabotti.

"Nearly done, sir. We think you may be correct about the age. This seems to be going much more smoothly than our previous procedures."

"And the application of the electrical current?" Mr. Siemons scratched his sideburns.

The man looked down at his notations, twiddling the side of his glassicals for focus. "Within the hour, sir, within the hour."

Mr. Siemons rubbed his hands together delightedly. "Excellent, quite excellent. I shall not disturb Dr. Neebs; he looks to be concentrating deeply. I know how involved he gets in his work."

"We are trying to moderate the intensity of the shock, sir. Dr. Neebs thinks this might extend survival time in the recipient," explained the second young scientist, looking up from some large levers he was fiddling with on the side of the machine.

"Fascinating thought. Very interesting approach. Proceed, please, proceed. Do not mind me. Just bringing in a new specimen." He turned and gestured at Miss Tarabotti.

"Very good, sir. I'll just get on, then," said the first scientist, who went back to what he had been doing before they entered the room with barely a glance in Miss Tarabotti's direction.

Alexia looked Mr. Siemons full in the face. "I am beginning to understand," she said in a quiet, deadly voice, "who is the monster. What you are doing is farther from natural than vampires or werewolves could ever get. You are profaning creation, not only with this"—she gestured rudely with her thumb at the automaton holding her tightly—"but with that." She pointed to the machine with its suckerlike metal tubes reaching hungrily inside the body of her dear friend. The horrible contraption seemed to be drinking him dry, more hungry for blood than any vampire she had ever seen. "It is you, Mr. Siemons, who is the abomination."

Mr. Siemons stepped forward and slapped her hard across the face. The sound, a sharp crack, caused Dr. Neebs to look up from his work. No one said anything, though, and all three scientists immediately returned to their activities.

Alexia recoiled back against the cold stillness of the automaton. Instantly, she jerked forward away from it once more, blinking away tears of frustration. When her vision had cleared, she could see that Mr. Siemons was once more smiling his tight little psychopathic smile.

"Protocol, Miss Tarabotti," he said. Then he said something in Latin.

The automaton hauled Alexia over to one of the other sets of platforms. One of the young scientists stopped what he was doing and came to strap her down while the creature held her immobile. Mr. Siemons helped to secure her ankles and wrists with rope tied so tight Miss Tarabotti was certain she would lose all circulation to her extremities. The platform was decked out with massive manacles made of solid metal that looked to be iron coated in silver, and there were more of those awful wooden stakes, but the scientists clearly did not think she needed such extreme measures.

"Bring in a new test recipient," Mr. Siemons ordered once she was secure. The gray-coated young man nodded, put his leather notebook on a small shelf, took off the glassicals, and left the room.

The automaton took up residence in front of the closed door, a silent wax-faced sentry.

Alexia twisted her head to one side. She could see Lord Akeldama to her left, still lying silent and unmoving on his platform. The older scientist, Dr. Neebs, seemed to have completed his task. He was now hooking another machine into the one with all the tubes. This new apparatus was a small engine of some kind, all gears and cogs. At its heart was a glass jar with metal plates at each end.

The remaining gray-clad young scientist came around and began to rigorously turn a crank attached to this device.

Eventually there issued a sharp crackling sound, and a vibrating beam of extraordinarily white light ran up the tube attached to Lord Akeldama's arm and penetrated his body. The vampire jerked and writhed, pulling involuntarily on the wooden stakes impaling his hands and feet. His eyes shot open, and he let out a keening scream of pain.

The young scientist, still cranking with one hand, pulled a small lever down with his other, and the beam of light shifted through the exsanguination machine to run up the tube attached to the seemingly comatose human subject on the platform next to Lord Akeldama.

This man's eyes also opened. He, too, jerked and screamed. The scientist stopped cranking, and the electrical current, for Alexia surmised that must be what it was, dissipated. Ignoring Lord Akeldama, who slumped with eyes closed, looking small and sunken and very old, Mr. Siemons, Dr. Neebs, and the young scientist rushed over to the other man. Dr. Neebs checked his pulse and then lifted his now-closed eyelids to check his pupils, staring hard through the glassicals. The man lay perfectly still.

Then, suddenly, he began to whimper, like a child at the end of a tantrum—out of tears, with only small dry heaving sobs left. All the muscles in his body seemed to lock up, his bones stiffened, and his eyes practically bulged right out of his head. The three scientists backed away but continued to watch him intently.

"Ah, there he goes," said Mr. Siemons with satisfaction.

"Yes, yes." Dr. Neebs nodded, slapping his hands together and rubbing. "Perfect!"

The gray-clad youngster busily scratched notes into his leather pad.

"A much more rapid and efficient result, Dr. Neebs. This is commendable progress. I shall write a most favorable report," said Mr. Siemons, smiling widely and licking his lips.

Dr. Neebs beamed with pride. "Much obliged, Mr. Siemons. However, I am still concerned by the charge current intensity. I should like to be able to direct soul transfer with even greater accuracy."

Mr. Siemons looked over at Lord Akeldama. "Do you think you left any behind?"

"Difficult to tell with such an ancient subject," Dr. Neebs prevaricated, "but perhaps—"

He was cut off by a loud knock on the door.

"Me, sir!" said a voice.

"*Expositus*," said Mr. Siemons.

The automaton turned stiffly and opened the door.

In came the other young scientist accompanied by Mr. MacDougall. They carried between them the body of a man, wrapped tightly in a long length of linen, looking like nothing so much as an ancient Egyptian mummy.

Upon seeing Miss Tarabotti, strapped to her own platform, Mr. MacDougall dropped his end of the body and rushed over to her.

"Good evening, Mr. MacDougall," said Alexia politely. "I must say, I do not think very highly of your friends here. Their behavior is"—she paused delicately—"immodest."

"Miss Tarabotti, I am so very sorry." The American worried his hands together in a little ball and fluttered about her anxiously. "If I had only known *what* you were at the commencement of our acquaintance, I might have prevented this. I would have taken proper precautions. I would have . . ." He covered his mouth with both pudgy hands, shaking his head in an excess of troubled emotion.

Alexia attempted a little smile. *Poor thing*, she thought. *It must be hard to be so weak all the time.*

"Now, Mr. MacDougall," Mr. Siemons interrupted their little tête-à-tête. "You know what is at stake here. The young lady refuses to cooperate willingly. So this is how it must be. You may stay to observe, but you must behave yourself and not interfere with the procedure."

"But, sir," the American protested, "shouldn't you test the extent of her abilities first? Make some notations, formulate a hypothesis, take a more scientific approach? We know so little about this so-called preternatural state. Shouldn't you utilize caution? If she is as unique as you say, you can hardly afford to take unnecessary risks with her well-being."

Mr. Siemons raised an autocratic hand. "We are only performing a preliminary transfer procedure. The vampires call her kind 'soulless.' If our predictions are correct, she will not require any kind of electroshock treatment for revival. No soul, you see?"

"But what if it is *my* theory that is correct and not yours?" Mr. MacDougall looked worried beyond all endurance. His hands were shaking, and a sheen of sweat had appeared across his brow.

Mr. Siemons smiled maliciously. "We had better hope, for her sake, that it is not." He turned away and issued instructions to his compatriots. "Prepare her for exsanguination. Let us analyze the true extent of this woman's capabilities. Dr. Neebs, if you are finished with that subject?"

Dr. Neebs nodded. "For the time being. Cecil, please continue to monitor his progress. I want immediate notification of dental protuberance." He began rummaging about, unhooking the two machines from each other and then from Lord Akeldama and his companion sufferer. He pulled the tubes out of their respective arms roughly. Alexia was disturbed to see that the gaping hole in Lord Akeldama's flesh did not immediately begin to close and heal itself.

Then there was no more time for her to worry about Lord Akeldama, for they were moving the machine in her direction. Dr. Neebs approached her arm with a very sharp-looking knife. He ripped away the sleeve of her gown and poked about with his fingers at the underside of her elbow, looking for a vein. Mr. MacDougall made nonsensical murmurs of distress the entire time but did nothing to help her. In fact, he backed timidly away and turned his head as though afraid to watch. Alexia struggled futilely against her restraints.

Dr. Neebs focused his glassicals and placed the knife into position.

A great crash reverberated through the room.

Something large, heavy, and very angry hit the outside of the door hard enough to jar the automaton that stood in front of it.

"What the hell's that?" Dr. Neebs asked, pausing with the knife resting against her skin.

The door reverberated again.

"It will hold," said Mr. Siemons confidently.

But with the third great crash, the door began to split.

Dr. Neebs lifted the knife he had been about to use on Alexia and took up a defensive position with it instead. One of the younger scientists began to scream. The other ran about looking for a weapon of some kind among the scientific paraphernalia littering the room.

"Cecil, calm yourself!" yelled Mr. Siemons. "It will hold!" Clearly, he was trying to convince himself as much as anyone else.

"Mr. MacDougall," Alexia hissed under the hubbub, "could you, perhaps, see yourself toward untying me?"

Mr. MacDougall, trembling, looked at her as though he could not understand what she was saying.

The door cracked and caved inward, and through the splintered mess charged a massive wolf. The fur about his face was matted and clotted with blood. Pink-tinged saliva dribbled from around long sharp white teeth. The rest of his pelt was brindled black and gold and brown. His eyes, when they turned toward Miss Tarabotti, were hot yellow, with no humanity in them at all.

Lord Maccon probably weighed a good fourteen stone. Alexia now possessed intimate knowledge supporting the fact that a good deal of that weight of his was muscle. This made for a very large, very strong wolf. And all of it was angry, hungry, and driven by full-moon madness.

The werewolf hit the exsanguination chamber in a vicious storm of fang and claw and began unceremoniously tearing everything apart. Including the scientists. Suddenly, there was noise and blood and panic everywhere.

Miss Tarabotti turned her head away as much as possible, flinching from the horror of it. She tried Mr. MacDougall again. "Mr. MacDougall, please untie me. I can stop him." But the American had pressed himself back into a far corner of the room, trembling with fear, eyes riveted on the rampaging wolf.

"Oh!" said Miss Tarabotti in frustration. "Untie me this instant, you ridiculous man!"

Where requests had failed, orders seemed to work well enough. Her sharp words broke through his terror. Trancelike, the American began fumbling at her bonds, eventually freeing her hands enough for her to bend down and untie her ankles herself. She swung to the edge of the platform.

A stream of Latin sang out above the sounds of carnage, and the automaton slid into action.

By the time Alexia could stand—it took a few moments for the blood to return to her feet—the automaton and the werewolf were grappling in the doorway. What was left of Dr. Neebs and the two young scientists lay crumpled on the floor, swimming in small pools of blood, glassical parts, and entrails.

Miss Tarabotti tried very hard not to be sick or faint. The smell of carnage was truly appalling—fresh meat and molten copper.

Mr. Siemons remained unscathed, and while his construct fought the supernatural creature, he turned to seek out Alexia.

He picked up Dr. Neebs's long sharp surgical knife and moved at her unexpectedly fast for such a well-fed man. Before Alexia had time to react, he was upon her, knife pressed to her throat.

"Do not move, Miss Tarabotti. You neither, Mr. MacDougall. Stay where you are."

The werewolf had its massive jaw about the throat of the automaton and appeared to be putting concerted effort into decapitating it. It was to no avail, however, because the construct's bones were made of a substance too strong even for a werewolf's jaw. The head remained attached. Wobbly, but attached. The automaton's sluggish blackened blood spilled out of massive neck gashes over the wolf's muzzle. The supernatural creature sneezed and let go.

Mr. Siemons began inching toward the door, which was mostly blocked by the battling monsters. He pushed Miss Tarabotti in front of him, knife to her throat, trying for a side approach behind the wolf.

The werewolf's massive head swung toward them, and his lips pulled back in a snarl of warning.

Mr. Siemons jerked back, slicing through the first few layers of skin on Alexia's neck. She squeaked in alarm.

The wolf sniffed at the air, and its bright yellow eyes narrowed. It turned its attention completely onto Alexia and Mr. Siemons.

The automaton charged from behind and grabbed for the wolf's throat, trying to choke it to death.

"Godth's truth, I am hungry!" someone lisped. All forgotten, the human half of the Lord Akeldama experiment stood up from his platform. He had long, well-developed fangs and was looking around the room with single-minded interest. His eyes flitted about, dismissing Lord Akeldama, the werewolf, and the automaton but lingering with interest on Miss Tarabotti and Mr. Siemons before zeroing in on the most accessible meal in the chamber: Mr. MacDougall.

The American, huddled in his corner, shrieked as the newly created vampire vaulted over Lord Akeldama and across the intervening space with supernatural agility and speed.

Miss Tarabotti did not have time to watch further, as her attention was drawn back to the entranceway. She heard Mr. MacDougall scream again and then the thumping sounds of fighting.

The werewolf was trying to shake the automaton off his back. But the construct had established a death grip around his furry neck and would not budge. With the wolf momentarily distracted, the broken door was partly freed up, and Mr. Siemons began forcing Alexia once more toward it.

Miss Tarabotti wished, for about the hundredth time that evening, for her trusty parasol. Not having it, she did the next best thing. She elbowed Mr. Siemons hard in the gut while stomping down onto his insole with the heel of her boot.

Mr. Siemons cried out in pain and surprise and let her go.

Miss Tarabotti twisted away with a yell of triumph, and the werewolf's attention switched back toward them at the sound.

Choosing his own safety above all else, Mr. Siemons gave Miss Tarabotti up for a bad risk and fled the chamber, calling for his fellow scientists at the top of his lungs as he ran pell-mell down the hallway outside.

The automaton continued to fight, its hands tightening ever more surely around the wolf's brindled throat.

Alexia did not know what to do. Lord Maccon undoubtedly stood a better chance against the automaton in werewolf form. But, wheezing from restricted air flow, he was coming toward *her* and ignoring the automaton attempting to strangle him. She could not allow him to touch her if she wanted him to survive.

A hoarse voice said, "Rub out the word, my darling *tulip*."

Alexia glanced over. Lord Akeldama, still pale and clearly in unmitigated pain, had tilted his head up from where he lay. He was watching the brutal proceedings with glazed eyes.

Miss Tarabotti gave a cry of relief. He was alive! But she did not understand what he wanted her to do.

"The word," he said again, his voice wrecked by his suffering, "on the *homunculus simulacrum*'s forehead. Rub it out." He collapsed back, exhausted.

Miss Tarabotti dodged sideways, positioning herself. Then, shuddering in revulsion, she reached forward and brushed her hand over the automaton's waxy face. She missed all but the very end of the word so that VIXI became VIX.

It seemed sufficient to do some good. The automaton stiffened and let go enough for the werewolf to shake him off. The creature was still moving but now did so with apparent difficulty.

The werewolf turned all his concentrated yellow attention on Miss Tarabotti.

Before he could even begin to spring at her, Alexia moved forward, unafraid, and wrapped both arms about his furry neck.

The change was a little less horrible the second time around. Or, perhaps, she was simply getting used to the feel of it. Fur retreated from where she touched him, bone and skin and flesh re-formed, and she held, once again, the naked body of Lord Maccon in her arms.

He was coughing and spitting.

"That automaton thing tastes awful," he announced, wiping his face with the back of one hand. It did nothing more effective than smudge the red over his chin and cheek.

Miss Tarabotti refrained from pointing out he had also been snacking on scientists and wiped his face with the skirt of her dress. It was already beyond salvation anyway.

Tawny brown eyes turned to her face. Alexia noted with relief that they were full of intelligence and entirely lacking in ferocity or hunger.

"You are unharmed?" he asked. One big hand came up, stroking over her face and down. He paused upon reaching the cut on her neck.

His eyes, even though he was touching her, went slightly back to feral yellow. "I'll butcher the bastard," he said softly, all the more anger in his voice for its quiet tone. "I'll pull his bones out through his nostrils one by one."

Alexia shushed him impatiently. "It is not that deep." But she did lean into his touch and let out a shaky breath she had not even known she was holding.

His hand, now trembling in fury, kept up its gentle assessment of her injuries. It smoothed softly over the bruises appearing on her exposed upper torso and down her shoulder to the slice on her arm.

"The Norse had it right—flay a man open from the back and eat out his heart," he said.

"Do not be disgusting," admonished the object of his interest. "Besides, I did that one to myself."

"What?!"

She shrugged dismissively, "You needed a trail to follow."

"You little fool," he said affectionately.

"It worked, didn't it?"

His touch became insistent for just a moment. Pulling her in against his large naked form, he kissed her roughly, a deeply erotic and oddly desperate melding of tongue and teeth. He kissed as though he needed her to subsist. It was unbearably intimate. Worse than allowing one's ankles to be seen. Alexia leaned into him, opening her mouth eagerly.

"I do so *hate* to intrude, my little lovebirds, but if you could see your way clear to maybe releasing me?" came a soft voice, interrupting their embrace. "And your business here, it is not quite finished."

Lord Maccon surfaced and looked about, blinking as though he had just woken from sleep: half nightmare, half erotic fantasy.

Miss Tarabotti shifted so that their only point of contact was her hand nested inside his big one. It was still enough contact to be comforting, not to mention preternaturally effective.

Lord Akeldama still lay on his platform. In the space between him and where Alexia had been strapped down, Mr. MacDougall still fought with the newly created vampire.

"Goodness me," said Miss Tarabotti in surprise, "he is still alive!" No one was sure, even her, whether she meant Mr. MacDougall or the manufactured vampire. They seemed equally matched, the vampire unused to his new strength and abilities, and Mr. MacDougall stronger than expected in his desperation and panic.

"Well, my love," said Alexia with prodigious daring to Lord Maccon, "shall we?"

The earl started to move forward and then stopped abruptly and looked down at her, not moving at all. "Am I?"

"Are you what?" She peeked up at him through her tangled hair, pretending confusion. There was no possible way she was going to make this easy for him.

"Your love?"

"Well, you are a werewolf, Scottish, naked, and covered in blood, and I am *still* holding your hand."

He sighed in evident relief. "Good. That is settled, then."

They moved over to where Mr. MacDougall and the vampire fought. Alexia was not certain she could effectively change two supernatural persons at once, but she was willing to try.

"Pardon me," she said, and grabbed the vampire by one shoulder. Surprised, the man turned toward this new threat. But his fangs were already retracting.

Miss Tarabotti smiled at him, and Lord Maccon had him by the ear like a naughty schoolboy before he could even make an aggressive move in her direction.

"Now, now," said Lord Maccon, "even new vampires may choose only willing victims." Releasing the ear, he punched the man extremely hard up under the chin. It was an expert boxer's move that laid the poor man out flat.

"Will it last?" Alexia asked of the fallen vampire. She was no longer touching him, so he should recuperate quickly.

"For a few minutes," said Lord Maccon in his BUR voice.

Mr. MacDougall, bleeding only slightly from a row of punctures in one side of his neck, blinked at his saviors.

"Tie him up, would you? There is a good lad. I have only one working hand, you see?" said Lord Maccon to the American, handing him rope from one of the platforms.

"Who, sir, are you?" Mr. MacDougall asked, looking the earl up and down and then focusing in on his and Alexia's linked hands. Or Alexia assumed that is what he was focusing in on.

Miss Tarabotti said, "Mr. MacDougall, your questions will have to wait."

Mr. MacDougall nodded submissively and began to tie the vampire.

"My love." Alexia looked at Lord Maccon. It was much easier to say the words the second time around, but she still felt very daring. "Perhaps you might see to Lord Akeldama? I dare not touch him in such a weakened state."

Lord Maccon refrained from commenting that when she called him "my love," he was pretty much willing to do whatever she asked.

They walked together over to Lord Akeldama's platform.

"Hello, princess," said Lord Maccon to the vampire. "Got yourself into quite a pickle this time, didn't you?"

Lord Akeldama looked him up and down. "My *sweet* young naked boy, you are *hardly* one to talk. Not that *I* mind, of course."

Lord Maccon blushed so profoundly it extended all the way down his neck to his upper torso. Alexia thought it entirely adorable.

Without another word, the earl untied Lord Akeldama and, as gently as possible, slid his hands and feet off the wooden stakes. The vampire lay still and silent for a long time after he had finished.

Miss Tarabotti worried. His wounds should be healing themselves. But, instead, they remained large, gaping holes. There wasn't even any blood dripping from them.

"My *dearest* girl," said the vampire finally, examining Lord Maccon with an exhausted but appreciative eye, "such a banquet. Never been one to favor werewolves myself, but he is *very* well equipped, now, is he not?"

Miss Tarabotti gave him an arch look. "My goodies," she warned.

"Humans," chuckled the vampire, "so possessive." He shifted weakly.

"You are not well," commented Lord Maccon.

"Quite right, Lord Obvious."

Miss Tarabotti looked at the vampire's wounds more closely, still careful not to touch him. She wanted desperately to hug her friend and offer some consolation, but any contact with her and he was certain to die. He was near enough to it already, and returning to human form would end him undoubtedly.

"You are dry," she remarked.

"Yes," agreed the vampire. "It all went into him." He gestured with his chin toward where the new vampire lay under Mr. MacDougall's ministrations.

"I suppose you might take a donation from me?" suggested Lord Maccon dubiously. "Would that work? I mean to say, how fully human does preternatural touch make me?"

Lord Akeldama shook his head weakly. "Not enough for me to feed from you, I suspect. It might work, but it also might kill you."

Lord Maccon unexpectedly jerked backward, pulling Alexia with him. Two hands were wrapped around his throat, squeezing tightly. The fingers on those hands had no fingernails.

The automaton had crawled all the way across the floor, slowly but surely, and was trying to fulfill the last order given to it: to kill Lord Maccon. This time, with the earl in human form, it stood a fairly good chance of succeeding.

CHAPTER FOURTEEN

Royal Interference

Lord Maccon sputtered and gasped for breath, trying to fight off the repulsive creature with only one hand. Miss Tarabotti beat at the automaton with her free arm. But nothing they did seemed capable of wresting the construct from around the earl's neck. Alexia was about to let go of Lord Maccon's hand and back away, knowing he could free himself in werewolf form, when Lord Akeldama stood shakily up from the platform on which he rested.

The vampire produced a still miraculously immaculate white lace handkerchief from a waistcoat pocket, stumbled over, and wiped the rest of the smudged word off the automaton's forehead.

The monstrosity let go of Lord Maccon and collapsed onto the floor.

The most remarkable thing then occurred. Its skin began melting away in slow rivulets, like warm honey. Slow black blood, mixed with some black particulate matter, leaked out and intermingled with the skin substance. Both slid off a mechanical skeletal structure. Soon, all that was left of the automaton was a metal frame wearing shabby clothing and lying in a gooey puddle of old blood, wax, and small black particles. Its internal organs appeared to be all gears and clockwork mechanisms.

Miss Tarabotti's attention was drawn away from the fascinating mess by Lord Maccon saying, "Oops, whoa there," and reaching for Lord Akeldama with his free arm.

The vampire was toppling over as well, having utterly exhausted what few resources of energy he had left in administering the deadly handkerchief. Lord Maccon, attached to Alexia with one hand, managed only to slow his fall with the other but not catch him completely. The vampire crumpled to the floor in a sad little heap of plum-colored velvet.

Miss Tarabotti bent over him, still desperately careful not to touch him in any way. He was still, miraculously, alive.

"Why?" she stuttered, glancing over at the automaton, or what *had* been the automaton. "Why did that work?"

"You only wiped off the *I*?" asked Lord Maccon, looking thoughtfully at the puddle of *homunculus simulacrum* residue.

Alexia nodded.

"So you turned VIXI—*to be alive*—into VIX, *with difficulty*. Thus, the automaton could still move, but only barely. In order to destroy it entirely, you needed to remove the word and the activation particulate completely, breaking the aetheromagnetic connection."

"Well," huffed Miss Tarabotti, "how was I supposed to know that? That was my first automaton."

"And a *very* good job you made of it, too, *my pearl*, on such short acquaintance," complimented Lord Akeldama tenderly from his prone position without opening his eyes. He had yet to succumb to the Grand Collapse, but he looked in imminent danger of doing so.

They heard a great clattering and a quantity of yelling from the hallway behind them.

"Arse over apex, what now?" wondered Lord Maccon, standing up and dragging Miss Tarabotti with him.

A conglomeration of impeccably well-dressed young men bustled into the room, carrying with them the trussed and bound form of Mr. Siemons. They let out a collective shriek upon seeing

Lord Akeldama crumpled on the floor. Several rushed over and began billing and cooing about him in an excess of emotional concern.

"Lord Akeldama's drones," Alexia explained to Lord Maccon.

"I would never have known," he replied sarcastically.

"Where did they all come from?" wondered Miss Tarabotti.

One of the young men whom Alexia remembered from before—had it only been a few hours ago?—deduced the cure to his master's ailments quickly enough. He pushed the other dandies aside, pulled off his blue silk evening jacket, rolled up his shirt-sleeve, and offered his arm to the destabilized vampire. Lord Akeldama's eyes blinked slowly open.

"Ah, my capable Biffy. Do not let me drink too long from you alone."

Biffy leaned forward and kissed Lord Akeldama on the fore-head, as though he were a small child. "Of course not, my lord." Gently he put his wrist to the vampire's pale lips.

Lord Akeldama bit down with a sigh of relief.

Biffy was both smart enough and strong enough to pull away halfway through the feeding. He summoned one of the other drones to take his place. Lord Akeldama, as thirsty as he was from his recent abuse, could easily damage a solo donor beyond repair. Luckily, none of his drones was foolish enough to try and stay the course. The second young man gave way to a third and then a fourth. At this point, Lord Akeldama's wounds began to close, and his skin went from frighteningly gray to its normal porcelain white.

"Explain yourselves, my darlings," ordered Lord Akeldama as soon as he was able.

"Our little information-gathering excursion into high society's festivities yielded up far more fruit than we had hoped, and more quickly, my lord," said Biffy. "When we returned home early to find you gone, we proceeded immediately to act upon the information most recently acquired—namely, that which bespoke suspicious activity and bright white lights late at night emanating from the recently opened scientific club, near the Duke of Snodgrove's town residence."

"And a good thing we did too," continued Biffy, wrapping a salmon-pink embroidered handkerchief about his own wrist and tying a knot with his teeth. "Not that I doubt your ability to handle the situation, sir," he said respectfully to Lord Maccon, without the sarcasm the statement ought to have elicited considering the Alpha was still entirely naked. "I will say that the moving room contraption transport device gave us some stick. Figured it out in the end, though. We ought to get one of those installed at the town house, my lord."

"I will think about it," said Lord Akeldama.

"You did very well," complimented Miss Tarabotti to the dandies. She believed in giving praise where it was due.

Biffy rolled down his sleeve and pulled his evening jacket back on over broad muscular shoulders. A lady was present, after all— even if her hair was most scandalously loose.

Lord Maccon said, "Someone must go to BUR and get a couple of agents over here to handle the formalities." He looked about, taking stock: three dead scientists, one new vampire, a trussed-up Mr. Siemons, a blathering Mr. MacDougall, the other mummy-like body intended for Alexia's blood, and the remains of an automaton. The chamber was a veritable battlefield. He winced at the mounds of paperwork ahead of him. His own three kills alone would not be too much of a bother. He *was* chief sundowner, sanctioned killer for queen and country. But explaining the automaton would require eight forms that he could think of, and probably a few more that he could not.

He sighed. "Whoever we send will also need to tell BUR we need sweeps here posthaste to clean up the mess. Have them check to see if there is a local ghost tethered nearby. See if it can be recruited to check for hidden chambers. This is a logistical nightmare."

Miss Tarabotti stroked his knuckles with her thumb sympathetically. Absentmindedly, Lord Maccon raised her hand to his lips and kissed the inside of her wrist.

Biffy signaled to one of the other drones. With a grin of eagerness, the man clapped his topper to his head and minced out of
the room. Alexia wished she had that kind of energy. She was
starting to feel the strain of the evening. Her muscles were sore,
and all the little points of abuse—the rope burns about her ankles,
the cut on her throat, the slice on her arm—had started to ache.

Lord Maccon said to Biffy, "We will need the potentate if we
are to shut this operation down completely. Does your master
have any drones with high enough rank to get into the Shadow
Council without question? Or will I need to do that myself?"

Biffy gave the Alpha an appreciative but courteous once-over.
"Looking like that, sir? Well, I am certain many a door might be
opened to you, but not the potentate's."

Lord Maccon, who seemed to be periodically forgetting he
was naked, sighed at this. Alexia figured, delightedly, that this
meant he did, in fact, tend to traipse around his private apart-
ments in the altogether. Marriage was becoming more and more
of an attractive prospect. Though, she suspected, such a practice
might get distracting in the long term.

Biffy continued, unabashed, to rib the Alpha's appearance.
"To the best of our knowledge, the potentate's inclinations lie
elsewhere. Unless he is with the queen, of course, in which case
you might get right inside." He paused significantly. "We all know
the queen likes a bit of Scottish now and again." He waggled his
eyebrows in a highly suggestive manner.

"You do not say?" gasped Miss Tarabotti, genuinely shocked
for the first time that evening. "Those rumors about Mr. Brown,
they were true?"

Biffy settled in. "Every word, my dear. You know what I heard
just the other day? I heard—"

"Well?" interrupted Lord Maccon.

Biffy shook himself and pointed to one of the young men
fussing solicitously over Lord Akeldama: a slight, effete blond,
with an aristocratic nose, wearing top-to-toe butter-yellow
brocade. "See the canary over there? That is Viscount Trizdale,

believe it or not. Heya Tizzy, come over here. Got a bit of sport for you."

The yellow-clad dandy pranced over.

"Our lord does not look well, Biffy. I am telling you. Quite ill, in fact," he said.

Biffy patted a yellow shoulder reassuringly. "Not to worry your pretty head. He will be just fine. Now, Lord Maccon here has a bit of a task for you. Should only take a jiffy. Wants you to nip round to old Bucky and rustle up the potentate. Needs some political clout, if you know what I mean, and it is not like the dewan's going to be much use this night. Full moon and all, haw haw. Go on now, shove off."

With one more worried look in Lord Akeldama's direction, the young viscount wandered out.

Alexia stared at Biffy. "Does the Duke of Trizdale know his only son is a drone?"

Biffy pursed his lips in a cagey manner. "Not as such."

"Huh," said Miss Tarabotti thoughtfully—so much gossip in one night!

A different dandy appeared, proffering one of the long gray frock coats sported by the younger scientists around the club.

Lord Maccon took it with a grumbled "thank you" and pulled it on. He was such a large man that it was quite scandalously short on him without trousers, but it covered the most important bits.

Alexia was a little disappointed.

So, apparently, was Biffy. "Now, Eustace, what did you go and do a thing like that for?" he said to his fellow drone.

"It was getting incommodious," said the unapologetic Eustace.

Lord Maccon interrupted them all by issuing forth a series of orders, which, with only minor dissembling, the assembled gentlemen took in hand. They did, collectively, keep trying to arrange matters so that Lord Maccon had to bend over. There was a twinkle in the earl's eye suggesting the Alpha knew what they were about and was humoring their attempts.

One small gaggle left to canvass the premises for other scientists, upon whom they pounced and locked away in the very cells formerly dedicated to vampires. Lord Akeldama's boys might *look* like fruits of the first water, but they all boxed at Whites, and at least a half dozen wore clothing specially cut to *disguise* musculature. As per Lord Maccon's instructions, they left his imprisoned pack alone. No need to test Miss Tarabotti's abilities any further than was necessary. The trapped vampires they released, asking them to please stay behind and help with the BUR reports. A few did, but most needed desperately to get home to their respective territories or down to the blood alley for a feeding. A few took off about the club tracking down and exterminating, in a most horrific manner, those last remaining scientists who had until then believed themselves lucky in evading Lord Akeldama's dandies.

"Bah," said Lord Maccon upon hearing this, "more paperwork, and on a night without Lyall too. How aggravating."

"I will help," said Miss Tarabotti brightly.

"Oh, you will, will you? I knew you were going to take every opportunity to interfere with my work, insufferable woman."

Miss Tarabotti knew how to handle his grumbling well enough now. She glanced about: everyone seemed to be suitably busy, so she slid in close to him and nibbled delicately at one side of his neck.

Lord Maccon jumped a little and clapped his hand to the front of the gray frock coat. The hemline rose slightly.

"Stop that!"

"I am very effective," Alexia insisted, breathing into his ear. "You should put me to good use. Otherwise, I will have to come up with other ways to entertain myself."

He groaned. "Fine, right. You can help with the paperwork."

She sat back. "Was that so hard?"

He raised both eyebrows and shifted his protective hand so she could partly see the result of her teasing.

Miss Tarabotti cleared her throat. "Was that so difficult?" She rephrased her question.

"I suspect you are much better at paperwork than I am anyway," he admitted grudgingly.

Miss Tarabotti had a brief horrific flashback to the state of his office last she had visited. "I am certainly more organized."

"You and Lyall are going to run me ragged, aren't you?" grumbled the earl, sounding most put-upon.

After that, cleanup proceeded with remarkable rapidity. Miss Tarabotti was beginning to understand how Lord Akeldama always seemed to know so much. His young men were amazingly efficacious. They managed to be everywhere at once. She wondered how many occasions in her past had contained some young fop, apparently too silly or too drunk, watching everything.

By the time the five BUR agents—two vampires, two humans, and a ghost—arrived, everything was basically in order. The premises had been searched thoroughly, vampire statements taken, prisoners and werewolves secured, and someone had even managed to find Lord Maccon a pair of ill-fitting knickerbockers. Above and beyond the call of duty, Biffy, utilizing a few stray metal coils from one of Dr. Neebs's machines, had twisted Miss Tarabotti's hair into a beautiful rendition of the latest updo out of Paris.

Lord Akeldama, now sitting on one of the platforms, watching, with the eyes of a proud parent, his boys work, said approvingly to Biffy, "Lovely job, my *dear*." Then to Alexia, "Do you see, my little marshmallow, you simply *must* get yourself a nice French maid."

Mr. Siemons was carted off to prison by two of the BUR agents. Miss Tarabotti had to speak most severely to Lord Maccon about not paying him a call when she was no longer around.

"Justice must take its course," she insisted. "If you are going to work for BUR and support the system, you must do so all the time, not simply when you find it convenient."

Eyes riveted on the line of congealed blood across the lower part of her neck, he wheedled, "Just a short visit, enough for a mild dismemberment?"

She gave him a dour look. "No."

The rest of the BUR agents and a competent-looking sweeps crew bustled about, scribbling notations and passing things to the earl to sign. At first they had been entirely shocked to find him in human form, but the sheer mountain of cleanup to be done at the Hypocras Club made them quickly more grateful than surprised to have him available and competent.

Miss Tarabotti tried to be helpful, but her eyes were becoming scratchy, and she was leaning more and more heavily against Lord Maccon's broad side. Eventually, the earl shifted his operation to the entry room of the club and sat them both down on the red couch there. Someone made tea. Lord Akeldama enthroned himself in the brown leather studded armchair. Despite the indignity, Miss Tarabotti soon found herself curled up on the couch, head pillowed on Lord Maccon's hard thigh, snoring softly.

The earl, issuing orders and signing forms, stroked her hair with one hand, in defiance of Biffy's protestations that this would mess up her new hairdo.

Miss Tarabotti, dreaming of brass octopuses, slept through the remains of the night. She did not awaken upon the arrival or the departure of the potentate and his argument with Lord Maccon, whose growls of annoyance at the politician's obtuseness only seemed to lull her further into dreamland. Nor was she awake to see Lord Maccon square off against Dr. Caedes over the disposition of the Hypocras Club's gadgetry and research notes. She slept through Lord Akeldama and his young men leaving, the sunrise, the release of the werewolves—now back in human form—and Lord Maccon's explanation of events to his pack.

She even slept through the earl gently transferring her into Professor Lyall's arms and the Beta carrying her rapidly past the arriving press, her head, and thus identity, covered by one of Lord Akeldama's ever-present lace handkerchiefs.

She did not, however, sleep through her mother's shrieks upon her arrival back at the Loontwill town house. Mrs. Loontwill was waiting up for them in the front parlor. And she was *not* pleased.

"Where have you been all night, young lady?" said her mother in the sepulchral tones of the deeply put-upon.

Felicity and Evylin appeared in the doorway of the parlor, wearing nightdresses and draped in heavy pelisses and shocked expressions. Upon noticing Professor Lyall, they squeaked in alarm and dashed back up to their rooms to dress as quickly as possible, horrified that decorum dictate they miss any part of the undoubted drama occurring downstairs.

Miss Tarabotti blinked at her mother sleepily. "Uh . . ." She could not think. *I was off meeting with a vampire, got abducted by scientists, attacked by a werewolf, and then spent the remainder of the night holding hands with a naked peer of the realm.* She said, "Uh . . ." again.

"She was with the Earl of Woolsey," said Professor Lyall firmly, in a tone of voice that brooked no objection, as though that settled the matter.

Mrs. Loontwill ignored his tone entirely and made a move as if to strike her daughter. "Alexia! You wanton hussy!"

Professor Lyall twisted fast so that his charge, still held in his arms, was well out of the woman's reach and glared furiously.

Mrs. Loontwill turned her wrath on him, like a rabid poodle. "I will have you know, young man, no daughter of mine spends an entire night away from home with a gentleman without being securely married to that gentleman first! I do not care if he *is* an earl. You werewolf types may have different rules for this kind of affair, but this *is* the nineteenth century, and we do not hold with such shenanigans. Why, I ought to have my husband call your Alpha out right now!"

Professor Lyall raised one refined brow. "He is welcome to the attempt. I would not recommend that particular course of action. To the best of my recollection, Lord Maccon has never actually lost a fight." He looked down at Alexia. "Except to Miss Tarabotti, of course."

Alexia grinned up at him. "You can put me down now, Professor. I am quite awake and able to stand. Mama will do that to a person. She is like a glass of cold water."

Professor Lyall did as she requested.

Miss Tarabotti found that she had not actually spoken the truth. Her whole body ached most awfully, and her feet did not seem to wish to work as instructed. She stumbled heavily to one side.

Professor Lyall made to grab her and missed.

With the majestic efficiency of all good butlers, Floote appeared at her side and took her arm, preventing her from falling.

"Thank you, Floote," said Alexia, leaning gratefully against him.

Felicity and Evylin, both properly attired in cotton day dresses, reappeared and went immediately to sit on the chesterfield before they could be told to leave.

Alexia looked about and noticed one family member still absent. "Where *is* the squire?"

"Never you mind that, missy. What is going on? I demand an immediate explanation," insisted her mother, waggling a finger.

Just then, there came the most imperious knocking on the front door. Floote transferred Alexia back to Professor Lyall and went to answer it. Lyall ushered Miss Tarabotti over to the wingback chair. With a nostalgic smile, Alexia sat down in it.

"We are *not* at home!" yelled Mrs. Loontwill after Floote. "To anyone!"

"You are at home to me, madam," said a very autocratic voice.

The Queen of England swept into the room: a petite woman, in late middle life but wearing it very well.

Floote trailed in after and said, in tones of shock Alexia had never thought to hear from her unflappable butler, "Her Most Royal Highness, Queen Victoria, to see Miss Tarabotti."

Mrs. Loontwill fainted.

Alexia thought it the best, most sensible thing her mama had done in a very long while. Floote uncorked a bottle of smelling salts and went to revive her, but Alexia shook her head firmly. Then she made to rise and curtsy, but the queen raised her hand.

"No formality, Miss Tarabotti. I understand you have had an interesting night," she said.

Miss Tarabotti nodded mutely and made a polite gesture for the queen to sit. She was mortified by what now seemed the shabby clutter of her family's front parlor. Her Most Royal Highness did not seem to notice, sitting down on a mahogany side chair next to Alexia, moving it so her back was to the collapsed form of Mrs. Loontwill.

Miss Tarabotti turned to her sisters. Both had their mouths open and were flapping about like ineffectual fish.

"Felicity, Evylin, out, now," she ordered quite curtly.

Professor Lyall helped hustle the two girls from the room and would have followed, but the queen said curtly, "Stay, Professor. We may need your expertise."

Floote glided out with an expression that said he would keep all prying ears at bay, although probably not his own.

The queen looked at Alexia a long moment. "You are not at all what I expected," she said at last.

Miss Tarabotti refrained from saying, "Neither are you." Instead she said, "You knew to expect something?"

"Dear girl, you are one of the only preternaturals on British soil. We approved your father's immigration papers all those many years ago. We were informed the moment of your birth. We have watched your progress since then with interest. We even considered interfering when all this folderol with Lord Maccon began to complicate matters. It has gone on quite long enough. You will be marrying him, I understand?"

Alexia nodded mutely.

"Good, we approve." She nodded as though she had somehow had a hand in this outcome.

Professor Lyall said, "Not everyone does."

The queen actually snorted at that. "*We* are the one whose opinion counts, are we not? The potentate and the dewan are trusted advisers, but they are only that: advisers. No legal records for our empire or any previous one forbid marriage between supernatural and preternatural outright. Yes, the potentate informs us hive tradition bans such a union, and werewolf legend warns against fraternization, but we require this business settled. We will not have our best BUR agent distracted, and we need this young lady married."

"Why?" Alexia asked, confused that her single state should concern the Queen of England.

"Ah, that. You are aware of the Shadow Council?" The queen settled herself in the hard chair, as much as queens do, which is to say her shoulders relaxed slightly.

Alexia nodded. "The potentate acts as your official vampire consultant and the dewan in the werewolf capacity. Rumors are that most of your political acumen comes from the potentate's advice and your military skill from the dewan's."

"Alexia," Professor Lyall growled a warning.

The queen looked more amused than insulted at this. She even dropped the royal "we" for the space of a few moments. "Well, I suppose my enemies must blame somebody. I will say that those two are invaluable, when they are not bickering with each other. But there is a third post that has been vacant since before my time. An adviser meant to break the stalemate between the other two."

Miss Tarabotti frowned. "A ghost?"

"No, no. We have plenty of those flitting around Buckingham Palace; cannot keep them quiet half the time. We certainly do not need one in any official capacity. Not when they cannot maintain solidity that long. No, what we require is a muhjah."

Alexia looked confused.

The queen explained. "Traditionally the third member of the Shadow Council is a preternatural, the muhjah. Your father declined the post." She sniffed. "Italians. Now, there simply is not enough of your set left to vote on your nomination, so it will have to be an appointed position. But voting is mostly a formality, even for the positions of dewan and potentate. At least it has been during my reign."

"No one else wants the job," said Professor Lyall with feeling.

The queen gave him a reproving look.

He leaned forward and explained further. "It is a political post," he said. "Lots of arguing and paperwork and books being consulted all the time. It is not at all like BUR, you understand?"

Miss Tarabotti's eyes positively sparkled. "Sounds delightful." Yet she remained suspicious. "Why me? What could I possibly offer against two such experienced voices?"

The queen was not used to being questioned. She looked at Professor Lyall.

He said, "I told you she was difficult."

"Aside from breaking a stalemate, our muhjah is the only truly mobile unit of the three councilors. Our potentate is confined to a narrow territory, like most vampires, and cannot function during the day. Our dewan is more mobile, but he cannot travel by dirigible and is incapacitated every full moon. We have relied upon BUR to make up for the Shadow Council's weakness in this regard, but we would prefer a muhjah whose attention is solely on the Crown's concerns and who can come to us directly."

"So there *will* be some active duty?" Miss Tarabotti was even more intrigued.

"Uh-oh," muttered Professor Lyall, "I do not think Lord Maccon fully comprehended this aspect of the position."

"The muhjah is the voice of the modern age. We have faith in our potentate and our dewan, but they are old and set in their ways. They require balance from someone who keeps up with current lines of scientific inquiry, not to mention the interests and suspicions of the daylight world. We are concerned that this Hypocras Club is a symptom of greater unrest. We are worried that our BUR agents did not uncover it sooner. You have proven yourself an able investigator and a well-read young woman. As Lady Maccon, you would also possess the standing needed to infiltrate the highest levels of society."

Alexia looked between Professor Lyall and the queen. Lyall looked worried. That decided her. "Very well, I accept."

The queen nodded happily. "Your future husband indicated you would not be averse to the position. Most excellent! We convene twice a week, Thursday and Sunday nights, unless there is a crisis of some kind, in which case you are expected to be readily available. You will be answerable to the Crown alone. We will expect you to start the week after your wedding. So do hurry it up."

Alexia smiled foolishly and looked at Professor Lyall from under her lashes. "Conall approves?"

The werewolf grinned. "He recommended you to the job months ago. The first time you interfered in one of his operations and he knew BUR would not be allowed to hire you. Of course, he did not know the muhjah engaged in active investigations on the queen's behalf."

The queen said, "Of course, initially we objected to the recommendation. We cannot have a single young lady in such a powerful position. It simply is *not* done." She looked almost mischievous and lowered her voice. "In all confidentiality, my dear, we do believe the Woolsey Alpha thinks being muhjah will keep you out of his way."

Alexia slapped a hand to her mouth in an excess of embarrassment. To have the Queen of England thinking of her as an interfering busybody!

Professor Lyall crossed his arms and said, "Begging your pardon, Your Majesty, but I think he wants to set Miss Tarabotti at the dewan and watch the fur fly."

Queen Victoria smiled. "They never have gotten along, those two."

Professor Lyall nodded. "Both are too much Alpha."

Miss Tarabotti looked suddenly worried. "That is not why he is marrying me, is it? So I can be muhjah?" A little bit of her old insecurity came back to haunt her.

"Do not be ridiculous," admonished the queen curtly. "He has been mad for you these many months, ever since you prodded him in the nether regions with a hedgehog. It has been driving everyone barmy, all this dancing about. Glad it is finally getting settled. This wedding of yours is going to be *the* social event of the season. Half the guests in attendance will be there simply to make certain you both go through with it. Outside of enough, that is our opinion."

Miss Tarabotti, for one of the first and last times in her life, was entirely at a loss for words.

The queen stood up. "Well, that is settled, then. We are most pleased. And now we suggest you go to bed, young lady. You look exhausted." With that, she swept from the house.

"She is so short," said Miss Tarabotti to Professor Lyall once the queen had gone.

"Alexia," said a tremulous voice from the other side of the room. "What *is* going on?"

Alexia sighed and struggled to her feet, wobbling over to her confused mama. All of Mrs. Loontwill's anger had evaporated upon waking to find her daughter in conversation with the Queen of England.

"Why was the queen here? Why were you discussing the Shadow Council? What is a muhjah?" Mrs. Loontwill was very confused. She seemed to have utterly lost control of the situation.

Me, thought Alexia with pleasure. *I will be muhjah. This is going to be such fun.* Aloud she said the only thing calculated to shut her mother up. "Do not worry about a thing, Mama. I am going to marry Lord Maccon."

It worked. Mrs. Loontwill's mouth snapped closed. Her expression evolved rapidly from perturbation to uncontrollable elation. "You caught him!" she breathed in delight.

Felicity and Evylin reentered the room, both wide-eyed. For

the first time in their entire lives, they regarded their older sister with something other than mild contempt.

Noticing her other two daughters had arrived, Mrs. Loontwill added hastily, "Not that I approve your methods of catching him, of course. Out all night, indeed. But thank heavens you did!" Then in an aside, "Girls, your sister is going to *marry* Lord Maccon."

Felicity and Evylin looked even more shocked, but they recovered quickly enough.

"But, Mama, why was the queen here?" Evylin wanted to know.

"Never mind that now, Evy," said Felicity impatiently. "The important question is, what will you wear for a wedding dress, Alexia? You look horrible in white."

The afternoon papers reported the bulk of the news accurately enough. Miss Tarabotti and Lord Akeldama's names were left out, and the exact makeup of the experiments was omitted in favor of emphasizing their sensational grisliness and illegal nature.

The reports threw all of London into a fervor of speculation. The Royal Society scrambled to deny any association with the Hypocras Club, but BUR commenced a whirlwind of undercover operations. A good many other scientists, some with well-known names indeed, suddenly found themselves without funding, on the run, or in prison. No one ever explained the octopuses.

The Hypocras Club was shut down permanently and its premises impounded and placed on the market. It was bought by a nice young couple from East Duddage whose success in the chamberpot business had brought them up in the world. The Duchess of Snodgrove regarded the entire affair as a travesty designed solely to impinge on her social standing. The fact that her new neighbors, nice young couple or no, hailed from Duddage and were involved in *trade* sent her into a fit of hysteria so pervasive her husband removed her instantly to the country ducal estates in

Berkshire for the sake of everyone's health. He sold their town house.

As far as Miss Tarabotti was concerned, the worst thing to result from the whole sordid affair was that, although both club premises and Lord Akeldama's house had been searched top to bottom, BUR never did recover her brass parasol.

"Bah," she complained to her intended as they strolled through Hyde Park late one evening, "I did so love that parasol."

A carriage of dowagers swept past. One or two nodded in their direction. Lord Maccon tipped his hat to them.

Society had come, albeit reluctantly, to accept the fact that one of the most eligible bachelors was going off the market by marrying a spinster nobody. One or two, witness the nods, had even come around to extending cautious overtures of friendship to Miss Tarabotti. Miss Tarabotti further improved her standing among the aristocracy as a force to be reckoned with by turning her large nose up at such sycophancy. Lady Maccon-to-be was clearly as formidable as her intended.

Lord Maccon took Miss Tarabotti's arm soothingly. "I shall have them make you a hundred such parasols, one for every dress."

Miss Tarabotti raised her eyebrows at him. "Silver tipped, you realize?"

"Well, you will be facing down the dewan several times a week; you might need some silver. Though I do not anticipate he will give you too much trouble."

Alexia, who had not yet had an opportunity to meet the other members of the Shadow Council and would not until after her wedding, looked at Lord Maccon curiously. "Is he really that fainthearted?"

"Nope. Simply ill-prepared."

"For what?"

"You, my love," the earl said, tempering the insult with an endearment.

Alexia sputtered in such a charming way that Lord Maccon

simply had to kiss her, right there, in the middle of Hyde Park. Which made her sputter even more. Which made him kiss her more. It was a vicious cycle.

Of course, it was Mr. MacDougall who had taken possession of the brass parasol. The poor young man had slipped everyone's mind, including Alexia's, as soon as the Hypocras investigation was put to rest. He took the parasol back to America with him— as a sort of memento. He had been genuinely heartbroken to read the announcement of Miss Tarabotti's engagement in the *Gazette*. He returned to his mansion in Massachusetts and threw himself with renewed scientific vigor and a more cautious attitude into measuring the human soul. Several years later, he married a veritable battle-ax of a woman and happily allowed himself to be bossed around for the remainder of his days.

EPILOGUE

Miss Alexia Tarabotti did not wear white to her wedding. Apart from the fact that Felicity was perfectly correct in stating that it clashed something terrible with her skin tone, she figured that when one has seen one's affianced naked and covered in blood, one is no longer quite pure enough for white.

Instead, she wore ivory: a sumptuous French-made dress selected and designed with Lord Akeldama's consummate assistance. It took into account the new trend in cleaner lines and long sleeves, hugging her upper torso and showing her curves to perfection. The square neckline of the bodice was cut quite low, much to Lord Maccon's approval, but it came up high in the back and around her neck in a demi-collar, reminiscent of some exotic robe from the Rococo era. It was held closed by an exquisite opal brooch at her throat and started a fashion trend in necklines that persisted for nearly three whole weeks.

Miss Tarabotti told no one the dress's design was a last-minute alteration due entirely to the fact that, two days before the wedding, the earl got her alone in the dining room for almost an hour. As always, the bite marks *she* had left on *him* faded the moment they separated. She sighed, not unhappily. *Really, the amount of attention he paid to her neck, one would think he was a vampire.*

Biffy did her hair for the prestigious event. He had been loaned to Miss Tarabotti for the duration of the wedding planning. He knew a phenomenal amount about who *must* be invited, who *should* be invited, what the invitations ought to look like, which flowers to order, and so forth. As bridesmaid, Ivy Hisselpenny did her best, but the poor thing was a tad overwhelmed by the particulars. Biffy developed a dab hand at keeping Ivy well out of tasks that involved style of any kind, so that, in the end, everything looked lovely and managed not to clash. Even Ivy.

The ceremony was to take place just after sunset on a quartermoon night so that everyone could attend. Just about *everyone* did: including the queen, Lord Akeldama and *all* his drones, and the cream of London society. Most notably absent were the vampires, who had not even bothered to politely refuse invitations but instead snubbed the couple outright.

"They have good reason to object," said Lord Akeldama.

"But not you?"

"Oh, I have good reason, too, but I trust you, little innovator. And I like change." He left it at that, despite Alexia's pointed further inquiries.

The Westminster hive proved the exception of the mass vampire cut direct. Countess Nadasdy sent Lord Ambrose to observe the ceremony, but clearly under duress. She also sent Alexia an unexpected gift, which arrived while she was dressing the afternoon of the wedding.

"Did I not say she would get rid of me?" said Angelique with a self-deprecating smile.

Miss Tarabotti was a little overwhelmed. "You are in favor of a new position? With me?"

The violet-eyed girl shrugged in a blasé French kind of way. "My master, he iz dead because of ze scientists. Lady's maid, it iz better than housemaid."

"But what about your drone status?"

Angelique looked coy. "Zer iz always claviger, yez?"

"Very well, then, welcome," said Miss Tarabotti. Of course, the French girl must, perforce, be a spy, but Alexia reasoned it was better to know and keep her close than force the hive into more desperate maneuvering. It did cause a twinge of worry. Why were the vampires fussing so?

Angelique began immediately to assist Biffy in finishing the last of Alexia's coiled updo, arguing mildly on the subject of a flower above the right ear.

They both protested when Alexia stood, not yet fully dressed, and waved them off.

"I must pay someone a visit," she said imperiously. It was late afternoon: the sun had not yet set, and there was still much to do before the big event that night.

"But right now?" sputtered Biffy. "It is your wedding evening!"

"And we have only just finished ze hair!"

Miss Tarabotti could tell that these two were going to be a force to be reckoned with. But so was she. Alexia instructed them to get her dress ready and that she would be back within the hour, so not to fret. "It is not like anything can actually occur without me, is it? I have to see a friend about the sun."

She took the Loontwills' carriage without asking and went round to Lord Akeldama's gilt-edged town house. She sailed in the front door past various drones and woke Lord Akeldama from his deadlike daytime sleep with a touch.

Human, he blinked at her groggily.

"It is almost sunset," said Miss Tarabotti with a tiny smile, her hand on his shoulder. "Come with me."

Clad only in his sleeping robe, she took the vampire firmly by the hand and led him up through the splendor of his gilt house and out onto the rooftop into the waning light.

Alexia rested her cheek on his shoulder, and they stood silently together and watched the sun set over the city.

Lord Akeldama refrained from pointing out she would be late for her own wedding.

Miss Tarabotti refrained from pointing out that he was crying.

She figured it was a good way to end her career as a spinster.

Lord Akeldama also cried during the ceremony, which took place at Westminster Abbey. Well, he was a bit of a weeper. So did Mrs. Loontwill. Miss Tarabotti, rather callously, figured her mama's tears were more for the loss of her butler than for the loss of her daughter. Floote had given notice and moved, along with Alexia's father's entire library, into Woolsey Castle that very morning. Both were settling in nicely.

The wedding was hailed as a masterpiece of social engineering and physical beauty. Best of all, as Alexia's bridesmaid, Miss Hisselpenny was not permitted to choose her own hat. The ceremony went unexpectedly smoothly, and in no time at all, Miss Tarabotti found herself Lady Maccon.

Afterward, everyone assembled in Hyde Park, which was admittedly unusual, but exceptions had to be made when werewolves were involved. And there certainly were a goodly number of werewolves. Not simply Lord Maccon's pack but all the loners, other packs, and clavigers within traveling distance had attended the celebration.

Luckily, there was enough meat for them all. The only aspect of wedding procedure Alexia had invested genuine involvement and time into was the food. As a result, the tables set about their corner of the park fairly groaned under their burdens. There were galantines of guinea fowl stuffed with minced tongue quivering in aspic jelly and decorated with feathers made of lemon-soaked apple peel. No fewer than eight pigeons in truffle gravy nesting in coils of pastry made their appearance and disappearance. There were stewed oysters, fried haddock fillets in anchovy sauce, and grilled sole with peach compote. Having noted Lord Maccon's fondness for poultry, the Loontwill cook provided woodcock pie, roast pheasant in butter sauce with peas and celery, and a brace of grouse. There was a baron of beef, a forequarter of mutton glazed with red wine, and lamb cutlets with fresh mint and broad beans—all offered on the rarer side. Corner dishes included lobster salad, spinach and eggs, vegetable fritters, and baked potatoes. In addition to the massive bride's cake and the piles of nutty groom's cakes for the guests to take home, there were rhubarb tarts, stewed cherries, fresh strawberries and purple grapes, gravy boats of clotted cream, and plum pudding. The food was declared an unqualified success, and many a plan was made to visit Woolsey Castle for luncheon once Alexia took over supervision of its kitchens.

Miss Hisselpenny took the entire event as an excuse to flirt with anything male and on two legs, and a few on four. This seemed perfectly acceptable, until Alexia spotted her going goggle-eyed over the repulsive Lord Ambrose. The new Lady Maccon crooked an imperious finger at Professor Lyall and sent him to salvage the situation.

Professor Lyall, muttering something about "new brides having more to concern themselves with than meddling," did as ordered. He insinuated himself seamlessly into the conversation between Lord Ambrose and Miss Hisselpenny, and hustled Ivy away for a waltz without anyone the wiser to his militarylike intervention tactics. He then carried Ivy off to the other side of the lawn, which was serving as the dance floor, and introduced her to Lord Maccon's redheaded claviger, Tunstell.

Tunstell looked at Ivy.

Ivy looked at Tunstell.

Professor Lyall noted with satisfaction that they wore identical expressions of the stunned-donkey variety.

"Tunstell," instructed the Beta, "ask Miss Hisselpenny if she would like to dance."

"Would you, um, like to, um, dance, Miss Hisselpenny?" stuttered the normally loquacious young man.

"Oh," said Ivy. "Oh yes, please."

Professor Lyall, all forgotten, nodded to himself. Then he dashed off to deal with Lord Akeldama and Lord Ambrose who seemed to be getting into some sort of heated argument on the subject of waistcoats.

"Well, wife?" asked Alexia's new husband, whisking her about the lawn.

"Yes, husband?"

"Think we can officially escape yet?"

Alexia looked about nervously. Everyone seemed to be suddenly fleeing the dance floor, and the music was changing. "Um, I think, perhaps, not just yet."

They both stopped and looked about.

"This was not part of the wedding plan," she said in annoyance. "Biffy, what is happening here?" she yelled.

From the sidelines, Biffy shrugged and shook his head.

The clavigers were causing the disturbance. They had arranged themselves in a large circle about Lord Maccon and Alexia and were slowly pushing everyone else away. Alexia noticed that Ivy, little traitor, was helping them.

Lord Maccon slapped his forehead with his hand. "God's truth, they aren't really? That old tradition?" He trailed off as the howling began. "Aye, they are. Well, my dear, best get used to this kind of thing."

The wolves burst into the open circle like a river of fur. Under the quarter moon, there was no anger or bloodlust in their movements. Instead it was like a dance, liquid and beautiful. The fuzzy throng was comprised of not just the Woolsey Pack but also all the visiting werewolves. Almost thirty of them jumped and pranced and yipped as they coiled around the newly married couple.

Alexia held very still and relaxed into the dizzying movement. The wolves circled closer and closer until they pressed against her skirts, all hot predator breath and soft fur. Then one wolf stopped directly next to Lord Maccon—a thin, sandy, vulpinelike creature—Professor Lyall.

With a wink at Alexia, the Beta threw his head back and barked, once, sharply.

The wolves stopped stock-still and then did the most organized, politely amusing thing. They lined up in a neat circle all about and one by one came forward. As each wolf stood before the newly married pair, he lowered his head between his forelegs, showing the back of his neck in a funny little bow.

"Are they paying homage to you?" Alexia asked her husband.

He laughed. "Lord, no. Why would they bother with me?"

"Oh," replied Alexia, realizing it was meant to honor her. "Should I *do* something?"

Conall kissed her cheek. "You are wonderful as you are."

The last to come forward was Lyall. His bow was somehow more elegant and more restrained than anyone else's.

Once completed, he barked again, and they all leaped into action: running three times around the couple and dashing off into the night.

After that, everything else was anticlimactic, and as soon as civility allowed, Alexia's new husband hustled her into the waiting carriage and on the road out of London toward Woolsey Castle.

A few of the werewolves returned then, still in wolf form, to run alongside the carriage.

Just outside of town, Lord Maccon stuck his head out the coach window and told them unceremoniously to "shove off."

"I gave the pack the evening out," he informed Alexia, retracting his head and closing the window.

His wife issued him an arch look.

"Oh, very well. I told them if they showed their furry faces round Woolsey Castle for the next three days, I would personally eviscerate them."

Alexia smiled. "Good gracious, where will they all stay?"

"Lyall muttered something about invading Lord Akeldama's town house." Conall looked smugly amused.

Alexia laughed. "Would I were a fly on that wall!"

Her husband turned about and without further ado began

unclasping the brooch that held the neck of her beautiful gown together.

"Intriguing design, this dress," he commented without real interest.

"Rather say, necessary design," replied his lady as the neck fell away to show a neat pattern of tiny love bites all about her throat. Lord Maccon traced them with proprietary pride.

"What are you up to?" Alexia asked as he gently kissed the tiny bruises. She was distracted by the delicious tingly sensation this caused, but not enough to forgo noticing his hands were round the back of the bodice of her dress, sliding open the row of buttons there.

"I should think that would be obvious by now," he replied with a grin. He pushed back the top of her dress and became intent on undoing her corset. His lips moved down from her neck to delve into the region of her décolletage.

"Conall," Alexia murmured hazily, almost losing her objections as new and delicious sensation extended from nipples turned strangely tight and hard. "We are in a moving *carriage*! Why this constant preference for inappropriate locations for amorous activities?"

"Mmm, not to worry," he purposefully misconstrued her protestations. "I gave the coachman instructions to take the long way round." He helped her to stand and shucked her out of her dress, skirts, and corset with consummate rapidity.

Alexia, in only a shift, stockings, and shoes, crossed her arms over her breasts self-consciously.

Her new husband ran large calloused hands around the hem of her chemise, stroking at the soft skin of her upper thighs. Then he lifted the material up to cup her buttocks before raising that last bastion of her admittedly deteriorated dignity over her head and discarding it.

Until that moment, Alexia realized she had never before seen real hunger in his eyes. They were in physical contact, supernatural and preternatural, but nevertheless, his eyes had turned to pure wolf yellow. He looked at her, clad in nothing but stockings and ivory button boots, as though he wanted to eat her alive.

"You are trying to get back at me, are you?" she said accusingly, trying to calm him a little. The intensity was scaring her. She was, after all, relatively new to this kind of activity.

He paused and looked at her, yellow fading in genuine surprise. "For what?"

"Back at the Hypocras Club, when you were naked and I was not."

He pulled her toward him. She had no idea how he managed to attend to himself as well as her, but somehow he had opened the flap at the front of his breeches. Everything else remained covered. "I'll admit the thought had crossed my mind. Now sit."

"What, there?"

"Aye, there."

Alexia looked dubious. However, there were destined to be some arguments in their relationship she could not hope to win. This was one of them. The carriage, rather too conveniently, pitched slightly to one side, and she stumbled forward. Conall caught her and guided her into his lap in one smooth movement.

He did not do anything else with that particular proximity for a moment; instead he turned his attention to her generous breasts, first kissing, then nibbling, then biting, a progression that had Alexia squirming in such a way as to force the very tip of him inside her whether she willed it or no.

"Really," she insisted, panting, "this is a most unseemly location for such activities."

Just then, the carriage lurched over a rut in the road and silenced all further objections. The movement brought her flush on top of him, naked thighs pressed against the material of his breeches. Lord Maccon groaned, a rapt expression on his face.

Alexia gasped and winced. "Ouch!" She leaned forward against her husband and bit his shoulder hard in revenge. Hard enough to draw blood. "That hurt."

He took the bite without complaint and looked worried. "Does it still?"

The carriage bumped again. This time Alexia sighed. Something extremely odd and tingly was beginning to occur in her nether regions.

"I shall take that as a no," said her husband, and began to move, rocking with the motion of the carriage.

What happened after that was all sweat, and moans, and pulsing sensation to which Alexia decided, after about one second of deep deliberation, she was not averse. It culminated in the most intriguing second heartbeat emerging right around the area where he had impaled himself. Shortly thereafter, her husband gave a long low groan and collapsed back on the carriage cushions, cradling her against him.

"Ooo," said Alexia, fascinated, "it shrinks back down again. The books didn't detail that occurrence."

The earl laughed. "You must show me these books of yours."

She folded forward on top of him and nuzzled down into his cravat, pleased to be with a man who was strong enough to be untroubled at having her draped atop him. "Books of my father's," she corrected.

"I hear he had an interesting reputation."

"Mmmm, so his library would suggest." She closed her eyes, relaxing against her husband. Then she thought of something, reared back, and whacked him on the waistcoat with one balled-up fist.

"Ouch," said her long-suffering husband. "Now what are you upset about?"

"Isn't that just *like* you!" she said.

"What?"

"You took it as a challenge, didn't you? My stopping you from seducing me back at the Hypocras Club."

Lord Maccon grinned wolfishly, though his eyes had gone back to their human tawny brown color. "Naturally."

She frowned, considering how best to handle this situation. Then she shifted back toward him and began busily untying his cravat and divesting him of coat, waistcoat, and shirt.

"Well, then," she said.

"Aye?"

"I am still holding that the carriage is an entirely inappropriate place for conjugal activities. Would you like to prove me wrong a second time?"

"Are you challenging me, Lady Maccon?" asked Lord Maccon in mock annoyance. But he was already lifting himself up to facilitate her removal of his clothing.

Alexia smiled down at his bare chest and then looked once more into his eyes. The yellow was back. "All the time."

extras

about the author

Ms. Carriger began writing in order to cope with being raised in obscurity by an expatriate Brit and an incurable curmudgeon. She escaped small-town life and inadvertently acquired several degrees in higher learning. Ms. Carriger then traveled the historic cities of Europe, subsisting entirely on biscuits secreted in her handbag. She now resides in the Colonies, surrounded by a harem of Armenian lovers, where she insists on tea imported directly from London and cats that pee into toilets. She is fond of teeny tiny hats and tropical fruit. Find out more about Ms. Carriger at www.gailcarriger.com.

Find out more about Gail Carriger and other Orbit authors by registering for the free monthly newsletter at www.orbit books.net

interview

Have you always known that you wanted to be a writer?
Actually, I'm still not entirely convinced I am one. I seem to have stumbled upon authordom inadvertently. I'm not complaining—never that—just startled.

When you aren't writing, what do you like to do in your spare time?
Drink tea. Although, come to think on it, I do that while I'm writing as well. Truth be told, eating, reading, sleeping, and breathing occupy a considerable amount of my time (generally in that order and often all at the same time).

Who/what would you consider to be your influences?
Jane Austen, P. G. Wodehouse, Gerald Durrell, a tea-obsessed expatriate British mum, years of historical study, and a lifetime of BBC costume dramas have all played pivotal roles in Alexia's inception.

Soulless has such a clever melding of alternate history, romance, and the supernatural. How did you derive the idea for this novel?
I knew I wanted to write urban fantasy, and there's one thing I've never been able to understand in the genre: if immortals were mucking about, wouldn't they have been mucking about for a very long time? A speculation arose: what if all

those strange and unexplainable bends in history were the result of supernatural interference? At which point I asked myself, what's the weirdest most eccentric historical phenomenon of them all? Answer: the Great British Empire. Clearly, one tiny little island could only conquer half the known world with supernatural aid. Those absurd Victorian manners and ridiculous fashions were obviously dictated by vampires. And, without a doubt, the British army regimental system functioned on werewolf pack dynamics. Of course, as soon as I started scribbling away about a land of bustles and top hats, romance and comedy had to enter the fray. I mean to say, bustles! Then I tossed nineteenth-century science into the mix and realized that if the Victorians were studying vampires and werewolves (which they would do, if they knew about them), not to mention developing weapons against them, technology would have evolved differently. Enter a sprinkling of steampunk, and suddenly, I was juggling more subgenres than Ivy has ugly hats! But then again, you can never have too many hats.

Do you have a favorite character? If so, why?
I'm torn between Professor Lyall and Floote. I have a little bit of a thing for capable and efficient gentlemen with quiet humors and calm dispositions.

What adventures can we look forward to seeing Alexia in next?
I shall say only that Alexia has always wanted to travel by dirigible . . .

Finally, if you had the opportunity to have tea with Lord Maccon, Alexia, or Lord Akeldama, who would you choose and why?
Oh, Lord Akeldama without a doubt. Alexia and I should never get along—we are far too much alike—and Lord Maccon

hasn't any manners to speak of. Now, Lord Akeldama may be outrageous, but he's a charming conversationalist, and he knows such fascinating things.

if you enjoyed
SOULLESS

look out for

TEMPEST RISING

book one of the Jane True series

by

NICOLE PEELER

I eyeballed the freezer, trying to decide what to cook for dinner that night. Such a decision was no mean feat, since a visiting stranger might assume that Martha Stewart not only lived with us but was preparing for the apocalypse. Frozen lasagnas, casseroles, pot pies, and the like filled our icebox nearly to the brim. Finally deciding on fish chowder, I took out some haddock and mussels. After a brief, internal struggle, I grabbed some salmon to make extra soup to—you guessed it—freeze. Yeah, the stockpiling was more than a little OCD, but it made me feel better. It also meant that when I actually had something to do for the entire evening, I could leave my dad by himself without feeling too guilty about it.

My dad wasn't an invalid—not exactly. But he had a bad heart and needed help taking care of things, especially with my mother gone. So I took up the slack, which I was happy to do. It's not like I had much else on my plate, what with being the village pariah and all.

It's amazing how being a pariah gives you ample amounts of free time.

After putting in the laundry and cleaning the downstairs bathroom, I went upstairs to take a shower. I would have loved to walk around all day with the sea salt on my skin, but not even in Rockabill was Eau de Brine an acceptable perfume. Like many twentysomethings, I'd woken up early that day to go exercise. Unlike most twentysomethings, however, my morning exercise took the form of an hour or so long swim in the freezing ocean. And in one of America's deadliest whirlpools. Which is why I am so careful to keep the swimming on the DL. It might be a great cardio workout, but it probably would get me burned at the stake. This is New England, after all.

As I got dressed in my work clothes—khaki chinos and a long-sleeved pink polo-style shirt with *Read It and Weep* embroidered in navy blue over the breast pocket—I heard my father emerge from his bedroom and clomp down the stairs. His job in the morning was to make the coffee, so I took a moment to apply a little mascara, blush, and some lip gloss, before brushing out my damp black hair. I kept it cut in a much longer—and admittedly more unkempt— version of Cleopatra's style because I liked to hide my dark eyes under my long bangs. Most recently, my nemesis, Stuart Gray, had referred to them as "demon eyes." They're not as Marilyn Manson as that, thank you very much, but even I had to admit to difficulty determining where my pupil ended and my iris began.

I went back downstairs to join my dad in the kitchen, and I felt that pang in my heart that I get sometimes when I'm struck by how he's changed. He'd been a fisherman, but he'd had to retire about ten years ago, on disability, when his heart condition worsened. Once a handsome, confident, and brawny man whose presence filled any space he entered, his long illness and my mother's disappearance had diminished him in every possible way. He looked so small and gray in his faded old bathrobe, his hands trembling from the anti-arrhythmics he takes for his screwed-up heart, that it took every ounce of self-control I had not to make him sit down and rest. Even if his body didn't agree, he still felt himself to be the man he had been, and I knew I already walked a thin line between caring for him and treading on his dignity. So I put on my widest smile and bustled into the kitchen, as if we were a father and daughter in some sitcom set in the 1950s.

"Good morning, Daddy!" I beamed.

"Morning, honey. Want some coffee?" He asked me that question every morning, even though the answer had been yes since I was fifteen.

"Sure, thanks. Did you sleep all right?"

"Oh, yes. And you? How was your morning?" My dad never asked me directly about the swimming. It's a question that lay under the auspices of the "don't ask, don't tell" policy that ruled our household. For example, he didn't ask me about my swimming, I didn't ask him about my mother. He didn't ask me about Jason, I didn't ask him about my mother. He didn't ask me whether or not I was happy in Rockabill, I didn't ask him about my mother . . .

"Oh, I slept fine, Dad. Thanks." Of course I hadn't, really, as I only needed about four hours of sleep a night. But that's another thing we never talked about.

He asked me about my plans for the day, while I made us a breakfast of scrambled eggs on wholewheat toast. I told him that I'd be working till six, then I'd go to the grocery store on the way home. So, as usual for a Monday, I'd take the car to work. We performed pretty much the exact same routine every week, but it was nice of him to act like it was possible I might have new and exciting plans. On Mondays, I didn't have to worry about him eating lunch, as Trevor McKinley picked him up to go play a few hours of cheeky lunchtime poker with George Varga, Louis Finch, and Joe Covelli. They're all natives of Rockabill and friends since childhood, except for Joe, who moved here to Maine about twenty years ago to open up our local garage. That's how things were around Rockabill. For the winter, when the tourists were mostly absent, the town was populated by natives who grew up together and were more intimately acquainted with each other's dirty laundry than their own hampers. Some people enjoyed that intimacy. But when you were more usually the object of the whispers than the subject, intimacy had a tendency to feel like persecution.

We ate while we shared our local paper, *The Light House*

News. But because the paper mostly functioned as a vehicle for advertising things to tourists, and the tourists were gone for the season, the pickings were scarce. Yet we went through the motions anyway. For all of our sins, no one could say that the True family wasn't good at going through the motions. After breakfast, I doled out my father's copious pills and set them next to his orange juice. He flashed me his charming smile, which was the only thing left unchanged after the ravages to his health and his heart.

"Thank you, Jane," he said. And I knew he meant it, despite the fact that I'd set his pills down next to his orange juice every single morning for the past twelve years.

I gulped down a knot in my throat, since I knew that no small share of his worry and grief was due to me, and kissed him on the cheek. Then I bustled around clearing away breakfast, and bustled around getting my stuff together, and bustled out the door to get to work. In my experience, bustling is always a great way to keep from crying.

Tracy Gregory, the owner of Read It and Weep, was already hard at work when I walked in the front door. The Gregorys were an old fishing family from Rockabill, and Tracy was their prodigal daughter. She had left to work in Los Angeles, where she had apparently been a successful movie stylist. I say apparently because she never told us the names of any of the movies she'd worked on. She'd only moved back to Rockabill about five years ago to open Read It and Weep, which was our local bookstore, café, and all-around tourist trap. Since tourism replaced fishing as our major industry, Rockabill can just about support an all-year-round enterprise like Read It and Weep. But other things, like the nicer restaurant—rather unfortunately named The Pig Out Bar and Grill—close for the winter.

"Hey girl," she said, gruffly, as I locked the door behind me. We didn't open for another half hour.

"Hey Tracy. Grizelda back?"

Grizelda was Tracy's girlfriend, and they'd caused quite a stir when they first appeared in Rockabill together. Not only were they lesbians, but they were as fabulously lesbionic as the inhabitants of a tiny village in Maine could ever imagine. Tracy carried herself like a rugby player, and dressed like one, too. But she had an easygoing charisma that got her through the initial gender panic triggered by her reentry into Rockabill society.

And if Tracy made heads turn, Grizelda practically made them spin *Exorcist* style. Grizelda was not Grizelda's real name. Nor was Dusty Nethers, the name she used when she'd been a porn star. As Dusty Nethers, Grizelda had been fiery haired and as boobilicious as a *Baywatch* beauty. But in her current incarnation, as Grizelda Montague, she sported a sort of Gothic-hipster look—albeit one that was still very boobilicious. A few times a year Grizelda disappeared for weeks or a month, and upon her return home she and Tracy would complete some big project they'd been discussing, like redecorating the store or adding a sunroom onto their little house. Lord knows what she got up to on her profit-venture vacations. But whatever it was, it didn't affect her relationship with Tracy. The pair were as close as any husband and wife in Rockabill, if not closer, and seeing how much they loved each other drove home to me my own loneliness.

"Yeah, Grizzie's back. She'll be here soon. She has something for you . . . something scandalous, knowing my lady love."

I grinned. "Awesome. I love her gifts."

Because of Grizzie, I had a drawer full of naughty underwear, sex toys, and dirty books. Grizzie gave such presents for *every* occasion; it didn't matter if it was your high school graduation, your fiftieth wedding anniversary, or your baby's baptism. This particular predilection meant she was a prominent figure on wedding shower guest lists from Rockabill to

Eastport, but made her dangerous for children's parties. Most parents didn't appreciate an "every day of the week" pack of thongs for their eleven-year-old daughter. Once she'd given me a gift certificate for a "Hollywood" bikini wax and I had to Google the term. What I discovered made me way too scared to use it, so it sat in my "dirty drawer," as I called it, as a talking point. Not that anyone ever went into my dirty drawer with me, but I talked to myself a lot, and it certainly provided amusing fodder for my own conversations.

It was also rather handy—no pun intended—to have access to one's own personal sex shop during long periods of enforced abstinence . . . such as the last eight years of my life.

"And," Tracy responded with a rueful shake of her head, "her gifts love you. Often quite literally."

"That's all right, somebody has to," I answered back, horrified at the bitter inflection that had crept into my voice.

But Tracy, bless her, just stroked a gentle hand over my hair that turned into a tiny one-armed hug, saying nothing.

"Hands off my woman!" crowed a hard-edged voice from the front door. Grizelda!

"Oh, sorry," I apologized, backing away from Tracy.

"I meant for Tracy to get off *you*," Grizzie said, swooping toward me to pick me up in a bodily hug, my own well-endowed chest clashing with her enormous fake bosoms. I hated being short at times like these. Even though I loved all five feet and eleven inches of Grizzie, and had more than my fair share of affection for her ta-ta-riddled hugs, I loathed being manhandled.

She set me down and grasped my hands in hers, backing away to look me over appreciatively while holding my fingers at arm's length. "Mmm, mmm," she said, shaking her head. "Girl, I could sop you up with a biscuit."

I laughed, as Tracy rolled her eyes.

"Quit sexually harassing the staff, Grizzly Bear," was her only comment.

"I'll get back to sexually harassing you in a minute, passion flower, but right now I want to appreciate our Jane." Grizelda winked at me with her florid violet eyes—she wore colored lenses—and I couldn't help but giggle like a schoolgirl.

"I've brought you a little something," she said, her voice sly.

I clapped my hands in excitement and hopped up and down in a little happy dance.

I really did love Grizzie's gifts, even if they challenged the tenuous grasp of human anatomy imparted to me by Mrs. Renault in her high school biology class.

"Happy belated birthday!" she cried as she handed me a beautifully wrapped package she pulled from her enormous handbag. I admired the shiny black paper and the sumptuous red velvet ribbon tied up into a decadent bow—Grizzie did everything with style—before tearing into it with glee. After slitting open the tape holding the box closed with my thumbnail, I was soon holding in my hands the most beautiful red satin nightgown I'd ever seen. It was a deep, bloody, blue-based red, the perfect red for my skin tone. And it was, of course, the perfect length, with a slit up the side that would rise almost to my hip. Grizzie had this magic ability to always buy people clothes that fit. The top was generously cut for its small dress size, the bodice gathered into a sort of clamshell-like tailoring that I knew would cup my boobs like those hands in that famous Janet Jackson picture. The straps were slightly thicker, to give support, and crossed over the *very* low-cut back. It was absolutely gorgeous—very adult and sophisticated—and I couldn't stop stroking the deliciously watery satin.

"Grizzie," I breathed. "It's gorgeous . . . but too much! This must have cost a fortune."

"You are worth a fortune, little Jane. Besides, I figured you might need something nice . . . since Mark's 'special deliveries' should have culminated in a date by now."

Grizzie's words trailed off as my face fell and Tracy, behind her, made a noise like Xena, Warrior Princess, charging into battle.

Before Tracy could launch into just how many ways she wanted to eviscerate our new letter carrier, I said, very calmly, "I won't be going on any dates with Mark."

"What happened?" Grizzie asked, as Tracy made another grunting declaration of war behind us.

"Well . . ." I started, but where should I begin? Mark was new to Rockabill, a widowed employee of the U.S. Postal Service, who had recently moved to our little corner of Maine with his two young daughters. He'd kept forgetting to deliver letters and packages, necessitating second, and sometimes third, trips to our bookstore, daily. I'd thought he was sweet, but rather dumb, until Tracy had pointed out that he only forgot stuff when I was working.

So we'd flirted and flirted and flirted over the course of a month. Until, just a few days ago, he'd asked me out. I was thrilled. He was cute; he was *new*; he'd lost someone he was close to, as well. And he "obviously" didn't judge me on my past.

You know what they say about assuming . . .

"We had a date set up, but he cancelled. I guess he asked me out before he knew about . . . everything. Then someone must have told him. He's got kids, you know."

"So?" Grizzie growled, her smoky voice already furious.

"So, he said that he didn't think I'd be a good influence. On his girls."

"That's fucking ridiculous," Grizzie snarled, just as Tracy made a series of inarticulate chittering noises behind us. She was normally the sedate, equable half of her and Grizzie's partnership, but Tracy had nearly blown a gasket when I'd called her crying after Mark bailed on me. I think she would have torn off his head, but then we wouldn't have gotten our inventory anymore.

I lowered my head and shrugged. Grizzie moved forward, having realized that Tracy already had the anger market cornered.

"I'm sorry, honey," she said, wrapping her long arms around me. "That's . . . such a shame."

And it was a shame. My friends wanted me to move on, my dad wanted me to move on. Hell, except for that tiny sliver of me that was still frozen in guilt, *I* wanted to move on. But the rest of Rockabill, it seems, didn't agree.

Grizzie brushed the bangs back from my eyes, and when she saw tears glittering she intervened, Grizelda-style. Dipping me like a tango dancer, she growled sexily, "Baby, I'm gonna butter yo' bread . . ." before burying her face in my exposed belly and giving me a resounding zerbert.

That did just the trick. I was laughing again, thanking my stars for about the zillionth time that they had brought Grizzie and Tracy back to Rockabill because I didn't know what I would have done without them. I gave Tracy her own hug for the present, and then took it to the back room with my stuff. I opened the box to give the red satin one last parting caress, and then closed it with a contented sigh.

It would look absolutely gorgeous in my dirty drawer.

We only had a few things to do to get the store ready for opening, which left much time for chitchat. About a half hour of intense gossip later, we had pretty much exhausted "what happened when you were gone" as a subject of conversation and had started in on plans for the coming week, when the little bell above the door tinkled. My heart sank when I saw it was Linda Allen, self-selected female delegate for my own personal persecution squad. She wasn't quite as bad as Stuart Gray, who hated me even more than Linda did, but she did her best to keep up with him.

Speaking of the rest of Rockabill, I thought, as Linda headed toward romance.

She didn't bother to speak to me, of course. She just gave

me one of her loaded looks that she could fire off like a World War II gunship. The looks always said the same things. They spoke of the fact that I was the girl whose crazy mother had shown up in the center of town out of nowhere, *naked*, in the middle of a storm. The fact that she'd *stolen* one of the most eligible Rockabill bachelors and *ruined him for life*. The fact that she'd given birth to a baby *without being married*. The fact that I insisted on being *that child* and upping the ante by being *just as weird as my mother*. That was only the tip of the vituperative iceberg that Linda hauled into my presence whenever she had the chance.

Unfortunately, Linda read nearly as compulsively as I did, so I saw her at least twice a month when she'd come in for a new stack of romance novels. She liked a very particular kind of plot: the sort where the pirate kidnaps some virgin damsel, rapes her into loving him, and then dispatches lots of seamen while she polishes his cutlass. Or where the Highland clan leader kidnaps some virginal English Rose, rapes her into loving him, and then kills entire armies of Sassenachs while she stuffs his haggis. Or where the Native American warrior kidnaps a virginal white settler, rapes her into loving him, and then kills a bunch of colonists while she whets his tomahawk. I hated to get Freudian on Linda, but her reading patterns suggested some interesting insights into why she was such a complete bitch.

Tracy had received a phone call while Linda was picking out her books, and Grizelda was sitting on a stool far behind the counter in a way that clearly said "I'm not actually working, thanks." But Linda pointedly ignored the fact that I was free to help her, choosing, instead, to stand in front of Tracy. Tracy gave that little eye gesture where she looked at Linda, then looked at me, as if to say, "She can help you," but Linda insisted on being oblivious to my presence. Tracy sighed and cut her telephone conversation short. I knew that Tracy would love to tell Linda to stick her attitude where the sun don't shine, but Read It and Weep couldn't afford to lose a customer who was as good at buying books as she was at being a snarky snake face. So Tracy rang up Linda's purchases and bagged them for her as politely as one can without actually being friendly and handed the bag over to Linda.

Who, right on cue, gave me her parting shot, the look I knew was coming but was never quite able to deflect.

The look that said, *There's the freak who killed her own boyfriend*.

She was wrong, of course. I hadn't actually killed Jason. I was just the reason he was dead.